Flu

Stephen Baxter applied to become an astronaut.
He didn't make it, but achieved the next best thing by
becoming a science fiction writer, and his novels and
short stories have been published and have won
awards around the world. His science background is in
maths and engineering. He is married and lives in
Buckinghamshire.

'Stephen Baxter proves what a cosmic thinker he is'
Washington Post Book World

'Baxter has emerged as a master of cosmological hard
SF, a writer enamored of alien viewpoints and radical
settings, with a sense of sublime immensities and an
ingenuity at working permutations on the question of
what is human'
Locus

BY THE SAME AUTHOR

Novels and stories in the Xeelee Sequence

Raft
Timelike Infinity
Flux
Ring
Vacuum Diagrams

Anti-Ice
The Time Ships
Voyage
Titan
Traces
Moonseed

Voyager

STEPHEN BAXTER

Flux

HarperCollins*Publishers*

Voyager
An Imprint of HarperCollins*Publishers*
77–85 Fulham Palace Road,
Hammersmith, London W6 8JB

This paperback edition 1998
3 5 7 9 8 6 4

Previously published in paperback by
HarperCollins Science Fiction & Fantasy 1994

First published in Great Britain by
HarperCollins*Publishers* 1993

ISBN 0 00 647620 1

Set in Palatino

Printed and bound in Great Britain by
Caledonian International Book Manufacturing Ltd, Glasgow

1

Dura woke with a start.

There was something wrong. The photons didn't smell right.

Her hand floated before her face, dimly visible, and she flexed her fingers. Disturbed electron gas, spiralling dizzily around the Magfield lines, sparkled purple-white around the fingertips. The Air in her eyes was warm, stale, and she could make out only vague shapes.

For a moment she hung there, curled in a tight ball, suspended in the elastic grip of the Magfield.

She heard voices, thin and hot with panic. They were coming from the direction of the Net.

Dura jammed her eyes tight shut and hugged her knees, willing herself to return to the cool oblivion of sleep. *Not again. By the blood of the Xeelee*, she swore silently, *not another Glitch; not another spin storm*. She wasn't sure if the little tribe of Human Beings had the resources to respond to more disruption . . . nor, indeed, if she herself had the strength to cope with fresh disaster.

The Magfield itself trembled now. Encasing her body, it rippled over her skin, not unpleasantly, and she allowed it to rock her as if she were a child in its arms. Then – not so pleasantly – it prodded her more rudely in the small of the back . . .

No, that wasn't the Magfield. She uncurled again, stretching against the confines of the field. She rubbed her eyes – the fleshy rims of the cups were crusted with sleep-deposits and felt sharp against her fingers – and shook her head to clear the clouded Air out of the cups.

The prod in her back was coming from the fist of Farr, her brother. He'd been on latrine duty, she saw; he still carried his plaited waste bag, empty of the neutron-rich shit he'd taken

5

out away from the Net and dumped in the Air. His skinny, growing body trembled in response to the instabilities in the Magfield and his round face was upturned to her, creased with an almost comical concern. In one hand he gripped a fin of his pet Air-pig – a fat infant about the size of Dura's fist, so young that none of its six fins were yet pierced. The little animal, obviously terrified by the Glitch, struggled to escape, feebly; it pumped out superfluid jetfarts in thin blue streams.

His fondness for the animal made Farr seem even younger than his twelve years – a third of Dura's age – and he clung to the piglet as if clinging to childhood itself. Well, Dura thought, the Mantle was huge and empty, but there was precious little room in it for childhood. Farr was having to grow up fast.

He was so like their father, Logue.

Dura, still misty with sleep, felt a surge of affection and concern for the boy and reached out to stroke his cheek, to run gentle fingers around the quiet brown rims of his eyes.

She smiled at her brother. 'Hello, Farr.'

'Sorry for waking you.'

'You didn't. The Star was kind enough to wake me, long before you got around to it. Another Glitch?'

'The worst one yet, Adda says.'

'Never mind what Adda says,' Dura said, stroking his floating hair; the hollow tubes were, as always, tangled and grubby. 'We'll get by. We always do, don't we? You get back to your father. And tell him I'm coming.'

'All right.' Farr smiled at her again, twisted stiffly, and, with his Air-pig's fin still clutched tight, he began to Wave awkwardly across the Magfield's invisible flux paths towards the Net. Dura watched him recede, his slim form diminished by the shimmering, world-filling vortex lines beyond him.

Dura straightened to her full length and stretched, pressing against the Magfield. She kept her mouth wide open as she worked stiffness out of her limbs and back. She felt the feathery ripple of the Air as it poured through her throat to her lungs and heart, rushing through superleak capillaries and filling her muscles; her body seemed to tingle with its freshness.

She gazed around, sniffing the photons.

Dura's world was the Mantle of the Star, an immense cavern of yellow-white Air bounded below by the Quantum Sea and above by the Crust.

The Crust itself was a rich, matted ceiling, purple-streaked with grass and the hairlike lines of tree trunks. By squinting – distorting the parabolic retinae of her eyes – she could make out dark motes scattered among the roots of the trees fixed to the underside of the Crust. Perhaps they were rays, or a herd of wild Air-pigs, or some other grazing creatures. It was too distant to see clearly, but the amphibian animals seemed to be swirling around each other, colliding, confused; she almost imagined she could hear the cool sound of their distress.

Far below her, the Quantum Sea formed a purple-dark floor to the world. The Sea was mist-shrouded, its surface indistinct and deadly. The Sea itself, she saw with relief, was undisturbed by the Glitch. Only once in Dura's memory had there been a Glitch severe enough to cause a Seaquake. She shuddered like the Magfield as she remembered that ghastly time; she had been no older than Farr, she supposed, when the neutrino founts had come, sweeping half the Human Beings – including Phir, Dura's mother and Logue's first wife – away and on, screaming, into the mysteries beyond the Crust.

All around her, filling the Air between Crust and Sea, the vortex lines were an electric-blue cage. The lines filled space in a hexagonal array, spaced about ten mansheights apart; they swept around the Star from far upflux – from the North – arced past her like the trajectories of immense, graceful animals, and converged into the red-soft blur that was the South Pole, millions of mansheights away.

She held her fingers up before her face, trying to judge the spacing and pattern of the lines.

Through her fingers she could see the encampment, a little knot of frantic detail and activity – jostling, terrified Air-pigs, scrambling people, the quivering Net – all embedded in the shuddering bulk of the Air. Farr with his struggling Air-piglet was a pathetic scrap, wriggling through the invisible flux tubes.

Dura tried to ignore the small, messy knot of humanity, to focus on the lines.

Normally the motion of the lines was stately, predictable

– regular enough for the Human Beings to measure their lives by it, in fact. Overlaid on the eternal drift of the lines towards the Crust there were pulses of line-bunching: the tight, sharp crowdings that marked the days, and the slower, more complex second-order oscillations which humans used to count their months. In normal times it was easy for the Human Beings to avoid the slow creep of the lines; there was always plenty of time to dismantle the Net, repitch their little encampment in another corner of the empty sky.

Dura even knew what caused the lines' stately pulsations, much good the knowledge did her: the Star had a companion, far beyond the Crust – a *planet*, a ball like the Star but smaller, lighter – which revolved, unseen, over their heads, pulling at the vortex lines as if with invisible fingers. And, of course, beyond the planet – the childish ideas returned to her unbidden, like fragments of her lingering sleep – beyond the planet were the stars of the Ur-humans, impossibly distant and forever invisible.

The drifting vortex lines were as stable and secure, in normal times, as the fingers of some friendly god; humans, Air-pigs and others moved freely between the lines, fearlessly and without any danger...

Except during a Glitch.

Now, across the frame of her spread fingers, the vortex array was shifting visibly as the superfluid Air sought to realign with the Star's adjusted rotation. Instabilities – great parallel sets of ripples – already marched majestically along the length of the lines, bearing the news of the Star's new awakening from Pole to magnetic Pole.

The photons emitted by the lines smelled thin, sharp. The spin storm was coming.

Dura had chosen a sleep place about fifty mansheights from the centre of the Human Beings' current encampment, in a place where the Magfield had felt particularly thick, comfortingly secure. Now she began to Wave towards the Net. Wriggling, rippling her limbs, she felt electricity course through her epidermis; and she pushed with arms and legs at the invisible, elastic resistance of the Magfield as if it were a ladder. Fully awake now, she found herself filled with a belated anxiety – an anxiety healthily laced with guilt at her tardiness – and as she slid across the Magfield she spread the webbed fingers of her hands and beat at the Air, trying to work up still more speed. Neutron superfluid made up most of the bulk of the Air, so there was barely any resistance to her hands; but still she clawed at the Air, her impatience mounting, seeking comfort in activity.

The vortex lines slid like dreams across her field of vision now. Ripples hurtled in great even chains, as if the vortex lines were ropes shaken by giants located in the mists of the Poles. As the waves beat past her they emitted a low, cool groan. The amplitude of the waves was already half a mansheight. *By Bolder's guts*, she thought, *maybe that old fool Adda is right for once; maybe this really is going to be the worst yet*.

Slowly, painfully slowly, the encampment grew from a distant abstraction, a melange of movement and noise, to a community. The encampment was based around the crude cylindrical Net made of plaited tree-bark, slung out along the Magfield lines. Most people slept and ate bound up to the Net, and the length of the cylinder was a patchwork of tied-up belongings, privacy blankets, cleaning brushes, simple clothes – ponchos, tunics and belts – and a few pathetic bundles of food. Scraps of half-finished wooden artifacts and flags of untreated Air-pig leather dangled from the Net ropes.

The Net was five mansheights across and a dozen long. It was at least five generations old, according to the older folk like Adda. And it was the only home of about fifty humans – and their only treasure.

As she neared it, clawing her way through the clinging Magfield, Dura suddenly saw the flimsy construct with an objective eye – as if she had not been born in a blanket tied to its filthy knots, as if she would not die still clinging to its fibres. How fragile it was: how pathetic, how defenceless they truly were. Even as she approached to join her people in this moment of need, Dura felt depressed, weak, helpless.

The adults and older children were Waving all around the Net, working at knots which dwarfed their fingers. She saw Esk, picking patiently at a section of the Net. Dura thought he watched her approach, but it was hard to be sure. In any event Philas, his wife, was with him, and Dura kept her face averted. Here and there Dura could make out small children and infants still attached to the Net by tethers of varying lengths. Each child, left tethered up by labouring parents and siblings, was a small, wailing bundle of fear and loneliness, Waving futilely against its constraints, and Dura felt her heart go out to every one of them. Dura spotted the girl Dia, heavily pregnant with her first child. Working with her husband Mur, Dia was pulling tools and bits of clothing from the Net and stuffing them into a sack; Air-sweat glistened from her swollen, naked belly. Dia was a small-limbed, childlike woman whose pregnancy had served to make her only more vulnerable and young-looking; watching her work now, her every movement redolent of fear, made something move inside childless Dura, an urge to protect.

The animals – the tribe's small herd of a dozen adult Air-pigs and about as many piglets – were restrained inside the Net, along its axis. They bleated, their din adding a mournful counterpoint to the shouts and cries of humans; they huddled together at the heart of the Net in a trembling mass of fins, jet orifices and stalks erect with huge, bowl-shaped eyes. A few people had gone inside the Net and were trying to calm the animals, to attach leaders to their pierced fins. But the dismantling of the Net was proceeding slowly and unevenly, Dura saw as she approached, and the herd was a mass of panicky noise, uncoordinated movement.

She heard voices raised in fear and impatience. What had seemed from a little further away to be a reasonably controlled operation was actually little more than a shambles, she realized.

There was something in her peripheral vision – a motion, blue-white and distant . . . More ripples in the vortex tubes, coming from the distant North: immense, jagged irregularities utterly dwarfing the small instabilities she'd observed so far.

There wasn't much time.

Logue, her father, hung in the Magfield a little way from the Net. Adda, too old and slow for the urgent work of dismantling the encampment, hovered beside Logue, his thin face twisted, sour. Logue bellowed out orders in his huge baritone, but, Dura could already see, with very little effect on the Human Beings' coordination. Still Dura had that odd feeling

10

of timelessness, of detachment, and she studied her father as if meeting him for the first time in many weeks. Logue's hair, plastered against his scalp, was crumpled and yellowed; his face was a mask through which the round, boyish features shared by Farr could still be discerned, obscured by a mat of scars and wrinkles.

As Dura approached, Logue turned to her, his brown eyecups wide, his cheek muscles working. 'You took your time,' he growled at her. 'Where have you been? You're needed here. Can't you see that?'

His words cut through her detachment, and despite herself, despite the urgency of the moment, she felt resentment building in her. 'Where? I've been to the Core in a Xeelee night-fighter. Where do you think I've been?'

Logue turned from her in apparent disgust. 'You shouldn't blaspheme,' he muttered.

She wanted to laugh. Impatient with him, with herself, with the continual friction between them, she shook her head. 'Oh, into the Ring with it. What do you want me to do?'

Now old Adda leaned forward, the open pores among his remaining hair sparkling Air-sweat. 'Don't know there's much you *can* do,' he said sourly. 'Look at them. What a shambles.'

'We're not going to make it in time, are we?' Dura asked him. She pointed North. 'Look at that ripple. We won't get out of the way before it hits.'

'Maybe. Maybe not.' The old man raised his empty eyes to the South Pole; its soft glow illuminated the backs of his eyes, the cup-retinae there; fragments of debris swirled around the rims and tiny cleansing symbiotes swam constantly in and out of the cups.

Logue bellowed suddenly, 'Mur, you damn fool. If that knot is stuck then cut it. Rip it. Gnaw it through if you have to! – but don't just leave it there, or half the Net is going to go flapping off into the Quantum Sea when the storm hits us . . .'

'Worst I've ever seen,' Adda muttered, sniffing. 'Never known the photons to smell so sour. Like a frightened piglet . . . Of course,' he went on after a few moments, 'I remember one spin storm when I was a kid . . .'

Dura couldn't help but smile. Adda was the wisest amongst them, probably, about the ways of the Star. But he relished his

11

role as doomsayer . . . he could never let go of the mysteries of his own past, of the wild, deadly days which only he could remember . . .

Logue turned on her with fury, his face as unstable as the quivering Magfield. 'While you grin, we could die,' he hissed.

'I know.' She reached out and touched his arm, feeling the hot tide of Air which superleaked from his clenched muscles. 'I know. I'm – sorry.'

He frowned, staring at her, and reached forward, as if to touch her. But he drew the hand back. 'Perhaps you're not as strong as I like to think you are.'

'No,' she said quietly. 'Perhaps I'm not.'

'Come,' he said. 'We'll help each other. And we'll help our people. No one's dead yet, after all.'

Dura scrambled across the Magfield flux lines to the Net. Men, women and older children were gathered in tight huddles, their thin bodies bumping together as they floated in the turbulent Magfield, labouring at the Net. They cast fearful, distracted glances at the approaching vortex instabilities, and from all around the Net Dura could hear muttered – or shouted – prayer-chants, pleas for the benevolence of the Xeelee.

Watching the Human Beings, Dura realized they were huddling together for *comfort*, not for efficiency. Rather than working evenly and systematically around the Net, the people were actually impeding each other from working effectively at the dismantling; whole sections of the tangled Net were being left unattended.

Dura's feeling of depressed helplessness deepened. Perhaps she could help them organize better – act as Logue's daughter for once, she admonished herself wearily, act as a *leader*. But as she studied the frightened faces of the Human Beings, the round, staring eyecups of the children, she recognized the weary terror which seemed to be numbing her own reactions.

Maybe huddling and praying was as rational a response as any to this latest disaster.

She twisted in the Air and Waved towards an empty section of Net, keeping well away from Esk and Philas. Logue would have to do the leading; Dura would remain one of the led.

The first of the massive ripples neared the encampment. Feeling the growing tension in the Air, Dura grasped the Net's sturdy rope and pulled her body against its shuddering bulk. For a moment her face was pressed against the Net's thick mesh, and she found herself staring at an Air-pig, not an arm's length from her. The rope-threaded holes punched through its fins were widened with age, ringed by scar tissue. The Air-pig seemed to be looking into her eyes, its six eyestalks pushed straight out from its brain pan, the cups swivelled at her. The beast was one of the oldest of the Air-pigs – as a kid, she recalled wistfully, she would have known the names of each one of the meagre herd – and it must have seen plenty of spin storms before. *Well*, she thought. *What's your diagnosis? Do you think we've a chance of getting through this storm any better than we have all the others? Will you live to see the other side of it? What do you think?*

The creature's fixed, mournful stare, the brown depths of its eyecups, afforded her no reply. But its musty animal warmth stank of fear.

The mat of rope before her face glimmered suddenly, blue-white; her head cast a shadow before her.

She turned to see that one vortex line had drifted to within a couple of mansheights of her position; it shimmered in the Air, quivering, a cable emitting an electric-blue glow almost too clamorous for her eyes.

The tribesfolk appeared to have given up any attempts at dismantling the Net; even Logue and Adda had come Waving across to the illusory safety of the habitat. People simply clung on where they were, arms wrapped around each other and around the smallest of the children, the opened-up Net flapping uselessly around them. The crying of children resounded.

And now, with sudden brutality, the spin storm hit. A jagged discontinuity a mansheight deep surged along the nearest vortex line past the Net, faster than any human could Wave, faster even than any wild Air-pig could jet through the Air. Dura tried to concentrate on the solidity of the fibrous rope in her hands, the comforting Magfield which, as always, confined her body with a gentle grip . . . But it was impossible to ignore the sudden thickness of the Air in her lungs, the

13

roaring heat-noise blasting through the Air so powerfully she feared for her ears, the quivering of the Magfield.

She clenched her eyes closed so hard that she could feel the Air in the cups squeeze away. *Concentrate*, she told herself. *You understand what's happening here. That wretched Air-pig, bound up inside the Net, is as ignorant as the youngest piglet in its first storm. But not you; not a Human Being.*

And it is through understanding that we will prevail . . . But, even as she intoned the words to herself like a prayer, she could not find any truth in that pious hope.

The Air was a neutron liquid, a superfluid. Superfluids could not sustain spin over extended distances. So, in response to the rotation of the Star, the Air became filled with vortex lines, tubes of vanishing thinness within which the Air's rotation was confined. The vortex lines aligned themselves in regular arrays, aligned with the Star's rotation axis – closely parallel to the magnetic axis followed by the Magfield. The vortex lines filled the world. They were safe as long as you stayed away from them; every child knew that. But in a Glitch, Dura thought ruefully, the lines sometimes came looking for you . . . and the Air's superfluidity broke down around a collapsing vortex line, transforming the Air from a thin, stable, lifegiving fluid into a thing of turmoil and turbulence.

The worst of the first spin gust seemed to be passing now. Still clinging to the Net, she opened her eyes and cast rapidly around the sky.

The vortex lines, parallel beams receding into infinity, were still marching grandly across the sky, seeking their new alignment. It was quite a magnificent sight; and for a moment Dura felt wonder thrill through her as she imagined the arrays of spin lines which stretched right around the Star realigning, gathering and spreading, as if the Star were bound up in the integrated thoughts of some immense mind.

The Net shuddered in her grip, its coarse fibres abrading her palms; the sharp pain jolted her rudely back to the here and now. She sighed, gathering her strength, as weariness closed around her again.

'Dura! Dura!'

The childish voice, thin and scared, came drifting to her from a few mansheights away. Gripping the Net with one

14

hand, she twisted to see Farr, her little brother, suspended in the Air like a discarded fragment of cloth and flesh. He was Waving towards her.

When Farr reached her, Dura enfolded him in her free arm, helping him wrap his arms and legs around the security of the Net's ropes. He was breathing hard and trembling, and she could see the short hairs which coated his scalp pulsing as superfluid surged through them.

'I was thrown off,' he gasped between gulps of Air. 'I lost my piglet.'

'So I see. Are you okay?'

'I think so.' He stared up at her, his eyes wide and empty, and he raked his gaze across the sky as if searching for the source of this betrayal of his safety. 'This is terrible, isn't it, Dura? Are we going to die?'

She ran her fingers casually through his stiff hair. 'No,' she said, with a conviction she could never have mustered for herself alone. 'No, we won't die. But we are in danger. Now come on, we should get to work. We need to get the Net taken apart, folded up, before the next instability hits us and wrecks it.' She pointed to a small, open-looking knot. 'There. Undo that. As quick as you can.'

He buried his trembling fingers in the knot and began prising out lengths of rope. 'How long before the next ripple?'

'Long enough to finish the job,' she said firmly. For confirmation, with her own fingers still dragging at the stubborn knots, she glanced upflux – Northwards – to the source of the next ripple.

Instantly she saw how wrong she had been. From around the Net she heard voices raised in wonder and rising alarm; within a few heartbeats, it seemed, she was hearing the first screams.

The next ripple was closing on them; already she could hear its rising clamour of heat fluctuations. This new instability was huge, at least five or six mansheights deep. Dura watched, mesmerized, her hands frozen. Already the ripple was hurtling at her faster than any she could remember, and as it approached its amplitude seemed to be deepening, as if it were feeding on Glitch energy. And, of course, with greater amplitude came still greater speed. The instability was a complex superposition of wave shapes clustered along the length of the migrating vortex line, a superposition which spiralled around the line like some malevolent animal clambering towards her . . .

Farr said, 'We can't escape that. Can we, Dura?'

There was a moment of stillness, almost of calm. Farr's voice, though still cracked by adolescence, had sounded suddenly full of a premature wisdom. It was some comfort that Dura wasn't going to have to lie to him.

'No,' she said. 'We've been too slow. I think it's going to hit the Net.' She felt distant from the danger around her, as if she were recalling events from long ago, far away.

Even as it rushed up towards them the ripple bowed away from the trend of the vortex line in ever more elaborate, fantastic shapes. It was as if some elastic limit had been passed and the vortex line, under intolerable strain, was yielding.

It was almost beautiful, captivating to watch. And it was only mansheights away.

She heard the thin voice of old Adda, from somewhere on the other side of the Net. 'Get away from the Net. Oh, get away from the Net!'

'Do as he says. Come on.'

The boy slowly lifted his head; he still clung to the rope, and his eyes were empty, as if beyond fear or wonder. She drove a fist into one of his hands. 'Come on!'

The boy cried out and withdrew his hands and legs from the Net, staring at her with a round face full of betrayal . . . but a face that looked once more like that of an alert child rather than a bemused, petrified adult. Dura grabbed his hand. 'Farr, you have to Wave as you've never Waved before. Hold my hand; we'll stay together . . .'

With a thrust of her legs she pushed away. For the first moments she seemed to be dragging Farr behind her; but soon his body was Waving in synchronization with hers, wriggling against the cloying thickness of the Magfield, and the two of them hurried away from the doomed Net.

As she Waved, gasping, Dura looked back. The spin instability, recoiling, wafted through the Air like a deadly, blue-white wand. It scythed towards the Net with its cargo of wriggling humans. It was like some wonderful toy, Dura thought; it glowed intensely brightly, and the heat-noise it emitted was a roar, almost drowning out thought itself. The bleating of trapped Air-pigs was cold-thin, and Dura thought briefly of the old animal with whom she had shared that brief, odd moment of half-communication; she wondered how much that poor creature understood of what was to happen.

Maybe half the Human Beings had heeded Adda's advice to get away. The rest, apparently paralysed by fear and awe, still clung to the Net. The pregnant Dia was lumbering away into the Air with Mur; the woman Philas still picked frantically, uselessly, at the Net, despite the pleas of her husband Esk to come away. It was as if, Dura thought, Philas imagined that the work was a magic spell which would drive the instability away.

Dura knew that rotation instabilities lost energy rapidly. Soon, very soon, this fantastic demon would wither to nothing, leaving the Air calm and empty once more. And, glowing, roaring, stinking of sour photons, the instability was indeed visibly shrinking as it bore down on the Net.

But, it was immediately obvious, not shrinking fast enough . . .

With a heat-wail like a thousand voices the instability tore into the Net.

It was like a fist driving into cloth.

The Air inside the Net ceased to be superfluid and became a stiff, turbulent mass, whipping and whorling around the vortex instability like some demented animal. Dura saw knots burst open; the Net, almost gracefully, disintegrated into fragments of rope, into rough mats to which adults and children clung.

The Air-pig herd was hurled away into the Air as if scattered by a giant hand. Dura could see how some of the beasts, evidently dead or dying, hung where they were thrown, limply suspended against the Magfield; the rest squirted away through the Air, their bellow-guts puffing out farts of blue gas.

One man, clinging alone to a raft of rope, was sucked towards the instability itself.

It was too far away to be sure, but Dura thought she recognized Esk. Dozens of mansheights from the site of the Net, she was much too far away even to call to him – let alone to help – but nevertheless she seemed to see what followed as clearly as if she rode at her lost lover's shoulder towards the deadly arch.

Esk, with his mat of rope, tumbled through the plane of the quivering, arch-shaped instability and was hurled around the arch itself, as limp as a doll. His trajectory rapidly lost energy and, unresisting, he spiralled inwards, orbiting the arch like some demented Air-piglet.

Esk's body burst open, the chest and abdominal cavities peeling back like opening eyes, the limbs coming free almost easily, like a toy's.

Farr cried out, wordless. It was the first sound he'd made since they'd pushed away from the Net.

Dura reached for him and clutched his hand, hard. 'Listen to me,' she shouted over the arch's continuing heat-clamour. 'It looked worse than it was. Esk was dead long before he hit the arch.' And that was true; as soon as he had entered the region in which superfluidity broke down, the processes of Esk's body – his breathing, his circulatory system, his very muscles, all reliant on the exploitation of the Air's superfluidity – would have collapsed. To Esk, as the strength left his limbs, as the Air coagulated in the superleak capillaries of his brain, it must have been like falling gently asleep.

She thought. She hoped.

The instability passed through the site of the Net and sailed on into the sky, continuing its futile mission towards the South. But even as Dura watched, the arch shape was dwindling, shrinking, its energy expended.

It left behind an encampment which had been torn apart as effectively as poor Esk's body.

Dura pulled Farr closer to her, easily overcoming the gentle resistance of the Magfield, and stroked his hair. 'Come on,' she said. 'It's over now. Let's go back, and see what we can do.'

'No,' he said, clinging to his sister. 'It's never over. Is it, Dura?'

*

18

Little knots of people moved through the glistening, newly stable vortex lines, calling to each other. Dura Waved between the struggling groups, searching for Logue, or news of Logue; she kept a tight grip on Farr's hand.

'Dura, help us! Oh, by the blood of the Xeelee, help us!'

The voice came to her from a dozen mansheights away; it was a man's – thin, high and desperate. She turned in the Air, searching for its source.

Farr took her arm and pointed. 'There. It's Mur, over by that chunk of Net. See? And it looks as if he's got Dia with him.'

Heavily pregnant Dia . . . Dura pulled at her brother's hand and Waved rapidly through the Air.

Mur and Dia hung alone in the Air, naked and without tools. Mur was holding his wife's shoulders and cradling her head. Dia was stretched out, her legs parting softly, her hands locked around the base of her distended belly.

Mur's young face was hard, cold and determined; his eyes were pits of darkness as he peered at Dura and Farr. 'It's her time. She's early, but the Glitch . . . You'll have to help me.'

'All right.' Dura lifted Dia's hands away from her belly, gently but firmly, and ran her fingers quickly over the uneven bulge. She could feel the baby's limbs pushing feebly at the walls which still restrained it. The head was low, deep in the pelvis. 'I think the head's engaged,' she said. Dia's young, thin face was fixed on hers, contorted with pain; Dura tried to smile at her. 'It feels fine. A little while longer . . .'

Dia hissed, her face creased with pain, 'Get on with it, damn you.'

'Yes.'

Dura looked around desperately; the Air around them was still empty, the nearest Human Beings dozens of mansheights away. They were on their own.

She closed her eyes for a moment, trying to resist the temptation to search the Air for Logue. She delved deep inside herself, looking for strength.

'It's going to be all right,' she said. 'Mur, hold her neck and shoulders. You'll have to brace her there; if you Wave a little you'll hold yourself in place, and . . .'

'I know what to do,' Mur snapped. Still holding Dia's small

head against his chest, he grasped her shoulders and Waved slowly, his strong legs beating at the Air.

Dura felt awkward, inadequate. *Damn it*, she thought, aware of the pettiness of her own reaction, *damn it, I've never done this on my own before. What do they expect?*

What next? 'Farr, you'll have to help me.'

The boy hovered in the Air a mansheight away, his mouth gaping. 'Dura, I . . .'

'Come on, Farr, there's nobody else,' Dura said. As he came close to her she whispered, 'I know you're frightened. I'm frightened too. But not as much as Dia. It's not so difficult as all that, anyway. We'll do fine . . .'

As long as nothing goes wrong, she thought.

'All right,' Farr said. 'What do I do?'

Dura took hold of Dia's right leg, wrapping her fingers tightly around the lower calf. The woman's muscles were trembling and slick with Air-sweat, and Dura could feel the legs pushing apart; Dia's vagina was opening like a small mouth, popping softly. 'Take her other leg,' she told Farr. 'Like I've done. Get a tight hold; you're going to have to pull hard.'

Farr, hesitant and obviously scared, did as he was told.

The baby moved, visibly, further into the pelvic area. It was like watching a morsel of food disappear down some huge neck. Dia arched back her head and moaned; the muscles in her neck were stiff and prominent.

'It's time,' Dura said. She glanced around quickly. She and Farr were in position, holding Dia's ankles; Mur was already Waving, quite hard, pushing at his wife's shoulders, so that the little ensemble drifted slowly through the Air. Both Mur's and Farr's eyes were locked on Dura's face.

Dia called out again, wordlessly.

Dura leaned back, grasping Dia's calf, and pushed firmly with her legs at the Magfield. 'Farr! Do what I'm doing. We have to open her legs. Go on; don't be afraid.'

Farr watched her for a moment, then leaned back and Waved in a copy of his sister's movements. Mur cried out and shoved hard at his wife's shoulders, balancing Farr and Dura.

Dia's legs parted easily. She screamed.

Farr's hands slid over Dia's convulsing calf; in his shock he seemed to stumble in the Air, his eyes wide. Dia's thighs twitched back towards each other, the muscles shuddering.

'No!' Mur shouted. 'Farr, keep going; you mustn't stop now!'

Farr's distress was evident. 'But we're hurting her.'

'No.'

Damn it, Dura thought, *Farr should know what's happening here.* Dia's pelvis was hinged; with the birth so close the cartilage locking the two segments of the pelvis together would have dissolved into Dia's blood, leaving her pelvis easily opened. Her birth canal and vagina were already stretching, gaping wide. Everything was working together to allow the baby's head an easy passage from the womb to the Air. *It's easy*, Dura thought. *And it's easy because the Ur-humans designed it to be easy, maybe even easier than for themselves . . .*

'It's meant to be like this,' she shouted at Farr. 'Believe me. You'll hurt her if you stop now, if you don't help us. And you'll hurt the baby.'

Dia opened her eyes. The cups brimmed with tears. 'Please, Farr,' she said, reaching towards him vaguely. 'It's all right. Please.'

He nodded, mumbling apologies, and pulled once more at Dia's leg.

'Easy,' Dura called, trying to match his motion. 'Not too fast, and not jerkily; nice and smooth . . .'

The birth canal gaped like a green-dark tunnel. Dia's legs parted further than it would have seemed possible; Dura could see, under the thin flesh around the girl's hips, how the pelvis had hinged wide.

Dia screamed; her stomach convulsed.

The baby came suddenly, wriggling down the birth passage like an Air-piglet. It squirted into the Air with a soft, sucking noise; droplets of dense, green-gold Air sprayed around it. As soon as it was out of the canal the baby started to Wave, instinctively but feebly, across the Magfield within which it would be embedded for all of its life.

Dura's eyes locked on Farr. He was following the baby's uncertain progress through the Air, his mouth slack with wonder; but he was still firmly holding Dia's leg. 'Farr,' Dura commanded. 'Come back towards me now. Slowly, steadily – that's it . . .'

Dia's only danger now was that her hinged bones would not settle neatly back into place without dislocation; and even if all went well, for a few days she would be barely able to move as the halves of her pelvis knitted together once more. With Dura and Farr guiding them, her legs closed smoothly; Dura could see the bones around Dia's pelvis sliding smoothly back into place.

Mur had managed to snatch a rag, a remnant of some piece of clothing, from the littered Air; now he wiped tenderly at Dia's relaxing, half-sleeping face. Dura took some of the rag and mopped at Dia's thighs and belly.

Farr Waved slowly towards them. He had chased after and caught the baby, Dura saw; now he held the child against his chest as proudly as if it were his own, uncaring of the birth fluid which pooled on his chest. The infant's mouth was still distorted into the characteristic horn-shape it had needed to lock on to the womb-wall nipples which sustained it before its birth; and its tiny penis had popped out of the protective cache between its legs.

Farr, grinning, held the baby out to its mother. 'It's a boy,' he said.

'Jai,' Dia whispered. 'He's Jai.'

Forty Human Beings had survived, of fifty. All but six adult Air-pigs, four of them male, were gone. The Net, torn and scattered, was irreparable.

Logue was lost.

The tribe huddled together in the Magfield, surrounded by featureless Air. Mur and Dia clung together, cradling their new, mewling baby. Dura uncomfortably led the Human Beings through a brief service of prayers, calling down the beneficence of the Xeelee. Adda stayed close to her, silent and strong despite his age, and Farr's hand was a constant presence in hers.

Then the bodies they'd managed to retrieve were released into the Air; they slid, dwindling, down to the Quantum Sea.

Philas, wife of the dead Esk, approached Dura after the service, Waving stiffly. The two women studied each other, not speaking; Adda and the rest moved away, averting their faces.

Philas was a thin, tired-looking woman; her uneven hair was tied back with a piece of rope, making her face look skeletal. She stared at Dura, as if daring her to grieve.

The Human Beings were monogamous . . . but there were more adult women than men. *So monogamy doesn't make sense,* Dura thought wearily, *and yet we practise it anyway. Or rather, we pay lip-service to it.*

Esk had loved them both . . . at any rate, he had shown tenderness to them both. And his relationship with Dura had been no secret to Philas, or to anyone else, for that matter. It had certainly done Philas no harm.

Perhaps Philas and Dura could help each other now, Dura thought. Perhaps hold each other. But they wouldn't even speak about it.

And she, Dura, would not even be allowed to grieve openly.

At last Philas spoke. 'What are we going to do, Dura? Should we rebuild the Net? What should we do?'

Staring into the woman's dull eyecups, Dura wanted to retreat into herself, to bring forward her own grief for her father, for Esk, as a shield against Philas's demands. *I don't know. I don't know. How could I know?*

But there was nowhere to retreat.

2

Ten Human Beings – Dura with Farr in tow, Adda, the newly
widowed Philas, and six other adults – climbed out of the site
of the devastated encampment. They Waved steadily across
the Magfield and towards the Crust, in search of food.

Adda, as was his custom, stayed a small distance away
from the rest as they Waved across the field-lines. One of his
eyes was matted over with the scars of age – thinking about it
now he gave that cup a quick poke with a fingertip to
dislodge some of the less welcome little creatures who were
continually trying to establish residence in there – but the
other eye was as keen as it had ever been, and as he Waved he
swept his gaze through the Air above, below and all around
them. He liked to stay apart to keep an eye on things. . . and it
allowed him to hide the fact that he sometimes had trouble
keeping up with the rest. It was his boast that he could still
Wave as good as any damn kid. It wasn't true, of course, but it
was his boast. He used to wriggle across the Magfield like an
Air-piglet with a neutrino fount up its arse, he recalled wistfully, but that was a long time ago. Now he must look like a
Xeelee's grandmother. Adda's vertebrae seemed to be seizing
up one by damn one as time wore away, so that his Waving
was more like thrashing; it took a conscious effort to thrust his
pelvis back, to let his legs flop behind the motion of his hips,
to let his head drive ahead of the bending of his spine. And
his skin was coarsened by age, too, tough as old tree-bark in
places; that had its advantages, but it meant that he had trouble feeling the places where the electric currents induced in
his epidermis by his motion across the Magfield were
strongest. Damn it, he could barely *feel* the Magfield now; he
was, he thought sourly, Waving from memory.

Much like sex these days.

As always he carried his battered and trusted spear, a sharpened pole of wood prised from a tree trunk by his own father hundreds of months ago. His fingers nestled comfortably in the gripping grooves carved expertly in the shaft, and electrical currents Magfield-induced in the wood tingled in his palm. As his father had taught him, he kept the spear pointed along the direction of the Magfield across which they climbed . . . for, of course, the wood – in fact any material – was stronger in the direction of the Magfield than across it. And as any child knew, if danger did approach it would most likely come along the Magfield lines, in which direction motion was invisibly easy.

There weren't many predators who would attack humans, but Adda had seen a few, and his father had told him of worse. The rays, for instance . . . Even a mature Air-boar – the tougher cousin of the Air-pig – could give a man or woman a hard fight, and could carry away a child as easy as snipping krypton grass away from the Crust, if it was hungry enough.

Even half as hungry as the Human Beings were going to grow before much longer.

He looked along the gleaming cage of vortex lines which swept to red-mist infinity at the South Pole, slicing up the sky around his companions. As always – whenever he travelled even a short distance from the illusory completeness of the tribe's tiny human environ – he was struck by the immensity of the Mantle-world; and as his eye followed the converging parallels of the vortex lines he felt as if his tiny spirit, helpless with awe, was somehow drawn along the lines. The island of scattered debris which marked the site of their devastated encampment was a dirt-coloured mote Air-marooned in the clean, yellow-white immensities of the Star. And his companions – nine of them still, he counted automatically – were Waving across the field lines with unconscious synchronization, ropes and nets wrapped loosely around their waists, their faces upturned to the Crust. One man had peeled away from the rest; he had found an abandoned spin-spider web slung across the vortex lines, and was searching it efficiently for eggs.

Human Beings looked so beautiful when they moved. And when a shoal of the kids went whirling along the Magfield

25

– flapping their legs so hard you could see the glow of the induced fields shining in their limbs, and spiralling around the flux lines fast enough to turn them into blurs – well, it was hard to imagine a better sight in this or any of the fabled, lost worlds of the Ur-humans.

But at the same time humans looked so fragile, dwarfed as they were by the immensities of the vortex-line cage and by the deep and deadly mysteries of the Quantum Sea far below. Somehow an Air-pig looked the part for this environment, he thought. Round and fat and solid . . . Why, even a neutrino fount didn't have to be the end for an Air-pig; all it had to do was to tuck in its eyes, fold down its fins and ride out the storm. Unless it got blasted out of the Star altogether, what could happen? When the fount was done the pig could just unfold, graze on whatever foliage it could find – for trees were trees, whichever part of the Crust they were growing out of – and mate with the first Air-pig it came across. Or get mated with, Adda thought with a grin.

Humans weren't like that. Humans were *delicate*. Easily smashed up, broken apart. He thought of Esk: a damn fool, but nobody deserved to die like that. And, more than anything else, humans were *strange*. If Adda were to pluck one of these irritating little nibblers out of his dud eye now and look at it up close, he knew he'd find the same basic design as the average Air-pig: six fins, symmetrically placed, an intake-mouth to the front, jet vents to the rear, six tiny eyes. All Mantle animals were the same, just scaled big and small, or with differences of proportion; the basic features could be recognized even in superficially different creatures like rays.

. . . Except for humans. There was nothing, no other animal, like a human in all this world.

That wasn't a surprise, of course. Every kid learned at his mother's breast how the Ur-humans had come from some- where far away – a place much better than this, of course; Adda suspected every human on every world grew up believ- ing that – and had left children here to grow, to be strong, and to join the community of mankind one day, all under the beneficial and all-too-abstract gaze of that multiple God, the Xeelee.

So the Human Beings had been *put* there. Adda had no

doubt about the basic truth of the old story – damn it, you only had to watch humans in flight to see the blinding self-evidence of it – but on the other hand, he thought as he watched the flock of Human Beings soar across the sky, he wouldn't really *want* to be built like an Air-pig. Fat and round and flying by farts?

Mind you, flatulence was one skill he *had* bettered as he had got older. Maybe it wouldn't have been such a bad idea to have been an Air-pig after all.

Adda was the oldest surviving Human Being. He knew what the others thought of him: that he was a sour old fool, too gloomy for his own good. But he didn't care much about that. He hadn't survived longer than any of his contemporaries by accident. But he was, and always had been, essentially a simple man, not gifted with the power over people and language shown by, say, a Logue. Or even a Dura, he thought, even though she mightn't realize it yet. So if he irritated folk with anecdotes of his boyhood . . . but, even as they laughed at him, if they soaked up any one of the small lessons which had kept him alive . . . well, that was all right by Adda.

Of course, there were fragments from the past he didn't share with anyone. He'd no doubt, for instance, that the Glitches were changing.

There had always been Glitches, spin storms. He even knew what caused them, in an abstract sort of way: the slowing of the Star's rotation, and the consequent explosive equalizations of spin energy. But over the last few years the Glitches had got worse . . . far worse, and much more frequent.

Something else was causing Glitches now. Something unknowably powerful, disrupting the Star . . .

Of course, his crotchety exterior had a major advantage – one he'd never admitted to anyone else, and only half-allowed to himself. By acting so sour he never had to show the unbearable love he felt for his fellow humans as he watched their alien, vulnerable, impossibly beautiful flight across the Magfield, or the heartbreak he endured at the loss of even the most wasted, most spoiled life.

Hefting his dragging spear in tiring fingers, Adda kicked on towards the treetops of the Crust with renewed vigour.

*

Farr hovered in the Air, his knees tucked against his chest. With four or five brisk pushes he emptied his bowels. He watched the pale, odourless pellets of shit sail sparkling into the empty Air and sink towards the underMantle. Dense with neutrons, the waste would merge into the unbreathable underMantle and, perhaps, sink at last into the Quantum Sea.

He'd never been so high.

The treetops were only a few minutes' Waving above him now: only a score of mansheights or so. The round, bronzed leaves of the trees, all turned towards the Quantum Sea, formed a glimmering ceiling over the world. As he Waved he stared up at that ceiling longingly, as if the leaves somehow represented safety – and yet he looked nervously too. For beyond the leaves were the tree trunks, suspended in darkness; and beyond the trunks lay the Crust itself, where all manner of creatures prowled . . . At least according to old Adda, and some of the other kids.

But still, Farr realized, he'd rather be up there amidst the trees than – *suspended* – out here.

He pushed at the Magfield and shimmered upwards.

Farr, young as he was, was used to the feeling of fear. Of mortal terror, even. But he was experiencing a kind of fear new to him – a novelty – and he probed at it, trying to understand.

The nine adults around him Waved steadily upwards, their faces turned up to the trees like inverted leaves. Their bodies moved efficiently and with varying degrees of grace, and Farr could smell the musky photons they exuded, hear the steady rhythm of their breathing as they worked, wordless. His own breath was rapid; the Air up here felt thin, shallow. And he was growing colder, despite the hard work of Waving.

Somehow, without realizing it, Farr had gotten himself to the centre of the Waving group, so they formed a protective barrier around him. In fact, he realized, he was Waving close to his sister, Dura, as if he were some little kid who needed his hand holding.

How embarrassing.

Discreetly, without making it too obvious, he leaned forward so that he slid out towards the edge of the group, away from Dura. And at the edge that strange new flavour of fear – a feeling of exposure – assailed him again. Shaking his head as if to clear out musty Air, he forced himself to turn away from the group, twisting in the Air, so that he faced outwards, across the Mantle.

Farr knew that the Mantle was tens of millions of mansheights deep. But humans could survive only in a band about two million mansheights thick. Farr knew why . . . or some of it anyway. The complex compounds of heavy tin nuclei which composed his body (so his father had explained earnestly) could remain stable – remain bonded by exchanges of neutron pairs – only within this layer. It was all to do with neutron density: too far up and there weren't enough neutrons to allow the complex bonding between nuclei; too far down, in the cloying underMantle, there were *too many* neutrons – in the underMantle the very nuclei which composed his body would begin to dissolve, liquefying at last into smooth neutron liquid.

And here – close to the treetops, nearing the top of the habitable band – he was tens of thousands of mansheights above the site of the ruined Net.

Farr looked down, beyond his Waving feet, back the way he had climbed. The vortex lines crossed the enormous sky, hundreds of them in a rigid parallel array of blue-white streaks which melted into misty vanishing-points to left and right. The lines blurred below him, the distance between them foreshortening until the lines melted into a textured blue haze above the Quantum Sea. The Sea itself was a purple bruise below the vortex lines, its surface mist-shrouded and deadly.

. . . And the surface of the Sea curved downwards.

Farr had to suppress a yell by gulping, hard. He looked again at the Sea and saw how it fell subtly away in every direction; there seemed no doubt that he was looking down at a huge sphere. Even the vortex lines dipped slightly as they arced away, converging, towards the horizons of the Sea. It was as if they were a cage which encased the Sea.

Farr had grown up knowing that the world – the Star – was a multilayered ball, a *neutron star*. The Crust was the outer surface of the ball, with the Quantum Sea forming an impenetrable centre; the Mantle, including the levels inhabited by humans, was a layer inside the ball filled with Air. But it was one thing to know such a fact; it was quite another to *see* it with your own eyes.

He was *high*. And he *felt* it. He stared down now, deep down, past his feet, at the emptiness which separated him from the Sea. Of course, the Net was long since lost in the Air, a distant speck. But even that, had he been able to see it, would have been a comforting break in this looming immensity . . .

A break from what?

Suddenly he felt as if his stomach were turning into a mass of Air, and the Magfield he was climbing seemed – not just invisible – but intangible, almost irrelevant. It was as if there was nothing keeping him up . . .

He shut his eyes, tight, and tried to retreat into another world, into the fantasies of his childhood. Perhaps once more he could be a warrior in the Core Wars, the epic battles with the Colonists at the dawn of time. Once humans had been strong, powerful, with magical four-walled 'wormhole Interfaces' which let them cross thousands of mansheights in a bound, and great machines which allowed them to fly through the Star and beyond.

But the Colonists, the mysterious denizens of the heart of the Star, had emerged from their glutinous realm to wage war on humanity. They had destroyed, or carried off, the marvellous Interfaces and all the rest – and would have scraped mankind out of the Mantle altogether if not for the wily cunning of Farr: Farr the Ur-human, the giant god-warrior . . .

At length he felt a touch on his shoulder; he opened his eyes to see – not a Colonist – but Dura hovering before him, a look of careful neutrality on her face. She pointed upward. 'We're there.'

Farr looked up.

Leaves – six of them arranged in a neat, symmetrical pattern – hung down just above his head. With a surge of absurd gratitude Farr pulled himself up into the darkness beyond the leaves.

A branch about the thickness of his waist and coated with slick-dark wood led from the leaf into a misty, blue-glowing darkness above him . . . no, he thought, that was the wrong way round; somewhere up there was the trunk of the tree, suspended from the Crust, and from it grew this branch, and from that in turn grew the leaves which faced the Sea. He ran a hand along the wood of the branch; it was hard and smooth, but surprisingly warm to the touch. A few twigs dangled from the main stem, and tiny leaves sought chinks of light between their larger cousins.

He found himself clinging to the branch, his arms wrapped around it as if around the arm of his mother. The warmth of the wood seeped through his chilled body. Embarrassment flickered through his mind briefly, but he ignored it; at last he felt safe.

Dura slid through the leaves and came to rest close to him. The subdued shadow-light of the tree picked out the curves of her face. She smiled at him, looking self-conscious. 'Don't worry about it,' she said, quietly enough that the others couldn't hear. 'I know how you feel. I was the same, the first time I came up here.'

Farr frowned. Reluctantly he released the branch and pushed himself away. 'You were? But I feel as if – as if I'm about to be pulled out of this tree . . .'

'It's called being frightened of falling.'

'But that's ridiculous. Isn't it?' To Farr, 'falling' meant losing your grip on the Magfield when Waving. It was always over in a few mansheights at the most – the tiny resistance of the Air and the currents induced in your skin soon slowed you down. Nothing to fear. And then you could just Wave your way around the Magfield to where you wanted to get to.

Dura grinned. 'It's a feeling as if . . .' She hesitated. '. . . as if you could let go of this tree, right now, and not be able to stop yourself sliding down, across the Magfield and across the vortex lines, faster and faster, all the way to the Sea. And your belly clenches up at the prospect.'

'That's exactly it,' he said, wondering at how precise her description was. 'What does it mean? Why should we feel like that?'

She shrugged, plucking at a leaf. The heavy plate of flesh came free of its attaching branch with a sucking sound. 'I don't know. Logue used to say it's something deep inside us. An instinct we carried with us, when humans were brought to this Star.'

31

Farr thought about that. 'Something to do with the Xeelee.'

'Perhaps. Or something even older. In any event, it's not something you need to worry about. Here.' She held out the leaf towards him.

He took it from her cautiously. It was a bronze-gold plate, streaked radially with purple and blue, about as wide as a man's hand. It was thick and pulpy – springy between his fingers – and, like the wood, was warm to the touch, although, away from its parent branch, it seemed to be cooling rapidly. He turned it over, prodding it with a fingertip; its underside was dry, almost black. He looked up at Dura. 'Thanks,' he said. 'What shall I do with it?'

She laughed. 'Try eating it.'

After a cautious inspection of her face to make sure this wasn't some kind of joke – Dura didn't usually play tricks on him; she was a little too serious for that . . . but you never knew – Farr lifted the leaf to his lips and bit into it. The flesh of the leaf was thin, surprisingly insubstantial, and it seemed to melt against his tongue; but the taste it delivered was astonishingly sweet, like the meat of the youngest Air-piglet, and Farr found himself cramming his mouth.

Within seconds he was swallowing the last of the leaf, savouring the lingering flavour on his tongue. It had been delicious but really quite light, and had done little but whet his hunger further. He looked around avidly. Here on the upper side of the treetop ceiling he could see the leaves turned downwards towards the Quantum Sea, like a layer of broad, flattened child-faces. Farr reached down to pluck another leaf.

Dura, laughing, restrained him. 'Take it easy. Don't strip the whole damn tree.'

Around a full mouth Farr said, 'It's delicious.'

She nodded. 'I know. But it won't fill your belly. Not unless you really do strip the tree . . . That's why we have to hunt the Air-pigs, who eat the leaves – and the grass – for us.' She pursed her lips. Then, in a tone suddenly and, to Farr, shockingly similar to their lost father's, she said, 'Let's have a little lesson. Why do you think the leaves are so tasty?'

Farr thought about that. 'Because they're full of protons.'

Dura nodded seriously. 'Near enough. Actually they are laced with proton-rich isotopes – of krypton, strontium, zirconium, molybdenum . . . even a little heavy iron. Each nucleus of krypton, for instance, has a hundred and eighteen protons, while the tin nuclei of our bodies have just fifty each. And our bodies need protons for their fuel.' The heavy nuclei fissioned in human stomachs. Protons combined with neutrons from the Air to make more tin nuclei – tin was the most stable nucleus in the Air – and gave off energy in the process. 'Now. Where does the proton-rich material come from?'

'From the Crust.' He smiled. 'Everyone knows that.'

The Crust, no more substantial than Air, was a gossamer solid. Its outermost layer was composed of iron nuclei. Further in, steepening pressures drove neutrons into the nuclei of the solid, forming increasingly heavy isotopes . . . until the nuclei became so soft that their proton distributions began to overlap, and the neutrons dripped out to form the Air, a superfluid of neutrons.

'All right,' said Dura. 'So how do the isotopes get all the way from the Crust to these leaves?'

'That's easy,' Farr said, reaching to pluck another succulent leaf. 'The tree pulls them down, inside its trunk.'

'Using veins filled with Air. Right.'

Farr frowned, feeling his cheeks bulge around the leaf. 'But why? What's in it for the tree?'

Dura's mouth opened and closed, and then she smiled, her eyes half-closed. 'That's a good question,' she said. 'One I wouldn't have thought of at your age . . . The isotopes make the leaves more opaque to the neutrinos shining out of the Quantum Sea.'

Farr nodded, chewing.

A flood of neutrinos, intangible and invisible, shone continually from the Sea – or perhaps from the mysterious Core deep beneath the Sea itself – and sleeted through the vortex lines, through the bodies of Farr and the other humans as if they were ghosts, and through the Crust to space. The trees turned slightly neutrino-opaque leaves to that unseen light, absorbing its energy and turning it into more leaves, branches, trunk. Farr pictured trees all over the interior of the Crust, straining towards the Sealight with their leaves of krypton, strontium and molybdenum.

33

Dura watched him eat for a moment; then, hesitantly, she reached out to ruffle his hair-tubes. 'I'll tell you a secret,' she said.

'What?'

'I'm glad you're here.'

Briefly he considered pushing her hand away, of saying something funny, or cruel, to break up the embarrassing moment. But something made him hold back. He studied her face. It was a strong face, he supposed, square and symmetrical, with small, piercing eyes and shining yellow nostrils. Not beautiful, but with something of the strength of their father; and now with the first lines of age it was acquiring a bit more depth.

But there was uncertainty in that face. Loneliness. Indecision, a need for comfort.

Farr thought about it. He felt safe with Dura. Not as safe as when Logue was alive . . . But, he thought ruefully, as safe as he would ever feel again. Dura wasn't really all that strong, but she did her best.

And this moment, as the others moved away from them, being together and talking quietly and tasting the leaves, seemed to be important to her. So he said, gruffly: 'Yes. Me too.'

She smiled at him, then bent to pluck a leaf for herself.

Adda slid silently through the treetops, following the circumference of a rough circle twenty mansheights wide. Then he moved a little further up into the suspended forest, working parallel to the lines of the trunks. The trees grew along the Magfield flux lines, and he kept his spear pointing along the Magfield as he worked his way along the smooth bark.

Save for the low, tinkling rustle of the leaves, the subdued talk of his companions, he found only silence.

He pulled himself back along the length of the tree trunk to the inverted canopy of leaves. None of the Human Beings – except, maybe, Logue's boy Farr, who was looking a little lost – had even noticed he'd been absent. Adda relaxed a little, munching on the thin, deceptively tasty meat of a leaf. But he kept his good eye wide open.

The Human Beings were bunched together around one

trunk, nibbling leaves desultorily and clinging, one-handed, to branchlets. They were huddled together for warmth. Here, where the Air was attenuated by height, it was cold and hard to breathe: so hard, in fact, that Adda felt his reflexes – his very thinking – slowing down, turning sluggish. And it wasn't as if he had a lot of margin in that area, he reflected. It was as if the very Air which drove his bones was turning to a thin, sour soup.

The boy Farr was crouched against a section of bark a mansheight or so from everyone else. He looked as if he were suffering a bit: visibly shivering, his chest rising and falling rapidly in the attenuated Air, his hands pushing leaves into his downturned mouth with an urgency that looked more like a craving for comfort than for food.

Adda, with a single flip of his legs, Waved briskly over to the boy; he leaned towards Farr and winked with his good eye. 'How are you doing?'

The boy looked up at him, lethargic despite the shivering, and his voice, when he spoke, was deepened by the cold. 'I can't seem to get warm.'

Adda sniffed. 'That's the way it is, up here. The Air's too thin for us, see. And if you go higher, towards the Crust, it gets thinner still. But there's no need to be cold.'

Farr frowned. 'What do you mean?'

For answer Adda grinned. He raised his spear of hardened wood and aligned it parallel to the tree trunk, along the direction of the Magfield flux lines. He hefted it for a few seconds, feeling its springy tension. Then he said, 'Watch and remember.'

The boy, eyeing the quivering spear with wide eyes, scrambled back out of the way.

Adda braced himself against the Magfield. With a single movement – he remained lithe in spite of everything, Adda congratulated himself – Adda thrust the spearpoint deep into the bulk of the tree. The first stab took the spearpoint through the bark and perhaps a hand's length into the wood. By working the haft of the spear, twisting it in his hands, Adda was able to drive the spear further into the flesh of the branch, to perhaps half an arm's length.

That done, feeling his chest drag at the thin Air, Adda

35

turned to make sure Farr was still watching. 'Now,' he rasped. 'Now comes the magic.'

He twisted in the Air and placed his feet against the branch, close to the line of his half-buried spear. Then he bent and wrapped both hands around the protruding shaft of the spear, squatted so that his legs were bent and his back was straight, and heaved upwards, using the spear as a lever to prise open the wood of the branch.

. . . Actually it was a long time since he'd done this, he realized a few heartbeats after starting. His palms grew slick with superfluid sweat, a steady ache spread along his back, and for some reason the vision of his good eye was starting to tremble and blur. And, though the spear bowed upwards a bit as he strained, the branch did little more than groan coldly.

He let go of the spear and wiped his palms against his thighs, feeling the breath rattle in his chest. He carefully avoided eye contact with the boy.

Then he bent to the spear again.

This time, at last, the branch gave way; a plate of it the size of his chest yielded and lifted up like a lid. Adda felt his aching legs spring straight, and he tumbled away from the branch. Quickly recovering his dignity, he twisted in the Air, ignoring the protests from his back and legs, and Waved back to Farr and the opened branch. He looked down at his handiwork appraisingly and nodded. 'Not as difficult as it looks,' he growled at the boy. 'Used to do that one-handed . . . But trees have got tougher since I was your age. Maybe something to do with this damn spin weather.'

But Farr wasn't listening; he crept forward to the wound in the branch and stared into it with fascination. Close to the rim of the ripped bark the wood was a pale yellow, the material looking much like that of the spear Adda had used. But further in, deeper than a hand's length, the wood was glowing green and emitting a warmth which – even from half a mansheight away – Adda could feel as a comforting, tangible presence against his chest. The glow of the wood sparkled against Farr's face and evoked verdant shadows within his round eyes.

Dura, Logue's ungainly daughter, joined them now; she shot a brief smile of thanks to Adda as she crouched beside

36

her brother and raised her palms to the warmth of the wood. The green fire scattered highlights from her limbs and face which made her look, Adda thought charitably, half-attractive for once. As long as she didn't move about too much and reveal her total lack of grace, anyway.

Dura said to Farr, 'Another lesson. What's making the wood burn?'

He smiled at her, eyecups full of wood-glow. 'Heavy stuff from the Crust?'

'Yes.' She leaned towards Farr so that the heads of brother and sister were side by side over the glowing wood, their faces shining like two leaves. Dura went on, 'Proton-rich nuclei on their way to the leaves. The tree branch is like a casing, you see, enclosing a tube where the pressure is lower than the Air. But when the casing is breached the heavy nuclei inside fission, decaying rapidly. What you're seeing is nuclei burning into the Air . . .'

Adda saw how Farr's smooth young face creased with concentration as he absorbed this new bit of useless knowledge.

Useless?

Well, maybe, he thought; but these precious, abstract facts, polished by retelling and handed down from the earliest days of the Human Beings – from the time of their expulsion from Parz City, ten generations ago – were treasures. Part of what made them human.

So Adda nodded approvingly at Dura and her attempts to educate her brother. The Human Beings had been thrust into this upflux wilderness against their will. But they were not savages, or animals; they had remained civilized people. Why, some of them could even read; a handful of books scraped painfully onto scrolls of pigskin with styli of wood were among the Human Beings' principal treasures . . .

He leaned towards Dura and said quietly, 'You'll have to go on, you know. Deeper into the forest, towards the Crust.'

Dura started. She pulled away from the trunk-wound, the light of the burning nuclei shining from the long muscles of her neck. The other Human Beings, a few mansheights away, were still clustered about the treetops; most of them, having crammed their bellies full, were gathering armfuls of the succulent leaves. She said, 'I know. But most of them want to go back to the camp already, with their leaves.'

Adda sniffed. 'Then they're damn fools, and it's a shame the spin weather didn't take them instead of a few with more sense. Leaves taste good but they don't fill a belly.'

'No. I know.' She sighed and rubbed the bridge of her nose, ran a finger around the rim of one eyecup absently. 'And we have to replace the Air-pigs we lost in the spin storm.'

'Which means going on,' Adda said.

She said with a weary irritation, 'You don't need to tell me, Adda.'

'You'll have to lead them. They won't go by themselves; folk aren't like that. They're like Air-pigs: all wanting to follow the leader but none wanting to lead.'

'They won't follow me. I'm not my father.'

Adda shrugged. 'They won't follow anyone else.' He studied her square face, seeing the doubts and submerged strength in its thin lines. 'I don't think you really have a choice.'

'No,' she sighed, straightening up. 'I know.' She went to talk to the tribesfolk.

When she returned to the nuclear fire, only Philas, the widow of Esk, came with her. The two women Waved side by side. Dura's face was averted, apparently riven with embarrassment; Philas's expression was empty.

Adda wasn't really surprised at the reaction of the rest. Even when it was against their own damn interest, they'd snub Logue's daughter.

He was interested to see Philas with Dura, though. Everyone had known about Dura's relationship with Esk; it was hardly the sort of thing that could be kept quiet in a community reduced to fifty people, counting the kids.

It had been against the rules. Sort of. But it was tolerated, and hardly unique – as long as Dura obeyed a few unspoken conventions. Such as restricting her reaction to Esk's death, keeping herself away from the widowed Philas.

Just another bit of stupidity, Adda thought. The Human Beings had once numbered hundreds – even in the days of Adda's grandfather there had been over a hundred adults – and maybe then conventions about adultery might have made sense. But not now.

38

He shook his head. Adda had despaired of Human Beings long before Farr was born.

'They want to go back,' said Dura, her voice flat. 'But I'll go on. Philas will come.'

The woman Philas, her face drab and empty, her hair lying limply against her angular skull, looked to Adda as if she had nothing left to lose anyway. Well, he thought, if it helped the two women work out their own relationship, then fine.

Some hunting expedition it was going to be, though.

He lifted his spear.

Dura frowned. 'No,' she said. 'I can't ask you to . . .'

Adda growled a soft warning to shut her up.

Farr straightened up from the burning pit. 'I'll come too,' he said brightly, his face turned up to Dura.

Dura placed her hands on his shoulders. 'Now, that's ridiculous,' she said in a parent's tones. 'You know you're too young to . . .'

Farr responded with bleated protests, but Adda cut across him impatiently. 'Let the boy come,' he rasped to Dura. 'You think he'd be safer with those leaf-gatherers? Or back at the place where the Net used to be?'

Dura's anxious face swivelled from Adda to her brother and back again. At length she sighed, smoothing back her hair. 'All right. Let's go.'

They gathered their simple equipment. Dura knotted a length of rope around her waist and tucked a short stabbing-knife and cleaning brush into the rope, behind her back; she tied a small bag of food to the rope.

Then, without another word to the others, the four of them – Adda, Dura, Farr and the widow Philas – began the slow, careful climb towards the darkness of the Crust.

3

They moved in silence.

At first Dura found the motion easy. The tree slid beneath her, almost featureless, slowly widening as she climbed up its length. The tree trunk grew along the direction of the Magfield, and so moving along it meant moving in the easiest direction, parallel to the Magfield, with the superfluid Air offering hardly any resistance. It was barely necessary to Wave; Dura found it was enough to push at the smooth, warm bark with her hands.

She looked back. The leafy treetops seemed to be merging into a floor across the world now, and the open Air beyond was being sealed away from her. Her companions were threaded along the trunk behind her, moving easily: the widow Philas apparently indifferent to her surroundings, Farr with his eyecups wide and staring, his mouth wide open and his chest straining at the thin Air, and dear old Adda at the back, his spear clasped before him, his good eye constantly sweeping the complex darkness around them. The three of them – naked, sleek, with their ropes, nets and small bags bound to them – looked like small, timid animals as they moved through the shades of the forest.

They rested. Dura took her cleaning scraper from her belt of rope and worked at her arms and legs, dislodging fragments of leaf and bark.

Adda glided up the line to her, his face alert. 'How are you?'

Looking at him, Dura thought of her father.

She'd been involved in hunts before, of course – as had most adult Human Beings – but always she'd been able to rely on the tactical awareness, the deep, ingrained knowledge of the Star and all its ways, of Logue and the others.

She'd never *led* before.

Some of her doubt must have shown in her face. Adda nodded, his wizened face neutral. 'You'll do.'

She snorted. Keeping her voice low enough that only Adda could hear, she said, 'Maybe. But what good is it? Look at us . . .' She waved a hand at the little party. 'A boy. Two women, distracted by grief . . .'

'And me,' Adda said quietly.

'Yes,' she acknowledged. 'Thanks for staying with me, Adda. But even if by some miracle this collection of novices succeeds we'll return with only two, maybe three Air-pigs. We wouldn't have the capacity to restrain any more.' She remembered – in the better days of her childhood – hunting parties of ten or a dozen strong and alert men and women, returning in triumph to the Net with whole herds of wild pigs. 'And what good will that do? The Human Beings are going to starve, Adda.'

'Maybe. But it may not be as bad as that. We might find a couple of sows, maybe with piglets . . . enough to reestablish our stock. Who knows? And look, Dura, you can only lead those who wish to be led. Don't flog yourself too hard. Even Logue only led by consent. And remember, Logue never faced times as hard as what's to come now.

'Listen to me. When the people get hungry enough, they'll turn to you. They'll be angry, disillusioned, and they'll blame you because there's no one else to blame. But they'll be yours to lead.'

She found herself shuddering. 'I've no choice, have I? All my life, since the moment of my birth, has had a kind of logic which has led me to this point. And I've never had a choice about any of it.'

Adda smiled, his face a grim mask. 'No,' he said harshly. 'But then, what choices do any of us have?'

The forest seemed empty of Air-pigs.

The little party grew fretful and tired. After another half-day's fruitless searching, Dura allowed them to rest, to sleep.

When they woke, she knew she would have to lead them downflux. Downflux, and higher – deeper into the forest, towards the Crust.

41

Towards the South – downflux – the Air was richer, the Magfield stronger. The pigs must have fled that way, following the Glitch. But everyone knew downflux was a dangerous direction to travel.

The Human Beings followed her with varying degrees of enthusiasm.

The forest was dense, complex. Six-legged Crust-crabs scuttled from Dura as she approached, abandoning webs slung between the tree trunks. Cocoons of leeches and other unidentifiable creatures clustered thick on the trunks, like pale, bloated leaves.

A ray turned its blind face towards her.

Adda hissed a warning. Dura flattened herself against the tree trunk before her, wrapping her arms around it and willing her ragged breath to still. The wood pressing against her belly and thighs was hard and hot.

A breath of Air at her back, a faint shadow.

She shifted her head to the right, feeling the roughness of the bark scratch her cheek. Her eyecups swivelled, following the ray as it glided by, utterly silent. The ray was a translucent sheet at least a mansheight wide. At its closest it was no more than an arm's length from her. She could recognize the basic architecture of all the Mantle's animals: the ray was built around a thin, cylindrical spine, and six tiny, spherical eyes ringed the babyish maw set into the centre of its face. But the fins of the ray had been extended into six wide, thin sheets. The wings were spaced evenly around the body and they rippled as the ray moved; electron gas sparkled around the leading edges. The flesh was almost transparent, so that it was difficult even to see the wings, and Dura could see shadowy fragments of some meal passing along the ray's cylindrical gut.

The ray was the only animal – other than humans – that moved by Waving, rather than by squirting jetfarts like pigs or boar. Moving in silence, without the sweet stink of jetfarts, the ray was an effective predator. And its mouth, though tiny, was ringed by jagged, ripping teeth.

The ray slid over the four humans for several heartbeats, apparently unaware of their presence. Then, still silent, it floated away into the shadows of the forest.

Dura counted to a hundred before pushing herself away from the tree trunk.

The vortex lines were dense here, almost tangled together among the trees. The Star, its rotation continually slowing, gradually expelled the vortex lines from the Mantle . . . until a fresh Glitch struck, when the lines crumbled into deadly fragments before renewing.

The Air was noticeably thinner. Dura felt her chest strain at the stuff and her heart pumped as it sought to power her muscles; from various points in her body she heard the small pops of pressure equalizing. She knew what was happening, of course. The Air had two main components, a neutron superfluid and an electron gas. The neutrons were thinning out; more pressure here was supplied by the gas of free electrons. When she held up her hand before her face she could see the ghostly sparkle of electrons around her fingers, bright in the gloom and evoking dim highlights from the crowding leaves.

But now her vision seemed to be failing. The Air was growing poor at carrying the high-frequency, high-velocity sound waves which allowed her to see. And, worse, the Air – thin as it was – was losing its superfluidity. It started to feel sticky, viscous; and as she moved she began to feel a breeze, faint but unquestionably present, plucking at her face and hair-tubes, impeding her motion.

She found herself trembling at the thought of this sticky stuff congealing in the fine network of capillaries which powered her muscles – the network which sustained her very being.

Human Beings weren't meant to live up here. Even pigs spent no more time close to the Crust than they had to. She heaved at the sludgelike Air, feeling it curdle within her capillaries, and longed for the open space of the Mantle beneath the roof-forest, for clean, fresh, thick Air.

In all directions around her the tree trunks filled the world. As it became progressively more difficult to see, the trunks, parallel, curving slightly to follow the Magfield, seemed suddenly artificial, sinister in their regularity, like the threads of some huge Net around her. She found herself gripped by a slow panic. Her chest heaved at the unsatisfying Air, the breath noisy in her throat. It took a strong, conscious effort to keep moving, an exercise of will just to keep her hands working at the tree trunk.

She was concerned for Farr. Even in the gloom she could see how distressed he was: his face was white and seemed to be bulging, his eyes half-closed; he seemed barely aware of where he was, and he moved along the trunk stiffly.

Dura forced herself to look away, to carry on. There was no help she could give him. Not now. The best she could do was to move on, to bring home the results of a successful hunt. And as Adda had said, the boy was probably safer with her than anywhere else . . .

At least Adda was close to Farr. Dura found herself offering up a simple, childlike message of thanks to the watchful Xeelee for the old man's presence and support.

When the climb ended it was with a suddenness that startled her.

The tree trunk she'd followed had broadened only gradually, at last reaching a width just too great for her to stretch her arms around. Now, suddenly, the clean lines of the trunk exploded into a complex tangle of roots which formed a semicircular platform over her head. Peering up, she could see the roots receding into the dim, translucent interior of the Crust itself; they looked almost like human arms, reaching deep into the gossamer solid in search of neutron-rich nuclei of molybdenum, strontium or krypton.

Looking around, she saw how the root system of the tree merged with those of its neighbours in the forest, so that a carpet of wood formed an impenetrable ceiling over the forest. A few strands of purplish grass sprouted among the roots. The tree trunks, following the Magfield lines, met the root ceiling at an oblique angle.

Soon the others had joined her. The four Human Beings huddled together, clinging to loose roots for stability. It was so dim now that Dura could barely make out the faces of her companions, the outlines of their thin bodies. Philas's eyes were dull with exhaustion and apathy; Farr, trembling, had his arms wrapped around himself, and his mouth was wide as he strained at the residual Air. Adda was as uncomplaining as ever, but his face was set and pale, and Dura could see how his old shoulders were hunched over his thin, heaving chest. Adda took leaves from the bulging pack at his waist. Dura bit into the food gratefully. Insubstantial and unsatisfying as it was, the food seemed to boost what was left of her strength. Farr continued to shiver; Dura put an arm around him and drew him closer to her, hoping to transmit enough of her body warmth to stop the trembling.

Farr asked, 'Are we at the Crust?'

'No,' Adda growled. 'The true Crust is still millions of mansheights above us. But we've reached the roots; this is as far as we can go.'

Philas's voice was low and harsh in the thin Air. 'We can't stay here for long.'

'We won't need to,' Dura said. 'But maybe we should open up a trunk and start some nuclear burning again, before we congeal here. Adda, could you . . .'

The old man raised a hand, curtly. 'No time,' he breathed. 'Just listen . . . all of you.'

Dura frowned but said nothing. The four fell into a silence broken only by the rattle of their uneven breaths. Dura felt small, vulnerable, isolated, dwarfed by the immensities of the root systems over their heads. Every instinct ordered her to bolt, to slide back down the tree and plummet through the wall of treetops to the open Air where she belonged; and she could see the same urges in the set faces of the others.

There. A rustle, a distant grunting . . . It came from the root systems, somewhere to her left.

Adda's face crumpled with frustration. 'Damn it all,' he hissed. 'I can't hear; my ears are turning to mush.'

'I can hear them, Adda,' Farr said.

Dura pointed. 'That way.'

Adda nodded, his good eye half-closed with satisfaction. 'I knew it wouldn't take long. How many?'

Dura and Philas looked at each other, each seeking the answer in the other's face. Dura said, 'I can't tell, Adda . . . more than one, I think.'

For a few seconds Adda swore steadily, cursing his age, his failing faculties. 'Well, into the Ring with it,' he said finally. 'We'll just have to chance there aren't too many in the herd.'

In an urgent, harsh whisper he gave them careful instructions on how, in the event of attack by a boar, they should scatter . . . and work *across* the Magfield flux rather than try to flee along it. 'Because that's the way the boar will go. And, believe me, the boar will be a damn sight quicker than you.' His face was a murderous, chilling mask in the twilight.

Dura said, 'Philas, go with Adda and Wave around to the far side of the herd. Take the nets and rope and get downflux from them. Farr, stay with me; we'll wait until the others are in position and then we'll chase the pigs into the nets. All right?'

Hurriedly they passed round the equipment they would need. Dura took two short stabbing spears from the bundle carried by Philas. Then Adda and Philas slid silently into the darkness, working across the Magfield by Waving and by clambering across the parallel tree trunks.

Farr stayed close to Dura, still pressed close to her for warmth, trusting. For a few seconds she looked down at him – his eyes seemed vacant, as if he were not fully conscious – and she tried to imagine how she would feel if anything were to befall this boy, as a result of her own ignorance and carelessness.

Well, she thought ruefully, at least she'd done her best for him in the way she'd structured the hunt. It was undoubtedly safer to be upflux of the herd when the hunt started. And she would have been greatly more worried if she hadn't stayed with Farr herself.

With a last, brisk hug, she whispered, 'Come on, Farr. We've got work to do. Let's see how close we can get to those pigs without them spotting us.'

He nodded dully and drew away from her, still shivering.

Hefting a short spear in each hand, Dura began to pull herself across the lines of the fat trunks in the direction of the noises she'd heard. Moving in this direction, the resistance of the Magfield was added to the thickened viscosity of the Air, and the going was hard. She felt submerged and had to suppress a pang of panic at the feeling of being trapped up here, of being unable to free herself from this solidifying Air.

She did not look back, but was aware of Farr following her,

perhaps a mansheight behind; he moved silently save for his rattling breath, and she could hear how he was trying to control the noise of his breathing. *The brave little hunter*, she thought. *Logue would have been proud of him.*

It took only seconds to reach the pigs; soon Dura could see the blocky forms of several animals sliding between the tree trunks, still apparently oblivious to the humans.

Beckoning Farr to come close to her, Dura lodged herself amid the tree trunks perhaps ten mansheights below the root ceiling.

There were three Air-pigs. The animals, each about the size of a man's torso, worked steadily around the bases of the trees, scooping up purple-green krypton grass and other small plants. The pigs' fins waved languidly as they fed, and Dura could see how their eyestalks were fixed on the grass before them and their mouths were pursed, almost shut. When grazing on the thin foodstuff which floated in the free Air, a pig's mouth could open so wide that it exposed the entire front end of the pig, turning the animal into an open-ended tube, a crude eating machine trailing eyestalks and fins. But here in this failing Air the mouths were barely opening as they worked, lapping and chewing at the krypton grass. The pigs were keeping their squat bodies sealed up as much as possible, maintaining an inner reservoir of life-sustaining Air; in this way, she knew, the pigs could last for days up here – unlike fragile, weak and ill-adapted Human Beings.

She turned to Farr, who hovered beside her with his eyes barely protruding over the trunk. She mimed: *Just three of them. We're in luck.*

He nodded and pointed at one of the pigs. Dura, studying the animal more closely, saw that it was bigger than the others: bulkier, clumsier.

A pregnant sow.

She felt a smile spread across her face. Perfect.

She counted one hundred heartbeats, then lifted her spears. Philas and Adda should be in position by now.

She nodded to Farr.

The two humans erupted from behind their trunk. Dura yelled as loudly as the thin Air would permit; she hurled herself along the Magfield flux at the pigs, rattling her spears against the wood of the trunk. Beside her Farr did the same, his hair tangling almost comically.

At their approach the pigs' mouths snapped shut. Their eyestalks lifted, rigid, to fix straining gazes on their sudden assailants. Then, as if with one mind, the pigs turned and bolted.

The animals hurled themselves along the Magfield lines, seeking the easiest and quickest escape. They clattered against tree trunks and bounced over roots, their jet orifices farting clouds of green-stained, sweet-smelling Air. Dura and Farr gave chase, still roaring enthusiastically. Suddenly Dura found herself bound up by the excitement of the hunt, and a new energy coursed through her.

The pigs, of course, outran Dura and Farr easily. Within a few heartbeats the animals were disappearing into the darkness of distance, trailing clouds of jetfarts . . .

But there were Adda and Philas, waiting just a little further down the Magfield, with a net pulled tight between them and with stabbing spears at the ready.

The first two pigs were moving too rapidly to stop. They turned in the Air and tumbled against each other, their huge mouths popping open to emit childlike squeals, but they hurtled backside first into the net. Philas and Adda worked together, a little clumsily but effectively. Within a few heartbeats they had thrown the net around the two pigs and were prodding at them, trying to force them to subside. Green jetfarts squirted from the pigs, and the net bulged as the terrified animals strove vainly to escape. By the time Dura got there they would have the animals trussed up and then . . .

There was a scream behind her. Farr's scream.

She whirled in the Air, Adda and Philas forgotten. The third pig – the pregnant sow, she saw – had evaded Adda's net. Terrified and enraged, it had flown down, away from the root ceiling, and was now plummeting up through the trees, back along the Magfield flux . . . and straight at Farr.

The boy gazed at the animal's flapping fins and rigid, staring eyestalks, apparently transfixed. *He isn't going to get out of the way*, Dura realized. And the momentum of the pig would crush him in a moment.

She tried to call out, to move towards the boy – but she was plunged into a nightmare of slow motion. The Magfield was thick, clinging, the Air a soupy mass in which she was embedded. She struggled to get free, to shout to her brother, but the hurtling, blurring speed of the pig reduced her efforts to the trivial.

There was barely a mansheight between the pig and the boy. Dura, trapped in viscous Air, heard herself scream.

Suddenly the sow opened its mouth wide and bellowed in agony. Jetfarts staining the air, it veered abruptly. One ventral fin caught Farr with a side-swipe which sent him spinning against a tree trunk . . . but, Dura saw with a flood of relief, he was no more than shocked.

As the sow tumbled in the Air the reason for its distress revealed itself: Adda's long spear, protruding from the sow's belly. The spear quivered as the beast thrashed, seeking an escape from this sudden agony.

Now Adda himself raced along the Magfield, ungainly but determined. Behind him the two trapped pigs were struggling free of the abandoned net. Adda bellowed: 'She's gone rogue . . . Dura, get to the boy and keep him away.'

Now the pig settled in the Air, all six of its eyestalks triangulating on the old man. Adda slowed to a hover, arms and legs outspread, his gaze locked on the pig.

Dura said uncertainly, 'Adda, get out of the way . . . I think . . .'

'Get the damn boy.'

Dura hurried to obey, skirting the hovering pig.

With a howl that rent the glutinous Air, the pig charged Adda.

Adda twisted in the Air and began to Wave out of the way, his legs thrashing at the Magfield . . .

But, Dura saw instantly, not fast enough.

Clinging to the weeping Farr there was nothing she could do as the final, ghastly moments unfolded. Adda's face showed no fear – but no acceptance either, Dura saw; there was only a grimace of irritation, perhaps at this newest failure of his crumbling body.

As it closed on Adda, trailing green clouds of jetfarts, the sow opened its mouth.

The huge, circular maw closed on both Adda's legs. The

momentum of the hurtling sow carried away both pig and Adda, and Dura cried out as she saw Adda's fragile body smashed against a tree trunk. But he was still conscious, and fighting; with both fists he pounded on the sow's wide, quivering back.

Dura kicked away from the tree and Waved as hard as she could towards the pig. Philas was approaching the pig from the far side, her stabbing spears held out before her. The woman's eyes were wide, emptied by shock and terror.

The pig, halted by its impact with the tree, pulled back into clear Air now, and it began, with lateral squirts of gas, to rotate around its long axis. Adda seemed to realize what was happening. With his legs still trapped, he beat harder at the pig's flank, cursing violently. But still the pig twisted, ever faster, becoming at last a blur of fins and eyestalks. Jetfart gas trailed around its body in circular ribbons, and electron glow sparkled from its fins. Adda, at last, fell backwards and lay against the pig's long flank, his knees bent cruelly.

This was the way boars killed their prey, Dura knew: the boar would spin so fast that the superfluidity of the Air which sustained all animals in the Mantle, including humans, broke down. It was simple, but deadly effective. Even now, she knew, the pain of Adda's trapped legs, the agony induced by the whirling of the world around him, would be subsumed by a dull, disabling numbness as his muscles ceased to function, his senses dimmed, and at last even his mind failed.

With a yell from deep in her gut, Dura threw herself at the whirling animal. She scrabbled at its smooth, slippery hide, feeling her belly and legs brush against its hot flesh. She stabbed at its tough epidermis once, twice, before being hurled clear. She tumbled backwards through the Air, colliding with a trunk hard enough to knock the breath out of her.

One of her two short spears had snapped, she saw, and was now floating harmlessly away. But she had succeeded in ramming the other through the skin of the pig. The wounded animal, with Adda's spear still protruding from its belly, tried to maintain its rotation; but, distracted by pain, its motion became uneven, and the pig began to precess clumsily, the axis of its rotation dipping as it thrashed in the Air. Poor Adda, now evidently unconscious, was thrown back and forth by the pig, his limp body flopping passively against the animal's flank.

Philas fell on the pig now and drove another spear into the animal's hide, widening the wound Dura had made. The animal opened its huge mouth, its circular lip-face pulling back to reveal a green-stained throat, and let out a roar of pain. Adda, his legs freed from the mouth, fell limply away from the pig; Farr hurried to him.

Philas rammed her second spear into the thrashing pig's mouth, stabbing at the organs exposed within. Dura pushed away from the tree and hurled herself once more at the sow; she was weaponless, but she hauled at the spears already embedded in the pig's flanks, wrenching open the wounds, while Philas continued to work at the mouth.

It took many minutes. The pig thrashed and tore at the Air to the end, striving to use its residual rotation to throw off its attackers. But it had no escape. At last, leaking jetfarts aimlessly, its cries dying to a murmur, the sow's struggles petered away.

The two women, exhausted, hung in the Air. The sow was an inert mass, immense, its skin ripped, its mouth gaping loosely. Dura – panting, barely able to see – found it difficult to believe that even now the animal would not erupt to a ghastly, butchered semblance of life.

Dura Waved slowly through the Air to Philas. The two women embraced, their eyes wide with shock at what they had done.

Farr gingerly laid Adda along a tree trunk, relying on the gentle pressure of the Magfield to hold him in place. He stroked the old man's yellowed hair. He had retrieved Adda's battered old spear and laid it beside him.

Dura and Philas approached, Dura wiping trembling hands on her thighs. She studied Adda's injuries cautiously, scared even to touch him.

Adda's legs, below the knees, were a mangled mess: the long bones were obviously broken in several places, the feet reduced to masses of pulped meat. The surface of Adda's chest was unbroken but oddly uneven; Dura, fearful even to touch, speculated about broken ribs. His right arm dangled at a strange angle, limp in the Air; perhaps the shoulder had been broken. Adda's face was a soft, bruised mess. Both eyecups were filled by gummy blood, and his nostrils were dimmed . . . And, of course, the Xeelee alone knew about internal injuries. Adda's penis and scrotum had fallen from their cache between his legs; exposed, they made the old man look still more vulnerable, pathetic. Tenderly, Dura cupped the shrivelled genitalia in her hand and tucked them away in their cache.

'He's dying,' Philas said, her voice uneven. She seemed to be drawing back from the battered body, as if this, for her, was too much to deal with.

Dura shook her head, forcing herself to think. 'He'll certainly die up here, in this lousy Air. We've got to get him away, back into the Mantle . . .'

Philas touched her arm. She looked into Dura's face, and Dura saw how the woman was struggling to break through her own shock. Philas said, 'Dura, we have to face it. He's going to die. There's no point making plans, or struggling to get him away from here . . . all we can do is make him comfortable.'

Dura shook off the light touch of the widow, unable – yet – to accept that.

Adda's mouth was phrasing words, feebly shaping the breath that wheezed through his lips. '. . . Dura . . .'

Still scared to touch him, she leaned close to his mouth. 'Adda? You're conscious?'

A sketch of a laugh came from him, and he turned blind eye-cups to her. '. . . I'd . . . rather not be.' He closed his mouth and tried to swallow; then he said, 'Are you all right? . . . The boy?'

'Yes, Adda. He's fine. Thanks to you.'

'. . . And the pigs?'

'We killed the one that attacked you. The sow. The others . . .' She glanced to the nets which drifted in the Air, tangled and empty. 'They got away. What a disaster this has been.'

'No.' He stirred, as if trying to reach out to her, then fell back. 'We did our best. Now you must . . . try again. Go back . . .'

'Yes. But first we have to work out how to move you.' She

52

stared at his crushed body, trying to visualize how she might address the worst of the wounds.

Again that sketchy, chilling laugh. 'Don't be so . . . damned stupid,' he said. 'I'm finished. Don't . . . waste your time.'

She opened her mouth, ready to argue, but a great weariness fell upon her, and she subsided. Of course Adda was right. And Philas. Of course he would soon die. But still, she knew, she would have to try to save him. 'I never saw a pig behave like that. A boar, maybe. But . . .'

'We should have . . . expected it,' he whispered. 'Stupid of me . . . pregnant sow . . . it was bound to . . . react like that.' His breath seemed to be slowing; in a strange way, she thought as she studied him, he seemed to be growing more comfortable. More peaceful.

She said softly, 'You're not going to die yet, damn you.'

He did not reply.

She turned to Philas. 'Look, we'll have to try to bind up his wounds. Cut some strips from the hide of that sow. Perhaps we can strap this damaged arm across his body. And we could tie his legs together, use his spear as a splint.'

Philas stared at her for a long moment, then went to do as Dura had ordered.

Farr asked, 'What can I do?'

Dura looked around, abstracted. 'Go and retrieve that net. We're going to have to make a cradle, somehow, so we can haul him back home . . .'

'All right.'

When Philas returned, the women tried to straighten Adda's legs in preparation for binding them to the makeshift splint. When she touched his flesh, Dura saw Adda's face spasm, his mouth open wide in a soundless cry. Unable to proceed, she pulled her hands away from his ruined flesh and stared at Philas helplessly.

Then, behind her, Farr screamed.

Dura whirled, her hands reaching for Adda's spear.

Farr was still working on the tangled net – or had been; now he was backing away from it, his eyecups wide with shock. With the briefest of glances, Dura assured herself that the boy had not been harmed. Then, as she hurried to his side, she looked past him to discover what was threatening him . . .

She slowed to a halt in the Air, her mouth dangling, forgetting even her brother in her amazement.

A box, floating in the Air, approached them. It was a cube about a mansheight on a side made of carefully cut plates of wood. Ropes led to a team of six young Air-pigs which was patiently hauling the box through the forest. And, through a clear panel set into the front of the box, a man's face peered out at her.

He was frowning.

The box drifted to a halt. Dura raised Adda's spear.

4

Toba Mixxax hauled on his reins. The leather ropes sighed through the sealant membranes set in the face of the car, and he could see through the clearwood window – and feel in the rapid slackening of tension in the reins – how eagerly the team of Air-pigs accepted the break.

He stared at the four strangers.

. . . And how strange they were. Two women, a kid and a busted-up old man – all naked, one of the women waving a crude-looking wooden spear at him.

At first Mixxax had assumed, naturally, that these were just another set of coolies taking a break in the forest, here at the fringe of his ceiling-farm. But that couldn't be right, of course; even the dimmest of his coolies wouldn't wander so far without an Air-tank. In fact, he wondered how this little rabble was surviving so high, so badly equipped. All they had were spears, ropes, a net of what looked like untreated leather . . .

Besides, he'd recognize his own coolies. Probably, anyway.

He'd been patrolling the woodland just beyond the border of the ceiling-farm when he'd come across this group – or at least, he'd meant to be patrolling; it looked as if, daydreaming, he'd wandered a little further into the upflux forest than he'd meant to. Well, that wasn't so surprising, he told himself. After all there was plenty on his mind. He was only fifty per cent through his wheat quota, with the financial year more than three-quarters gone. He found his hands straying to the Corestuff Wheel resting against his chest. Any more spin weather like the last lot and he was done for; he, with his wife Ito and son Cris, would be joining the swelling masses in the streets of Parz itself, dependent on the charity of strangers for their very survival. And there was precious little charity in the Parz of Hork IV, he reminded himself with a shudder.

With an effort he brought his focus back to the present. He stared through the car's window at the vagrants. The woman with the spear – tall, streaks of age-yellow in her hair, strong-looking, square face – stared back at him defiantly. She was naked save for a rope tied around her waist; affixed to the rope was some kind of carrying-pouch that looked as if it was made from uncured pigskin. She was slim, tough-looking, with small, compact breasts; he could see layers of muscles in her shoulders and thighs.

She was, frankly, terrifying.

Who were these people?

Now he thought about it, this far upflux from Parz they couldn't possibly be stray coolies, even runaways from another ceiling-farm. Toba's farm was right on the fringe of the wide hinterland around Parz . . . just on the edge of culti-vation, Toba reminded himself with an echo of old bitterness; not that it allowed him to pay less tax than anyone else. Even the farm of Qos Frenk, his nearest neighbour, was several days' travel downflux from here without a car.

No, these weren't coolies. They must be upfluxers . . . *wild people.*

The first Toba had ever encountered.

Toba's left hand circled in a rapid, half-involuntary Sign of the Wheel over his chest. Maybe he should just yank on the reins and get out of here, before they had a chance to do anything . . .

He chided himself for lack of courage. What could they do, after all? The only man looked old enough to be Toba's father, and it seemed to be all the poor fellow could do just to keep breathing. And even the two women and the boy working together couldn't get through the hardened wood walls of a sealed Air-car . . . could they?

He frowned. Of course, they could always attack him from the outside. Kill the Air-pigs, for instance. Or just cut the reins.

He lifted the reins. Maybe it would be better to come back with help – get some of the coolies into a posse, and then . . .

Fifty per cent of quota.

He dropped the reins, suddenly angry with himself. No, damn it; poor as it was, this was his patch of Crust, and he'd deserve to be Wheel-Broken if he let a gang of weaponless savages drive him away.

Full of a righteous resolve, Toba pulled the mouthpiece of the Speaker towards him and intoned into it, 'Who are you? What are you doing here?'

The upfluxers startled like frightened Air-pigs, he was gratified to see. They Waved a little further from the car and poked their short spears towards him. Even the old fellow looked up – or tried to; Toba could see how the injured man's eyecups were sightless, clouded with pus-laced, stale Air.

Toba was filled with a sudden sense of confidence, of command of the situation. He had nothing to fear; he was intimidating to these ignorant savages. They'd probably never even *heard* of Parz City. His anger at their intrusion seemed to swell as his apprehension diminished.

Now the strong-looking woman approached the car – cautiously, he saw, and with her spear extended towards him – but evidently not paralysed by fear . . . as, he conceded, he might have been were the positions reversed.

The woman shouted through the clearwood at him now, emphasizing her words with stabs of her spearpoint at his face; the voice was picked up by the Speaker system's external ear.

'Who do you think you are, a Xeelee's grandmother?'

Toba listened carefully. The voice of the upfluxer was distorted by the limitations of the Speaker, of course; but Toba was able to allow for that. He knew how the Speaker system worked, pretty well. Working a ceiling-farm as far from the Pole as Toba's – so far upflux, in such an inhospitable latitude – the car's systems kept him alive. The strongest of the coolies could survive for a long time out here and maybe some of them could even complete the trek back to the Pole, to Parz City. But not Toba Mixxax, City-born and bred; he doubted he would last a thousand heartbeats.

So he had assiduously learned how to maintain the systems of the car on which his life depended . . . The Speaker system, for instance. The Air he breathed was supplied by reservoirs carved into the thick, heavy wooden walls of the car. The Speaker system was based on fine tubes which pierced the reservoirs; the tubes linked membranes set in the inner and outer walls. The tubes were filled with Air, kept warmed to perfect superfluidity by the reservoirs around them, and so capable of transmitting without loss the small temperature fluctuations which human ears registered as sound.

But the narrowness of the tubes did tend to filter out some lower frequencies. The upfluxer savage's voice sounded thin and without depth, and the resonances gave her a strange, echoing timbre. Despite that, her words had been well formed – obviously in his own language – and tainted by barely a trace of accent.

He frowned at his own surprise. Was he so startled that the woman could speak? These were upfluxers – but they were people, not animals. The woman's few words abruptly caused him to see her as an intelligent, independent being, not capable of being cowed quite so easily, perhaps, by his technological advantage.

Maybe this wouldn't be so simple after all.

'What's wrong?' the woman rasped. She shook her spear at him. 'Too scared to speak?'

'My name is Toba Mixxax, freeman of Parz. This is my property. And I want you out of here.'

The injured old fellow swivelled sightless eyecups at Toba. He shouted – weakly, but loud enough for Toba to hear: 'Parz bastards! Think you own the whole damn Mantle, don't you?' A fit of coughing interrupted the old fool, and Toba watched as the stronger woman bent over him, apparently asking him what he was talking about. The man ignored her questions, and once his coughing had subsided he called out again: 'Bugger off, Pole man!'

Toba pursed his lips. They knew about Parz. Definitely not as ignorant as he had supposed, then. In fact, maybe *he* was the ignorant one. He bent to his Speaker membrane, trying to load his voice with threat: 'I won't warn you again. I want you off my property. And if you don't I . . .'

'Oh, shut up.' Now the strong woman thrust her face into his window; Toba couldn't help but recoil. 'What do you think that means to us, "your property"? And anyway . . .' She pointed at the injured old fellow. 'We can't go anywhere with Adda in that state.' The old man, Adda, called something to her – perhaps an order to leave him – but she ignored him.

'We're not going to move. Do what you have to do. And we . . .' — she raised her spear again – 'will do whatever we can to stop you.'

Toba stared into the woman's clear eyecups.

At his side was a collection of small, finely carved wooden levers. Maybe now was the time to pull on those levers, to use the car's crossbows and javelin tubes . . .

Maybe.

He leaned forward, unsure of his own motives. 'What's happened to him?'

The woman hesitated, but the boy piped up loyally, his thin, clear voice transmitted well by the Speaker tubes. 'Adda was gored by a boar.'

The old man spat a harsh laugh. 'Oh, rubbish. I was mangled by a pregnant sow. Stupid old fool that I am.' Now he seemed to be struggling to push himself away from his tree trunk to reach for a weapon. 'But not so stupid, or old, that I can't turn your last few minutes of life into hell, Pole man.'

Toba locked eyes with the strong woman. She raised her spear and grimaced . . . and then, shockingly, disarmingly, her face broke up into laughter.

Toba, startled, found himself laughing back.

The woman jabbed her spear at Toba, barely threatening now. 'You. Toba Paxxax.'

'Mixxax. Toba Mixxax.'

'I am Dura, daughter of Logue.'

He nodded to her.

She said, 'Look, you can see we're in trouble here. Why don't you get out of your pig-box and give us some help?'

He frowned. 'What kind of help?'

She looked towards the old man, apparently exasperated. 'With him, of course.' She stared at the car with new eyes, as if appraising the subtlety of its design. 'Maybe you could help us fix up his wounds.'

'Hardly. I'm no doctor.'

Dura frowned, as if the word wasn't familiar to her. 'Then at least you can help us get him out of the forest. Your box would be safe here until you got back.'

'It's called a car,' he said absently. 'Carry him where? Your home?'

She nodded and jabbed a spear along the line of the trees, down towards the interior of the Star. 'A few thousand mansheights that way.'

Mansheights? he thought, distracted. A practical measure, he supposed . . . but what was wrong with microns? A mansheight would be about ten microns – a hundred-thousandth of a metre – if it meant what it sounded like . . .

'What kind of facilities do you have there?'

'. . . Facilities?'

Her hesitation was answer enough. Even if Toba were inclined to risk his own health carting this old chap around the forest, there was evidently nothing waiting for him at home but more of these naked savages living in some unimaginable squalor. 'Look,' he said, trying to be kind, 'what's the point? Even if we got there in time . . .'

'. . . there'd be nothing we could do for him.' Dura's eyes were narrow and troubled. 'I know. But I can't just give up.' She looked at Toba, through his window, with what looked like a faint stab of hope. 'You talked about your property. Is it far from here? Do you have any – ah, facilities?'

'Hardly.' Of course there were basic medical facilities for the coolies, but nothing with any more ambition than to patch them up and send them back to work. Frankly, if one of his coolies were injured as badly as old Adda he'd expect him to die.

He'd write him off, in fact.

Only in Parz itself would there be treatment of the quality needed to save Adda's life.

He picked up his reins, trying to refocus his attention on his own affairs. He had plenty of problems of his own, plenty of work to finish before he'd see Ito and Cris again. Maybe he could be charitable – give these upfluxers the chance to get away. After all, they weren't really likely to damage his ceiling-farm . . .

'I'm sorry,' he said, trying to get out of this surprisingly awkward situation with some kind of dignity. 'But I don't think . . .'

The woman, Dura, stared through his window, her eyecups deep and sharp, acute; Toba felt himself shudder under the intensity of her perception. 'You know a way to help him,' she said slowly. 'Or you think you do. Don't you? I can see it in your face.'

Toba felt his mouth open and close, like the vent of a farting Air-piglet. 'No. Damn it . . . Maybe. All right, maybe. *If* we could get him to Parz. But even then there'd be no guarantee . . .' He laughed. 'And anyway, how do you plan to pay for the treatment? Who are you, Hork's long-lost niece? If you think I have funds to cover it . . .'

'Help us,' she said, staring straight into his eyecups.

It wasn't a request now, he realized, or a plea; it was an *order*.

He closed his eyes. *Damn it*. Why did these things have to happen to him? Didn't he have enough problems? He almost wished he'd simply blasted this lot with the crossbows before they had a chance to open their mouths and confuse him.

Unwilling to let himself think about it further, he pulled an Air-tank from beneath his seat, and reached out to open the door of the car.

A circular crack appeared in one previously seamless wall of Toba Mixxax's wooden box – of his *car*. At this latest surprise Dura couldn't help but flinch backwards, raising her spear at the lid of wood which began to hinge inwards into the car.

The door opened fully with a sigh of equalizing pressure. The richness of the car's Air wafted out over her, so thick it almost made her cough; she got one deep breath of it, and for a few heartbeats she felt invigorated, filled with energy. But then the Air dispersed into the stale, sticky thinness of the forest; and it was gone, as insubstantial as a dream. Obviously there had been more Air inside the compartment than out . . . but that made sense, of course. Why else ride around in a wooden prison, dependent on the cooperation of young pigs, other than to carry with you enough Air to sit in comfort?

Toba Mixxax emerged from his car. Dura watched, wary and wide-eyed. Mixxax stared back at her. For long seconds they hung there, eyes raking over each other.

Mixxax was wearing *clothes*. Not just a belt, or a carrying-pouch, but a suit of some kind of leather which encased him all over. She'd never seen anything so restrictive. And useless.

It wasn't as if it had a lot of pockets, even. And he wore a hat on his head, with a veil of some clear, light material dangling over his face. Tubes led from the veil to a pack on his back. A medallion, a wheel shape, hung on a chain around his neck.

Mixxax was a good five years older than Dura herself, and only perhaps fifteen years younger than her father at the time of his death. Old enough for his hair – what she could see of it – to have mostly yellowed and for a network of lines to have accumulated around shallow eyecups. In the forest's thin Air he seemed breathless, despite his hat and veil. He was short – a head shorter than she was – and looked well fed: his cheeks were round and his belly bulged under his clothes. But, despite his cargo of fat, Mixxax was not well muscled. His neck, arms and upper legs were thin, the muscles lost under the concealing layers of leather; his covered head wobbled slightly atop a neck that was frankly scrawny.

In a fair contest, Dura realized slowly, Mixxax would be no match for her. In fact, he'd be hard pressed to defend himself against Farr. Had all the people of his strange home – *Parz City* – become so atrophied by riding around in pig-drawn cars?

Dura began to feel confident again. Toba Mixxax was strange, but he obviously wasn't much of a threat.

She found her gaze drawn back to the medallion suspended from his neck. It was about the size of her palm, and consisted of an open wheel against which was fixed a sketchy sculpture of a man, with arms and legs outstretched against the wheel's five spokes. The work was finely done, with the expression on the face of the little carved man conveying a lot of meaning: pain, and yet a kind of patient dignity.

But it wasn't the form of the pendant but its material which was causing her to stare. It was carved of a substance she'd never seen before. Not wood, certainly; it looked too smooth, too heavy for that. What, then? Carved bone? Or . . .

Mixxax seemed to become aware of her gazing at the pendant; with a start, oddly guilty, he masked the device in the palm of his hand and tucked it inside the neck of his jacket, out of sight.

She decided to puzzle over this later. One more mystery among many . . .

'Dura,' Toba said. His voice sounded a lot better than the distorted croak she'd heard through the walls of the car.

'Thank you for helping us.'

He frowned, his fat cheeks pulling down. 'Don't thank me until we find out if there's anything to be done. Even if he survives the trip back to Parz, there's no guarantee I'll find a doctor to treat an upfluxer like him.'

Upfluxer?

'And even if I do I don't know how you're going to pay . . .'

She dismissed this with a wave of her hand. 'Toba Mixxax, I'd rather deal with these mysterious problems when I come to them. For now, we should concentrate on getting Adda into your box . . . your *car.*'

He nodded, and grinned. 'Yes. And that's not going to be so easy.'

With a few brisk Waves, and with Mixxax clumsily following, Dura crossed to the little group of Human Beings. Farr's eyes swivelled between Dura's face, Mixxax's hat, and back again; and his mouth gaped like a third, huge eyecup. Dura tried not to smile. 'All right, Farr. Don't stare.'

Philas was cradling Adda's battered head. Adda turned his blinded face to them. 'Clear off, Parz man.' His voice was a bubbling croak.

Mixxax ignored the words and bent over the old man. Dura seemed to see Adda's wounds through the stranger's eyes – the splayed right arm, the crushed feet, the imploded chest – and she felt a knife twist in her heart.

Mixxax straightened up. His expression was obscured by his veil. 'I was right. It's not going to be easy, even getting him as far as the car,' he said quietly.

'Then don't bother,' Adda hissed. 'Dura, you bloody fool . . .'

'Shut up,' Dura said. She tried to think her way through the situation. 'Maybe,' she said slowly, 'if we could bind him up – tie him closely to splints made out of our spears – it wouldn't be so bad.'

'Yes.' Mixxax looked around. 'But those ropes you have, and the nets, would just cut into him.'

'I know.' She looked appraisingly at Mixxax's clothes. 'So maybe . . .'

After a while, he grasped what she was asking; and with a resigned sigh he started to peel off his trousers and jacket. 'Why me?' he muttered, almost too quietly for her to hear.

He wore clothes even *under his clothes*. His chest, arms and legs were bare, but he wore substantial shorts of leather which covered his crotch and lower stomach. He kept his hat on.

He looked even scrawnier of limb, flabbier of belly, without his clothes. In fact, he looked ridiculous. Dura forbore to comment.

The Human Beings wore simple garments sometimes, of course – ponchos and capes, if the Air blew especially cold. But clothes under clothes?

Adda swore violently as they strapped him – with knotted trouser legs and sleeves – to a makeshift frame of spears. But he was too weak to resist, and within a few minutes he was encased in a cocoon of soft leather, his blind face twisting to and fro as if in search of escape.

Dura and Mixxax, with a scared Philas still cradling Adda's fragile head, slid Adda's cocoon carefully into the pig-car. Mixxax climbed in after it and set to work fixing it in place at the rear of the cabin with lengths of rope. Even now, Dura could hear from outside the car, Adda continued to curse his saviour.

Dura smiled at Philas, tired. 'Old devil.'

Philas did not respond. Her eyes, as she stared at the car, were wide . . . in fact, Dura slowly realized, her fear now was the strongest emotion the woman had shown since the death of Esk.

Dura reached out and took Philas's hand. It trembled against her palm, like a small animal. 'Philas,' she said carefully. 'I need your help.'

Philas turned her face, long, grief-lined, towards Dura.

Dura went on, 'I need to return to the Human Beings. To organize another hunt . . . You see that, don't you? But someone has to go with Adda, in the car, to this – Parz City.'

Philas almost spat the word. '*No.*'

'Philas, you must. I . . .'

'Farr. Send him.'

Dura stared at the woman's hard, empty-eyed expression;

64

anger and fear radiated out, shocking her. 'Farr's just a kid. You can't be serious, Philas.'

'Not me.' Philas shook her head stiffly, the muscles of her neck stiff with rage. 'I'm not getting in that thing, to be taken away. No. I'd rather die.'

And Dura, despairing, realized that the widow meant it. She tried for some while to persuade Philas, but there was no chink in the younger woman's resolution.

'All right, Philas.' Problems revolved in her head: the tribe, Farr . . . Her brother would have to come with her, in the car, of course. Adda had been correct in intuiting that Dura would never be able to relax if Farr were out of her sight for long. She said to Philas, 'Here is what you must do.' She squeezed the woman's hand, hard. 'Go back to the Human Beings. Tell them what has happened. That we are safe, and that we're going to get help for Adda. And we'll return if we can.'

Philas, her transfixing terror abating, nodded carefully.

'They must hunt again. Tell them that, Philas; try to make them understand. Despite what's befallen us. Otherwise they'll starve. Do you understand? You must tell them all this, Philas, and make them hear.'

'I will. I'm sorry, Dura.'

Dura felt an impulse to embrace the woman then; but Philas held herself away. The two women hovered in the Air, unspeaking, awkward, for a few heartbeats.

Dura turned away from Philas to face the door of the car. It was dark in there, like a mouth.

Terror spurted in her, sudden and unexpected. She fought to move forward, to keep from shivering.

She was scared of the car, of Parz City, of the unknown. Of course she was. She wondered now if that fear, lurking darkly at the back of her head, was truly what had impelled her to order Philas to go with Toba, regardless of any other justification. And she wondered if Philas had perceived that, too.

Here was another layer, she thought tiredly, to add to an already overcomplex relationship. Well, maybe that was the nature of life.

Dura turned and climbed slowly into the car; Farr, wordless, meek, followed.

The man from the Pole, much less impressive without his

outer garments, watched them climb aboard. The car proved to be cramped with the four of them – plus Adda's improvised cocoon and an expansive seat for Mixxax before an array of controls. Mixxax pulled off his hat and veil with every expression of relief. He pulled a lever; the heavy door swung outward.

Just before she was sealed away from the forest, Dura called out: 'And Philas! Give them our love . . .'

The door settled into its frame with a dull impact. Mixxax pulled another lever: a hiss, startlingly loud, erupted from the walls around them.

Air flooded the cabin. It was sweet, invigorating, and it filled Dura's head – but it was, she reminded herself, *alien*. She found a corner and huddled into it, pulling her knees to her chest.

Mixxax looked around. He seemed puzzled. 'Are you all right? You look – ill.'

Dura fought the urge to lunge at him, to batter at the clear panels of wood set in the walls. 'Toba Mixxax, we are Human Beings,' she hissed. 'We have never, in our lives, been confined inside a box before. Try to understand how it feels.'

Toba seemed baffled. Then he turned away and, looking self-conscious, hauled on reins that passed through the wooden walls.

Dura's belly lurched as the car jerked into motion. 'Toba. Where is this City of yours?'

'At the South Pole,' he said. 'Downflux. As far downflux as it's possible to go.'

Downflux . . .

Dura closed her eyes.

5

Dura emerged reluctantly from sleep.

She could feel the laxness of her muscles, the slow rhythm of her heart, the rich, warm Air of the car pulsing through her lungs and capillaries. She opened her eyecups slowly and glanced around the cramped, boxy interior of the car.

The only light came from four small, clear sections of wall – *windows*, Mixxax had called them – and the little wooden room was immersed in semi-darkness. It was a bizarre situation: to take a shit, she'd had to open a panel and squat over a tube; when she pulled a little lever the waste had been sucked away into the Air. The cabin itself was constructed of panels of wood fixed to a framework of struts and spars. The frame surrounded her, she thought fancifully, like the rib cage of some immense, protective creature. Still half-asleep, she remembered absently her feelings of threat when first climbing into the car. Now, after less than a day, she felt only a womb-like security; it was astonishing how quickly humans could adjust.

Adda's stretcher was still secured to the struts to which they had strapped it. Adda himself seemed to be asleep – or rather, unconscious. He breathed noisily, his mouth gaping and dribbling fluid; his eyes were half-open, but even his good eye was a small lake of pus which leaked slowly onto his cheek and forehead; small, harmless symbiotes covered his cheeks, lapping at the pus. Farr was curled, asleep, into a tight ball, wadded into one corner of the boxy cabin; his face was tucked into his knees and his hair waved gently as he breathed.

Mixxax sat in his comfortable-looking seat before his array of levers and gadgets. He had his back to her, his eyes focussed on the journey ahead of them. As he sat in his undershorts she

67

could see afresh how thin and bony this man from the City really was, how pale his flesh. But, at this moment, in control of his vehicle, he radiated calm and competence. It was that very calmness, the feeling of being in a controlled, secure environment – coupled with the exhaustion of the abortive hunt, the stress of Adda's injuries, the thinness of the forest Air – that had lulled Dura and Farr to fall asleep almost instantly, once the car had begun its journey.

Well, Dura was grateful for this brief interlude of peace. Soon enough the pressures of the outside world would return – the responsibilities of Adda's illness, Farr's vulnerability and need for protection, the unimaginable strangeness of the place to which they were being taken. Before long she would be looking back on this brief, secure interlude in the confining walls of the car with nostalgic affection.

Unwinding slowly, stretching to get the stiffness out of her muscles, she pushed out of her corner and glided across the small cabin to Mixxax's seat. She anchored herself by holding on to the back of the chair and peered past him out of his window.

Toba Mixxax gave a start, flinching away from her. Dura had to suppress a laugh at the moment of near-panic on his broad face.

'I'm sorry,' he said quietly. 'I thought you were asleep.'

'The others still are, I think. How long was I out?'

He shrugged. 'A while.'

She peered out of Mixxax's window, squinting a little at the golden brightness of the Air. From the front face of the car, leather leaders led to a light wooden framework which constrained the strong young Air-pigs Mixxax called his 'team'. The labouring pigs were emitting green clouds of jetfart, so dense they half-obscured the animals themselves; but they were making the car sail along the vortex lines, she saw. Thin leather ropes – reins – were attached to the pierced fins of the pigs and led, through a tight membrane in the front face of the cabin, to Mixxax's hands; Mixxax held the reins almost casually, as if his control of the pigs and car was unthinking, automatic. Dura fantasized briefly about living in such a place as this magical Parz City, where the ability to direct a car like this came as naturally as Waving.

Her eye followed the tunnel of vortices far ahead of the car to the distinct point where they merged, obscuring infinity. And just beyond that red-white point at infinity she made out the dull glow of the South Pole... and perhaps, she wondered, the glow of Parz City itself.

The Crust sailed over them like an immense ceiling, detail whipping past her with disconcerting speed. The trees through which she had hunted still grew here. They dangled from the diaphanous substance of the Crust and following the Magfield lines like hair-tubes; the cup-shapes of their neutrino leaves sparkled as her view of them shifted. But the trees seemed to be thinning: she discerned patches of Crust separating small, regular-looking stands of trees.

... And the exposed Crust was not bare: rectangular markings coated it, each perhaps a hundred mansheights across. The rectangles were characterized by slight differences of colour, varieties of texture. Some contained markings which swept across the patches in the direction of the Magfield like trapped vortex lines, but the patterns in others worked aslant from the Magfield direction – even perpendicular to it. And some bore no markings at all, save for random stipples of deeper colour.

She stared into the South. The rectangular enclosures covered the Crust from this point in, she saw, marking it out in a patchwork that receded into the misty infinity beyond the end of the vortex lines. Small forms moved across the enclosures, patiently working: humans, dwarfed by distance and by the scale of the enclosures. Here and there she made out the boxy forms of Air-cars drifting through groups of humans, supervising and inspecting.

She felt humbled, dwarfed. The cap of Crust around the Pole was *cultivated* – but on an immense scale.

Before this journey she had never seen any artifact larger than the Human Beings' Net. The car of Toba Mixxax, with its unending complexity, was impressive enough, she supposed – but these markings across the Crust were of another order entirely: artifice on a grand enough scale to challenge the curvature of the Star itself.

And put there by humans, like herself. She fought back awe.

She sought for the words Mixxax had used. *'Ceiling-farm,'* she recalled at last. 'Toba Mixxax, this is your . . . ceiling-farm.'

He laughed, an edge of bitterness in his voice. 'Hardly. These fields are much too lush for the likes of me. No, we passed the borders of my ceiling-farm long ago, while you were sleeping . . . poor as it is, you probably wouldn't have been able to distinguish it from the forest. When I picked you up we were about thirty metres from the Pole. We're within about five metres of Parz now; here the Air is thicker, warmer – the structure of the Star is different, just over the Pole itself – and people can live and work much higher, close to the Crust itself.' He waved a hand, the reins resting casually in his grasp. 'We're getting into the richest arable area. The Crust farms from this point in are owned by much richer folk than me. Or better connected . . . You wouldn't think it possible for one man to have as many brothers-in-law as Hork IV. Even worse than his father was. And . . .'

'What are they doing?'

'Who?'

She pointed to the fields. 'The people up there.'

He frowned, apparently surprised by the question. 'They're coolies,' he said. 'What I mistook your people for. They're working the fields.'

'Growing pap for the City,' came a growl from behind them.

Dura turned, startled. Adda was awake; though his pus-filled eyecups were as sightless as before, he held himself a little stiffer in his cocoon of clothes and rope and his mouth was working, bubbles of spittle erupting from its corner.

Dura swam quickly to his side. 'I'm sorry we woke you,' she whispered. 'How are you feeling?'

His mouth twisted and his throat bubbled, in a ghastly parody of a laugh. 'Oh, terrific. What do you think? If you were any better-looking I'd invite you in here to keep me warm.'

She snorted. 'Don't waste your Air on stupid jokes, you old fool.' She tried to adjust the position of his neck, smoothing out rucks in the rolled-up cloth around it.

Each time she touched him he winced.

Toba Mixxax turned. 'There's food in that locker,' he said, pointing. 'We've still a long way to go.'

In the place he'd indicated there was a small door cut into the wall, fixed by a short leather thong; opening it, Dura found a series of small bowls, each covered by a tight-fitting leather skin. Peeling away one of the skins she found pads of some pink, fleshy substance, each about the size of her palm. She took a pad and nibbled at it.

It was about as dense as meat, she supposed, but with a much softer texture. And it was delicious – like the leaves of the trees, she thought. But, as far as she could tell from her small sample, a lot denser and more nutritious than any leaf.

When was the last time she had eaten? It was all she could do not to cram the strange food into her own mouth.

She pulled three of the food pads out of the bowl, then covered over the bowl and stowed it away in its cupboard, desperate that the heavily scented photons which seeped from the food shouldn't wake up Farr.

She held a pad to Adda's lips. 'Eat,' she ordered.

'City man's pap,' he grumbled; but, feebly, he bit into the pad and chewed at it.

'There's nothing wrong with it,' she whispered as she fed him. 'It's just food.'

'And it's good for you,' Toba Mixxax called in a loud whisper, turning in his seat to watch. 'It's better for your health than meat, in fact. And . . .'

'But what is it?' Dura asked.

'Why, it's bread, of course,' he said. 'Made from wheat. From my ceiling-farm. What did you think it was?'

'Ignore him,' Adda rasped. 'And don't give him the satisfaction of asking what wheat is. I can see you want to.'

'You can't see any damn thing,' she said absently. She paused. 'Well, what *is* wheat, anyway?'

'Cultivated grass,' Toba said. 'The stuff which grows wild in the forest is good enough for Air-pigs, but it wouldn't keep you or I alive long. But wheat is a special type of grass, a strain which needs to be tended and protected – but which contains enough proton-rich compounds from the Crust to feed people.'

'On pap,' Adda growled.

'Not pap. Bread,' Mixxax said patiently.

71

Dura frowned. 'I don't think I understand. Air-pigs eat grass and we eat pigs. That's the way things work. What's wrong with that?'

Mixxax shrugged. 'Nothing, if you don't have the choice. And if you want to spend your life chasing around forests in search of pigs. But the fact is, per cubic micron of Crust root ceiling, you can get more food value out of wheat than grazing pigs. And it's economically more efficient in terms of labour to run wheat ceiling-farms rather than pig farms.' He laughed, with infuriating kindness. 'Or to hunt wild pigs, as you people do. After all, wheat stays in one place. It doesn't jetfart around the forest, or attack old men.' He looked sly. 'Anyway, there are some things you won't get except from cultivated crops. Beercake, for instance . . .'

'*Efficient*,' Adda hissed. 'That was one of the words they used when they drove us away from the Pole.'

Dura frowned. 'Who drove us away?'

'The authorities in Parz,' he said, his sightless eyes leaking disconcertingly. 'I'm talking of a time ten generations ago, Dura . . . We don't talk of these things any more. The princelings, the priests, the Wheelwrights. Drove us away from the thick, warm Air of the Pole and out into the deserts upflux. Drove us out for our faith, because we looked to a higher authority than them. Because we wouldn't work on their ceiling-farms; we wouldn't accept slavery. Because we wouldn't be *efficient*.'

'Coolies aren't slaves,' Toba Mixxax said heatedly. 'Every man and woman is free in the eyes of the law of Parz City, and . . .'

'And I'm a Xeelee's grandmother,' Adda said wearily. 'In Parz, you are as free as you can afford to be. If you're poor – a *coolie*, or a coolie's son – you've no freedom at all.'

Dura said to Adda, 'What are you talking about? Is this how you knew where Toba was from – because we were from Parz City too, once?' She frowned. 'You've never told me this. My father . . .'

Adda coughed, his throat rattling. 'I doubt if Logue knew. Or, if he did, if he cared. It was *ten generations ago*. What difference does it make now? We could never return; why dwell on the past?'

Mixxax said absently, 'I still haven't worked out what to do if you incur costs for the old man's medical treatment.'

'It doesn't take much imagination to guess,' Adda hissed. 'Dura, I told you to drive away this City man.'

'Hush,' she told him. 'He's helping us, Adda.'

'I didn't want his help,' Adda said. 'Not if it meant going into Parz itself.' He thrashed, feebly, in his cocoon of clothes. 'I'd rather die. But I couldn't even manage that now.'

Frightened by his words, Dura pressed against Adda's shoulders with her hands, forcing him to lie still.

Toba Mixxax called cautiously, 'You mentioned "Xeelee" earlier.'

Dura turned to him, frowning.

He hesitated. 'Then that's your faith? You're Xeelee cultists?'

'No,' Dura said wearily. 'If that word means what I think it means. We don't regard the Xeelee as gods; we aren't savages. But we believe the goals of the Xeelee represent the best hope for . . .'

'Listen,' Toba said, more harshly, 'I don't see that I owe you any more favours. I'm doing too much for you already.' He chewed his lip, staring out at the patterned Crust through his window. 'But I'll tell you this anyway. When we get to Parz, don't advertise your faith – your belief, about the Xeelee. Whatever it is. All right? There's no point looking for trouble.'

Dura thought that over. 'Even more trouble than following a wheel?'

Adda turned blind eyes to her. Mixxax twisted, startled. 'What do you know about the Wheel?'

'Only that you wear one around your neck,' she said mildly. 'Except when you think you need to hide it.'

The City man yanked on his reins angrily.

Adda had closed his eyes and breathed noisily but steadily, evidently unconscious once more. Farr still slept. With a pang of guilt, Dura rammed the last morsels of the food – the *bread* – into her mouth, and slid forward to rejoin Mixxax at his reins.

She gazed through the windows. Bewildering Crust detail billowed over her head. Even the vortex lines seemed to be racing past her, and she had a sudden, jarring sensation of immense speed; she was plummeting helplessly towards the mysteries of the Pole, and the future.

Toba studied her, cautious but with traces of concern. 'Are you all right?'

She tried to keep her voice steady. 'I think so. I'm just a little taken aback by the speed of this thing, I suppose.'

He frowned and squinted out through his window. 'We're not going so fast. Maybe a metre an hour. After all, it's not as if we've got to work across the Magfield; we're simply following the flux lines home . . . To my home, anyway. And, this far downflux, the pigs are getting back the full strength they'll have at the Pole. There they could reach maybe twice this speed, with a clear run.' He laughed. 'Not that there's any such thing as a clear run in Parz these days, despite the ordinances about cars inside the City. And the top teams . . .'

'I've never been in a car before,' she hissed, her teeth clenched.

He opened his mouth, and nodded. 'No. True. I'm sorry; I'm not very thoughtful.' He mused, 'I guess I'd find it a little disconcerting if I'd never ridden before – if I hadn't been riding since I was a child. No wonder you're feeling ill. I'm sorry; maybe I should have warned you. I . . .'

'Please stop apologizing.'

'Anyway, we've made good time. Considering it's such a hell of a long way from the Pole to my ceiling-farm.' His round face creased with anger. 'Humans can't survive much more than forty, fifty metres from the Pole. And my ceiling-farm is right on the fringe of that, right on the edge of the hinterland of Parz. So far upflux the Air tastes like glue and the coolies are weaker than Air-piglets . . . How am I supposed to make a living in conditions like that?' He looked at her, as if expecting an answer.

'What's a metre?'

'. . . A hundred thousand mansheights. A million microns.' He looked deflated, his anger fading. 'I don't suppose you know what I'm talking about. I'm sorry; I . . .'

'How deep is the Mantle?' she asked impulsively. 'From Crust to Quantum Sea, I mean.'

He smiled, his anger evaporating visibly. 'In metres, or mansheights?'

'Metres will do.'

'About six hundred.'

She nodded. 'That's what I've been taught, too.'

He studied her curiously. 'You people know about things like that?'

'Yes, we know about things like that,' she said heavily. 'We're not animals; we educate our children . . . even though it takes most of our energy just to keep alive, without clothes and cars and Air-boxes and teams of captive Air-pigs.'

He winced. 'I won't apologize again,' he said ruefully. 'Look . . . here's what I know.' Still holding his reins loosely, he cupped his long-fingered, delicate-looking hands into a ball. 'The Star is a sphere, about twenty thousand metres across.'

She nodded. *Two thousand million mansheights.*

'It's surrounded by the Crust,' he went on. 'There's three hundred metres of that. And the Quantum Sea is another ball, about eighteen thousand metres across, floating inside the crust.'

She frowned. 'Floating?'

He hesitated. 'Well, I think so. How should I know? And between the Crust and the Quantum Sea is the Mantle – the Air we breathe – about six hundred metres deep.' He looked into her face, a disconcerting mixture of suspicion and pity evident there. 'That's the shape of the Star. The world. Any kid in Parz City could have told you all that.'

She shrugged. 'Or any Human Being. Maybe there was no difference once.'

She wished Adda were awake, so she could learn more of the secret history of her people. She turned her face to the window.

In the last hours of the journey the inverted Crust landscape changed again.

Dura, with Farr now awake and at her side, stared up, fascinated, watching the slow evolution of the racing Crustscape. There was very little left of the native forest here, although a few trees still straggled from small copses. The clean, orderly regularity of the fields they'd passed under to the North – further *upflux*, as she was learning to call it – was breaking up into a jumble of forms and textures.

Farr pointed excitedly, his eyes round. Dura followed his gaze.

They weren't alone in the sky, she realized: in the far, misted distance something moved – not a car; it was long, dark, like a blackened vortex line. And like Mixxax's car it was heading for the Pole, threading along the Magfield.

She said, 'That must be thousands of mansheights long.'

Toba glanced dismissively. 'Lumber convoy,' he said. 'Coming in from upflux. Nothing special. Damn slow, actually, if you get stuck behind one.'

Soon there were many more cars in the Air. Mixxax, grumbling, often had to slow as they joined streams of traffic sliding smoothly along the Magfield flux lines. The cars came in all shapes and sizes, from small one-person buggies to grand chariots drawn by teams of a dozen or more pigs. These huge cars, covered in ornate carvings, quite dwarfed poor Mixxax's; Toba's car, thought Dura, which had seemed so grand and terrifying out in the forest upflux, now appeared small, shabby and insignificant.

Much, she was coming to realize, like its owner.

The colours of the Crust fields were changing: deepening and becoming more vivid. Farr asked Mixxax, 'Different types of wheat?'

Mixxax showed little interest in these rich regions from which he was excluded. 'Maybe. Flowers, too.'

'Flowers?'

'Plants bred for their beauty – their shape, or colour; or the scent of the photons they give off.' He smiled. 'Actually, Ito grows some blooms which . . .'

'Who's Ito?'

'My wife. Nothing as grand as this, of course: after all, we're flying over the estates of Hork's court now.'

Farr had his face pressed to a window of the car. 'You mean people grow plants just for the way they look?'

'Yes.'

'But how do they live? Don't they have to hunt for food, as we do?'

Dura shook her head. 'Folk here don't hunt, Farr. I've learned that much. They grow special kinds of grasses, and eat them.'

Mixxax laughed bitterly. '"Folk here", as you call them, don't even do that. *I* do that, in my scrubby farm on the edge of the upflux desert. I grow food to feed the rich folk in Parz . . . and I pay them taxes so they can afford to buy it. And that,' he finished bitterly, 'is how Hork's courtiers have enough leisure time to grow flowers.'

The logic of that puzzled Dura, but – understanding little – she let it pass.

Now, suddenly, the queue of cars in front of them cleared aside, and the view ahead was revealed.

Dura heard herself gasp.

Farr cried out, sounding like a small child. 'What is it?'

Mixxax turned and grinned at him, evidently enjoying his moment of advantage. 'That,' he said, 'is Parz City. We have arrived.'

6

Muub arrived at the Reception Gallery shortly before the start of the Grand Tribute. He moved to the front of the Gallery, so that he could see down the full depth of Pall Mall, and selected a body-cocoon close to Vice-Chair Hork's customary place. A servant drifted around him for a few moments, adjusting the cocoon so it fit snugly, and offered him drinks and other refreshments. Muub, unable to shake off weariness, found the harmless little man as irritating as an itch, and he chased him away.

Muub looked down. Pall Mall was the City's main avenue. Broad and light-filled, it was a rectangular corridor cut vertically through the complex heart of Parz – from the elaborate superstructure of the Palace buildings at the topmost Upside, down through hundreds of dwelling levels, all the way to the Market, the vast, open forum at the centre of the City. The Reception Gallery was poised at the head of Pall Mall, just below the Palace buildings themselves; Muub, trying to relax in his cocoon, was bathed in the subtly shaded light filtering down through the Palace's lush gardens, and was able to survey, it seemed, the whole of the City as if it were laid open before him. Pall Mall itself glowed with light from the Airshafts and wood-lamps which lined its perforated walls; threads of the shafts, glowing green and yellow, converged towards the Market itself, the City's dusty heart. The great avenue – normally thronged with traffic – was deserted today, but Muub could make out spectators peering from doors and viewing-balconies: ordinary little faces turned up towards him like so many flowers. And in the Market itself – all of five thousand mansheights below the Palace – the Tribute procession was almost assembled, as thousands of common citizens gathered to present the finest fruit of this quarter's labour to the Committee. No cocoons down there, of course; instead the Market was criss-crossed by ropes and bars to which people clung with their hands or legs, or hauled themselves along in search of vantage points. To Muub, staring down at the swarming activity, it was like gazing into a huge net full of young piglets.

The Gallery itself was laced with ropes of brushed leather – to guide those Committee members and courtiers, Muub thought sourly, too poor to be simply carried to their cocoons. The Gallery's cool, piped Air was scented with fine Crust-flowers. Vice-Chair Hork was already in his place close to Muub, alongside the vacant cocoon reserved for his father, Hork IV. Hork glared ahead, sullen and silent in his bulk and glowering through his beard. Perhaps half the courtiers were in their places; but they had congregated towards the rear of the Gallery, evidently sensing, in their dim, self-seeking way, that today was not a good day to attract the attention of the mercurial Vice-Chair.

So already the elaborate social jostling had begun. It would be a long day.

In fact – thanks to the recent Glitch – it had already been a long day for Muub. The latest in a series of long days. He was principal Physician to the First Family, but he also had a hospital to run – indeed, the retention of his responsibilities at the Hospital of the Common Good had been a condition of his acceptance of his appointment to Hork's court – and the burden placed on his staff by the Glitch had still to unravel. He studied the vapid, pretty, ageing faces of the courtiers as they preened in their finery, and wondered how many more ravaged bodies he would have to tend before sleep claimed him.

Vice-Chair Hork seemed to notice him at last. Hork nodded to him. Hork was a bulky man whose size gave him an appearance of slowness of wit – a deceptive appearance, as more than one courtier had found to his cost. Under his extravagant beard – extravagantly manufactured, actually, Muub reflected wryly – Hork's face had something of the angular nobility of his father's, with those piercing, deep black eyecups and angular nose; but the features tended to be lost in the sheer bulk of the younger Hork's fleshy face, so that whereas the Chair of the Central Committee had an appearance of gentle, rather bruised nobility, his son and heir appeared hard, tough and coarse, the refined elements of his looks serving only to accentuate his inherent violence. Today, though, Hork seemed calm. 'So, Muub,' he called. 'You've decided to join me. I was fearful of being shunned.'

Muub sighed as he worked his way deeper into his cocoon. 'You glower too much, sir,' he said. 'You frighten them all away.'

Hork snorted. 'Then through the Ring with them,' he said, the ancient obscenity coming easily to his lips. 'And how are you, Physician? You're looking a little subdued yourself.'

Muub smiled. 'I'm afraid I'm getting a little old for my burden of work. I've spent most of the last few days in the Hospital. We're – very busy, sir.'

'Glitch injuries?'

'Yes, sir.' Muub rubbed a hand over his shaven scalp. 'Of course we should have seen the worst now . . . or rather, the more serious cases we have not yet reached must, sadly, be beyond our care. But there remains a steady stream of lesser injuries which . . .'

'Minor?'

'Lesser,' Muub corrected him firmly. 'Which is very different. Not life-threatening, but still, perhaps, disabling. Most of them patients from the central districts, of course. When Longitude I failed . . .'

'I know,' Hork said, chewing his lip. 'You don't need to tell me about it.'

Longitude I was an anchor-band, one of four superconducting toroids wrapped around the City to maintain the structure's position over the South Pole. Longitudes I and II were aligned vertically, while their twins Latitudes I and II were placed horizontally, so that the toroids criss-crossed around the City.

The Glitch had largely spared the Polar regions, the City itself. But at the height of the Glitch, with vortex lines tangling around the City, Longitude I had failed. The City had rattled in its superconducting cage like a trapped Air-pig. The anchor-band's current had been restored quickly, and the effects on the external parts of the structure – such as the Spine and the Committee Palace – had been minimal. But it had been in the hidden interior of the City, where thousands of clerks and artisans toiled their lives away, that the most serious injuries had been incurred.

'Do we have any figures on the casualties yet?'

Muub looked at the Vice-Chair. 'I'm surprised you're asking me. I'm your father's Physician, but I'm really just one Hospital Administrator – one of twelve in all of Parz.'

Hork waved fat fingers. 'I know that. All right, forget I asked. I just wanted your view. The trouble is that the agencies which gather statistics like that for us are precisely those which were wrecked by the Glitch itself.' He shook his head, the jowls wobbling angrily. 'People think gathering information is a joke – unnecessary. A luxury. I suspect even my highly intelligent father shares that view.' The last few words were spat out, venomously. 'But the fact is, without such data a government can scarcely operate. I've tried to justify this to my father often enough. You see, Doctor, without central government functions, the state is like a body without a head. We can't even raise tithes successfully, let alone allocate expenditure.' Hork grimaced. 'It makes today's Grand Tribute look a little pointless, doesn't it, Physician?'

Muub nodded. 'I understand, sir.'

'I tell you, Muub,' Hork said, still nervously chewing on his bearded underlip, 'one more Glitch like that and we could be done for.'

Muub frowned. 'Who are "we"? The government, the Committee?'

Hork shrugged. 'There are plenty of hotheads, out in the ceiling-farms, in the dynamo sheds, in the Harbour . . . There seems no way of rooting such vermin out. Even Breaking them on the Wheel serves only to create martyrs.'

Muub smiled. 'A wise observation.'

Hork laughed, displaying well-maintained teeth. 'And you're a patronizing old fool who pushes his luck . . . Martyrs. Yet another subtlety of human interaction which seems to evade my poor, absent father.' Now Hork looked piercingly at Muub; the Physician found himself flinching. 'And you,' Hork said. 'Do you scent rebellion in the Air?'

Muub thought carefully. He knew he wasn't under any personal suspicion; but he also knew that the Vice-Chair

– unlike his father – took careful note of anything said to him. And Hork had dozens, hundreds of informants spread right throughout Parz and its hinterland. 'No, sir. Although there are plenty of grumbles – and plenty of folk ready to blame the Committee for our predicament.'

'As if we had called the Glitches down on our own heads?' Hork wriggled in his cocoon, folds of brushed leather rippling over his ample form. 'You know,' he mused, 'if only that were true. If only the Glitches were human in origin, to be cancelled at a human command. But then, the scholars tell us – repeating what little wisdom was allowed to survive the Reformation – man was brought to this Mantle by the Ur-humans, modified to survive here. If once we had such control over our destiny, why should we not regain it, ultimately?' He smiled. 'Well, Physician?'

Muub returned the smile. 'You've a lively mind, sir, and I enjoy debating such subjects with you. But I prefer to restrict my attention to the practical. The achievable.'

Hork scowled, his plaited hair-tubes waving with an elegance that made Muub abruptly aware of his own baldness. 'Maybe. But let's not forget that that was the argument of the Reformers, ten generations ago. And their purges and expulsions left us in such ignorance we can't even measure the damage they did . . .

'Anyway, it's not revolt I fear, Physician. It's more the feasibility of government itself – I mean the viability of our state, regardless of whoever sits in my father's chair.' The man's wide, fleshy face turned to Muub now, full of unaccustomed doubt. 'Do you understand me, Muub? Damn few do, I can tell you, inside this wretched court or out.'

Muub was impressed – not for the first time – by the younger Hork's acuity. 'Perhaps, you fear, the Glitches will render an organized society like Parz City impossible. Revolts will become irrelevant. Our civilization itself will fall.'

'Exactly,' Hork said, sounding almost grateful. 'No more City – no more tithe-collectors, or Crust-flower parks, or artists or scientists. Or Physicians. We'll all have to Wave off to the upflux and hunt boar.'

Muub laughed. 'There are a few who would like to see the back of the tithes.'

'Only fools who cannot perceive the benefits. When every man must not only maintain his own scrubby herd of pigs, but must make, *by hand*, every tool he uses, like the poorest upfluxer . . . then, perhaps, he will look back on taxation with nostalgic affection.'

Muub frowned, scratching at one eyecup. 'Do you think such a collapse is near?'

'Not yet,' Hork said. 'Not unless the Glitches really do smash us wide open. But it's possible, and growing more so. And only a fool closes his eyes to the possible.'

Muub, wary of what traps might lie under the surface of that remark, turned to stare down through the dusty, illuminated Air of Pall Mall.

Hork growled, 'Now I've embarrassed you. Come on, Muub, don't start acting like one of these damn piglet-courtiers. I value your conversation. I didn't mean to imply my father is such a fool.'

'. . . But he does not necessarily share your perspective.'

'No. Damn it.' Hork shook his head. 'And he won't give me the power to do anything about it. It's frustrating.' Hork looked at Muub. 'I hear you saw him recently. Where is he?'

Shouldn't you know? 'He's at his garden, at the Crust. He can't take the thin Air, of course, so he mostly stays in his car, watching the coolies getting on with their work.'

'So he's healthy?'

Muub sighed. 'Your father is an old man. He's fragile. But – yes; he is well.'

Hork nodded. 'I'm glad.' He glanced at the Physician, seeking his reaction. 'I mean it, Muub. I get frustrated with him because I'm not always sure he addresses the key issues. But Hork *is* still my father. And besides,' he went on pragmatically, 'the last thing we need right now is a succession crisis.'

There was a buzz of conversation from around the Gallery.

Hork leaned forward in his cocoon. 'What's going on?'

Muub pointed. 'The pipers are moving into position.' There were a hundred of the pipers, dressed in bright, eye-catching clothes, now Waving out of doorways all along Pall Mall and taking up their positions, lining the route of the parade. The closest pipers – four of them, one to each of the Mall's complex walls – were earnest young men, efficiently stoking the small furnaces they carried on belts around their waists. Fine, tapered tubes led from the furnaces in elaborate whorls to wide, flower-like horns; the horns of polished wood gaped above the head of the pipers like the mouths of shining predators.

'There!' Hork cried, pointing down the avenue, his face illuminated with a mixture of excitement and avarice.

Muub, suppressing a sigh, leaned further forward and squinted down the Mall, trying to pick out the distant specks in the Air that would be the approaching Tribute parade: earnest, overweight citizens bearing vast sheaves of wheat, or grotesquely bloated Air-pigs.

The pipers pushed valves on their furnace-boxes. Within each horn, complex Air patterns swirled, sending pulses of heat along the necks of the horns – pulses which emerged from the horns, by a process which had always seemed magical to the resolutely non-musical Muub, as stirring peals of sound.

Far below, in the Market, the crowd roared.

Toba Mixxax twitched his reins and stared unblinking out of his window. 'I'm going to take him straight into the Hospital. The Common Good. It's a decent place. Hork's own Physician runs it . . .'

Cars of all sizes came hurtling past them in a constant, random stream. Pig teams farted clouds of green gas. Speakers blared. Toba yelled back through his own car's system, but the amplified voices were too distorted for Dura to understand what was being said.

It was, frankly, terrifying. Dura, hovering with Farr behind Toba's seat and staring out at the chaotic whirl of hurtling wooden boxes, bit the back of her hand to avoid crying out.

But somehow Toba Mixxax was managing not only to avoid collisions but also to drive them forward – slowly, but forward – to the staggering bulk of the City itself.

'Of course it's not the cheapest. The Common Good, I mean.' Toba laughed hollowly. 'But then, frankly, you're not going to be able to afford even the cheapest. So you may as well not be able to afford the best.'

'Your talk means little, Toba Mixxax,' Dura said. 'Perhaps you should concentrate on the cars.'

Toba shook his head. 'Just my luck to come into town with three upfluxers on the day of the Grand Tribute. Today of all days. And . . .'

Dura gave up listening. She tried to ignore the cloud of hurtling cars in the foreground of her vision, to see beyond them to Parz itself.

The South Magnetic Pole itself was spectacular enough – like a huge artifact, an immense sculpting of Magfield and spin lines. Vortex lines followed – almost – the shape of the Magfield, so it was easy to trace the spectacular curvature of the magnetic flux. It was nothing like the gentle, easy, Star-girdling curvature of her home region, far upflux; here, at the furthest downflux, the vortex lines converged from all over the Mantle and plunged into the bulk of the Star around the Pole itself, forming a funnel of Magfield delineated by sparkling, wavering vortex lines.

And, suspended right over the mouth of that immense funnel, as if challenging the Pole's very right to exist, the City of Parz hung in the Air.

The City was shaped like a slender, upraised arm, with a fist clenched at its top. The 'arm' was a spine of wood which thrust upwards, out of the Pole's plunging vortex funnel, and the 'fist' was a complex mass of wooden constructions which sprawled across many thousands of mansheights. Four great hoops of some glittering substance – 'anchor-bands', Toba called them, two aligned vertically and two horizontally – surrounded the fist-mass; Dura could see struts and spars attaching the hoops to the mass of the 'fist'.

The 'fist', the City itself, was a perforated wooden box, suspended within the hoops. Ports – circular, elliptical and rectangular – punctured the box's surface, and cars streamed in and out of many of the ports like small creatures feeding off some greater beast. Towards the base of the City the ports were much wider: they gaped like mouths, dark and rather forbidding, evidently intended for bulk deliveries. Into one of these Dura could see tree-stalks being hauled from a great lumberjacking convoy.

Sparkling streams, hundreds of them, flowed endlessly

from the base of the City and into the Air, quite beautiful: they were sewer streams, Toba told her, rivers of waste from Parz's thousands of inhabitants.

As the car veered around the City – Toba, braying incoherently into his Speaker tube, was evidently looking for a port to enter – Dura caught tantalizing glimpses through the many wide shafts of complex structures, layers of buildings *within* the bulk of the City itself. A complex set of buildings perched on the crown of the City, grand and elegant even to Dura's half-baffled eyes. There were even small Crust-trees arcing into the Air from among those upper buildings. When she pointed this out to Toba he grinned and shrugged. 'That's the Committee Palace,' he said. 'Expense is little object if you live that far Upside . . .'

Light filled the City, shining from its many ports and casting beams across the dusty Air surrounding it, so that Parz was surrounded by a rich, complex mesh of green-yellow illumination. The City was immense – almost beyond Dura's imagination – but it seemed to her bright, Air-filled, full of light and motion. People swarmed around the buildings, and streams of Air-cars laced around the spires of the Palace. Even the 'arm' below the City-fist, the Spine (as Toba called it) that grew down towards the Pole, bore tiny cars which clambered constantly up and down ropes threaded along the Spine's length.

The City grew as they approached – growing so huge, at last, that it more than filled the small window of the car. Dura began to find the whole assemblage overwhelming in detail and complexity. She recalled – with a strange feeling of nostalgia – her feelings of panic on first encountering Toba's car. She'd soon learned to master her panic then, and had come to feel almost in control of this strange, weak person, Toba Mixxax. But now she was confronted by strangeness on an unimaginably huger scale. Could she ever come to terms with all this – ever again take control over her own destiny, let alone influence events around her?

Her discomfiture must have shown in her expression. Toba grinned at her, not unsympathetically. 'It must be pretty overwhelming,' he said. 'Do you know how big the City is? Ten thousand mansheights, from side to side. And that's not counting the Spine.' The little car continued to edge its way, cautiously, around the City, like a timid Air-piglet looking for a place to suckle. Toba shook his head. 'Even the Ur-humans would have been impressed by ten thousand mansheights, I'll bet. Why, that's almost a centimetre...'

The car entered – at last – a narrow rectangular port which seemed to Dura to be already filled with jostling traffic. The car pushed deeper into the bulk of the City along a narrow tunnel – a 'street', Toba Mixxax called it – through which cars and people thronged. These citizens of Parz were all dressed in thick, heavy, bright clothing, and all seemed to Dura utterly without fear of the streams of cars around them. Dura's impressions from without of the airiness and brightness of the City evaporated now; the walls of the street closed in around her, and the car seemed to be pushing deeper into a clammy darkness.

At last they came to a gap in the wall of the street, a port leading to a brighter place. This was the entrance to the Hospital, Toba said. Dura watched, silent, as Toba with unconscious skill slid his car through the last few layers of traffic and encouraged the pigs to draw the car gently into the Hospital bay. When the car had been brought to rest against a floor of polished wood, Toba knotted the reins together, pushed his way out of his chair and stretched in the Air.

Farr looked at him strangely. 'You're tired? But the pigs did all the work.'

Toba laughed and turned bruised-looking eyes to the boy. 'Learn to drive, kid, and you'll know what tiredness is.' He looked to Dura. 'Anyway, now comes the hard part. Come on; I'll need you to help me explain.'

Toba reached for the door of the car. As he released its catch Dura flinched, half-expecting another explosive change of pressure. But the door simply glided open, barely making a noise. Heat washed into the opened interior of the car; Dura felt the prickle of cooling superfluid capillaries opening all over her body.

Toba led Dura and Farr out of the car, wriggling stiffly through the doorway. Dura put her hands on the rim of the doorway, pulled – and found herself plunging forward, her face ramming into Toba's back hard enough to make her nose ache.

Toba staggered in the Air. 'Hey, take it easy. What's the rush?'

Dura apologized. She looked down at her arms uncertainly. What had that been all about? She hadn't misjudged her own strength like that since she was a child. It was as if she had suddenly become immensely strong . . . or else as light as a child. She felt clumsy, off balance; the heat of this place seemed overwhelming.

Her confidence sank even more. She shook her head, irritated and afraid, and tried to put the little incident out of her mind.

The Hospital bay was a hemisphere fifty mansheights across. Dozens of cars were suspended here, mostly empty and bereft of their teams: harnesses and restraints dangled limply in the Air, and one corner had been netted off as a pen for Air-pigs. One car, much larger than Toba's, was being unloaded of patients: injured, even dead-looking people, tied into bundles like Adda's. A tall man was supervising; he was quite hairless and dressed in a long, fine robe. People – all clothed – moved between the cars, hurrying and bearing expressions of unfathomable concern. A few of them found time to glance curiously at Dura and Farr.

The walls, of polished wood, were so clean that they gleamed, reflecting curved images of the bustle within the bay. Wide shafts pierced the walls and admitted the brightness of the Air outside to this loading bay. Huge rimless wheels – *fans*, Toba told her – turned in the shafts, pushing Air around the bay. Dura breathed in slowly, assessing the quality of the Air. It was fresh, although clammy-hot and permeated by the stench-photons of pigs. But there was something else, an aroma that was at once familiar and yet strange, out of context . . .

People.

That was it; the Air was filled with the all-pervading, stale smell of *people*. It was like being a little girl again and stuck at the heart of the Net, surrounded by the perspiring bodies of adults, of other children. She was hot and claustrophobic, suddenly aware that she was surrounded, here in the City, by more people than had lived out their lives in her tiny tribe of Human Beings in many generations. She felt naked and out of place.

Toba touched her shoulder. 'Come on,' he said anxiously. 'Let's get the stretcher out of the car. And then we'll find someone to . . .'

'Well. What have we here?' The voice was harsh, amused, and shared Toba's stilted accent.

Dura turned. Two men were approaching, Waving stiffly through the Air. They were short, blocky and wore identical suits of thick leather; they carried what looked like coiled whips, and wore masks of stiffened leather which muffled their voices and made it impossible to read their expressions.

The eyes of these anonymous beings raked over Dura and Farr.

She dropped her hands to her hips. The rope she'd taken Crust-hunting was still wrapped around her waist, and she could feel the gentle pressure of her knife, her cleaning scraper, tucked into the rope at her back. She found the presence of these familiar things comforting, but – apart from that little knife – *all their weapons were still in the car*. Stupid, stupid; what would Logue have said? She edged backwards through the Air, trying to find a clear path back to the car.

Toba said, 'Sirs, I am Citizen Mixxax. I have a patient for the Hospital. And . . .'

The guard who had spoken earlier growled, 'Where's the patient?'

Toba waved him to the car. The man peered in suspiciously. Then he withdrew his head from the car, visibly wrinkling his nose under his mask. 'I don't see a patient. I see an upfluxer. And here . . .' – he waved the butt of his whip towards Dura and Farr – 'I see two more upfluxers. Plus a pig's-ass in his underpants. But no patients.'

'It's true,' Toba said patiently, 'that these people are from the upflux. But the old man's badly hurt. And . . .'

'This is a Hospital,' the guard said neutrally. 'Not a damn zoo. So get these animals out of here.'

Toba sighed and held out his hands, apparently trying to find more words.

The guard was losing patience. He reached out and poked at Dura's shoulder with one gloved finger. 'I said get them out of here. I won't tell . . .'

Farr moved forward. 'Stop that,' he said. And he shoved, apparently gently, at the guard.

The man flew backwards through the Air, at last colliding with a wooden-panelled wall. His whip trailed ineffectually behind him.

Farr tipped backwards with the reaction; he looked down at his own hands with astonishment.

The second guard started to uncoil his whip. 'Well,' he said softly, 'maybe a few spins of the Wheel would help you learn your place, little boy.'

'Look, this is all going wrong,' Toba said. 'I didn't mean for any of this to happen. Please; I . . .'

'Shut up.'

Dura clenched her fists, ready to move forward. She had no doubt that she and Farr could account for this man, leather armour or not – especially with the immense new strength they seemed to have acquired here. Of course, there were more than two guards in Parz City; and beyond the next few minutes she could envisage a hundred dim and dark ways for events to unfold, flowering like deadly Crust-flowers out of this incident . . . But this moment was all she could influence.

The guard raised the whip to her brother. She reached for her knife and prepared to spring . . .

'Wait. Stop this.'

Dura turned, slowly; the guard was lowering his whip.

The man who had been supervising the unloading of the other car – tall, commanding, dressed in a fine but begrimed robe, and with a head shockingly denuded of hair-tubes – was coming towards them.

Dura was aware of Toba cringing backwards. The guard looked at Farr and Dura with frustrated hunger.

Dura said, 'Who are you? What do you want?'

The newcomer frowned. He was about Logue's age, she judged. 'Who am I? It's a long time since I was asked that. My name is Muub, my dear. I am the Administrator of this Hospital.' He studied her curiously. 'And you're an upfluxer, aren't you?'

'No,' she said, suddenly heartily sick of that word. 'I am a Human Being.'

He smiled. 'Indeed.' Muub glanced at the guards, and then turned to Toba Mixxax. 'Citizen, what is happening here? I don't welcome disturbances in my Hospital; we have enough to cope with without that.'

Toba bowed; he seemed to be trembling. His hands moved across the front of his body, as if he were suddenly embarrassed by his underwear. 'Yes. I'm sorry, sir. I am Toba Mixxax; I run a ceiling-farm about thirty metres upflux, and I . . .'

'Get on with it,' Muub said mildly.

'I found an injured upfluxer . . . an injured man. I brought him back. He's in the car.'

Muub frowned. Then he slid across to the car and pulled his head and shoulders through the doorway. Dura could see the Administrator efficiently inspecting Adda. He seemed fascinated by the spears and nets of the Human Beings, the artifacts which had been used to improvise splints for Adda.

Adda opened one eye. 'Bugger off,' he whispered to Muub.

The Administrator studied Adda, Dura thought, as one might consider a leech, or a damaged spider.

Muub withdrew from the car. 'This man's seriously hurt. That right arm . . .'

'I know, sir,' Toba said miserably. 'That was why I thought . . .'

'Damn it, man,' Muub said, not unkindly, 'how do you expect them to be able to pay? They're upfluxers!'

Toba dropped his head. 'Sir,' he said, his voice wavering but dogged, 'there is the Market. Both the woman and the boy are strong and fit. And they're used to hard work. I found them at the Crust, working in conditions no coolie would withstand.' He fell silent, keeping his head averted from the others.

Muub brushed his soiled fingers against his robe and gazed vacantly into the car. At length he said mildly, 'All right. Bring him in, Citizen Mixxax . . . Guard, help him. And bring the woman and the boy. Keep your eye on them, Mixxax; if they run wild, or foul the place, I'll hold you responsible.'

Mixxax's misery seemed to lift a little. 'Yes, sir. Thank you.'

Another car sailed into the bay, evidently bringing in more patients for the Hospital; Muub Waved away, tired responsibility etched into his face.

7

Toba grudgingly offered to let Dura and Farr stay at his home in the City while Adda's injuries were treated at the Hospital. At first Dura refused, but Toba gave her a look of exasperation. 'You haven't any choice,' he said heavily. 'Believe me. If you had, I'd tell you about it; I've got my own life to get back to, eventually . . . Look, you've nowhere to go, you've no money – not even any clothes.'

'We don't need charity.'

'The noble savage,' Toba replied sourly. 'Do you know how long it would take for you to be picked up as vagrants? You saw the guards at the Hospital. And at the Hospital, they're picked specially for their warm bedside manner. Vagrants aren't popular. *No tithes to the Committee, no room in the City*, as the saying goes . . . You'd be on a Committee-run ceiling-farm doing forced labour, or worse, before you could turn around. And then who's going to pay poor old Adda's bills?'

Dura could see there was indeed no choice. In fact, she thought, they had every reason to be grateful to this irritable little man – if he weren't offering to take them in, they could be in real difficulty. So she nodded, and tried, embarrassed, to form a phrase of thanks.

Toba said, 'Oh, just get in the car.'

Toba drove them through the still-crowded streets away from the Hospital. The streets – wood-lined corridors of varying widths – were a baffling maze to Dura, and after a few twists and corners her orientation was gone. Cars and people were everywhere, and more than once Toba's team of Air-pigs came into jostling contact with others, forcing Toba to haul on his reins. Speaker-amplified voices blared. Here in the City, Toba drove with the car door open. The Air in the streets was noisy, thick, hot, and laden with the stink of people and

Air-pigs; beams of brightness shone through the dust and the green clouds of jetfart.

At length they left the busiest streets behind and came to an area which seemed quieter – less full of rushing cars and howling pigs. The corridor-streets here were wide and lined by rows of neat doors and windows which marked out small dwelling-places. Evidently these had been virtually identical when constructed, but now they had been made unique by their owners, with small plants confined in globe-baskets by the windows, elaborate carvings on the doorways, and other small changes. Many of the carved scenes depicted the Mantle outside the City: Dura recognized vortex lines, Crust trees, people Waving happily through clear Air. How strange that these people, still longing for the open Air, should closet themselves inside this stuffy box of wood.

Toba tugged his reins and drove the car smoothly through a wide, open portal to a place he described as a 'car park'. He slowed the car. 'End of the line.' Dura and Farr stared back at him, confused. 'Go on. Out you get. You have to Wave from here, I'm afraid.'

The car park was a large, dingy chamber, its walls stained by pig faeces and splintered from multiple collisions. There were a half-dozen cars, hanging abandoned in the Air, and thirty or forty pigs jostled together in a large area cordoned off by a loose net. The animals seemed content enough, Dura observed; they clambered slowly over each other, munching contentedly at fragments of food floating in the Air.

Toba loosened the harnesses around his own pigs and led them one by one over to the cordoned area. He guided the pigs competently through a raised flap in the net, taking care to seal the net tight after himself each time.

When he was done he wiped his hands on his short under-trousers. 'That's that. Someone will come by shortly to feed and scrape them.' He sniffed, peering at the grubby walls of the car park. 'Tatty place, isn't it? And you wouldn't believe the quarterly charges. But what can you do? Since the ordinances banning so much on-street parking it's become impossible to find a place. Not that it seems to stop a lot of people, of course . . .'

Dura strained to follow this. But like much of Toba's

conversation it was largely meaningless to her, and – she suspected – contained little hard information anyway.

After a while, and with no reply from the silent, staring Human Beings, Toba subsided. He led them from the car park and out into the street.

Dura and Farr followed their host through the curving streets. It was oddly difficult to Wave here; perhaps the Magfield wasn't as strong outside. Dura felt very conscious of people all around her, of strangers behind these oddly uniform doorways and windows. Occasionally she saw thin faces peering out at them as they passed. The stares of the people of Parz seemed to bore into her back, and it was difficult not to whirl around, to confront the invisible threats behind her.

She kept an eye on Farr, but he seemed, if anything, less spooked than she was. He stared around wide-eyed, as if everything was unique, endlessly fascinating. His bare limbs and graceful, strong Waving looked out of place in this cramped, slightly shabby street.

After a few minutes Toba stopped at a doorway barely distinguishable from a hundred others. 'My home,' he explained, an odd note of apology in his voice. 'Not as far Upside as I'd like it to be. But, still, it's home.' He fished in a pocket of his under-shorts and produced a small, finely carved wooden object. He inserted this into a hole in the door, turned it, and then pushed the door wide. From inside the house came a smell of hot food, the greenish light of wood-lamps. 'Ito!'

A woman came Waving briskly to the door. She was quite short, plump and with her hair tied back from her forehead; she wore a loose suit of some brightly coloured fabric. She seemed about the same age as Dura, although – oddly – there was no yellow coloration in her hair. The woman smiled at Toba, but the smile faded when she saw the upfluxers.

Toba's hands twisted together. 'Ito, I've some explaining to do . . .'

The sharp eyes of the woman, Ito, travelled up and down the bodies of the Human Beings, taking in their bare skin, their unkempt hair, their hand-weapons. 'Yes, you bloody well have,' she said.

*

95

Toba's dwelling-place was a box of wood about ten mansheights across. It was divided into five smaller rooms by light partitions and coloured sheets; small lamps, of nuclear-burning wood, glowed neatly in each room.

Toba showed the Human Beings a place to clean themselves – a room containing chutes for waste and spherical bowls holding scented cloth. Dura and Farr, left alone in this strange room, tried to use the chutes. Dura pulled the little levers as Toba had shown them, and their shit disappeared down gurgling tubes into the mysterious guts of the City. Brother and sister peered into the chutes, open-mouthed, trying to see where it all went.

When they were done Toba led them to a room at the centre of the little home. The centrepiece was a wooden ball suspended at the heart of the room; there were handholds set around the globe's surface and fist-sized cavities carved into it. Ito – who had changed into a lighter, flowing robe – was ladling some hot, unrecognizable food into the cavities. She smiled at them, but her lips were tight. There was a third member of the family in the room – Toba's son, who he introduced as Cris. Cris seemed a little older than Farr, and the two boys stared at each other with frank, not unfriendly curiosity. Cris seemed better muscled than most City folk to Dura. His hair was long, floating and mottled yellow, as if prematurely aged; but the colour was vivid even in the dim lamplight, and Dura suspected it had been dyed that way.

At Ito's invitation the upfluxers came to the spherical table. Dura, still naked, her knife still at her back, felt large, clumsy, ugly in this delicate little place. She was constantly aware of the Pole-strength of her muscles, and she felt inhibited, afraid to touch anything or move too quickly for fear of smashing something.

Copying Toba, she shovelled food into her mouth with small wooden utensils. The food was hot and unfamiliar, but strongly flavoured. As soon as she started, Dura found she was ravenously hungry – in fact, save for the few fragments of the bread Toba had offered to Adda during the long journey to the City, she hadn't eaten since their ill-fated hunt – and how long ago that seemed now!

They ate in silence.

After the meal, Toba guided the Human Beings to a small room in one corner of the home. A single lamp cast long shadows, and two tight cocoons had been suspended across the room. 'I know it's small, but there should be room for the two of you,' he said. 'I hope you sleep well.'

The two Human Beings clambered into the cocoons; the fabric felt soft and warm against Dura's skin.

Toba Mixxax reached for the lamp – then hesitated. 'Do you want me to dampen the light?'

It seemed a strange request to Dura. She looked around, but this deep inside Parz City there were, of course, no light-ducts, no access to the open Air. 'But then it would be dark,' she said slowly.

'Yes . . . We sleep in the dark.'

Dura had never been in the dark in her life. 'Why?'

Toba looked puzzled. 'I don't know . . . I've never thought about it.' He drew back his hand from the lamp, and smiled at them. 'Sleep well.' He Waved briskly away, sealing shut the room behind him.

Wriggling inside her cocoon, Dura uncoiled her length of rope from her waist, and wrapped it loosely around one of the cocoon's ties. She knotted the rope around her knife, close enough that she could reach the knife if she needed to. Then she squirmed deeper into the cocoon, at last drawing her arms inside it. It was an odd experience to be completely enclosed like this, though oddly comforting.

She glanced across at Farr. He was already asleep, his head tucked down against his chest. She felt a burst of protective affection for her brother – and yet, she realized ruefully, he seemed less in need of protection than she did herself. Farr seemed to be absorbing the wonders and mysteries of this complex place with much more resilience and openness than Dura could find.

Dura sighed, clinging to the fragments of her dissipating feeling of protectiveness. Looking after her brother, at least nominally, made her able to forget her own sense of isolation and threat. Perhaps in an odd way, she thought drowsily, she needed Farr more than he needed her. In the quiet of the room, she became aware of noises from beyond the walls around her. There were murmured words from Toba, the uneven voice of the boy, Cris; and then it was as if her sphere of awareness expanded out beyond this single house, so that she could hear the soft insect-murmurings of thousands of humans all around her in this immense hive of people. The wooden walls creaked softly, expanding and contracting; she felt as if the whole City were breathing around her.

The cocoon soon grew hot, confining; impatiently she shoved her arms out into the marginally cooler Air. It took her a long time to find sleep.

The next day Ito seemed a little friendlier. After feeding them again she told them, 'I've a day off work today . . .'

'Where do you work?' Dura asked.

'In a workshop just behind Pall Mall.' She smiled, looking tired at the thought of her job. 'I build car interiors. And I'm glad of a bit of free time. Sometimes, at the end of my shift, I can't seem to get the smell of wood out of my fingers . . .'

Dura listened to all this carefully. The conversation of these City folk was like an elaborate puzzle, and she wondered where to start the process of unravelling. 'What's a Pall Mall?'

Cris, the son, laughed at her. 'It's not *a* Pall Mall. It's just – Pall Mall.'

Ito hushed him. 'It's a street, dear, the main one leading from the Palace to the Market . . . All this must be very strange to you. Why don't you come see the sights with me?'

Uncertain, Dura looked to Toba. He nodded. 'Go ahead. I've got to head back to the ceiling-farm, but you take your time; it's going to be a few days before Adda's ready for visitors. And maybe Cris can look after Farr for a while.'

Ito was eyeing Dura's bare limbs doubtfully. 'But I don't think we should take you out like that. Nudity's all right for shock value – but in Pall Mall?'

Ito lent Dura one of her own garments, a one-piece coverall of some soft, pliant material. The cloth felt smoothly comfortable against Dura's skin, but as she sealed up the front of the outfit she felt enclosed, oddly claustrophobic. She tried Waving around the room experimentally; the material rustled against her skin, and the seams restricted her movements.

After a little thought she wrapped her battered piece of rope around her waist, and tucked her wooden knife and scraper inside the coverall. The homely feel of the objects made her feel a little more secure.

Cris stared at her with a sceptical grin. 'You won't need a knife. It isn't the upflux here, you know.'

Again Ito hushed him; the two adults politely refrained from comment.

Leaving Farr with Cris, the two women left the home with Toba. He led them to his car, waiting in the 'car park'. Dura helped him harness up a team of fresh pigs from the pen in the corner.

Toba took them through a fresh maze of unfamiliar streets. Soon they left behind the quiet residential section and arrived in the bustling central areas. Dura tried to follow their route, but once again found it impossible. She was used to orienting herself against the great features of the Mantle: the vortex lines, the Pole, the Quantum Sea. She suspected that keeping a sense of direction while tracking through this warren of wooden corridors was a skill which the children of Parz must acquire from birth, but which she would have to spend many months learning.

Toba brought them to the widest avenue yet. Its walls – at least a hundred mansheights apart – were lined with green-glowing lamps and elaborate windows and doorways. Toba pulled the car out of the traffic streams and hauled on his reins. 'Here you are – Pall Mall,' he announced. He embraced Ito. 'I'll head off to the farm; I'll be back in a couple of days. Enjoy yourselves . . .'

Ito led Dura out of the car. Dura watched, uncertain, as the car pulled away into the traffic.

The avenue was the largest enclosed space Dura had ever seen – surely the largest in the City itself. It was an immense, vertical tunnel, crammed with cars and people and full of noise and light. The two women were close to one wall; Dura could see how the wall was lined with windows, all elaborately decorated and lettered, beyond which were arrays of multicoloured clothes, bags, scrapers, bottles and globes, elaborately carved lamps, finely crafted artifacts Dura could not even recognize. People – hundreds of them – swarmed across the wall like foraging animals; they chattered excitedly to each other as they plunged through doorways.

Ito smiled. 'Shops,' she said. 'Don't worry about the crush. It's always like this.'

All four walls of the avenue were lined with the 'shops'. The wall opposite, a full hundred mansheights away, was a distant tapestry of colour and endless human motion, rendered a little indistinct by the dusty Air; lamps sparkled in rows across its face and shafts of light shone from round ducts.

Pall Mall was alive with traffic. At first the swarming, braying cars seemed to move chaotically, but slowly Dura discerned patterns: there were several streams, she saw, moving up and down the avenue parallel to its walls, and every so often a car would veer – perilously, it seemed to her – from one stream to another, or would pull off Pall Mall into a side-street. The Air was thick with green jetfart, alive with the squealing of pigs. For a while Dura managed to follow Toba's car as it worked its way along the avenue, but she soon lost it in the swirling lanes of traffic.

There was a strong, sweet smell, almost overpowering. It reminded Dura of the scented towels in Ito's bathroom.

Ito, touching her arm, drew her towards the shops. 'Come on, dear. People are starting to stare . . .'

Dura could hardly help goggle at the people thronging the shops. Men and women alike were dressed in extravagantly coloured robes and coveralls shaped to reveal flashes of flesh; there were hats and jewels everywhere, and hair sculpted into huge, multicoloured piles.

Ito led Dura through two or three shops. She showed her jewellery, ornaments, fine hats and clothes; Dura handled the goods, wondering at the fine craftsmanship, but quite unable to make sense of Ito's patient explanations of the items' use.

Ito's persistence seemed to be wearing a little now, and they returned to the main avenue. 'We'll go to the Market,' Ito said. 'You'll enjoy that.'

They joined a stream of people heading – more or less – for that end of Pall Mall deepest inside the City. Almost at once Dura was thumped in the small of her back by something soft and round, like a weak fist; she whirled, scrabbling ineffectually at her clothes in search of her knife.

A man hurried past her. He was dressed in a flowing,

sparkling robe. In his soft white hands he held leaders to two fat piglets, and he was being dragged in an undignified way – it seemed to Dura – after the piglets, his feet dangling through their clouds of jetfart. It had been one of the piglets that had hit Dura's back.

The man barely glanced at her as he passed.

Ito was grinning at her.

'What's wrong with him? Can't he Wave like everyone else?'

'Of course he can. But he can afford not to.' Ito shook her head at Dura's confusion. 'Oh, come on, it would take too long to explain.'

Dura sniffed. The sweet smell was even stronger now. 'What *is* that?'

'Pig farts, of course. Perfumed, naturally . . .'

They dropped gently down the avenue, Waving easily. Dura found herself embarrassed by the awkward silences between herself and this kindly woman – but there was so little common ground between them.

'Why do you live in the City?' Dura asked. 'I mean, when Toba's farm is so far away . . .'

'Well, there's my own job,' Ito said. 'The farm is large, but it's in a poor area. Right on the fringe of the hinterland, so far upflux that it's hard even to get coolies to work out there, for fear of . . .' She stopped.

'For fear of upfluxers. It's all right.'

'The farm doesn't bring in as much as it should. And everything seems to cost so much . . .'

'But you could live in your farm.' The thought of that appealed to Dura. She liked the idea of being out in the open, away from this stuffy warren – and yet being surrounded by an area of cultivation, of *order*; to know that your area of control extended many hundreds of mansheights all around you.

'Perhaps,' Ito said reluctantly. 'But who wants to be a subsistence farmer? And there's Cris's schooling to think of.'

'You could teach him yourself.'

Ito shook her head patiently. 'No, dear, not as well as the professionals. And they are only to be found here, in the City.' Her tired, careworn look returned. 'And I'm determined Cris

101

is going to get the best schooling we can afford. *And* stick it to the end, despite his dreams of Surfing.'

Surfing?

Dura fell silent, trying to puzzle all this out.

Ito brightened. 'Besides – with all respect to you and your people, dear – I wouldn't want to live on some remote farm, when I could be surrounded by all this. The shops, the theatres, the libraries at the University . . .' She looked at Dura curiously. 'I know this is all strange to you, but don't you feel the buzz of life here? And if, one day, we could move a bit further Upside . . .'

'Upside?'

'Closer to the Palace.' Ito pointed upwards, back the way they had come. 'At the top of the City. All of this side of the City, above the Market, is Upside.'

'And below the Market . . .'

Ito blinked. 'Why, that's the Downside, of course. Where the Harbour is, and the dynamo sheds, and cargo ports, and sewage warrens.' She sniffed. '*Nobody* would live down there by choice.'

Dura Waved patiently along, the unfamiliar clothes scraping across her legs and back.

As they descended, the walls of Pall Mall curved away from her like an opening throat, and the avenue merged smoothly into the Market. This was a spherical chamber perhaps double the width of Pall Mall itself. The Market seemed to be the end-point of a dozen streets – not just the Mall – and traffic streams poured through it constantly. Cars and people swarmed over each other chaotically; in the dust and noise, Dura saw drivers lean out of their cars, bellowing obscure profanities at each other. There were shops here, but they were just small, brightly coloured stalls strung in rows across the chamber. Stallkeepers hovered at all angles, brandishing their wares and shouting at passing customers.

At the centre of the Market was a wheel of wood, about a mansheight across. It was mounted on a huge wooden spindle which crossed the chamber from side to side, cutting through the shambolic stalls; the spindle must have been hewn from a single Crust-tree, Dura thought, and she wondered how the carpenters had managed to bring it here, into the heart of the

City. The wheel had five spokes, from which ropes dangled. The shape of the wheel looked vaguely familiar to Dura, and after a moment's thought she recalled the odd little talisman which Toba wore around his neck, the man spreadeagled against a wheel. Wasn't that five-spoked too?

Ito said, 'Isn't this great? These little stalls don't look like much but you can get some real bargains. Good quality stuff, too . . .'

Dura found herself backing up, back towards the Mall they'd emerged from. Here, right in the belly of this huge City, the noise, heat and constant motion seemed to crowd around her, threatening to overwhelm her.

Ito followed her and took her hand. 'Come on,' she said. 'Let's find somewhere quieter and have something to eat.'

Cris's room was a mess. Crumpled clothes, all gaudily coloured, floated through the Air like discarded skin; from among the clothes' empty limbs, bottles of hair-dye protruded, glinting in the lamplight. Cris pushed his way confidently into this morass, shoving clothes out of the way. Farr didn't find it so easy to enter the room. The cramped space, the clothes pawing softly at his flesh, gave him an intense feeling of claustrophobia.

Cris misread his discomfiture. 'Sorry about the mess. My parents give me hell about it. But I just can't seem to keep all this junk straight.' He tipped back in the Air and rammed at a mass of clothing with both feet; the clothing wadded into a ball and compressed into one corner, leaving the Air marginally clearer; but even as Farr watched the clothes slowly unravelled, reaching out blindly with empty sleeves.

Farr peered around, wondering what he was supposed to say. 'Some of your belongings are – attractive.'

Cris gave him an odd look. 'Attractive. Yeah. Well, not half as attractive as they could be if we had a little more money to spare. But times are hard. They're always hard.' He dived into the bundles of clothing once more, pulling them apart with his hands, evidently searching for something. 'I suppose money doesn't mean a thing, where you grew up.'

'No,' Farr said, still unsure what money actually was. Oddly, he had heard envy in Cris's voice.

Cris had retrieved something from within the cloud of clothing: a board, a thin sheet of wood about a mansheight long. Its edges were rounded and its surface, though scored by grooves for gripping, was finely finished and polished so well that Farr could see his reflection in it. A thin webbing of some shining material had been inlaid into the wood. Cris ran his hand lovingly over the board; it was as if, Farr thought, he were caressing the skin of a loved one. Cris said, 'It sounds great.'

'What does?'

'Life in the upflux.' Cris looked at Farr uncertainly.

Again Farr didn't know how to answer. He glanced around at Cris's roomful of possessions – none of which he'd made himself, Farr was willing to bet – and let his look linger on Cris's stocky, well-fed frame.

'I mean, you're so *free* out there.' Cris ran his hand around the edge of his polished board. 'Look, I finish my schooling in another year. And then what? My parents don't have the money for more education – to send me to the University, or the Medical College, maybe. Anyway, I don't have the brains for any of that.' He laughed, as if proud of the fact. 'For someone like me there are only three choices here.' He counted them off on his callus-free fingers. 'If you're stupid, you end up in the Harbour, fishing up Corestuff from the underMantle – or maybe you can lumberjack, or you might end up in the sewage runs. Whatever. But if you're a little smarter you might get into the Civil Service, some-where. Or – if you can't stand any of that, if you don't want to work for the Committee – you can go your own way. Set up a stall in the Market. Or work a ceiling-farm, like my father, or build cars like my mother. And spend your life breaking your back with work, and paying over most of your money in tithes to the Committee.' He shrugged, cling-ing to his board; his voice was heavy with despondency, with world-weariness. 'And that's it. Not much of a choice, is it?'

If Farr had closed his eyes he might have imagined he was listening to an old, time-beaten man like Adda rather than a boy at the start of his life. 'But at least the City keeps you fed, and safe, and comfortable.'

'But not everyone wants to be comfortable. Isn't there more to life than that?' He looked at Farr again with that odd tinge of envy. 'That's what Surfing offers me . . . Your life, in the upflux, must be so – *interesting*. Waking up in the open Air, every day. Never knowing what the day is going to bring. Having to go out and find your own food, with your bare hands . . .' Cris looked down at his own smooth hands as he said this.

Farr didn't know what to reply to all this. He had come to think of the City folk as superior in wisdom, and it was a shock to find one of them talking such rubbish.

Looking for something to say, he pointed to the board Cris was still cradling. 'What's this?'

'My board. My Surfboard.' Cris hesitated. 'You've never seen one before?'

Farr reached out and ran his fingertips over the polished surface. It was worked so finely that he could barely feel the unevenness of the wood; it was like touching skin – the skin of a very young child, perhaps. The mesh of shining threads had been inlaid into a fine network of grooves, just deep enough to feel.

'It's beautiful.'

'Yes.' Cris looked proud. 'It's not the most expensive you can get. But I've put a hell of a lot of work into it, and now I doubt there's a better board this side of Pall Mall.'

Farr hesitated, embarrassed by his utter ignorance. 'But what's it for?'

'For Surfing.' Cris held the board out horizontally and flipped up into the Air, bringing his bare feet to rest against the ridged board. The board drifted away from him, of course, but Farr could see how expertly Cris's feet moved over the surface, almost as if they were a second pair of hands. Cris held his arms out and swayed in the Air. 'You ride along the Magfield, like this. There's nothing like it. The feeling of power, of speed . . .'

'But how? Do you Wave?'

Cris laughed. 'No, of course not.' Then he looked more thoughtful. 'At least, not quite.' He flipped off the board, doing a neat back-somersault in the cramped room, and caught the board. 'See the wires inlaid into the surface? That's

Corestuff. Superconducting. That's what makes the boards so damn expensive.' He rocked the board in the Air with his arms. 'You work it like this, with your legs. See? It's like Waving, but with the board instead of your body. The currents in the superconductors push against the Magfield, and . . .' He shot his hand through the Air. 'Whoosh!'

Farr thought about it. 'And you can go faster than Waving?'

'Faster?' Cris laughed again. 'You can be faster than any car, faster than any farting pig – when you get a clear run, high above the Pole, you feel as if you're going faster than thought.' His expression turned misty, dreamlike.

Farr watched him, fascinated and curious.

'So that's what the board is for . . . sort of. But it's also my way out of here. Out of my future. Maybe.' Cris seemed awkward now, almost shy. 'I'm good at this, Farr. I'm one of the best in my age group; I've won a lot of the events I've been eligible for up to now. And in a couple of months I qualify for the big one. The Games. I'll be up against the best, my first chance . . .'

'The Games?'

'The biggest. If you do well there, become a star of the Games, then Parz just opens her legs for you.' Cris laughed coarsely at that, and Farr grinned uncertainly. 'I mean it,' Cris said. 'Parties at the Palace. Fame.' He shrugged. 'Of course it doesn't last forever. But if you're good enough you never lose it, the *aura*. Believe me . . . Will you still be around, for the Games?'

'I don't know. Adda . . .'

'Your friend in the Hospital. Yeah.' Cris's mood seemed to swing to embarrassment again. 'Look, I'm sorry for going on about Surfing. I know you're in a difficult situation.'

Farr smiled, hoping to put this complex boy at his ease. 'I enjoy hearing you talk.'

Cris studied Farr speculatively. 'Listen, have you ever tried Surfing? No, of course you haven't. Would you like to? We could meet some people I know . . .'

'I don't know if I'd be able to.'

'It looks simple,' Cris said. 'It *is* simple in concept, but difficult to do well. You have to keep your balance, keep the board pressed between you and the Magfield, keep pushing down

106

against the flux lines to build up your speed.' He closed his eyes briefly and rocked in the Air.

'I don't know,' Farr said again.

Cris eyed him. 'You should be strong enough. And, coming from the upflux, your sense of balance and direction should be well developed. But maybe you're right. You're barrel-chested, and your legs are a little short. Even so it mightn't be impossible for you to stay aboard for a few seconds . . .'

Farr found himself bridling at this cool assessment. He folded his arms. 'Let's do it,' he said. 'Where?'

Cris grinned. 'Come on. I'll show you.'

Ito took Dura to the Museum.

This was situated in the University area of the City – far Upside, as Dura was learning to call it; in fact, not very far below the Palace itself. The University was a series of large chambers interconnected by richly panelled corridors. Ito explained that they weren't allowed to disturb the academic calm of the chambers themselves, but she was able to point out libraries, seminar areas filled with groups of earnest young people, arrays of small cells within which the scholars worked alone, poring over their incomprehensible studies.

The University was close to the City's outer wall, and was so full of natural light the Air seemed to glow. There was an atmosphere of calm here, an intensity which made Dura feel out of place (even more than usual). They passed a group of senior University members; these wore flowing robes and had shaved off their hair, and they barely glanced at the two women as they Waved disdainfully past.

She leaned close to Ito and whispered, 'Muub. That Administrator at the Hospital. He shaved his head. Does he belong here too?'

Ito smiled. 'I've never met the man; he sounds a little too grand for the likes of us. But, no, if he works at the Hospital he has no connection now with the University. But he may once have studied here, and he wears the bald fashion as a reminder to the rest of us that once he was a scholar.' Her smile was thin, Dura thought, and tired-looking. 'People do that sort of thing, you know.'

'Did you – study – at the University? Or Toba?'

'Me?' Ito laughed, gently. 'Do I look as if I could ever have afforded it? . . . It would be wonderful if Cris could make it here, though. If only we could find the fees – it would give him something higher, something better to aim for. Maybe he wouldn't waste so much time on that damn Surfboard.'

The Museum was a large cube-shaped structure at the heart of the University complex. It was riddled with passageways and illumination shafts, so that light seeped through the whole of its porous bulk. As they moved slowly through the maze of passageways, the multitude of ports and doorways seemed to conceal a hundred caches of treasure.

One corridor held rows of pigs, rays and Crust-spiders. At first the creatures, looming out of the darkness, made Dura recoil; but she soon realized that these animals were no threat to her – and never would be to anyone else. They were dead, preserved somehow, fixed to the walls of this place in grim parodies of their living postures: gazing at the magnificent, outstretched wings of a ray, pinned against a frame of wood, Dura felt unaccountably sad. A little further along a display showed an Air-pig – dead like the others, but cut open and splayed out with its organs – small masses of tissue fixed to the inner wall of the body – now glistening, exposed for her inspection. Dura shuddered. She had killed dozens of Air-pigs, but she could never have brought herself to touch this cold, clean display.

Oddly, there was no smell in these corridors, either of life or death.

They came to an area containing human artifacts. Much of it was from the City itself, Dura gathered, but from ages past; Ito laughed as she pointed to clothes and hats mounted on the walls. Dura smiled politely, not really seeing the joke. There was a model of the City, finely carved of wood and about a mansheight tall. There was even a lamp inside so that the model was filled with light. Dura spent some time peering at this in delight, with Ito pointing out the features of the City. Here was a toy lumber train entering one of the great ports Downside, and here was the Spine leading down into the underMantle; tiny cars carrying model Fishermen descended along the Spine, seeking lodes of precious Corestuff. And the Palace at the very crown of the City – at the farthest Upside of all – was a rich tapestry glowing with life and colour.

Further along, there were small cases containing artifacts from outside the City. Ito touched her arm. 'Perhaps you'll recognize some of this.' There were spears and knives, all carved from wood; she saw nets, ponchos, lengths of rope.

Upfluxer artifacts.

None of them looked as if they had come from the Human Beings themselves. But, said Ito, that wasn't so surprising; there were upfluxer bands all around the fringe of Parz's hinterland, right around the Star's Polar cap. Dura studied the objects, aware of her own knife, her rope still wrapped around her waist. The things she carried wouldn't be out of place inside one of these displays, she realized. With a tinge of bitterness, she wondered if these people would like to pin her and her brother up on the walls, like that poor, dead ray.

Finally, Ito brought her to the Museum's most famous exhibit (she said). They entered a spherical room perhaps a dozen mansheights across. The light here was dim, coming only from a few masked wood-lamps, and it took some time for Dura's eyes to adapt to the darkness.

At first she thought there was nothing here, that the chamber was empty. Then, slowly, as if emerging from mist, an object took shape before her. It was a cloud about a mansheight across, a mesh of some shining substance. Ito encouraged her to move a little closer, to push her face closer to the surface of the mesh. The exhibit was like a tangled-up net, composed of cells perhaps a handsbreadth across. And Dura saw that within the cells of the main mesh there was more detail: sub-meshes, composed of fine cells no wider than a hair-tube. Perhaps, Dura wondered, if she could see well enough she would find still more cells, almost invisibly tiny, within the hair-scale mesh.

Ito showed Dura a plaque on the wall, inscribed with text on the display. '"The structure is *fractal*."' Ito pronounced the word carefully. '"That is, it shows a similar structure on many scales. Corestuff lends itself to this property, being composed of hyperons, bags of quarks in which are dissolved the orderly nucleons – the protons and neutrons – of the human world.

'"In regions humans can inhabit Corestuff exists in large

metastable islands of matter – the familiar Corestuff bergs retrieved by Fishermen, and used to construct anchor-bands, among other artifacts . . .

'"But further in, in the deep Core, the hyperonic material can combine to form extraordinary, rich structures like this model. The representation here is based on guesswork – on fragmentary tales from the time of the Core Wars, and on half-coherent accounts of Fishermen. Nevertheless, the University scholars feel that . . ."'

'But,' Dura interrupted, 'what *is* it?'

Ito turned to her, her face round and smooth in the dim light. 'Why, it's a Colonist,' she said.

'But the Colonists were human.'

'No,' Ito said. 'Not really. They abandoned us, stealing our machines, and went down into the Core.' She looked sombre. 'And this is what they became. They lived in these structures of Corestuff.'

Dura stared into the deep, menacing depths of the model. It was as if, here in the belly of the City, she had been transported to the Core itself and left to face this bizarre, monstrous entity alone.

8

Clutching his Surfboard, Cris led Farr through the heart of the City.

They followed a tangle of subsidiary streets, avoiding the main routes. Farr tried to memorize their path, but his rudimentary sense of City-bound direction was soon overwhelmed. Lost, baffled, but following Cris doggedly, he involuntarily glanced around, looking for the Quantum Sea, the angle of the vortex lines to orient himself. But of course, here deep in the guts of Parz, the faceless wooden walls hid the world.

After a time, though, he realized that they must have passed below the City's rough equator and moved into the region called the Downside. The walled streets here were meaner, with illumination shafts and wood-lamps far separated. There were few cars and fewer Wavers, and the doors to dwelling-places off the Downside streets, battered and dirty, looked impenetrably solid. Cris didn't comment on the changed environment – he kept up his chatter of Surfing as if oblivious – but Farr noticed how the City boy kept his precious board clutched tight against his chest, shielding it with his body.

At length they came to a wide, oval port set in a street wall. The shaft beyond this port, about ten mansheights across, was much plainer than any City street – long and featureless, and with scuffed, unfinished-looking walls – but it led, Farr saw, to an ellipse of clear, precious Airlight. He stared hungrily into that light, marvelling at how the bright yellow glow glittered from scraped-smooth patches of wall.

'Are we going down here?'

'Through this cargo port? Out through the Skin? But that's against City ordinances . . .' Cris grinned. 'You bet we are.'

With a whoop, Cris placed one hand on the lip of the elliptical entrance and somersaulted into the shaft. His board clutched above his head, he flapped his arms, Waving in reverse feet-first down the shaft. Farr, clumsier, clambered over the lip of the port and plunged down. Laughing, their voices echoing from the wooden walls, the boys tumbled towards the open Air.

Farr shot out of the oppressive wall of the City and spread his arms and legs, drinking in the yellow-shining Air and staring up at the arc of the vortex lines.

Cris was looking at him sceptically. 'Are you okay?'

'I'm just glad to be out in the Air . . . even if it *is* this sticky Polar stuff.'

'Right. Not like back in the good old upflux, eh?' Cris levelled his board, flexed it with the palm of his hand experimentally against the Magfield.

Farr rolled luxuriously in the Air. The port they'd emerged from was a rough-rimmed mouth set in the wooden outer hull – the *Skin* – and it loomed around them still, as if threatening to snap down on them, to swallow them back into the City's wooden guts. But the boys were drifting in the Air, away from the City, and Farr saw that this port was just one of an array of similar entrances which stretched across the face of the City in all directions, as far as he could see. Farr tried to pick out identifying features of 'their' port, so he could find it again if he needed to. But it was simply a crudely finished gash in the wooden Skin, unmarked, with nothing to distinguish it from a hundred others. Farr soon gave up the effort of memorizing. After all, if he did get lost, even if he found this particular port again he'd never find his way back to the Mixxaxes' home through the City streets.

He flipped his legs and pulled a little further away from the City. The Skin was like a gigantic mask, looming over him. This close he could see its detail – how it was crudely cobbled together from mismatched sections of wood and Corestuff – but it was hugely impressive nevertheless. The dozens of cargo ports in this part of the Skin were, he thought, like mouths, continually ingesting; or perhaps like capillary pores, taking in a granular Air of wood and food. As he pulled back still further he saw the huge, unending falls from the sewage outlets spread across the base of the City; the roar of the semi-solid stuff tumbling into the underMantle seemed to fill the Air.

The City – battered and imperfect as it might be – was magnificent, he realized slowly; it was like an immense animal, noisily alive, utterly oblivious of his own tiny presence before its face.

He heard his name called.

He glanced around, but Cris had gone. Farr felt an absurd stab of disorientation – after all, he had a far smaller chance of getting lost out here than in the City's guts – and twisted, staring around. There was Cris, his orange coverall bright, a distant, waving figure suspended on his Surfboard. He was close to the Skin but far above Farr's head. He'd slipped away while Farr was daydreaming.

Embarrassed, a little irritated, Farr thrust at the Air, letting the upfluxer strength in his legs hurl him towards Cris.

Cris watched him approach, grinning infuriatingly. 'Keep up. There are people waiting for us.' He clambered back onto his board, turned and led the way.

Farr followed, perhaps a mansheight behind; one after the other the boys soared over the face of the City.

Cris's Surfing technique was spectacular, bearing little relation to the cut-down caricature he had shown Farr inside the City. Cris pivoted the gleaming board under one bare foot while thrusting with the other heel at the back of the board, making it Wave vigorously. His bare soles seemed able to grip at the surface's fine ridges. He kept his arms stretched out in the Air for balance, and the muscles in the City boy's legs worked smoothly. The whole process looked wonderfully easy, in fact, and Farr felt a dull itch – in the small of his back and in his calves – as he stared at Cris. He longed to try out the Surfboard for himself. Why, with his enhanced strength, here at the Pole, he could make the damn thing *fly* . . .

But he couldn't deny Cris's skill as he expertly levered his mass and inertia against the soft resistance of the Magfield. The speed and grace of Cris's motion, with electron gas crackling around the Corestuff strips embedded in the board, was nonchalant and spectacular.

They were climbing up and around the City's Skin, generally away from the sewage founts at the base but on a diagonal line across the face. They crossed one of the huge Longitude anchor-bands. Farr saw how the band was fixed to the Skin by pegs of Corestuff at intervals along its length. The gleaming Corestuff strip was wider than a mansheight, and – in response to the huge currents surging through the band's superconducting core – electron gas played unceasingly over its smooth surface. The Magfield here was distorted, constricted by the band's field; it felt uneven, harsh, tight around Farr's chest.

Cris clambered off his board and joined Farr in Waving away from the Skin, working cautiously past the anchor-band. 'Magfield's too spiky here,' Cris said curtly. 'You can't get a proper grip.'

Past the anchor-band, the Skin unfolded before Farr's gaze. He'd expected the Skinscape to be featureless, uniform, except for the random blemishes of its construction. But it was much too huge to allow such uniformity, he soon realized. As they climbed towards the City's equator, towards the Upside areas, the huge cargo ports and public Air-shafts became more sparse, to be replaced by smaller, tidier doorways evidently meant for humans and Air-cars, and by small portals which must be windows or light-shafts for private dwellings. A man leaned out of a window and hurled out a bowl of what looked like sewage; the stuff sparkled as it dispersed. Cris cupped his hands around his mouth and called down a greeting. The man – squat and yellow-haired – peered out into the sky, startled. When he spotted the boys he shook his fist at them, shouting something angry but indistinguishable. Cris yelled abuse back, and Farr joined in, shaking his fist in return. He laughed, exhilarated by this display of disrespect; he felt free, young, healthy, released from the confines of the City, and the comparison with the sour old man in his windowed cell made his condition all the sweeter.

They flew past an area of hull covered by a crude framework, a rectangular lattice of wood. Behind the framework the Skin was broken open, exposing small chambers within the City lit by dim green wood-lamps. Huge sections of wooden panelling drifted in the Air outside the City, attached loosely to the framework by lengths of rope; men and women clambered over the framework, hauling at the panels and hammering them into place in the gaps in the Skin.

'Repairs,' said Cris in uninterested response to Farr's question. 'They go on all the time. My father says the City's never really been finished; there's always some section of it that needs rebuilding.'

They arced high across a comparatively blank area of hull, unblemished by door, window or port. Farr looked back to see the last small portals recede over the City's tightly curving horizon, and soon there was no break in the Skin in sight. Cris Surfed on in silence, subdued. Moving over this featureless Skinscape Farr felt absurdly as if he had been rejected by the City, thrown out and shunned – as if it had turned its back.

Now they passed another group of humans clambering over the Skin. At first Farr thought this must be another set of repair workers, but the Skin here was unbroken, clearly undamaged. And there was no repair scaffolding – just a loose net spread across the Skin. A group of perhaps twenty adults were huddled in one corner of their net, engaged in some unidentifiable project. Peering down as they passed, Farr saw how belongings had been stuffed loosely into the net; he saw spears, crude clothing and smaller folded-up nets that wouldn't have seemed out of place among the belongings of the Human Beings. There was even a small colony of Air-pigs which jostled slowly against the wooden wall, bound by ropes to a peg which had been hammered into the Skin. An infant child squirmed inside the net, crying; its wails, sweet and distant, carried through the silent Air to Farr.

A woman, fat and naked, turned from whatever she was engaged in with her companions, and peered up at the boys. Farr saw how her fists were clenched. He looked to Cris for a lead, but the City boy simply Waved on with his board, keeping his eyes averted from the little colony below.

Farr, burning with curiosity, glanced down again. To his relief he saw that the woman had turned away and was returning to her companions, evidently forgetting the boys.

'Skin-riders,' Cris said dismissively. 'Scavengers. There are whole colonies of them, living off remote bits of the Skin like this.'

'But how do they survive?'

'They take stuff from the sewage founts, mostly. Filter it out with those nets of theirs. Some of it they consume themselves, and some they use to feed their pigs. Many of them hunt.'

'Doesn't anybody mind?'

Cris shrugged. 'Why should they? The Skin-riders are out of the way in places like this, and they don't absorb any of the City's resources. You could say they make Parz more efficient by extracting what they can out of everyone else's waste. The Committee only takes action against them when they go rogue. Turn bandit. Some tribes do, you know. They ring the exit portals, waiting to descend on slower-moving cars. They kill the drivers and steal the pigs; they've no use for the cars themselves. And sometimes they turn on each other, fighting stupid little Skin-wars no one else understands. *Then* the guards step in. But apart from that, I guess the City is big enough to support a few leeches on its face.' He grinned. 'Anyway, there'll always be Skin-riders; you could never wipe them out. Not everyone can live their lives inside six wooden walls.' He bent his knees, flourishing the board. 'Which is one reason I'm out here today. I'd have thought you'd understand that, Farr. Maybe the Skin-riders are a little like your people.'

Farr frowned. Maybe there was a surface comparison, he thought. But Human Beings would never allow themselves to become so – so filthy, he thought, so poor, to live so badly – as the Skin-riders he had seen.

And no Human Being would accept the indignity of living by scavenging the waste of others.

The squalid little colony of Skin-riders was soon hidden by the wooden limb of the City face, and Cris led Farr further across the featureless Skin.

Farr spotted the girl before Cris saw her.

She was a compact, lithe shape swooping around the vortex lines, high above the City. Electron gas sparkled around her Surfboard, underlighting the contours of her body. There was a grace, a naturalness about her movements which far eclipsed even Cris's proficiency, Farr thought. The girl saw them approaching and waved her arms in greeting, shouted something inaudible.

They came to another net, stretched over the wooden Skin between a series of pegs, just as the Skin-riders' had been. But this net was evidently abandoned: torn and fraying, the net flapped emptily, containing nothing but what looked like the sections of a Surfboard snapped in half, a few clothes tucked behind knots in the net, and some crude-looking tools.

Cris drifted to a halt over the net and locked an anchoring hand comfortably into a loop of rope. 'That's Ray,' he said enviously. 'The girl. That's what she calls herself anyway . . . after the rays of the Crust-forests, you see.'

Farr squinted up at the girl; she was spiralling lazily around a vortex line as she approached them, electron glow dazzling from her skin. 'She looks good.'

'She is good. Too bloody good,' Cris said with a touch of sourness. 'And she's a year younger than me . . . My hope is there's going to be room for both of us in the Games.'

'What is this place?'

Cris flipped his Surfboard in the Air and watched it somersault. 'Nowhere,' he said. His voice was deliberately casual. 'Just an old Skin-rider net, in a bit of the Skinscape that's hardly ever visited. We just use it as a base. You know, a place to meet, to Surf from, to keep a few tools for the boards.'

Just a base to Surf from . . . Cris's tone made it sound a lot more important than that, to him. Farr watched the girl approach, casually skilful, slowing as she rode the Magfield towards the Skin. He thought of what it must be like to be accepted by a group of people like Cris and this girl Ray – to have a place like this to come to, hidden from the gaze of families and the rest of the City.

He could barely imagine it. He realized suddenly that he'd never even been out of sight of his family before the Glitch that killed his father. A place like this must mean a great deal.

He wanted to ask Cris more questions. Who were these Surfers? What were they like? How many of them were there? . . . But he kept quiet. He didn't want to be the clumsy outsider from the upflux – not here, not with these two. He wanted them to accept him, to make him one of theirs – even just for a day.

Maybe if he kept his mouth shut as much as possible they would think he knew more than he did.

The girl, Ray, performed one last roll through the Air and stepped lightly off her board before them. With one small ankle she flipped the board up, caught it in one hand, and tucked it into a gap in the net. She hooked a hand into the net, close to Cris's, and smiled at him and Farr. She was nude, and her long hair was tied back from her face; there were streaks of yellow dye across her scalp, just as Cris affected.

'You're on your own today?' Cris asked.

She shrugged, breathing heavily. 'Sometimes I prefer it that way. You can get some real work done.' She turned to Farr, a look of lively interest on her face. 'Who's this?'

Cris grinned and clapped a hand on Farr's shoulder. 'He's called Farr. He's staying with us. He's from a tribe called the Human Beings.'

'Human Beings?'

'Upfluxers,' Cris said with an apologetic glance at Farr.

The girl's smile broadened, and Farr was aware of her light gaze flicking over him with new interest. 'An upfluxer? Really? So what do you make of Parz? Dump, isn't it?'

Farr tried to find something to say.

He couldn't take his eyes off the girl. Her face was broad, intelligent, vividly alive, her perfect nostrils shining. She was still breathing deeply after her exertions, and her chest and shoulders were rising and falling smoothly. The capillary pores across her chest and between her small breasts were wide and dark.

Cris was staring at him strangely, and Ray was watching him, interested, amused. He had to find something to say. 'It's okay. Parz is fine. Interesting.' *Interesting*. What a stupid thing to say. His voice sounded booming and uncontrolled, and he was aware of his bulky, overmuscled body, his hands huge and useless at his side.

She let herself drift a little closer to him. He tried to keep his eyes on her face. Her nakedness was spectacular. But that didn't make sense; the Human Beings had always gone naked, save for occasional toolbelts or ponchos, so why should he be so disturbed now? He must have become accustomed to bodies hidden by City clothes, like the light coveralls he and Cris were wearing; Ray's sudden nudity by contrast was impossible to ignore. Yes, that must be it . . .

118

But now he felt a deep warmth in his lower belly. *Oh, blood of the Xeelee, help me.* Like an independent creature – utterly without his volition – his penis was trying to push out of its cache. He leaned forward, hoping that folds in the cloth of his coveralls would hide him. But the girl's eyes were wide and appraising, and he could see a smile forming on her small mouth. *She knew.* She knew all about him.

'"Interesting",' she repeated. 'Maybe, if you haven't had to grow up in it.'

'We saw you practising,' Cris said. 'You're looking good.'

'Thanks.' She looked at Cris awkwardly. 'I've been selected for the Games. Had you heard that?'

'Already?' Farr could see envy battling with affection for the girl on Cris's face. 'No, I – I mean, I'm pleased for you. Really, I am.'

She brushed Cris's shoulder with her fingertips. 'I know. And it's not too late for you.' She took her board from the net. 'Come on, let's practise.'

Cris glanced at Farr. 'Yes, soon. But first . . .' He held out his board to Farr. 'Would you like to try it?'

Farr took the board hesitantly. He ran the palm of his hand across its surface. The wood was more finely worked than any object he'd ever held, and the inlaid strips of Corestuff were cold and smooth. 'Don't you mind?'

Cris laughed easily. 'As long as you bring it back whole, no. Go with Ray – she's a better Surfer than me, and a better teacher. I'll wait here until you're done.'

Farr looked at Ray. She smiled at him. 'Come on, it'll be fun.' She took the board from him – her fingers brushed the back of his hand, lightly, sending a thrill through him which caused his penis to stir again – and laid the board along the Magfield, flat. She patted its surface with its criss-cross inlay of Corestuff strips. 'Surfing's easy. It's just like Waving, but with your feet and your board instead of your legs. All you have to remember is to keep contact with your board, to keep pushing against the Magfield . . .'

With Ray's help, and Cris's, Farr clambered onto the board and learned how to rock it with his toes and heels. At first it seemed impossible – he kept kicking the board away, clumsily – and he was aware of the eyes of Ray on every galumphing movement. But each time he fell away he retrieved the board and climbed back on.

Then, suddenly, he had it. The secret was not strength, really, but gentleness, suppleness, a sensitivity to the soft resistance of the Magfield. It was enough to rock the board steadily and evenly across the Magfield flux paths, to keep the pressure of his feet less than the counterpressure of the Magfield so that the board stayed attached to the soles of his bare feet. When a downstroke with one foot was completed, he bent his legs slowly and pushed the other end of the board down in its turn. Gradually he learned to build up the tempo of this rocking motion, and wisps of electron gas curled about his toes as induced current began to flow in the Corestuff inlays.

The board – Waving just as the girl had said – carried him gracefully, effortlessly across the flux lines.

He learned to slow, to turn, to accelerate. He learned when to stop rocking the board, simply to allow his momentum to carry him arcing across the Magfield.

He had no idea how long it took him to learn the basics of Surfing. He was only peripherally aware of Cris's continuing patience, and he even forgot, for quite long periods, the nearness of Ray's bare, lithe body. He sailed across the sky. It was, he thought, like learning to Wave for the first time. The board felt natural beneath his feet, as if it had always been there, and he suspected that a small, inner part of him – no matter what he did or where he went – would always cling to the memory of this experience, utterly addicted.

Ray swooped down before him, inverted and with hands on bare hips. 'All right,' she said. 'You've got the basics. Now let's *really* Surf. Come on!'

High over the Pole, Farr surged along the corridors of light marked out by hexagonal arrays of vortex lines. The lines surged past him with immense, unimaginable speed. The soft bodies of floating spin-spider eggs padded at his face and legs as he flew, and the Air brushed at his cheeks, the tiny viscosity of its non-superfluid component resisting him feebly. The Quantum Sea was a purple floor far below him, delimiting the yellow Air; and the City was a vast, complex block of wood and light, hanging over the Pole, huge yet dwarfed by the Mantlescape.

Ahead of him the girl Ray looped around vortex lines with unconscious skill, electron light shimmering from her calves and buttocks.

His face was stretched into a fierce grin. He knew the grin was there, he knew Ray must be able to see it, and yet he couldn't keep it from his face. Surfing was *glorious*. His head rattled with the elements of complex, unrealistic schemes by which he might acquire his own board, join this odd, irregular little troupe of Skin-based Surfers, maybe even enter some future Games himself.

Ray turned and swept close to him. 'You're doing fine,' she shouted.

'I still feel as if I might fall off any moment.'

She laughed. 'But you're strong. That makes up for a lot. Come on. Try a spiral.'

She showed him how to angle his body back and push the board across the Magfield, so that he moved in slow, uneven, sweeping curves around a vortex line. Still he was hurtling forward through the sky, but now the huge panorama wheeled steadily around him. He stared down at his body, at the board; blue highlights from the corridors of vortex lines and the soft purple glow of the Sea cast complex shadows across his board.

He pushed at the Air harder, trying like Ray to tighten his spirals around the vortex lines. This was the most difficult manoeuvre he'd attempted, and he was forced to concentrate, to think about each motion of his arms and legs.

His foot slipped on the board's ridges. He stumbled through the Air, upwards towards the vortex line at the axis of his spiral. The board fell away from his feet. As he came within a mansheight of the vortex line he felt the Air thicken, drag at his chest and limbs. He was picked up and hurled around the vortex singularity, and sent tumbling away into the Air.

He rolled on his back and kicked easily at the Air, Waving himself to a stop. He lay against the soft resistance of the Magfield, laughing softly, his chest dragging at the Air.

Ray came slithering across the Magfield on her board; she

carried Cris's board under her arm. 'I bet you couldn't do that again if you tried.'

He took the board from her. 'I guess I should take this back to Cris. He's been very patient.'

She shrugged, and pushed a stray length of hair away from her face. 'I suppose so. You want one more run first?'

He hesitated, then felt his grin return. 'One more.'

Suddenly he twisted the board in the Air, bent his knees and slipped the board under his feet. He thrust at the length of wood as rapidly as he could, and soared away through a tunnel of vortex lines. Behind him he heard her laugh and clamber onto her own board.

He sailed over the Pole, over the passive bulk of Parz City once more. He thrust at the board, still awkwardly he knew, but using all his upfluxer strength now. The vortex lines seemed to shoot past like spears, slowly curving, and the weak breeze of the Air plucked at his hair.

The corridor of vortex light was infinite before him. The ease of movement, after the restriction of spiralling, was exhilarating. He was moving faster than he'd ever moved in his life. He opened his mouth and yelled.

He heard Ray shouting behind him. He glanced over his shoulder. She was still chasing him, but he'd given himself a good lead. It would take her a while to catch him yet. She was cupping a hand around her mouth and calling something, even as she Surfed. He frowned and looked more closely, but he couldn't make out what she was trying to tell him. Now she was pointing at him – no, *past* him.

He turned his head again, to face the direction of his flight. There was something in his path.

Spin-web.

The fine, shining threads seemed to cover the sky before him. He could see where the web was suspended from the vortex line array by small, tight rings of webbing which encircled the vortex lines without quite touching the glowing spin-singularities. Between the anchor rings, long lengths of thread looped across the vortex arrays. The complex mats of threads were almost invisible individually, but they caught the yellow and purple glow of the Mantle, so that lines of light formed a complex tapestry across the sky ahead.

It was really very beautiful, Farr thought abstractedly. But it was a wall across the sky.

The spin-spider itself was a dark mass in the upper left corner of his vision. It looked like an expanded, splayed-open Air-pig. Each of its six legs was a mansheight long, and its open maw would be wide enough to enfold his torso. It seemed to be working at its web, repairing broken threads perhaps. He wondered if it had spotted him – if it had started moving already towards the point where he would impact the net, or if it would wait until he was embedded in its sticky threads.

Only a couple of heartbeats had passed since he'd seen the web, and yet already he'd visibly reduced his distance to it.

He swivelled his hips and beat at the Magfield with his Surfboard, trying to shed his velocity. But he wouldn't be able to stop in time. He looked quickly around the sky, seeking the edges of the web. Perhaps he could divert rather than stop, fly safely around the trap. But he couldn't even *see* the edges of the web. Spin-spider webs could be hundreds of mansheights across.

Maybe he could break through the web, burst through to the other side before the spider could reach him. It had to be impossible – there were layers to the web, a great depth of sticky threads before him – but it seemed his only chance.

How could he have been so stupid as to fall into such a trap? He was supposed to be the upfluxer, the wild boy; and yet he'd made one of the most basic mistakes a Human Being could make. Ray and Cris would think him a fool. His *sister* would think him a fool, when she heard. He imagined her voice, tinged with the tones of their father: 'Always look up- and downflux. *Always*. If you scare an Air-piglet, which way does it move? Downflux, or upflux, along the flux paths, because it can move quickest that way. That's the easiest direction to move for any animal – cut across the flux paths and the Magfield resists your motion. And that's why predators set their traps across the flux paths, waiting for anything stupid enough to come fleeing along the flux direction, straight into an open mouth . . .'

The web exploded out of the sky. He could see more detail now – thick knots at the intersection of the threads, the glistening stickiness of the threads themselves. He turned in the Air and thrust with the board, trying to pick up as much speed as he could. He crouched over the board, his knees and ankles still working frantically, and tucked his arms over his head.

He'd remain conscious after he was caught in the thread. Uninjured, probably. He wondered how long the spin-spider would take to clamber down to him. Would he still be aware when it began its work on his body?

A mass came hurtling over his head, towards the web. He flinched, almost losing his board, and looked up. Had the spider left its web and come for him already? . . .

But it was the girl, Ray. She'd chased him and passed him. Now she dived, ahead of Farr, deep into the tangle of webbing. She moved in a tight spiral as she entered the web, and the edge of her board cut through the glistening threads. Farr could see the dangling threads brushing against her arms and shoulders, one by one growing taut and then slackening as she moved on, burrowing through the layers of web.

She was cutting a tunnel through the web for him, he realized. The ragged-walled tunnel was already closing up – the web seemed to be designed for self-repair – but he had no choice but to accept the chance she'd given him.

He *hurtled* deep into the web.

It was all around him, a complex, three-dimensional mesh of light. Threads descended before his face and laid themselves across his shoulders, arms and face; they tore at the fabric of his coverall and his skin and hair, and came loose with small, painful rips. He cried out, but he dared not drop his face into his hands, or close his eyes, or lift his arms to bat away the threads, for fear of losing his tenuous control of the board.

Suddenly, as rapidly as he had entered it, he was through the web. The last threads parted softly before him with a soft, sucking sigh, and he was released into empty Air.

Ray was waiting for him a hundred mansheights from the border of the web, with her board tucked neatly under her arm. He brought his board to a halt beside her and allowed himself to tumble off gracelessly.

He turned and looked back. The tunnel in the web had

already closed – all that remained of it was a dark, cylindrical path through the layers of webbing, showing where their passage had disrupted the structure of the web – and the spin-spider itself was making its slow, patient way past the vortex lines on its way to investigate this disturbance in its realm.

Farr felt himself shuddering; he didn't bother trying to hide his reaction. He turned to Ray. 'Thank you . . .'

'No. Don't say it.' She was grinning. She was showing no fear, he realized. Her pores were wide open and her eyecups staring, and again she exuded the vivid, unbearably attractive aliveness which had struck him when he'd first met her. She grabbed his arms and shook him. 'Wasn't it fantastic? What a ride. Wait till I tell Cris about this . . .'

She jumped on her board and surged away into the Air.

As he watched her supple legs work the board, and as the reaction from his brush with death worked through his shocked mind, Farr once again felt an unwelcome erection push its way out of his cache.

He climbed onto his board and set off, steering a wide, slow course around the web.

9

After a few days Toba returned, and told Dura and Farr that he had booked them into a labour stall in the Market. Dura was given to understand that Toba had done them yet another favour by this, and yet he kept his eyes averted as he discussed it with them, and when they ate Cris seemed embarrassed into an unusual silence. Ito fussed around the upfluxers, her eyecups deep and dark.

Dura and Farr dressed as usual in the clothes the family had loaned them. But Toba told them quietly that, this time, they should go unclothed. Dura peeled off the thick material of her coverall with an odd reluctance; she could hardly say she had grown used to it, but in the bustling streets she knew she would feel exposed – conspicuously naked.

Toba pointed, embarrassed, to Dura's waist. 'You'd better leave that behind.'

Dura looked down. Her frayed length of rope was knotted, as always, at her waist, and her small knife and scraper were comforting, hard presences just above her hips at her back. Reflexively her hands flew to the rope.

Toba looked at Ito helplessly. Ito came to Dura hesitantly, her hands folded together. 'It really would be better if you left your things here, Dura. I think I understand how you feel. I can't imagine how I'd cope in your position. But you don't *need* those things of yours, your weapons. You do understand they couldn't really be much protection to you here anyway . . .'

'That's not the point,' Dura said. In her own ears her voice sounded ragged and a little wild. 'The point is . . .'

Toba pushed forward impatiently. 'The point is we're getting late. And if you want to be successful today, Dura – and I assume you do – you're going to have to think about the

126

effect those crude artifacts of yours would have on a prospective purchaser. Most people in Parz think you're some kind of half-tamed animal already.'

'Toba . . .' Ito began.

'I'm sorry, but it's the truth. And if she goes down the Mall with a knife at her waist – well, we'll be lucky not to be picked up by the guards before we even reach the Market.'

Farr moved closer to Dura, but she waved him away. 'It's all right, Farr.' Her voice was steadier now. More *rational*. 'He's right. What use is this stuff anyway? It's only junk from the upflux.'

Slowly she unravelled the rope from her waist.

The noise of the Market heated the Air even above the stifling clamminess of the Pole. People swarmed among the stalls which thronged about the huge central Wheel, the colours of their costumes extravagant and clashing. Dura folded her arms across her breasts and belly, intimidated by the layers of staring faces around her.

Farr was quiet, but he seemed calm and watchful.

Toba brought them to a booth – a volume cordoned off from the rest of the Market by a framework of wooden bars. Inside the booth were ten or a dozen adults and children, all subdued, unkempt and shabbily dressed compared to most of the Market's inhabitants; they stared with dull curiosity at the nakedness of Dura and Farr.

Toba bade the Human Beings enter the booth.

'Now,' he said anxiously, 'you do understand what's happening here, don't you?'

'Yes,' said Farr, his eyes tight. 'You're going to sell us.'

Toba shook his round head. 'Not at all. Anyhow, it's nothing to do with me. This is a Market for work. Here, *you* are going to sell *your labour* – not yourselves.'

Four prosperous-looking individuals – three men and a woman – had already emerged from the Market's throng and come over to the booth. They were studying both the Human Beings curiously but seemed particularly interested in Farr. Dura said to Toba, 'I doubt it's going to make much practical difference. Is it?'

'It's all the difference in the world. You sign up for a

127

fixed-term contract . . . Your liberty remains your own. And at the end of it . . .'

'Excuse me.' The woman buyer had interrupted Toba. 'I want to take a look at the boy.'

Toba smiled back. 'Farr. Come on out. Don't be afraid.'

Farr turned to Dura, his mouth open. She closed her eyes, suddenly ashamed that she could do so little to protect her brother from this. 'Go on, Farr. They won't hurt you.'

Farr slid through the wooden bars and out of the booth.

The woman was about Dura's age but a good deal plumper; her hair-tubes were elaborately knotted into a gold-and-white bun, and layers of fat showed over her cheekbones. With the air of a professional she peered into the boy's eyecups, ears and nostrils; she bade him open his mouth and ran a finger around his gums, inspecting the scrapings she extracted. Then she poked at Farr's armpits, anus and penis-cache.

Dura turned away from her brother's misery.

The woman said to Toba, 'He's healthy enough, if underfed. But he doesn't look too strong.'

Toba frowned. 'You're considering him for Fishing?'

'Yes . . . He's obviously slim and light. But . . .'

'Madam, he's an upfluxer,' Toba said complacently.

'Really?' The woman stared at Farr with new curiosity. She actually pulled away from him a little, wiping her hands on her garment.

'And that means, of course, for his size and mass he's immensely strong, here at the Pole. Ideal for the Bells.' Toba turned to Dura, and his voice was smooth and practised. 'You see, Dura, the material of our bodies is changed, here at the Pole, because the Magfield is stronger.' He seemed to be talking for the sake of it – to be filling in the silence while the woman pondered Farr's destiny. 'The bonds between nuclei are made stronger. That's why it feels hotter here to you, and why your muscles are . . .'

'I'm sure you're right,' the woman cut in. 'But . . .' She hesitated. 'Is he . . .'

'Broken in?' Dura interrupted heavily.

'Dura,' Toba warned her.

'Lady, he is a Human Being, not a wild boar. And he can speak for himself.'

Toba said rapidly, 'Madam, I can vouch for the boy's good nature. He's been living in my home. Eating with my family. And besides, he represents good value at . . .' – his face puffed out, and he seemed to be calculating rapidly – 'at fifty skins.'

The woman frowned, but her fat, broad face showed interest. 'For what? The standard ten years?'

'With the usual penalty clauses, of course,' Toba said.

The woman hesitated.

A crowd was gathering around the Market's central Wheel. The noise level was rising and there was an air of excitement . . . of dangerous excitement, Dura felt; suddenly she wished the booth formed a more substantial cage around her.

'Look, I don't have time to haggle; I want to watch the execution. Forty-five, and I'll take his option.'

Toba hesitated for barely a moment. 'Done.'

The woman melted into the crowd, with a final intrigued glance at Farr.

Dura reached out of the booth-cage and touched Toba's arm. *'Ten years?'*

'That's the standard condition.'

'And the work?'

Toba looked uncomfortable. 'It's hard. I'll not try to hide that. They'll put him in the Bells . . . But he's strong, and he'll survive it.'

'And after he's too weak to work?'

He pursed his lips. 'He won't be in the Bells forever. He could become a Supervisor, maybe; or some kind of specialist. Look, Dura, I know this must seem strange to you, but this is our way, here in Parz. It's a system that's endured for generations . . . And it's a system you accepted, implicitly, when you agreed to come here in the car, to find a way to pay for Adda's treatment. I did try to warn you.' His round, dull face became defiant. 'You understood that, didn't you?'

She sighed. 'Yes. Of course I did. Not in every detail, but . . . I couldn't see any choice.'

'No,' he said, his voice hard. 'Well, you don't have any choice, now.'

She hesitated before going on. She hated to beg. But at least Toba and his home were fixed points in this new world, nodes of comparative familiarity. 'Toba Mixxax. Couldn't *you* buy us . . . our labour? You have a ceiling-farm at the Crust. And . . .'

'No,' he said sharply. Then, more sympathetically, he went on, 'I'm sorry, Dura, but I'm not a prosperous man. I simply couldn't afford you . . . Or rather, I couldn't afford a fair price for you. You wouldn't be able to pay off Adda's bills. Do you understand? Listen, forty-five skins for ten prime years of Farr, unskilled as he is, may seem a fortune to you; but believe me, that woman got a bargain, and she knew it. And . . .'

His voice was drowned by a sudden roar from the crowd around the huge Wheel. People jostled and barged each other as they swarmed along guide ropes and rails. Dura – listless, barely interested – looked through the crowd, seeking the focus of excitement.

A man was being hauled through the crowd. His two escorts, Waving strongly, were dressed in a uniform similar to the guards at Muub's Hospital, with their faces made supernaturally menacing by heavy leather masks. Their captive was a good ten years older than Dura, with a thick mane of yellowing hair and a gaunt, patient face. He was stripped to the waist and seemed to have his hands tied behind his back.

The crowds flinched as he passed, even as they roared encouragement to his captors.

Dura rubbed her nose, depressed and confused. 'I don't know what you're talking about. How are forty-five skins a fortune? Skins of what?'

He had to shout to make himself heard. 'It means, ah, forty-five Air-pig skins.'

That seemed clearer. 'So you're saying Farr's labour is worth as much as forty-five Air-pigs?'

'No, of course not.'

A new buyer came by the booth, a man who briefly asked about Farr. Toba had to turn him away but indicated Dura was available. The buyer – a coarse, heavy-set man dressed in a close-clinging robe – glanced over Dura cursorily before moving on.

Dura shuddered. There had been nothing threatening in the man's appraisal, still less anything sexual. In fact – and this was the ghastly, dispiriting part of it – there had been nothing personal in it at all. He had looked at her – *her*, Dura, daughter of Logue and leader of the Human Beings – the way she might weigh up a spear or knife, a carved piece of wood.

As a tool, not a person.

Toba was still trying to explain *skins* to her. 'You see, we're not talking about real pigs.' He smiled, patronizing. 'That would be absurd. Can you imagine people carting around fifty, a hundred Air-pigs, to barter with each other? It's all based on credit, you see. A skin is equivalent to the value of one pig. So you can exchange skins – or rather, amounts of credit in skins – and it's equivalent to bartering in pigs.' He nodded brightly at her. 'Do you see?'

'So if I had a credit of one skin – I could exchange it for one pig.'

He opened his mouth to agree, and then his face fell. 'Ah – not quite. Actually, a pig – a healthy, fertile adult – would cost you about four and a half skins at today's prices. But the cost of an actual *pig* is irrelevant . . . That isn't the point at all. Can't you see that? It's all to do with inflation. The Air-pig is the base of the currency, but . . .'

She turned her face away. She knew it was important to make sense of the ways of these people, if she were ever to extricate herself and her charges from this mess, but the flux lines of understanding across which she would have to Wave were daunting.

Now another man came to inspect her. This one was short, fussy and dressed in a loose suit; his hair-tubes were dyed a pale pink. He and Toba shook hands. They seemed to know each other. The man called her out of the booth and, to her shame, began to subject her to the intimate examination which Farr had suffered earlier.

Dura tried not to think about the strange little man's probing fingers. She watched the captive, who had now been led to the wooden Wheel. His arms and legs were crudely outstretched by the guards and fixed by ropes to four of the spokes, while a thong was drawn around his neck to attach his head to the fifth spoke. Dura, even as she endured her own humiliation, winced as the thong cut into the man's flesh.

The crowd bellowed, squirming around the Wheel in a frenzy of anticipation; despite the finery of their clothes, Dura was reminded of feeding Air-pigs.

Toba Mixxax touched her shoulder. 'Dura. This is Qos Frenk. He's interested in your labour . . . Only five years, though, I'm afraid.'

Qos Frenk, the pink-haired buyer, had finished his inspection. 'Age catches up with us all,' he said with sad sympathy. 'But my price is fair at fifteen skins.'

'Toba Mixxax, will this cover the costs of Adda, with Farr's fee?'

He nodded. 'Just about. Of course, Adda himself will have to find work once he's fit. And . . .'

'I'll take the offer,' she told Toba dully. 'Tell him.'

The Wheel started to turn about its axis.

The crowd screamed. At first the revolutions were slow, and the man pinned to it seemed to smile. But momentum soon gathered, and Dura could see how the man's head rattled against its spoke.

'Dura, I know Qos,' Toba said. 'He'll treat you well.'

Qos Frenk nodded at her, not unkindly.

'How close will I be to Farr?'

Toba hesitated, looking at her strangely. Qos Frenk seemed confused.

Now the victim's eyecups had closed; his fists were clenched against the pain of the rotation. Memories of Adda's attack by the sow returned to Dura. As the man was spun around, the Air in his capillaries would lose its superfluidity, begin to coagulate and slow; a sphere of agonizing pain would expand out through his body from the pit of his stomach, surrounding a shell of numbness. And . . .

'Dura, you don't understand. Qos owns a ceiling-farm which borders on mine. So you'll be working at the Crust . . . as a coolie. I explained to Qos how well adapted you upfluxers are for such work; in fact I found you at the Crust, and . . .'

'What about Farr?'

'He will be in the Harbour. He will be a Fisherman. Didn't you understand that? Dura . . .'

Now the man was rotating so fast that his limbs had become a blur. He must be unconscious already, Dura thought, and it was a mercy not to be able to see his face.

'Where is the Harbour, Toba Mixxax?'

He frowned. 'I'm sorry,' he said, sounding genuinely contrite. 'I forget sometimes how new all this is for you. The Harbour is at the base of the City, at the top of the Spine . . . the pillar of wood which descends from the base of the City. Bells from the Harbour follow the length of the Spine, diving deep into the underMantle. And . . .'

'And it's not acceptable,' she snarled. Qos Frenk flinched from her, eyecups wide. 'I must be with Farr.'

'No. Listen to me, Dura. *That's not an option.* Farr is ideal for the Harbour; he's young and light but immensely strong. You're too old for such work. I'm sorry, but that's the way it is.'

'We won't be parted.'

Toba Mixxax's face was hard now, his weak chin thrust forward. 'You listen to me, Dura. I've done my best to help you. And Ito and Cris have grown fond of you; I can see that. But I've my own life to lead. Accept this now or I just Wave away out of here. And leave you, and your precious brother, to the mercy of the Guards . . . and within half a day you'll be joining that man on the Wheel, two more unemployable vagrants.'

Now the Wheel was a blur. The crowd bellowed its excitement.

There was a popping sound, soft and obscene. The Wheel rapidly slowed; the man's hands, feet and head dangled as the Wheel turned through its final revolutions.

The prisoner's stomach cavity had burst; Air-vessels dangled amid folds of flesh like fat, bloody hair-tubes. The crowd, as if awed, grew silent.

Toba, oblivious, still stared into Dura's face. 'What's it to be, Dura?' he hissed.

The guards cut the Broken man down from the Wheel. The crowd, with a rising buzz of conversation, started to disperse.

Dura and Farr were allowed to visit Adda in his Hospital room – his *ward*, Dura remembered.

A huge fan turned slowly on one wall and the ward was pleasantly cool – it was almost like the open Air. The Hospital was close to the City's outer wall and the ward was connected to the outside world by only a short duct and was comparatively bright; entering it, Dura had an impression of cheerfulness, of competence.

But these initial impressions were rapidly dispelled by the sight of Adda, who was suspended at the centre of the room in a maze of ropes, webbings and bandages, almost all of his battered body obscured by gauzy material. A doctor – called Deni Maxx, a round, prissy-looking woman whose belt and pockets bristled with mysterious equipment – fussed around the suspended Human Being.

Adda peered at Dura and Farr from his nest of gauze. His right upper arm, which had been broken, was coated in a mound of bandages, and his lower legs were strapped together inside a cage of splints. Someone had scraped the pus from his good eye, and applied an ointment to keep out symbiotes.

Dura, oddly, felt more squeamish about Adda's wounds now than when she had been trying to cope with them with her bare hands in the Crust-forest. She was reminded, distressingly, of the dead, displayed animals in the Museum. 'You're looking well,' she said.

'Lying sow,' Adda growled. 'What by the bones of the Xeelee am I doing here? And why haven't you got out while you can?'

The doctor clucked her tongue, tweaking a bandage. 'You know why you're here.' She spoke loudly, as if Adda were a deaf child. 'You're here to heal.'

Farr said, 'Anyway, we'll be gone soon. I'm off to work in the Harbour. And Dura is going to the ceiling-farm.'

Adda fixed Dura with a one-eyed, venomous stare. 'You stupid bitch.'

'It's done now, Adda; I won't argue about it.'

'You should have let me die, rather than turn yourselves into slaves.' He tried to raise gauze-wrapped arms. 'What kind of life do you think I'm going to have now?'

Dura found Adda's tone repellent. It seemed wild, unconstructed, out of place in this huge, ordered environment. She found herself contrasting Adda's violence with the quiet timidity of Ito, who was living out her life in a series of tiny movements as if barely aware of the constraints of the crush of people around her. Dura would not have exchanged places with Ito, but she felt she understood her now. Adda's rage was crass, uncomprehending. 'Adda,' she said sharply. 'Leave it. It's done. We have to make the best of it.'

'Indeed we do,' the doctor sighed philosophically. 'Isn't that always the way of things?'

Adda stared at the woman. 'Why don't you keep out of it, you hideous old hag?'

Deni Maxx shook her head with no more than mild disapproval.

Dura, angry and unsettled, asked the doctor if Adda was healing.

'He's doing as well as we could expect.'

'What's that supposed to mean? Why can't you people talk straight?'

The doctor's smile thinned. 'I mean that he's going to live. And it looks as if his broken bones are knitting – slowly, because of his age, but knitting. And I've sewn up the ruptured vessels; most of his capillaries are capable of sustaining pressure now . . .'

'But?'

'He's never going to be strong again. And he might not be able to leave the City.'

Dura frowned; brief, selfish thoughts of extended periods of fee-paying crossed her mind. 'Why not? If he's healing up as you say . . .'

'Yes, but he won't be able to generate the same level of pneumatic pressure.' Maxx frowned quizzically. 'Do you understand what that means?'

Dura gritted her teeth. 'No.'

'Oh dear. It's so easy to forget you're all upfluxers . . .'

Adda closed his eyes and leaned back in his gauze net.

'Look,' said Maxx, 'our bodies function by exploiting the Air's mass transport properties . . . No? All right.' She pointed at the fan set into the wall. 'Do you know why that fan is there – why there are fans installed throughout the City? To *regulate the temperature* – to keep us cool, here in the heat of the South Pole. The Air we inhabit is a neutron gas, and it's made up of two components – a superfluid and a normal fluid. The superfluid can't sustain temperature differences – if you heat it, the heat passes straight through.

135

'Now – that means that if you add more superfluid to a mass of Air, its temperature will drop. And similarly if you take superfluid out the temperature rises, because normal fluid is left behind. And that's the principle the wall fans work on.'

Farr was frowning. 'What's that got to do with Adda?'

'Adda's body is full of Air – like yours, and mine. And it's permeated by a network of tiny capillaries, which can draw in superfluid to regulate his temperature.' Deni Maxx winked at Farr. 'We have tiny Air-pumps in our bodies . . . lots of them, including the heart itself. And that's what hair-tubes are for . . . to let Air out of your skull, to keep your brain the right temperature. Did you know that?'

'And it's that mechanism which may not work so well, now, for Adda.'

'Yes. We've repaired the major vessels, of course, but they're never the same once they're ruptured – and he's simply lost too much of his capillary network. He's been left weakened, too. Do you understand that Air also powers our muscles? . . . Look – suppose you were to heat up an enclosed chamber, like this room. Do you know what would happen to the superfluid? Unable to absorb heat, it would flee from the room – vigorously, and however it could. And by doing so it would raise pressure elsewhere.

'When Adda wants to raise his arm, he heats up the Air in his lungs. He's not aware of doing that, of course; his body does it for him, burning off some of the energy he's stored up by eating. And when his lungs are heated the Air rushes out; capillaries lead the Air to his muscles, which expand and . . .'

'So you're saying that because this capillary network is damaged, Adda won't be as strong again?'

'Yes.' She looked from Dura to Farr. 'Of course you do realize that our lungs aren't really *lungs*, don't you?'

Dura shook her head, baffled by this latest leap. 'What?'

'Well, we are artifacts, of course. Made things. Or at least our ancestors were. Humans – *real* humans, I mean – came to this world, this Star, and designed us the way we are, so that we could survive, here in the Mantle.'

'The Ur-humans.'

Maxx smiled, pleased. 'You know of the Ur-humans?

Good . . . Well, we believe that original humans had lungs – reservoirs of some gas – in their bodies. Just as we do. But perhaps their lungs' function was quite different. You see, our lungs are simply caches of Air, of working gas for the pneumatic systems which power our muscles.'

'What were they like, the Ur-humans?'

'We can't be sure – the Core Wars and the Reformation haven't left us any records – but we do have some strong hypotheses, based on scaling laws and analogies with ourselves. Analogous anatomy was my principal subject as a student . . . Of course, that was a long time ago. They were much like us. Or rather, we were made in their image. But they were many times our size – about a hundred thousand times as tall, in fact. Because he was dominated by balances between different sets of physical forces, the average Ur-human was a metre tall, or more. And his body can't have been based, as ours is, on the tin-nucleus bond . . . Do you know what I'm talking about? The tin nuclei which make up our bodies contain fifty protons and one hundred and forty-four neutrons. That's twelve by twelve, you see. The neutrons are gathered in a spherical shape in symmetries of order three and four. Lots of symmetry, you see; lots of easy ways for nuclei to fit together by sharing neutrons, plenty of ways for chains and complex structures of nuclei to form. The tin-nucleus bond is the basis of all life here, including our own. But not the Ur-humans; the physics which dominated their structure – the densities and pressures we think they inhabited – wouldn't have allowed any nuclear bonding at all. But they must have had *some* equivalent of the tin bond . . .'

She held out her arms and wiggled her fingers. 'So they were very strange. But they had arms, and legs, like us – so we believe, because otherwise why would they have given them to us?'

Dura shook her head. 'That doesn't make any sense.'

'Of course it does,' Maxx smiled. 'Oh, fingers have their uses. But haven't there been times when you'd have swapped your long, clumsy legs for an Air-pig's jetfart bladder? Or for a simple sheet of skin like a Surfer's board which would let you Wave across the Magfield ten, a hundred times as fast as you can now? You have to face it, my dear . . . We humans are a bad design for the environment of the Mantle. And the reason must be that we are scale models of the Ur-humans who built us. No doubt the Ur-human form was perfectly suited for whatever strange world they came from. But not here.'

Dura's imagination, overheating, filled her mind with visions of huge, misty, godlike men, prising open the Crust and releasing handfuls of tiny artificial humans into the Mantle...

Deni Maxx looked deeply into Dura's eyecups. 'Is that clear to you? I think it's important that you understand what's happened to your friend.'

'Oh, it's clear,' Adda called from his cocoon. 'But it doesn't make a blind bit of difference, because there's nothing she can do about it.' He laughed. 'Nothing, now she's condemned me to this living hell. Is there, Dura?'

Dura's anger welled like Deni's heated superfluid. 'I'm sick of your bitterness, old man.'

'You should have let me die,' he whispered. 'I told you.'

'Why didn't you tell us about Parz City? Why did you leave us so unprepared?'

He sighed, a bubble of thick phlegm forming at the corner of his mouth. 'Because we were thrown out ten generations ago. Because our ancestors travelled so far before building a home that none of us thought we would ever encounter Parz again.' He laughed. 'It was better to forget... What good would it do to know such a place existed? But how could we know they would spread so far, staining the Crust with their ceiling-farms and their Wheels? Damn them...'

'Why were we sent away from Parz? Was it because...' She turned, but Deni Maxx was making notes on a scroll with a Corestuff stylus, and did not appear to be listening. 'Because of the Xeelee?'

'No.' He grimaced in pain. 'No, not because of the Xeelee. Or at least, not directly. It was because of how our philosophy caused us to behave.'

The Human Beings believed that knowledge of the Xeelee predated the arrival of humans in the Star – that it had been brought there by the Ur-humans themselves.

The Xeelee, godlike, dominated spaces so large – it was said

– that by comparison the Star itself was no more than a mote in the eyecup of a giant. Humans, striving for supremacy, had resented the Xeelee – had even gone to hopeless war against the great Xeelee projects, the constructs like the legendary Ring.

But over the generations – and as the terrible defeats continued – a new strand had emerged in human thought. No one understood the Xeelee's grand purposes. But what if their projects were aimed, not at squalid human-scale goals like the domination of others, but at much higher aspirations?

The Xeelee were much more powerful than humans. Perhaps they always would be. And perhaps, as a corollary, they were much more *wise*.

So, some apologists began to argue, humans should trust in the Xeelee rather than oppose them. The Xeelee's ways were incomprehensible but must be informed by great wisdom. The apologists developed a philosophy which was accepting, compliant, calm, and trusting in an understanding above any human's.

Adda went on, 'We followed the way of the Xeelee, you see, Dura; not the way of the Committee of Parz. We would not obey.' He shook his head. 'So they sent us away. And in that we were lucky; now they might simply have destroyed us on their Wheels.'

Deni Maxx touched Dura's shoulder. 'You should leave now.'

'We'll be back.'

'No.' Adda was shifting with ghastly slowness in his cocoon of bindings, evidently trying to relieve his pain. 'No, don't come back. Get away. As far and as fast as you can. Get away...'

His voice broke up into a bubbling growl, and he closed his eyes.

10

'You dumb upfluxer jetfart!' Hosch screamed in Farr's face. 'When I want a whole damn tree trunk fed into this hopper I'll tell you about it!' Now the Harbour supervisor shoved his bony face forward and his tone descended into a barely audible, infinitely menacing hiss. 'But until I do... and if it wouldn't trouble you too much... maybe you could split the wood just a *little* more finely. Or...' – foul-smelling photons seeping from his mouth – 'maybe you'd like to follow your handiwork into the hopper and finish your work in there? Eh?'

Farr waited until Hosch was through. Trying to defend himself, he knew from bitter experience, would only make things worse.

Hosch was a small, wiry man with a pinched mouth and eyecups which looked as if they had been drilled into his face. His clothes were filthy and he always smelled to Farr like days-old food. His limbs were so thin that Farr was confident that, with his remarkable upfluxer strength here at the Pole, he – or Dura – could snap the supervisor in two, in a fair fight...

At last Hosch seemed to exhaust his anger, and he Waved away to some other part of the hopper line. The labourers who had gathered to relish Farr's humiliation – men and women alike – gave up their surreptitious surveillance and, with the smugness of spared victims, fixed their attention back on their work.

Air seethed in Farr's capillaries and muscles. *Upfluxer. He called me upfluxer, again.* He watched his fists bunch...

Bzya's huge hand enclosed both Farr's own, and, with an irresistible, gentle force, pulled Farr's arms down. 'Don't,' Bzya said, his voice a cool rumble from the depths of an immense chest. 'He's not worth it.'

140

Farr's rage seemed to veer between the supervisor and this huge Fisherman who was getting in the way. 'He called me . . .'

'I heard what he called you,' Bzya said evenly. 'And so did everyone else . . . just as Hosch intended. Listen to me. He wants you to react, to hit him. He'd like nothing better.'

'He'd be capable of liking nothing after I take off his head for him.'

Bzya threw his head back and roared laughter. 'And as soon as you did the guards would be down on you. After a beating you'd return to work – to Hosch, to a supervisor who really *would* hate you, and wouldn't pass up an opportunity to show it – and to an extra five, or ten, years here to pay his compensation.'

Farr, the remnants of his anger still swirling in him, looked up into Bzya's broad, battered face. 'But I've only just started this shift . . . At the moment I'll be happy just to get through that.'

'Good.' With an immense, powerful hand Bzya ruffled Farr's hair-tubes. 'That's the way to think of it . . . You don't have to get through your whole ten years at once, remember; just one shift at a time.'

Bzya was a huge man with muscles the size of Air-piglets. He was as bulky, powerful and gentle as the supervisor was small and needle-dagger vicious. Bzya's face was marred by a mask of scar tissue which obliterated one side of his head and turned one eyecup into a ghastly cavern that reached back into the depths of his skull. Farr had come to know him as a simple man who had lived his life in the poverty-stricken Downside, keeping himself alive by turning his giant muscles to the mundane, difficult and dangerous labour which allowed the rest of Parz City to function. He had a wife, Jool, and a daughter, Shar. Somehow, through a life of travail, he had retained a kind and patient nature.

Now he said to Farr, winking at him with his good eyecup, 'You shouldn't be hard on old Hosch, you know.'

Farr gaped, trying to suppress a laugh. 'Me, hard on him? Why, the old Xeelee-lover has it in for me.'

Bzya reached to the conveyor and raised a length of tree trunk longer than Farr was tall. With a single blow of his axe

141

he cracked it open to reveal its glowing core. 'See it from his point of view. He's the supervisor of this section.'

Farr snorted. 'Making himself rich out of our work. Bastard.'

Bzya smiled. 'You learn fast, don't you? Well, maybe. But he's also *responsible*. We lost another Bell, last shift. Had you heard? Three more Fishermen dead. Hosch is responsible for that too.'

Disasters seemed to hit the Harbour with a depressing regularity, Farr thought. Still, he remained impatient with Bzya's tolerance, and he began to list Hosch's faults.

'He's all of that, and then some you're too young to understand. Maybe he isn't up to the responsibility he has.

'But – I'll say it again – whether he can cope or not, he's *responsible*. And when one of us dies, a little of him must die too. I've seen it in his face, Farr, despite all his viciousness. Remember that.'

Farr frowned. He shoved more glowing wood into the hoppers. It was so complex. If only Logue or Dura were here to help him make sense of it all . . .

Or if only he could get out of here and *Surf*.

The rest of the shift wore away without incident. Afterwards Farr filed out with the rest of the labourers to the small, cramped dormitory they shared. The dormitory, home to forty people, was a stained box slung across with sleeping ropes. It stank of shit and food. Farr ate his daily ration – today, a small portion of tough bread – and looked for a stable nest in the web of sleeping-ropes. He wasn't yet confident enough to challenge the older, powerful-looking Fishermen, men and women both, who monopolized the chamber walls where the Air was slightly less polluted by the grunts and farts of others. He finished up, as usual, close to the centre of the dormitory.

One day, he told himself as he closed his eyes and sought sleep. One day.

At the start of his next shift, with eyecups still crusted with sleep deposits, he filed back to his post at the wood hoppers.

The Harbour was an irregular compound of large chambers constructed of stained wood and fixed to the base of the City

– in the shadow of the Downside, well away from the bright, fashionable sectors of the upper levels. It was just below the huge dynamos which powered the anchor-bands, and the deep, thrumming vibration of the machines above was a constant accompaniment to life for the Fishermen. The Harbour was a dark, hot, filthy place to work, and the contrast of the heat of the stoves, the grinding roar of the pistons and pulleys with the open Air of the upflux, made it all but unbearable for Farr.

Still, as his shift wore on, Farr relaxed into his work's heavy, steady rhythms. He hauled the next massive length of tree trunk from the conveyor belt that ran continually behind the row of labourers. He was forced to wrestle with the chunk of wood; its inertia seemed to turn it into a wilful, living thing, determined to plough its own path through the Air regardless of Farr's wishes. The muscles in his arms and back bulged as he braced himself against the floor of the chamber and swung at the section of trunk with his axe of wood, hardened with a tip of Corestuff. The trunk was tough, but split easily enough if he swung the blade along the direction of the grain. When the split was deep enough, Farr forced his hands into the cracked wood and prised the trunk section open, releasing a flood of warmth and green light from the nuclear-burning interior which bathed his face and chest. Then, with the nuclear fire still bright, he dumped the hot fragments into the gaping maw of the hopper before him.

Cutting the wood was the part of his work Farr enjoyed the most, oddly. There was a certain skill to be applied in finding exactly the right spot for his axe blade, a skill Farr found pleasure in acquiring and applying. And when the wood split open under his coaxing, releasing its energy with a sigh of warmth, it was like revealing some hidden treasure.

A line of labourers worked alongside Farr, stretching almost out of sight in the gloom of the Harbour; working in shifts, they fed the ravenous maw of the hoppers unceasingly. The work was heavy, but not impossibly so for Farr, thanks to his upfluxer muscles. In fact, he had to take care not to work too fast; exceeding his quota didn't earn him any popularity with his workmates.

The heat energy released by the wood's burning nuclei was

contained in great, reinforced vessels – boilers – in another part of the Harbour complex. Superfluid Air, fleeing the heat, was used to drive pistons. These pistons were immense fists of hardened wood twice Farr's height which plunged into their jackets as steady as a heartbeat.

The pistons, via huge, splintered rotary arms, turned pulleys; and it was the pulleys which sent Bells full of fearful Fishermen towards the mysterious and deadly depths of the underMantle.

It was so different from his life with the Human Beings, where there were no devices more complex than a spear, no source of power save the muscles of humans or animals. The Harbour was like an immense machine, with the sole purpose of sending Fishermen down into the underMantle. He felt as if he were a component of that huge machine himself, or as if he were labouring inside the heart of some giant built of wood and rope . . .

Bzya apart, the other workers showed no signs of accepting Farr. It was as if their unhappiness with their lot, here in this noisy, stinking inferno, had been turned inwards on themselves, and on each other. But still, once each new shift had settled in, the workers seemed to reach a certain rhythm, and a mood of companionship settled over the line – a mood which, Farr sensed, extended even to him, as long as he kept his mouth shut.

He missed Dura, and the rest of the Human Beings, and he missed his old life in the upflux. Of course he did. His sentence in this Harbour seemed to stretch off to eternity. But he was able to accept his lot, as long as he kept his mind focussed on the task in hand, and took comforts where he could find them. One shift at a time, that was the secret, as Bzya had told him. And . . .

'You.'

There was a hand on his shoulder, grasping at his grubby tunic. He was roughly dragged out of the line.

Hosch glared at him, his nostrils glowing sickly-white. 'Change of assignment,' he growled.

'What?'

'A Bell,' Hosch said.

*

As Dura approached – with twenty other new coolies in a huge car drawn by a dozen stout Air-pigs – Frenk's ceiling-farm seemed tiny at first, a child's palmprint against the immensity of the Crust itself. The other coolies seemed more interested in another farm, still more distant and harder to make out than Frenk's. This belonged to Hork IV, Chair of Parz City, Dura was told. The absent-minded Chair escaped his civic responsibilities – leaving Parz in the scheming hands of his son – by indulging in elaborate agricultural experiments, here at the Crust. On Hork's ceiling-farm there were said to be spears of wheat taller than a man, and Crust-trees no longer than a man's arm and bound up with lengths of Corestuff-wire . . .

Dura was barely able to keep her attention focussed on this prattle. The thought of being marooned at the Crust, with only these dullards for company, made her heart sink.

At last Frenk's ceiling-farm filled the clearwood windows. The car settled to rest at the centre of a group of crude wooden buildings, and the doors opened.

Dura scrambled out and Waved away from the others. She took a deep breath of clean, empty Air, relishing the sensation in her lungs and capillaries. The Air stretched away all around her, an immense, unbroken layer stretching right around the Star; it was like being inside the lungs of the Star itself. Well, the company might leave a bit to be desired, but at least here she could breathe Air which didn't taste like it had been through the lungs of a dozen people already.

Qos Frenk himself was there to greet them. He picked out Dura, smiling with apparent kindness at her, and while the other coolies dispersed among the buildings, he offered to show Dura around his farm.

Frenk – dapper, round and sleek, his pink hair flowing over an elaborate cloak – Waved confidently beside her. 'The work is straightforward enough, but it needs concentration and care . . . qualities, sadly, which not all coolies nowadays share. I'm sure you'll do a fine job, my dear.'

Dura was wearing a coverall woven of some crude vegetable-fibre cloth, given to her as a parting gift by Ito. As she Waved it grated against her skin constantly, as if chafing her all over, and she longed to tear it off. On her back she carried a round pod of wood – an Air-tank, like the one she'd seen Toba wear, with a small mask she was supposed to fit over her face to help her breathe the rarefied Air of the upper Mantle. The bulky, unnatural thing impeded her movement even more than the City-made clothes, but Frenk insisted she carry it. 'Health ordinances, you see,' he had said with a philosophical shrug, his ornate cloak bunching around his thin shoulders.

Under the coverall, she still wore her length of rope and her small knife.

The farm had largely been cleared of tree trunks; the exposed forest root-ceiling was seeded with neat rows of green-gold wheat, of altered grass. Here, hovering just a few mansheights below the wafting, swollen tips of mutant grass, she could no longer see the boundaries of the farm. It was as if the Crust's natural wildness had been banished, overrun by this claustrophobic orderliness.

Of course the orderliness covered only two dimensions. The third dimension led down to the clean, free Air of the Mantle which hung below her, huge and empty. The Parz folk had not yet succeeded in fencing off the Air itself . . . All she needed to do was to throw this Air-tank into the round, delicate face of Qos Frenk, and Wave away into infinity. These soft City-borns – even the coolies – could never catch her.

But she could never quit this place, abandon her obligations, until Adda's fees were paid off. Ties of obligation and duty would imprison her here as surely as any cage.

Qos Frenk blinked, studying her. 'I know this must be a strange situation for you. I want you to know you've nothing to fear but hard work. I own the ceiling-farm, and I own your labour, in that sense. But I don't make the mistake of imagining I own your soul.

'I'm not a cruel man, Dura. I believe in treating my coolies as well as I can afford. And . . .'

'Why?' Dura found herself snarling. 'Because you're such a noble person?'

He smiled. 'No. Because it's economically more efficient for me to have a happy and healthy workforce.' He laughed, and he looked a little more human to Dura. 'That should reassure you if nothing else does. I'm sure you'll be fine here, Dura.

146

Why, as soon as you learn the trade I don't see why we shouldn't be thinking of you as a future supervisor, or skills specialist.'

She forced herself to smile back. 'All right. Thank you. I understand you're doing your best for me. What will I have to do?'

He indicated the rows of ripening wheat dangling from the forest ceiling above them. 'In a few weeks we'll be ready for the harvest, and that's when the real work begins. But for now your job is to ensure that the growth of the wheat is unimpeded. Look for the obvious, like boars crushing the stems. Or trespassers.' He looked saddened. 'We get a lot of that nowadays . . . scavengers, I mean. A lot of poverty in the City, you see. Watch out for blight. Any kind of discoloration, or growth abnormalities . . . If we get any diseases we isolate the area and sterilize it fast, before the infection spreads.

'Look for wild grass, any plants growing among the roots, damaging the wheat. We don't want anything else absorbing the lovely Crust isotopes which were meant for our crop . . . And that includes young trees. You'd be surprised how fast they grow.' He spread his hands wide. His enthusiasm was almost endearing, Dura thought. 'You wouldn't think it but this part of the Crust was all native forest, once.'

'Remarkable,' Dura cut in drily, remembering the broad, unspoiled forests of her home area in the far upflux.

Frenk looked at her uncertainly.

They met another worker, a woman who drifted with her head lost in the green-gold crop and her legs dangling down into the Air. The woman was hauling small saplings down from between the green stems of the wheat and shoving the weeds into a sack bound to her waist.

'Ah,' Frenk said with a smile. 'One of my best workers. Rauc, meet Dura. Just arrived here. Perhaps you'd be good enough to show her around . . .'

The woman drifted slowly down from the dangling crop. Over her head, Rauc was wearing her Air-helmet, a veil of soft, semitransparent gauze which covered a broad-brimmed hat. The curtain bulged out a little, showing that it was being fed by Air from the woman's tank.

Frenk Waved fussily away.

Rauc was slim and wore a simple smock of grubby leather, though her arms were bare. After Frenk's departure she regarded Dura sombrely for a few moments without speaking. Then she untied her veil and lifted it. Her face was thin and tired, her eyecups dark; she looked about Dura's own age. 'So you're the upfluxer,' she said, her voice containing the flat whine of the City-born.

'Yes.'

'We heard you were coming. We were glad. Do you know why?'

Dura shrugged, uncaring.

'Because you upfluxers are strong . . . You'll work hard, help us meet our quotas.' She sniffed. 'As long as you don't show us up, you'll be popular enough.'

'I understand.' This woman was trying to warn her, she realized. 'Thanks, Rauc.'

Rauc led her beneath the golden ceiling-fields back towards the cluster of structures at the heart of the farm, where Dura had been dropped on first arrival. There was no sign of Qos Frenk's car; Dura imagined him returning to his cosy, stuffy home inside the City. Now, in mid-shift, the little huts seemed deserted: they were small, boxy buildings of wood, dangling by lengths of rope from the truncated stems of Crust-trees. There was a small, unkempt herd of pigs. Rauc said the herd was kept – not for commercial purposes — but to provide meat for the coolies, leather for smocks and hats. Rauc showed her small stores of clothing, Air-sacks and tools. There was a bakery, its inner walls blackened by heat; the coolies' staple food, bread, was made for them here. A large, overweight man laboured in the gloom of the bakery; he scowled at Dura and Rauc as they peered in at him. Rauc pulled a face. 'Well, the bread's fresh,' she said. 'But that's all you can say for it . . . The lowest-quality wheat ends up here, that and any gleanings we can find, while the best stuff is shipped off to Parz.'

There was a dormitory building, a small, cramped box packed with rows of cocoons. About half the cocoons were occupied. A woman's sleepy face lifted to stare at them before flopping back into sleep, mouth open and hair dangling. Rauc pointed out a vacant cocoon Dura would be able to claim for herself. But Dura couldn't imagine sleeping in here, breathing in the snores and farts of others, while the fresh Air of the Mantle swept away all around her. It made her realize, jarringly, that she was going to be as out of place here as in Parz itself. Most of the coolies were, after all, City-born – and mostly from the Downside where conditions were even more cramped than the average. So off-shift coolies shovelled themselves into this stinking box, listening to each other breathe and pretending that they weren't stranded out here in the Mantle, but were tucked away inside the cosy confines of Parz.

Rauc smiled at her. 'I think we'll get along, Dura. You can tell me about your people. And I'll show you how to get around here.'

'Frenk seems all right . . .'

Rauc looked surprised. 'Oh, he's decent enough. But that doesn't matter. Not day to day, it doesn't. I'll introduce you to our section supervisor, Leeh. *She* makes a difference . . . But not as much as she likes to think. Now Robis – who runs the stores – that's where the real power lies. Get him to smile on you and the world is a brighter place.'

Dura hesitated. 'Frenk says I might get to be a supervisor, eventually.'

'He says that to everyone,' Rauc said dismissively. 'Come on, let's find Leeh; she's probably off in the fields somewhere . . .' But she hesitated, looking searchingly at Dura. Then, glancing around to check they were unobserved, she dug into a deep pocket in her smock and drew out a small object. 'Here,' she said, placing the object in Dura's hand. 'This will keep you well.'

It was a tiny five-spoked Wheel, like the one she'd seen around the neck of Toba Mixxax . . . a model of the execution device in the Market Place. 'Thank you,' Dura said slowly. 'I think I understand what this means.'

'You do?' Now Rauc's look was becoming wary.

Dura hastened to reassure her. 'Don't worry. I won't betray you.'

'The Wheel is illegal in Parz City,' Rauc said. 'In theory it's illegal everywhere, throughout the Mantle . . . wherever the Guards' crossbows can reach. But we're a long way from Parz

149

here. The Wheel is tolerated on the ceiling-farms. Something to keep us happy . . . That old fool Frenk says it's economically efficient for us to be allowed to practise our faith.'

Dura smiled. 'That sounds like Frenk.'

'. . . But you never know. Do upfluxers follow the Wheel?'

'No.' She studied Rauc. She didn't seem very strong, or much of a rebel; but apparently this Wheel business gave her comfort. 'I saw a Wheel used as an execution tool.'

'Yes.'

'Then why is it a symbol of faith?'

'*Because* it's used to kill.' Rauc looked into her eyes, searching for understanding. 'So many human lives have been Broken that the Wheel, the very shape of it, has become something human in itself. Or more than human. Do you see? By keeping the Wheel close by us we are staying close to the noblest, bravest part of us.'

Rauc's speech was intense and earnest. Dura thumbed the little Wheel doubtfully. The cult must be quite widespread. After all, Toba Mixxax was an adherent . . . a ceiling-farm owner. Widespread through the Star, then, and through society itself.

If these Wheel cultists ever found a leader, they could be formidable opponents for the mysterious Committee which ran the City.

Rauc looked tired. 'Come on. Let's find Leeh, and get you started.'

Side by side the two women Waved through the orderly Air of the farm, the golden stalks of wheat suspended above them.

Farr was dimly aware of the other workers pulling away from him, sly looks conveying their pleasure at his discomfiture. Chunks of Crust-tree rolled past on their conveyor belt, ignored.

There was a growl. 'No.' Bzya, Farr realized, hovering close behind him.

Hosch's bony head swivelled at Bzya, eyecups deep and empty. 'You're questioning me, Fisherman?'

'This one's too young,' Bzya said, laying a huge hand on Farr's shoulder. Farr, unwilling to lead his friend into trouble, tried to shrug the hand away.

'But he was recruited for this.' A muscle in the supervisor's cheek was twitching. 'He's small and light, but he's got that upfluxer strength. And we're short of able-bodied . . .'

'He's got no skills. No experience. And we've taken a lot of losses recently, Hosch. It's too much of a risk.'

Hosch's cheek muscle seemed to have a life of its own. When he replied, it was in a sudden scream. 'I'm not asking your advice, you Xeelee-lover! And if you're so concerned for this Piglet-turd you can come down as well. Got that? Got that?'

Farr dropped his head. Of course, Hosch wasn't being logical. If he – Farr – was being taken down because of his size, then surely Bzya shouldn't be . . .

Bzya simply nodded, apparently unmoved by Hosch's anger or by his own sudden assignment to peril. 'Who's the third?'

'I am.' Hosch's rage still showed in the pulsing of muscles in his face, in the quivering of his eyecup rims. 'I am. Now get moving, you Pig-lovers, and maybe we've got a chance to get down there before the Quantum Sea congeals . . .'

Farr and Bzya followed Hosch out of the hopper chamber. Hosch's continued abuse passed unheard through Farr's head, and he could only remember what Bzya had told him about Hosch and responsibility.

11

The chamber where they were to board the Bell was at the very base of the City. The chamber had walls, an upper surface – but no floor. Farr, following Hosch and Bzya, clung to guide ropes and gazed down into clear Air, drinking in its freshness after days of the stale stenches of the Harbour. He was aware of the immense mass of the City above him; it creaked softly, like some brooding animal.

The Bell itself was a sphere of hardened, battered wood two mansheights across. Hoops of Corestuff were wrapped around it. The Bell was suspended from an immense pulley which was almost lost in the darkness above Farr's head. More cables attached the Bell loosely to the Spine. Farr could make out pale patches in the dimness above, faces of Harbour workers close to the pulley.

The Spine was a pillar of wood which plunged, trailing cables, out of this chamber and speared through the thick Air beneath the City. It turned into a dark line, barely visible, curving slowly to follow the flux of the Magfield. Cables trailed along its length to reach far, far down, into the distant, bruised-purple, lethal mass of the underMantle.

Farr, following the Spine's curve, felt his heart slow inside him.

The Bell seemed impossibly fragile. How could it possibly protect him from dissolution in the depths of the underMantle, hovering over the boiling surface of the Quantum Sea itself? Surely it would be crushed like a leaf; no wonder so many Fishermen lost their lives.

Hosch opened up a large door in the side of the Bell and clambered stiffly inside. Bzya prodded Farr forward. As he approached the sphere Farr saw how badly scuffed and scratched the outer surface was. He ran a finger along one deep scar; it looked as if some animal had attacked this frag-ile-looking device, gouging it with teeth or nails.

Reassuring, he thought drily.

Farr had expected the interior of the Bell to be something like Mixxax's car, with its comfortable seats and light-admit-ting windows. Instead he entered a pocket of gloom – in fact he almost collided with Hosch. The only windows were small panels of clearwood which hardly admitted any light; wood-lamps gave off a smoky, apologetic green glow. There was a pole running the length of the sphere's axis, and Farr clung to this. There was a small control panel – with two worn-looking switches and a lever – and the hull was bulky with lockers and what looked like tanks of Air.

Bzya lumbered into the Bell. The interior was suddenly crowded; and as the Fisherman's huge hands wrapped around the support pole the Bell was filled with Bzya's strong, homely stench. Hosch clambered around them both to pull closed the hatch – a massive disc of wood which fitted snugly into its frame.

They waited in the almost complete gloom. There was a busy scraping from all around the hull. Farr, peering through the windows, saw Harbour workers adjusting the position of the Corestuff hoops so that they surrounded the sphere evenly, covering the hatchway. Farr glanced from Hosch to Bzya. Bzya returned his stare with a patient acceptance, the darkness softening the lines of his scars. The supervisor glared into space, angry and tense.

There was a humming, strangely regular. The whole craft vibrated with it. It seemed to permeate his very being; he could feel his capillaries contracting. He looked at Bzya, but the Fisherman had closed his good eye, his face set; his damaged eyecup was a tunnel to infinity.

. . . And *something changed*. Something was taken away from Farr, lifted for the first time in his life. The only time he had felt anything remotely like this was during that last, fateful hunt with the Human Beings, when he had experienced that disorienting fear of falling. What was happening to him? He felt his grasp of the support pole loosen, his fingers slip from the wood. He cried out, drifting backward.

Bzya's strong hand grasped his hair-tubes and hauled him

back to the pole; Farr wrapped his arms and legs around the solidity of the wood.

Hosch was laughing, his voice grating.

Somebody rapped on the Bell with a heavy fist. Now there was a sensation of movement – jerking, swaying; Farr could hear cables rattle against the Bell and against each other.

So it had begun. In brisk, bewildering silence, they were descending towards the underMantle.

'The boy hasn't been prepared for any of this, Hosch.' There was no trace of anger in Bzya's voice. 'I told you. How can he function if his ignorance leaves him paralysed by fear?'

'Talk to the upfluxer if you want.' The supervisor turned his thin, creased, self-absorbed face away.

'What's happening to me, Bzya? I feel strange. Is it just because we're descending, following the Spine?'

'No.' Bzya shook his head. 'We are descending, but it's more than that. Listen carefully, Farr; it's important that you understand what's happening to you. Maybe it will keep you alive.'

These words, simply spoken, evoked more fear in the boy than all of Hosch's ranting. 'Tell me.'

'As we descend, the Air gets thicker. You understand that, don't you? . . .'

Farr understood. In the deadly depths of the underMantle, pressures and densities were so great that nuclei were crammed together, forced into each other. It was impossible for the structures of bonded nuclei which composed human bodies – and all the material which comprised Farr's world – to remain stable. The nuclei dissolved into the neutron superfluid that was the Air; and protons freed from the nuclei formed a superconducting fluid in the neutron mix.

At last, from the Quantum Sea inwards, the Star was like a single, immense nucleus; no nuclear-based life could persist.

'How can this Bell of wood protect us? Won't the wood just dissolve?'

'It would . . . if not for the Corestuff hoops.'

The hoops were hollow tubes of hyperonic Corestuff. The tubes contained proton superconductor, extracted from the underMantle. More tubes led up through the cables to dynamos in the Harbour which generated electrical currents in the Bell's hoops.

'The currents in the hoops generate huge magnetic fields,' Bzya said. 'Like our own Magfield. And they protect us. The fields are like an extra wall around the Bell, to insulate it from the pressures.'

'But what's making me feel so strange? Is it this magfield of the Bell's?'

'No.' Bzya smiled. 'The hoops are expelling the Magfield – the Star's Magfield, I mean – from the interior of the Bell.

'We all grow up in the Magfield. The Magfield affects us all the time . . . We use the Magfield to move about, when we Wave. Farr, for the first time in your life you can't feel the Magfield . . . For the first time, you can't tell which way up you are.'

There was no way of tracking time. The silence was broken only by the clatter of cables, the dull thud of the body of the Bell against the Spine, and the almost subvocal, angry mumblings of Hosch. Farr kept his eyes closed and hoped for sleep.

After an unknowable period the Bell gave a savage lurch, almost jolting the axial bar from Farr's hands. He clung to it, peering around the dimly lit cabin. Something had changed; he could feel it. But what? Had the Bell hit something?

The Bell was still moving, but the quality of its motion had changed – or so the pit of his stomach told him. They were still descending, he was sure; but now the Bell's descent was much smoother, and the occasional collisions of the Bell against the Spine had ceased.

It felt as if the Bell were floating, loose, through the underMantle.

Bzya laid a massive, kindly hand on his arm. 'It's nothing to fear.'

'I'm not . . .'

'We've come free of the Spine, that's all.'

Farr felt his eyes grow round. 'Why? Is something wrong?'

'No.' The cabin's small, woodburning lamps sent a soft glow into the pit of Bzya's ruined eye. 'It's designed to be this way. Look, the Spine only goes down a metre or so from the City. That's deeper than anyone could Wave unaided. But we have to go much, much deeper than that. Now our Bell is descending without the Spine to guide it.

'The cables still connect us to Parz. And the current they're carrying will continue to protect us, and the cable, from the conditions here, as long as we descend. But . . .'

'But we're drifting. And our cable could tangle, or break. What happens if it breaks, Bzya?'

Bzya met his gaze steadily. 'If it breaks, we don't go home.'

'Does that ever happen?'

Bzya turned his face to the lamp. 'When it does, they can tell almost immediately, up in the Harbour,' he said. 'The cable starts to run free. You know the worst straight away. You don't have to wait for the empty end to be returned . . .'

'And us? What would happen to us?'

Hosch pushed his thin face forward. 'You ask a lot of stupid questions. I'll give you some comfort. If the cable breaks, you won't know anything about it.' He made his hand into a loose fist and snapped it closed in Farr's face.

Farr flinched. 'Maybe you should tell me what else can kill me. Then at least I'll be prepared . . .'

There was a crash which jarred him loose from the support pole. The Bell swayed, rocking through the thick fluid of the underMantle.

Farr found himself floundering in the Bell's stuffy Air. Once again he needed Bzya to reach out and haul him back to the central post.

Bzya raised a silencing finger to his lips; Hosch merely glowered.

Farr held his breath.

Something scraped across the outside hull of the Bell; it was like fingernails across wood. It lasted a few heartbeats, and then faded.

After a few minutes of silence, the lurching, unsteady journey continued; Farr imagined metres of cable above his head, kinks mansheights tall running along its length.

'What was that?' He glanced up at the windows, which grudgingly admitted a diffuse purple light. 'Are we in the Quantum Sea?'

'No,' Bzya said. 'No, the Sea itself is still hundreds of metres below us. Farr, we're barely going to penetrate the upper layers of the underMantle. But we're already a couple of metres below the Spine now.'

'Yeah,' said Hosch, his deep eyes fixed on Farr. 'And that was a Colonist, come back from the dead to see who's visiting him.'

Farr felt his mouth drop open.

'It's a Corestuff berg,' Bzya said steadily. 'Corestuff. That's all.'

Hosch sneered, his gaze sliding around the cabin.

Farr knew Hosch was taunting him, but the sudden shock of the words had penetrated his imagination. He had always enjoyed Core War stories, had relished staring into the unachievable surface of the Quantum Sea and frightening himself with visions of the ancient, altered creatures prowling its depths. But the stories of the War, of humankind's loss, had seemed so remote from everyday experience as to be meaningless.

But Dura had told him of the fractal sculpture she had seen in Parz's University – a sculpture of a Colonist's physical form, Ito had said. And now he was descending into the underMantle himself, protected only by a rickety, barely understood technology.

He clung to the post, staring at the bruised light in the windows.

Again there was a scraping against the hull. Again the Bell swayed, causing Farr's stomach to lurch.

This time, Hosch and Bzya did not seem surprised. Hosch turned to press his face to a window, while Bzya relaxed his grip on the support post and flexed the fingers of his immense hands.

'What is it now?' Farr whispered.

'We think we've snagged a berg . . .'

Below the surface of the Quantum Sea, nuclei – clusters of protons and neutrons – could not survive. And deeper still, in the dark belly of the Sea itself, densities became so high that the nucleons themselves were brought into contact. Hyperons, exotic combinations of quarks, could form from the colliding nucleons. The hyperons could combine into stable islands of dense material – Corestuff bergs – which could persist away from the formative densities of the heart of the Star. The bergs drifted up, in Quantum Sea currents, to higher levels to be retrieved by the Fishermen and returned to Parz City.

'It's clinging to the outside of the Bell,' Bzya said. He mimed the impact of the berg against the Bell with his fists. 'See? It's drawn there by the magnetic field of the Bell, of its Corestuff hoops. And it stays, stuck by the Magfield set up in response in its own interior.'

Hosch grinned again, and Farr was aware of the supervisor's foul breath. 'Good Fishing. We were lucky. We can't be more than four metres below Parz. Now, boy. Watch.' With a grandiloquent gesture, Hosch closed the two switches on the small control panel beside him.

Farr held his breath, but nothing seemed to have changed. The Bell still swayed alarmingly through the underMantle – in fact it seemed to be rotating, his stomach told him, perhaps knocked into a twist by the impact of the berg.

Bzya said patiently, 'He's sent a signal to the Harbour, along the cables. That we're ready to be hauled up.'

Hosch grinned at him. 'And that's why we're here, boy. That's the reason they put men in these cages, and stuff them down into the underMantle. All to close those little switches. See? Otherwise, how else would the Harbour know when to haul up the Bells?'

'Why three of us? Why not just one Fisherman?'

'Double redundancy,' Hosch said. 'If something hit the mission – well, one of us might live long enough to throw the switches, and bring home the precious Corestuff.' He was obviously relishing teasing out Farr's fear.

Farr tried to bite back. 'Then you should have told me what was going on before. What if something had gone wrong, and I hadn't known what to do?'

Bzya regarded Hosch impassively. 'The boy has a point, Hosch.'

'Anyway,' Farr said, 'it can't take much skill to throw a simple switch . . .'

'Oh, that's not the skill,' Hosch said quietly. 'The skill is in staying alive long enough to do it.'

The Bell lurched alarmingly through the underMantle, unbalanced by the mass of Corestuff clinging to its side. Farr tried to judge their ascent, but he couldn't separate genuine indications of their rise to the light – the sensations in his belly, a lightening of the gloom in the small windows – from optimistic imagination. He gazed anxiously at the bruised-purple glow in the windows, unable to take any of the food Bzya offered him from a small locker set in the hull of the Bell.

The Bell shuddered under a fresh impact. Farr clung to his pole. There was a grinding noise, and the clumsy little craft shuddered to a halt.

Farr resisted the temptation to close his eyes and curl up. *What now? What else can they throw at me?*

He felt Bzya's rough fingertips on his shoulders. 'It's all right, lad. That's a sign that we're nearly home.'

'What was it?'

'That was our berg, scraping against the Spine. We're only a metre or so below Parz itself now.'

Hosch hauled at a lever on the control panel, grunting with the effort; the hum Farr had learned to associate with the currents supplying the Bell's protective magnetic field decreased in intensity. Hosch turned to him, his mood evidently swinging towards its calm, sly pole. 'Your buddy here is half-right. But we aren't safe yet. Not by a long way.'

In fact this was one of the most dangerous parts of the mission. The berg, rattling against the Spine, could easily sever their cables or damage the Spine itself.

'So,' Hosch said silkily, 'one of us has to go outside and do some work.'

'What work?'

'Wrap ropes around the berg. Lash it to the Bell,' Bzya said gently. 'That's all. Stops the berg from shaking loose, and protects the cables from collisions with the Corestuff.'

Hosch was staring at Farr.

Bzya held up his huge hands. 'No,' he said. 'Hosch, you can't be serious. You can't send the boy out there.'

'I've never been more serious,' Hosch said. 'As you've both been telling me, the boy won't last five heartbeats down here unless he learns the trade. And there's only one way to do that, isn't there?'

Bzya made to protest, but Farr stopped him. 'It's all right, Bzya. I'm not afraid. He's probably right, anyway.'

Bzya said, 'Listen to me. If you were not afraid you would be a fool, or dead. Fear keeps your eyecups open and clean.'

'Ropes in that locker,' Hosch said, pointing.

Bzya started to haul out the tightly packed, thick ropes; soon the little cabin seemed filled with the stuff. 'And you,' Hosch snapped at Farr. 'Get the hatch open.'

Farr looked through the window. The Air – if it could be called Air, this deep – was purple, almost Sea-like. He was still, after all, a full metre – a hundred thousand mansheights – below Parz.

He felt the sole of a foot in his back. 'Get on with it,' Hosch growled. 'It won't kill you. Probably.'

Farr put his shoulders to the circular hatch and pushed. It was heavy and stiff, and as he pushed he heard the scraping of the Corestuff hoops binding up the capsule as they slid away.

The hatch burst open, flying out of his reach. The Air outside the Bell was thick and glutinous, and it crowded into the cabin, overwhelming the thinner, clear Air within. The light of the cabin's lamps seemed immediately dimmed.

Farr held his breath, his mouth clamped closed almost of its own accord. There was a pressure on his chest, as if the thicker Air were trying to force itself into his lungs through his skin. With an effort of will he dragged his lips apart. The cloying, purple Air forced its way into his throat; he could feel it on his lips, viscous and bitter. He heaved, expanding his lungs; the stuff burned as it worked through his capillaries.

So, after a brief few heartbeats of struggle, he was embedded in the underMantle. He raised his arms experimentally, flexing his fingers. His movements were unimpaired, but he felt weaker, sluggish. Perhaps the superfluid fraction of this Air was lower than in the true Mantle.

'The hatch,' Bzya said, pointing. 'You'd better retrieve it.' Bzya's voice was obscured, as if he was speaking through a layer of cloth.

Farr nodded. He pushed his way out of the hatchway.

The yellow-purple Air was so thick it barely carried any illumination; it was as if he was suspended in a dark-walled bubble about four mansheights across. The Bell was suspended at the centre of the bubble, a drifting bulk. Beyond it the Spine was a wall, massive and implacable, its upper and lower extremes lost in the misty obscurity of the Air. Looking at the Spine now Farr could see cables of Corestuff wrapped around it and laid out along its length – cables which must provide a magnetic field like the Bell's, to keep the Spine from itself dissolving in the lower underMantle. The Bell's own cables snaked up and out of sight towards the world of the upper Mantle, a world which seemed impossibly distant to Farr.

The loose hatch was a short distance from him. He Waved to it easily enough, although the Air in which he was embedded was a cloying presence around him. He caught the hatch and returned it briskly to Bzya.

'Now the berg,' Hosch called. 'Can you see it?'

Farr looked. There was a shape, lumpen, lodged between the Bell and the Spine. It was half a mansheight long, dark and irregular, like a growth on the clean, artificial lines of the Bell.

'Don't I need the ropes?'

'Go and inspect the berg first,' Hosch called. 'See if it's done us any damage.'

He took deep breaths of the stale Air and flexed his legs. It would take only a few strokes to Wave to the lump of Corestuff.

As he neared, he saw that the berg's surface was made rough by small pits and escarpments. It was hard to imagine that this was the material that formed the gleaming hoops around the Bell, or the City's anchor-bands, or the fine inlays in Surfboards. He was within an arm's length of the berg, still Waving smoothly . . . If he lived long enough, he would like to see the workshops – the foundries, Bzya called them – where the transformation of this stuff took place . . .

Invisible hands grabbed his chest and legs, yanking him sideways. He found himself tumbling head over heels away from the Bell. He cried out. He scrabbled at the Air but could gain no purchase, and his legs thrashed at the emptiness in a futile effort to Wave.

Trembling, he paddled at the Air, trying to still his roll. Hosch was laughing at him, he realized; and Bzya, too, seemed to be having trouble suppressing a smile.

Just another little game, then; another test for the new boy.

He closed his eyes, willing the trembling of his limbs to still. He tried to think. *Invisible hands?* Only a magfield could have jolted him like that – the Bell's protective magfield. And of course he'd been knocked sideways; that was the way fields affected moving charged objects, like his body. That was why it was necessary, when Waving, to move legs and arms *across* the flux lines of the Magfield to generate forward motion.

So the Bell's own magfield shell had thrown him. Big joke.

Logue would probably have told him off for not anticipating this, he realized. Laughed at him as well, to drive home the point.

Farr's fear turned to anger. He looked forward to the day when he would no longer have so much to learn . . . and he could maybe administer a few lessons of his own.

His self-control returning, Farr began to make his clumsy way back to the Bell. 'Give me the ropes,' he said.

12

The huge lumber caravan was visible for many days before it reached Qos Frenk's ceiling-farm.

Dura, descending from a wheat-field at the end of a shift, watched the caravan's approach absently. It was a trace of darkness on the curving horizon, a trail of tree trunks toiling through the vortex lines from the wild forests on the upflux fringe of the hinterland, on its way to the City at the furthest downflux. She wasn't too interested. The hinterland sky, even this far from Parz, was never empty of traffic. The caravan would pass in a couple of days, and that would be that.

But this caravan didn't go by so quickly. As time wore on it continued to grow in her vision, and Dura slowly came to appreciate the caravan's true scale, and the extent to which distance and perspective had fooled her. The train of severed tree trunks, stretched along the vortex lines, must have extended for more than a centimetre. And it was only when the caravan approached its nearest point to the farm that Dura could make out people travelling with the caravan – men and women Waving along the lengths of the trunks, or tending the teams of Air-pigs scattered along the trunks' lengths, utterly dwarfed by the scale of the caravan itself.

Another shift wore away. Rubbing arms and shoulders left stiff by a long day's crop-tending, Dura slung her Air-tank over her shoulder and Waved slowly towards the refectory.

Rauc came up to her. Dura studied her curiously. Rauc had become something of a friend to Dura – as much of a friend as she had made here, anyway – but today the slim little coolie seemed different. Distracted, somehow. Although Rauc too had just finished a shift, she'd already changed into a clean smock and combed her hair free of dirt and wheat-chaff. The smile on her thin, perpetually tired face was nervous.

'Rauc? Is something wrong?'

'No. No, not at all.' Rauc's small feet twisted together in the Air. 'Dura, have you got any plans for your off-shift?'

Dura laughed. 'To eat. To sleep. Why?'

'Come with me to the caravan.'

'What?'

'The lumber caravan.' Rauc pointed down beneath her feet, to where the caravan toiled impressively across the sky. 'It wouldn't take us long to Wave down there.'

Dura tried to conceal her reluctance. *No thanks. I've already seen enough of the City, the hinterland, of new people, to last me a lifetime.* She thought with a mild longing of the little nest she'd been able to establish for herself on the fringe of the farm – just a cocoon, and her little cache of personal belongings, suspended in the open Air, away from the cramped dormitories favoured by the rest of the coolies. 'Maybe another time, Rauc. Thanks, but . . .'

Rauc looked unreasonably disappointed. 'But the caravans only pass about once a year. And Brow can't always arrange an assignment to the right caravan; if we're unlucky he ends up centimetres away from the farm when he passes this latitude, and . . .'

'Brow?' Rauc had mentioned the name before. 'Your husband? Your husband's with this caravan?'

'He'll be expecting me.' Rauc reached out and took Dura's hands. 'Come with me. Brow's never met an upfluxer before.'

Dura squeezed her hands. 'Well, I've never met a lumber-jack. Rauc, is this the only time you get to see your husband? Are you sure you want me along?'

'I wouldn't ask otherwise. It will make it special.'

Dura felt honoured, and she said so. She considered the distance to the caravan. 'Will we have the time to get there and back, all in a single off-shift? Maybe we ought to go to Leeh and postpone our next shift – do a double.'

Rauc grinned. 'I've already fixed it. Come on; find yourself something clean to wear, and we'll go. Why don't you bring your stuff from the upflux? Your knife and your ropes . . .'

Rauc followed Dura to her sleeping-nest, talking excitedly the whole way.

*

The two women dropped out of the ceiling-farm and descended lightly into the Mantle.

Dura dipped forward, extending her arms towards the caravan, and began to thrust with her legs. As she Waved she was still wondering if this was a good idea – her legs and arms still ached from her long shift – but after some time the steady, easy exercise seemed to work the pains from her muscles and joints, and she found herself relishing the comfortable, natural motion across the Magfield – so different from the cramped awkwardness of her work in the fields, with her head buried in an Air-mask, her arms straining above her head, her fingers thrust into the roots of some recalcitrant mutant plant.

The caravan spread out across the sky before her. It was a chain of Crust-tree trunks stripped of roots, branches and leaves; the trunks were bound together in sets of two or three by lengths of rope, and the sets were connected by more links of strong plaited rope. Dura had to swivel her head to see the leading and trailing ends of the chain of trunks, which dwindled with perspective among the converging vortex lines; in fact, she mused, the whole caravan was like a wooden facsimile of a vortex line.

Two humans hung in the Air some distance from the caravan. They seemed to be waiting for Rauc and Dura; as the women approached they called something and set off through the Air to greet them. It was a man and a woman, Dura saw. They were both around the same age as Rauc and Dura, and they wore identical, practical-looking loose vests equipped with dozens of pockets from which bits of rope and tools protruded.

Rauc rushed forward and embraced the man. Dura and the lumberjack woman hung back, waiting awkwardly. The woman was slim, strong-looking, with tough-looking, weathered skin; she – and the man, evidently Rauc's husband Brow – looked much more like upfluxers than any hinterland or City folk Dura had met up to now.

Rauc and Brow broke their embrace, but they stayed close with their arms linked together. Rauc pulled Brow towards Dura. 'Brow, here's a friend from the farm. Dura. She's an upfluxer . . .'

Brow turned to Dura with a look of surprised interest; his gaze flickered over her. He resembled Rauc quite closely. His body was lean, strong-looking under its vest, and his narrow face was kindly. 'An upfluxer? How do you come to be working on a ceiling-farm?'

Dura forced herself to smile. 'It's a long story.'

Rauc squeezed Brow's arm. 'She can tell you later.'

Brow rubbed his nose, still staring at Dura. 'We see upfluxers sometimes. In the distance. When we're working in the far upflux, right at the edge of the hinterland. You see, the further upflux you go towards the wild forests, the better the trees grow. But . . .' He stopped, embarrassed.

'But the more dangerous it gets?' Dura maintained her smile, determined for once to be tolerant. 'Well, don't worry. I don't bite.'

They laughed, but it was forced.

Rauc introduced the woman with Brow. She was called Kae, and she and Rauc embraced. Dura observed them curiously, trying to make sense of their relationship. There was a stiffness between Rauc and Kae, a wariness; and yet their embrace seemed genuine – as if on some level, beneath the surface strain, they shared a basic sympathy for each other.

Brow tugged at Rauc. 'Come and see the others; they've missed you. We're going to eat shortly.' He glanced at Dura. 'Will you join us?'

The woman Kae approached Dura with brisk friendliness. 'Dura, let's leave these two alone for a while. I'll show you around the caravan . . . I don't suppose you've met people like us before . . .'

Dura and Kae Waved side by side along the length of the caravan. Kae pointed out features of the caravan and described how it worked in a brisk, matter-of-fact way, her talk laced with endless references to Dura's assumed ignorance. Dura had long since grown tired of being treated as an amusing freak by these Parz folk, but – for today – she bit back the acid replies which seemed to come so easily to her. This woman, Kae, didn't mean any harm; she was simply trying to be kind to a stranger.

Maybe I'm learning to look beneath the surface of people, Dura

166

wondered. *Not to react to trivia.* She smiled at herself. Maybe she was growing up at last.

The chain of trunks slid through the Air at about half an easy Waving speed. There were teams of harnessed Air-pigs, their harness sets fixed – not to Air-cars – but to the rope links in the chain of trees. The pigs squealed and snorted as they hauled at their restraints of leather. Humans, some of them children, tended the animals. The pigs were fed bowls of mashed-up Crust-tree leaf, and their harnesses were endlessly adjusted to keep the teams hauling in the same direction, along the long line of trunks.

People hailed Kae as she passed, and they glanced curiously at Dura. Dura guessed there must be a hundred people travelling with this caravan.

The women paused to watch one team being broken up. The animals were released from their harnesses, but they were still restrained by ropes fixed to pierced fins. The animals were led away to be tied up in another part of the caravan to rest, while a fresh team was fixed into place.

Dura frowned at this. 'Wouldn't it be easier to stop the caravan, rather than try to change the pigs over in flight?'

Kae laughed. 'Hardly. Dura, when the caravan is assembled, back on the edge of the upflux, it takes several days, usually, for the pig-teams to haul it up to speed. And once this mass of wood is moving, it's much easier to maintain its motion than to keep stopping and starting it. Do you see?'

Dura sighed inwardly. 'I know what momentum is. So you don't even stop when you sleep?'

'We sleep in shifts. We sleep tied up to nets and cocoons fixed to the trunks themselves.' Kae pointed to the nearest pig-team. 'We rotate the pigs in flight. It isn't so difficult to steer a caravan; all you have to do is follow the vortex lines downflux until you get to the South Pole . . . Dura, a caravan like this never stops moving, once it sets off from the edge of the hinterland. Not until it's within sight of Parz itself. Then the pig-teams are turned around, and the caravan's broken up to be taken into the City.'

Dura tried to envisage the distance from the upflux to Parz. 'But at this speed it must take months to reach the City.'

'A full year, generally.'

'A year?' Dura frowned. 'But how can the City wait that long for lumber?'

'It can't. But it doesn't have to.' Kae was smiling, but there didn't seem to be any impatience in her tone at Dura's slowness. 'At any time, there's a whole stream of caravans like this, heading for the City from all around the circumference of the hinterland. From the point of view of Parz there's a steady flow of the wood it needs.'

'Rauc knew on exactly which day to come down to the caravan. In fact, you and Brow were waiting to greet us.'

'Yes. We were on time. We always are, Dura; all the caravans are, right across the hinterland. It's all carefully planned.'

Dura thought of dozens, hundreds perhaps, of caravans like this, endlessly converging on Parz with their precious lumber . . . and all *on time*. She felt awed at the idea of humans being able to plan and act systematically on such a scale, and with such precision.

They moved on along the length of the caravan. In some places the trunks had been opened up to expose the green glow of the wood's nuclear-burning core. Humans moved around the glowing spots and circles, purposeful and busy. There were nets and lengths of rope trailing from the trunks, and Dura saw sleep cocoons, tools, clothes, food bales tucked into the nets. In one place there was a little clutch of infants and small children, safely confined inside a fine-meshed net.

'Why,' she said, 'the caravan's like a little City in itself. A City on the move. There are whole families here.'

'That's right.' Kae smiled, a little sadly. 'But the difference is, it's a City that will be broken up in another few months, when we get to Parz. And we'll be shipped back to the hinterland in cars, to start work on another.'

They passed another netful of sleeping children.

Dura asked gently, 'Why doesn't Rauc travel with the caravan? With Brow?'

Kae stiffened slightly. 'Because she gets better pay where she is, doing coolie-work for Qos Frenk. They have a kid. Did she tell you? She and Brow are having her put through school in Parz itself. They have to work like this, to afford the fees.'

Dura let herself drift to a stop in the Air. 'So Rauc is on a ceiling-farm in the hinterland, her child is in that wooden box at the Pole, and Brow is lost somewhere in the upflux with the lumber caravans. And if they're lucky they meet – what? once a year?' She thought of the Mixxaxes, also constrained to spend so much of their time apart, and for much the same motives. 'What kind of life is that, Kae?'

Kae drew away. 'You sound as if you disapprove, Dura.' She waved a hand. 'Of all of this. The way we live our lives. Well, we can't all live as toy savages in the upflux, you know.' She bit her lip, but pressed on. 'This is the way things are. Rauc and Brow are doing the best they can, for their daughter. And if you want to know how they feel about so much separation, you should ask them.'

Dura said nothing.

'Life is complex for us – more than you can imagine, perhaps. We all have to make compromises.'

'Really? And what's your compromise, Kae?'

Kae's eyes narrowed. 'Come on,' she said. 'Let's find the others. It must be time to eat.'

They worked their way back along the complicated linear community in stiff silence.

A dozen people had gathered, close to the trunk of one of the great severed trees at the heart of the caravan. A Wheel design had been cut into the trunk: neat, five-spoked, large enough to curve around the trunk's cylindrical form. Small bowls of food had been jammed into the glowing trenches of the design.

The people anchored themselves to the trunk itself, or to ropes and sections of net dangling from the trunk, arranging themselves around the glow of the nuclear fire. Occasionally one of them reached into the fire and drew out a bowl.

Dura joined the group a little nervously. But she was greeted by neutral, even friendly nods. With their nomadic lives, criss-crossing the hinterland, these caravanners must be as used to accepting strangers as anyone in the huge, sprawling hinterland around Parz.

She found a short length of rope and wrapped it around her arm. The rope, leading to the tree trunk, hauled at her with a steady pressure. So, she realized, she had become part of the caravan, bound to it and swept along by its immense momentum. She glanced around at the group. Their faces, their relaxed bodies in their practical vests, formed a rough hemispherical shell over the exposed wood core. The green glow underlit their faces and limbs and cast soft light into their eyecups. Dura felt comfortable – accepted here – and she drifted closer to the warmth of the nuclear fire.

She spotted Rauc and Brow, huddled together on the far side of the little group. Rauc waved briefly to her, but quickly returned her attention to her husband. Glancing around discreetly, Dura saw that most of the party had separated out into couples, bonded loosely by conversation. Alone, she turned to stare into the steady glow of the fire.

There was a tap on her arm. She turned. Kae had settled into place next to her. She was smiling. 'Will you eat?'

Dura couldn't help but glance around surreptitiously. There seemed to be no one with Kae, no partner. There was no sign of Kae's earlier flash of hostility – she had the impression that there was a core of deep unhappiness in Kae, hidden not far beneath the surface. She smiled back, eager to show good grace. 'Thanks. I will.'

Kae reached towards the fire-trenches cut into the wood. She drew out one of the bowls embedded there, taking care to keep her fingers away from the hot wood itself. The bowl was a small globe carved of wood, and it held food, a dark brown, irregular mass. She held the bowl out to Dura.

Dura reached into the bowl and poked at the food tentatively. It was hot to the touch. She took hold of it and drew it out. The surface was furry, but the furs were singed to a crisp, and they crackled as she squeezed.

She looked at Kae doubtfully. 'What is it?'

'Try it first.' Kae looked sly in the green underglow.

Dura picked at the fur. 'The whole thing?'

'Just bite into it.'

Dura shrugged, raised the lump briskly, opened her mouth wide and bit into the fur. The surface was elastic, difficult to pierce with her teeth, and the furs tickled the roof of her mouth. Then the skin broke, and bits of hot, sticky meat spurted over her mouth and chin. She spluttered, but she wiped her face and swallowed. The stuff was rich, warm, meaty. She took a bite from the skin and chewed it slowly. It was tough and without much flavour. Then she sucked at the

170

remaining meat inside the shell. There was a hard inner core which she discarded.

'It's good,' she said at last. 'What is it?'

Kae let the empty bowl hang in the Air; she poked at it with her forefinger and watched it roll in the Air. 'Spin-spider egg,' she said. 'I knew you wouldn't recognize it. But it's the only way to eat it. It's actually a delicacy, in some parts of the hinterland. There's even a community on the edge of the wild forest who cultivate spiders, to get the eggs. Very dangerous, but very profitable. But you have to know how to treat the eggs, to bring out the flavour.'

'I don't think I would have recognized this as a spider egg at all.'

'It has to be collected when freshly laid – when the young spider hasn't yet formed, and there's just a sort of mush inside the egg. The hard part in the centre is the basis of the creature's exoskeleton; the young spider grows into its skeleton, consuming the nutrient.'

'Thanks for telling me,' Dura said drily.

Kae laughed, and opened up a sack at her waist. She drew out a slice of beercake. 'Here; have some of this. In Parz, there's a good market for exotic deep-hinterland produce like that. We make a good side-profit from it. Now. How about some Air-pig meat?'

'All right. Please. And then you can tell me how you came to join these lumber caravans.'

'Only if you tell me how you ended up here, so far from the upflux . . .'

With food warm inside her, and with the exhilarating buzz of beercake filling her head, Dura told Kae her tangled story; and a little later, in the steady glow of the nuclear-fire Wheel, she repeated her tale for the rest of the lumberjacks, who listened intently.

The food globes, nestling in the fire trenches, were finished. The conversation gradually subsided, and Dura sensed that the gathering was coming to an end.

Rauc drew her hand from her husband's, and pulled forward, alone, into the centre of the little group. She faced the Wheel cut into the tree trunk in silence.

The last trickles of conversation died. Dura watched, puzzled. The atmosphere was changing – becoming more solemn, sadder. The lumberjacks drew away from each other, their postures stiffening in the Air. Dura glanced at Kae's face. The lumberjack's eyecups were wide, illuminated by the fire-glow, fixed on Rauc.

Slowly Rauc began to speak. Her words consisted of names – all of them unknown to Dura – recited in a steady monotone. Rauc's voice was tired, quiet, but it seemed to enfold the intent gathering. Dura listened to the lulling, rhythmic chant of names as it went on, for heartbeat after heartbeat, read evenly by Rauc to the great Wheel carved into the wood.

These were the names of victims, Dura realized slowly. Victims of what? Of cruelty, of disease, of starvation, of accident; they were the names of the dead, remembered now in this simple ceremonial.

Some of the names must go back generations, she thought, their deaths so ancient that all details had been forgotten. But the names remained, preserved by this gentle, graceful Wheel cult.

And people who lived in the sky could have no other memorial than words.

At last the list came to a close. Rauc hung in the Air before the fading glow of the Wheel trenches, her face empty. Then she stirred and looked around at the faces watching her, as if waking up. She Waved back to her husband.

The group broke up. Brow enfolded his wife in his arms and led her away. All around the group, couples bid farewells and drifted off.

Dura observed Kae surreptitiously. The woman was watching Brow and Rauc, her expression blank. She became aware of Dura. She smiled, but her voice sounded strained. 'I've the feeling you're judging me again.'

'No. But I think I understand your compromises now.'

Kae shrugged. 'We're together, Brow and I, for most of the time. Rauc knows it, and has to live with that. But Brow – *loves* – Rauc. This day with her is worth a hundred with me. And I have to live with *that*. We all have to compromise, Dura. Even you.'

172

Dura thought of Esk, long dead now, and a similar painful triangle. 'Yes,' she said. 'We all have to compromise.'

Kae offered her a place to sleep, somewhere in the tangle of nets and ropes that comprised this strange, linear City. Dura refused, smiling.

She said farewell to Kae. The lumberjack nodded, and they regarded each other with a strange, calm understanding.

Dura pushed away from the trunk and kicked at the Air, Waving for the ceiling-farm and her secure, private little nest.

The caravan spread out beneath her, Wheel-shaped fires burning in a dozen places.

13

Accompanied by a nervous-looking nurse from the Hospital of the Common Good, the injured old upfluxer diffidently entered the Palace Garden. When Muub spotted him he beckoned to the nurse – over the heads of curious courtiers – that she should bring the upfluxer to join him at the Fount. Then he turned back to the slow ballet of the superfluid fountain.

The Garden was a crown perched atop Parz City, an expensive setting for the Palace of the City Committee. The Garden had been established generations before by one of the predecessors of Hork IV. But it had been the particular genius of the current Chair, and his fascination for the natural world around him, that had made this place into the wonder it was. Now it was a lavish park, with exotic plants and animals from all around the Mantle brought together in an orderly, tasteful display. The low – but extravagant – buildings which made up the Palace itself were studded around the Park, gleaming like Corestuff jewels set in rich cloth. Courtiers drifted through the Garden in little knots, huddling like groups of brightly coloured animals.

Muub was no lover of the great outdoors, but he relished the Garden. He tilted back his stiff neck, looking up into the yellow-gold Air. To be here beneath the arching, sparkling vortex lines of the Pole – and yet securely surrounded by the works of man – was a fulfilling, refreshing experience. It seemed to strengthen his orderly heart that the Garden was an artifact, a museum of tamed nature – but an artifact which stretched for no less than a square centimetre around him . . . The Garden was enough to make one believe that man was capable of any achievement.

He ran a discreet doctor's eye over the approaching upfluxer. Adda was recovering well but he could still barely move without assistance. Both his lower legs were encased in splints, and his chest was swathed in bandages; a cast of carved wood enclosed his right shoulder. His head, too, was a mass of strapped-up cloth, and an eye-leech patiently fed in the corner of the old fellow's only working eye.

'I'm glad you could join me,' Muub greeted him with a professional smile. 'I wanted to talk to you.'

Adda glowered past his leech at Muub's shaved head, his finery. 'Why? Who or what are you?'

Muub allowed himself a heartbeat's cold silence. 'My name is Muub. I am Physician to the Committee... and Administrator of the Hospital of the Common Good, where your injuries have been treated.' He decided to go on the offensive. 'Sir, we met before, when you were first carried into the Hospital by one of our citizens. On that occasion – though I don't expect you to remember – you told me to "bugger off". Well, I failed to accept that invitation, choosing instead to have you treated. I have asked you to view the Garden today as my guest, as a friendly gesture to one who is new to Parz and who is alone here. But frankly, if you're not prepared to be courteous then you are free to depart.'

'Oh, I'll behave,' Adda grumbled. 'Though I'll not swallow the pretence that you've done me any sort of favour by treating my injuries. I know very well that you're exacting a handsome price from the labour of Dura and Farr.'

Muub frowned. 'Ah, your companions from upflux. Yes, I understand they have found indentures.'

'Slave labour,' Adda hissed.

Muub made himself relax. Anyone who could survive at the court of Hork IV could put up with a little goading from an eyeless old fool from the upflux. 'I'll not let you needle me, Adda. I've invited you here to enjoy the Garden – the spectacle – and I fully intend that that is how we will spend the day.'

Adda held his stare for a few moments; but he did not pursue the discussion, and turned his head to view the Fount.

The superfluid fountain was the centrepiece of the Garden. It was based on a clearwood cylinder twenty microns across, fixed to a tall, thin pedestal. Inside the cylinder hovered a rough ball of gas, stained purple-blue, quivering slowly. The cylinder – fabulously expensive in itself, of course – was girdled by five hoops of polished Corestuff, and it bristled with poles which protruded from its surface. Barrels – boxes of wood embossed with stylized carvings of the heads of Hork IV and his predecessors – were fixed to the ends of the poles inside the cylinder.

Beautiful young aerobats – male and female, all naked – Waved spectacularly through the Air around the cylinder, working its elaborate mechanisms. The electric blue of the vortex lines cast shimmering highlights from the clearwood, and the soft, perfect skin of the aerobats glowed with golden Air-light.

The upfluxer, Adda, made a disgusting noise through his nose. 'You brought me here to see this?'

Muub smiled. 'I wouldn't expect you to understand what you're seeing.'

Adda scowled, his hostility evident. 'Then tell me.'

'Superfluidity.' Muub pointed. 'The cylinder contains a low-pressure region. There's hardly any Air in there, I mean . . . except for the sphere in the centre. That's just Air, but stained blue so you can see it. The hoops around the cylinder, there, are generating a localized magnetic field. Do you understand me? Like the Magfield, but artificial. Controllable. The magnetic field keeps the cylinder from being crushed by the pressure of the Air outside. And it's designed to keep the little Air inside the cylinder in that ball at the centre.'

'So what?'

'So we can view the Air – within which we are ordinarily immersed – from the outside, as it were.

'Adda, Air is a neutron superfluid – a quite extraordinary substance which, were inhabitants of some other world to discover it, would seem miraculous. Quantized circulation – the phenomena which causes all the spin in the Air to collect into vortex lines – is only one aspect. Watch, now, as the vessels are lowered and raised from the sphere of Air.'

A handsome young aerobat – a girl with blue-dyed hair – grasped one of the poles protruding from the cylinder and pushed it through the clearwood wall. The base of the ornate barrel at its far end dipped into the sphere of blue Air. The barrel wasn't completely immersed; the girl held the barrel still so that its rim protruded from the surface of the Air by a good two or three microns.

Blue-stained Air visibly crawled up the sides of the box and over the lip, pooling inside. It was like watching a living creature, Muub thought, fascinated and charmed as always by the spectacle.

When the box had filled itself to the level of the rest of the sphere, the aerobat drew it slowly out of the sphere and brought it to rest again, so that its base was placed perhaps five microns above the surface. Now the blue Air slid over the sides and, in a thin stream which poured from the base of the vessel, returned eagerly to the central sphere.

The aerobat troupe maintained this display at all hours of the day, at quite remarkable expense. Adda watched the cycle through a couple of times, his good eye empty of expression.

Muub watched him surreptitiously, then shook his head. 'Don't you have any interest in this? Even your eye-leech is showing more awareness, man!' He felt driven, absurdly, to justify the display. 'The Fount is demonstrating superfluidity. When the vessel is lowered into the pool, a thin layer of the fluid is adsorbed onto the vessel's surface. And the Air uses that fine layer – just a few neutrons thick – to gain access to the interior of the vessel. When the vessel's withdrawn the Air uses the same channel to return to the main bulk, the sphere. Quite remarkable.

'The hoops maintain a slight magnetic gradient from the geometric centre of the cylinder. That gradient restricts the residual Air to that sphere at the centre . . . and it is the resulting difference in electromagnetic potential energy which drives the cycle of the fountain. And . . .'

'Riveting,' Adda said drily.

Muub bit back a sharp comment. 'Well, I know you people have different priorities in life. Let's view the rest of the Garden . . . perhaps some of it will remind you of the world you have left behind. I'm curious as to how you lived, actually.'

'We *upfluxers*?' Adda asked acidly.

Muub replied smoothly, 'You Human Beings. For example, superfluidity . . . Have you retained much knowledge of such matters?'

Adda said, 'Much of the lore absorbed by our children is practical and everyday . . . how to repair a net; how to keep yourself clean; how to turn the battered corpse of an Air-pig into a meal, a garment, a source of weapons, a length of rope.'

Muub felt himself shudder delicately.

'But knowledge is our common heritage, City man,' Adda murmured. 'We would scarcely allow you to rob us of that, as you robbed us of our place here ten generations ago.'

Turning, Muub led Adda slowly away from the Fount. Beside the youthful grace of the aerobats, Adda's ungainly stiffness was laughable – and yet heartbreaking, Muub thought. They passed through one of Hork's experimental ceiling-farm areas. Here a new strain of wheat – tall and fat-stemmed – thrust from a simulated section of Crust-forest root-ceiling.

'Tell me, Adda. What are your plans now?'

'Why should you care?'

'I'm curious.'

Adda was silent for a while; then, grudgingly, he replied: 'I'm going to go back. Back to the upflux. What else?'

'And how do you propose to achieve that?'

'I'll damn well Wave there if I have to,' Adda growled. 'If I can't get one of your *citizens* to take me home in one of those pig-drawn cars you have.'

Muub was tempted to mock. He tried to summon up sympathy, to put himself in Adda's situation – alone and far from home in a place he must find frighteningly strange, despite his bravado. 'My friend,' he said evenly, 'with all respect to the skills of my staff in the Common Good, and to the remarkable progress you are making . . . I have to say it will be a long time before you are fit for such a journey. Even by car, the trek would kill you.'

Adda snarled. 'I'll take my chance.'

'And if you made it home you'd never be as strong as you were, frankly. Your pneumatic system has been weakened to well below its nominal level.'

Adda's response, when it came, seemed doubtful. 'I couldn't hunt?'

'No.' Muub shook his head firmly. 'Even if you were able to Wave fast enough to creep up on, let us say, an aged and unfit

Air-pig . . .' – that won a slight smile from the upfluxer – 'even so, you could never survive the low pressures, the thin Air of the upper Mantle. You see, you would be a burden on your people if you returned. I'm sorry.'

Adda's anger was apparently directed inwards now. 'I will not be a burden. I wanted to die, after my injury. You did not allow me to die.'

'It was the choice of your companions. *They* did not allow you to die; they sold their labour to pay for your continued health. Adda, you owe it to them to maximize the usefulness of your new life.'

Adda shook his head stiffly, the bandaging rustling at his neck. 'I cannot return home. But I have nothing here.'

'Perhaps you could find work. Anything you could earn would reduce the burden on your friends.' . . . And help besides, Muub forbore to add, to pay for Adda's own food and shelter once his medical treatment was concluded.

'What could I do? Do you hunt here? I can't see myself being much use stalking blades of mutated grass.'

They had come now to a simulation of the wild Crust-forest. Dwarf Crust-trees – slender whips no taller than a mansheight – thrust out of the roof of Parz. A clutch of young ray, shackled to the roof surface by short lengths of rope, snapped at them as they passed. Muub glanced at Adda, curious about the old man's reaction to this toy forest. But Adda had turned his face up to the vortex lines swooping over the City; his good eye was half-closed, as if he were peering at something, and the leech crawled, ignored, over his face.

Muub hesitated. 'When I first encountered you, you were swaddled in makeshift bandages. And you had splints . . . Do you remember? The splints seemed actually to be spears, of varying lengths and thicknesses. All decorated with fine engravings.'

'What of it? Are you suggesting I could get a price for them here? I thought your people, your *Guards*, were well enough equipped with their bows and whips.'

'Indeed. No, we do not need your weapons . . . as *weapons*. But as artifacts the spears have a certain – novelty.' Muub sought the right words. 'A kind of primitive artistry that is really rather appealing. Adda, I suspect you could get a decent price for your artifacts, especially from collectors of primitive materiel. And if, by chance, you were capable of producing more . . .'

There was an odd change in the quality of light around them. Muub glanced around, half-expecting to find that they had fallen into the shadow of an Air-car; but the sky was empty, save for the vortex lines. Still the feeling of change persisted, though, unsettling Muub; he pulled his robe closer around him.

Adda laughed. 'I'd rather die than whore myself.'

Muub opened his mouth, shaping a reply. *That may be the choice, old man* . . . But now there was some sort of disturbance among the courtiers around them. No longer drifting in their intense little knots of intrigue, the courtiers were gathering together as if for comfort, pointing at the sky. 'I wonder what's wrong. They seem scared.'

'Look up,' Adda said drily. 'Perhaps that has something to do with it.'

Muub looked into the old man's sour, battered face, and then lifted his head to the open Air.

The flux lines were moving. They were surging upwards, away from the City, rising like huge knife-blades towards the Crust.

'*Glitch*,' Adda said, his voice tight. 'Another one. And a bad one. Muub, you must do what you can to protect your people.'

'Is the City in danger?'

'I don't know. Perhaps not. But those in the ceiling-farms certainly are . . .'

Muub, in the last moment before rushing to his duties, found time to remember that Adda's own people too were exposed to all of this, lost somewhere in the sky.

The Air above him seemed to shimmer; somewhere a courtier screamed.

It was Rauc who first noticed the change in the sky.

Dura and Rauc were working together in a corner of Qos Frenk's ceiling-farm. Dura was wearing the mandatory Air-tank, but she wore the veil pushed back from her face; and the heavy wooden tank thumped against her back as she worked.

She had pushed her head and shoulders high into the stems of wheat, so that she was surrounded by a bottomless cage of the yellow-gold plants. She reached above her head with both hands, burrowing with her fingers among the roots of the wheat. Stems scratched her bare arms. Here was another sapling; it felt warm and soft, undeniably a living thing, a thin thread of heavy-nuclei material pulsing along its axis. Young Crust-trees were the most persistent danger to Frenk's crop, springing up endlessly despite continual weeding. The saplings – thinner than a finger's width – were difficult to see, but easy to pick out from among the wheat-stems by touch. She allowed her fingers to track along the sapling's length further up into the shadows of the wheat. She probed at its roots, which snaked up into the tangle of roots and plants which comprised the forest ceiling, and patiently prised them out.

It was dull, mindless work, but not without a certain satisfaction: she enjoyed the feel of the plants in her fingers, and relished deploying the simple skills she was learning. Maybe in some other life she might have been a good farmer, she thought. She liked the orderliness of the farm – although not the pressure of other people – and the work was simple enough to leave her mind free to wander, to think of Farr, of the upflux, and . . .

Rauc half-laughed. 'Look at that. Dura, look . . . How strange.'

Vaguely irritated at this irruption into her daydream, Dura dropped down from the inverted field. Emerging into the clear Air, she rubbed her hands free of dust. 'What is it?'

Rauc hovered in the Air, Waving gently; she pointed downwards. 'Look at the vortex lines. Have you ever seen them behave like that before?'

Vortex lines, acting strangely?

Dura snapped her head downwards and raked her gaze across the sky.

The vortex lines were *shimmering* – infested with so many small instabilities that it was difficult to see the lines themselves. At the limit of vision Dura could just make out individual ripples racing along the lines, like small, scurrying animals. And the lines were exploding upwards, out of the

Mantle and towards the Crust. Towards the farm. Towards her.

All of the lines were moving, as deep into the sky as she could see; the parallel ranks of them hurtled evenly out towards her.

There was something else, too: a dark shape far away, at the edge of her peripheral vision; it scored the yellow horizon with a pencil of blue-white light.

'Rauc,' she said. 'We have to move.'

Rauc looked up at her, the thin, tired face beneath its veiled hat registering unconcern. 'Why? What's wrong?'

Dura brushed the hat from her head, impatiently shrugging off the straps of her Air-tank. 'Give me your hand.'

'But why . . .'

'It's a Glitch. And if we don't move now we'll be killed. Give me your hand. Now!'

Rauc's mouth opened wide. Dura saw shock in her expression, but no fear yet. Well, there would be time enough for that. She grabbed Rauc's hand; the labourer's palm was toughened by her work but the hand was cool, free of the heat of terror. She kicked at the Magfield with both legs, Waving downwards, away from the Crust and towards the approaching flux lines. At first Rauc was dead inertia behind her; but after a few strokes Rauc, too, began to Wave.

When the Star suffered a Glitch the Mantle could not sustain its even, gently slowing pattern of rotation. The superfluid Air tried to expel the excess rotation from its bulk by pushing the arrays of vortex lines – lines of quantized vorticity – out towards the Crust. And the lines themselves suffered instabilities, and could break down . . .

The women dropped into the racing forest of vortex lines. The lines were usually about ten mansheights apart, so – in normal times – they were easy to avoid. But now, at the birth of this spin storm, they were already rising faster than a Human Being could Wave. The vortex lines fizzed past the women, sparkling electric blue. Instabilities the size of a fist raced along them, colliding, merging, collapsing.

Rauc whimpered. Unwelcome images of the last Glitch, of Esk imploding around the rogue vortex line, crowded Dura's head. She concentrated on the buffeting of the Air against her bare skin, the thin, unnatural taste of it on her lips, the deadly sparkle of the vortex lines. *Now* was all that mattered – now, and surviving into the future through this moment.

The vortex lines were growing denser as they crowded towards the Crust, seeking an impossible escape from the Star. It was becoming harder to dodge the lines as they swept past her like infinite blades; she was forced to twist backwards and forwards, slithering between lines. The instabilities were becoming more prominent, too; now ripples almost a mansheight high were marching along the soaring lines, deepening and quickening as they passed. There was a terrible beauty in the way the complex waveforms sucked energy from the vortex lines and surged forwards. The Air was filled with the deafening, deadening heat-roar of the lines.

Soon Dura's arms and legs, already stiff from a long shift, were aching, and the Air seemed to scrape through her lungs and capillaries. But now, as they penetrated the rushing vortex forest and moved deeper into the Mantle, the lines were starting to thin out. Dura, gratefully, looked down and saw that they were approaching a volume where the lines – though still cutting the Air with preternatural speed – were spaced at about their normal density. Further in still the Air seemed almost clear of lines, temporarily purged of its vorticity.

Dura released Rauc's hand and risked a look back.

The vortex lines soared upwards into the Crust, slicing through nuclear matter and embedding themselves amid the complex nuclei of the Crust material. As they entered the forest ceiling the lines thrashed with instabilities, sending bits of broken matter flying into the Air. The lines were tearing apart Qos Frenk's ceiling-farm. The crops she had tended only heartbeats earlier were now uprooted, fat wheat-stems scattered in the Air. Ironically Dura could see Crust-tree saplings, anchored by their deeper roots to the forest ceiling, surviving the spin storm where the mutated grass could not.

Further away the buildings at the heart of Frenk's farm had been torn loose of their moorings to the Crust ceiling; one of them exploded into a shower of wood splinters. Coolies and supervisors were emerging from the fields and buildings, all over the farm. They looked like a cloud of ungainly insects, dropping from the fields towards the hurtling spin lines. Even through the storm Dura could hear their shouts and cries; she wondered if the voice of Qos Frenk himself were among them. Some people squirmed desperately into the lethal rain of vorticity, as Dura and Rauc had done; but most had left it too late. Unable to squeeze through the barrage of twisting lines they were forced to turn back, to climb up towards the Crust.

But there was no haven there.

Dura saw a woman, her Air-mask still in place over her face, pull herself up into the wheat, as if burrowing into the Crust. When the vortex lines struck, her body folded around the lines, backwards, her arms and legs outstretched. The woman's cries rose, thin and clear, before cutting off sharply.

Dura concentrated on the light-smell of the disturbed Air, its sharp presence in her nostrils and on her palate and lips. She wasn't out of danger yet herself. She watched an instability emerge from a line close to her. The instability grew like a tumour and scythed through the Air, its motion along the line combining with the line's upward sweep to take it diagonally past her. As it exceeded a mansheight in depth the complex grace of its waveform became distorted; it seemed to be forming a neck at its base, and secondary instabilities rippled around its circumference like attendants.

The neck began to close. Dura stared, fascinated.

The sparkling vortex line crossed itself. The throat closed, and a ring of vorticity spun clear of the line, perhaps two mansheights in diameter. The line itself, freed of its irksome instability, recoiled from the ring in a smooth surge, and then soared on towards the Crust. The ring turned in the Air, quivering, cutting a diagonal path through the array of vortex lines.

A vortex ring.

Rings were believed to form perhaps once a generation, in extremes of spin weather. Dura had never seen one before, and as far as she knew neither had her father, in a long lifetime in the upflux.

She felt a prickle of deep unease. *A vortex ring. Something extraordinary is happening to the Star.*

She remembered the odd, distant movement she had seen at

184

the start of the storm, the needles of blue light on the concave horizon. Perhaps that blue light was the cause of all this. Making sure she wasn't in any immediate danger, she glanced around the sky, seeking out the strange vision . . .

A scream. *Rauc*.

Dura spun in the Air, her legs thrashing at the Magfield. Rauc had gone from her side, unnoticed. She felt a surge of anger at herself, her own carelessness, her dreamy fascination with the vortex ring.

The scream had come from the path of the vortex ring, as it rose towards the Crust. There was Rauc, high up in the thinning, rushing forest of vortex lines. She must have seen the damage being wrought at the farm, and had taken it into her head to return. To help. And now she was right in the path of the climbing vortex ring. Rauc's eyes and her round, gaping mouth were like three splashes of dark paint on her round face. The older woman was hanging in the Air, mesmerized by the ring's oscillations, making no effort to flee.

Dura wrenched her legs and arms through the Air, surging towards the remote tableau. 'Get out of the way! Rauc, oh, get out of the way! It will kill you . . .'

But she could not overtake the ring. Rauc seemed to be waiting, almost patiently, for the ring to come to her. The Air scraped in Dura's mouth and throat. She clawed through the Air, her concern for patient, harmless Rauc merging with layers of savage memory: her desolation at the loss of Esk and her father, her continual, helpless ache at the thought of Farr, so remote from her.

A ring was a mechanism for a vortex line to shed instability, to lose excess energy in a bid to regain lost equilibrium. But the ring itself was unstable. It quivered in the Air as it climbed, seeming almost fragile, and it was visibly shrinking: already it had lost perhaps half its original diameter and was reduced to no more than a mansheight in width. And its path curved in the Air, as its spin wrenched at the gas it passed through. For a moment Dura wondered wildly if the combined effects of the shrinkage and the deviation of its trajectory might take the ring away from Rauc. Perhaps if Rauc would just Wave a little way, away from the curve of the path . . .

No. It was too late. Rauc was still alive, fully breathing, aware; but it was as if she was already dead.

The ring struck Rauc in the midriff. She seemed to implode around the ribbon of vorticity. Her smock was torn open and dragged forward, exposing her back; Dura saw shards of bone protruding from broken flesh. One arm was twisted around and torn away, leaving a grisly, twisted stump of ligament and bone. Rauc's head remained intact, but it seemed to have been pulped; her face had been stretched, grotesquely, the mouth ripping at its corners.

The vortex ring passed on through the wreckage of Rauc, shrinking rapidly.

Dura let herself drift to a stop in a clear volume of Air. She felt the tension leave her muscles; she curled slowly into a ball, as if she were seeking sleep. *This shouldn't happen*, she thought. *It's not right. We don't deserve such a fate. It's – unnatural.*

And now there was another name to add to the litany of the caravans.

On the horizon, something moved. An object, slicing through the Air; it was like a ray, with shining, golden wings which beat at the Air . . . but it was far larger than any ray, large enough to be seen even though it was almost lost in the mists of the horizon. Blue-white light stabbed from the belly of the great sky-ray into the bruised purple mass of the Quantum Sea below.

More memories, legends from the mouths and staring eyecups of intense, lean old men, returned to her. *I know what that is. Could it be causing the Glitches, with those beams?*

I know what it is. It's a ship, from beyond the Star.

She let her head sink forward, against her knees.

Xeelee.

14

'*Xeelee.*'

Amidst the wreckage of ceiling-farm buildings, Hork cradled the head of his father in his lap. He looked up at Muub, despair and rage shining from his bearded face.

Muub studied the broken body of Hork, Chair of Parz Committee, determined to forget his own personal danger – exposed as he was to the mercurial anger of the younger Hork – and to view this shattered man as just another patient.

As soon as word of the latest Glitch reached Parz, Hork, fearing for his father's life, had summoned Muub. Now, less than a day later, here they were at the experimental Crust farm.

The small medical staff maintained here had clearly been overwhelmed by the disaster. They had greeted Muub on his arrival with a bizarre mixture of relief and fear – eager to hand over responsibility for the injured Chair, and yet fearful of the consequences if they were judged to be negligent. Well, the staff here had clearly done their best, and Muub doubted that the attention Hork had received could have been bettered even within his own Common Good Hospital. But the medics' work had been to no avail, Muub saw immediately. The large, delicate skull of the Committee Chair was clearly crushed.

A Guard, crossbow loaded, hovered over the body, watching Muub surreptitiously.

Hork lifted his face to Muub; Muub read bitterness, apprehension and determination in Hork's round, tough features. He tried to put aside the interest shown by the Guard in his movements. Hork was a grieving son, he told himself. 'Sir,' he said slowly. 'He's dead. I'm sorry. I . . .'

Hork's eyecups seemed to deepen. 'I can see that, damn

you.' He glanced over his father's crushed body, picking at the Chair's fine robes.

'The staff here were afraid to tell you,' Muub said.

'Do they have reason to be?'

Muub tried to judge Hork's mood. He was honest enough to admit to himself that he would have no compunction in delivering the hapless attendants here up to Hork's wrath, if he thought it were necessary to save himself. But Hork, though clearly shocked, seemed rational. And in his heart he wasn't a vindictive man. 'No. They did everything they could.'

Hork ran a hand over his father's thin, yellow hair. 'Make sure you tell them I appreciate their work. See they understand they're under no threat for their part in this . . . And see they get on with treating the rest of the injured here.'

'Of course.' There was plenty of work for the medics here. As the Air-chariot had hurtled beneath the devastated hinterland, Muub had caught shocking, vivid glimpses of smashed fields – of coolies and uprooted wheat-stems drifting alike in the placid Air – of shattered, exploded buildings. Air-pigs had nosed among drifting corpses, seeking food. He shuddered. 'I may be forced to stay here myself, sir, after you've departed. There is urgent work to be done, all around this area, finding and treating the wounded before . . .'

'No.' Hork still stroked his father's head, but his voice was brisk, businesslike. 'I intend to stay here one day, to ensure my father's affairs are in order. During that time you may do as you please here. But then I will return to Parz, and you must return with me.' He raised his face to the sky and stared around at the Crust, at the newly congealed vortex lines. 'The devastation is not restricted just to this farm, or even this part of the Crust. Muub, damage was done in a broad annulus right around the Pole, in a great swathe cutting through much of Parz's best hinterland. It's all to do with the Star's modes of vibration, I'm told.' He shook his head. 'If it's any consolation there must have been similar bands of destruction encompassing the Star at every latitude, all the way to the North Pole. The Star rang like a Corestuff Bell, one cheerful idiot told me . . . Now I have to ensure that the work of relief is co-ordinated as well as it can be – and to start to consider the consequences of so much damage to Parz's bread-basket hinterland. And I need you with me, Muub; you have thousands of patients throughout the hinterland, not just the few dozen here. And I have another assignment in mind for you . . .'

'As you say.'

Still Hork's eyes probed at the sky. '*Xeelee*,' he said again.

His mind full of images of destruction, Muub tried to focus on what the Chair-elect was saying . . . It seemed very important to Hork. And therefore, he thought wearily, it was important to Muub.

'I'm sorry, sir. I don't understand.'

'That's what they're saying.'

'Who?'

'The commoners . . . the ordinary people, here in the ceiling-farm. The coolies and their supervisors. Even some of the medical staff, who should be educated enough to know better.' Hork's face grimaced in a ghastly echo of a smile. 'They all saw the beams in the sky, the ship from beyond the Crust. The reality of these visions seems unquestionable, Muub. And the commoners have only one explanation . . . that the Xeelee have returned to haunt us.' He looked down at the devastated head of his father. 'To destroy us, apparently.'

Muub, disturbed, reached out and grasped Hork's fat-laden shoulder; he felt the tension in Hork's massive muscles. 'Sir, this is nonsense. The commoners know nothing. You must not . . .'

'Rubbish, Muub.' Again that wild look; but Muub, daring, kept his hand in place. 'Everyone knows all about the Xeelee, it seems, even after all this time. So much for generations of suppression since the Reformation, eh? These superstitions are like weeds in my father's fields, I'm starting to think. It's the same with the damn Wheel cult – no matter how many of the bastards you Break, they keep coming back for more. Quite ineradicable. Even within the Court itself, Muub! Can you believe that?'

Muub felt himself stiffen. 'Sir, a great disaster has befallen us. We must deal with the consequences of the Glitch. We cannot pay attention to the gossiping of ignorant folk. And . . .'

'Don't tell me my duties, Muub,' Hork said. 'Of course I have to deal with the impact of this Glitch. But *I cannot ignore what has been seen*, Physician.' Hork's round face was stern, determined. 'A huge ship, penetrating the Crust from the spaces beyond the Star. And appearing to fire some kind of weapon, a spear made of light, into the Quantum Sea. Muub, what if the ship is *causing* the Glitches? What then? Where would my duty lie?'

Muub pulled away from Hork. Despite his exhaustion and shock, he felt a thrill of awe run through him, deep and primitive. *Hork was planning to challenge the Xeelee themselves.*

'Now that my father's gone the Court will be a nest of intrigues. In the chaos of this disaster, perhaps there'll even be an assassination attempt . . . and I don't have time to deal with any of it. We have to find a way to combat the threat of the Xeelee. We need knowledge, Muub; we need to understand the enemy before we can fight them.'

Muub frowned. 'But so many generations after the Reformation our knowledge of the Xeelee mythos has been relegated to fragments of legend. I could consult scholars in the University, perhaps . . .'

Hork shook his heavy head. 'All the books were fed into Harbour hoppers generations ago . . . And the heads of those "scholars" are as empty as they are shaved of hair.'

Muub forced himself not to run a self-conscious hand over his own bare scalp.

'Muub, we have to think wider. Beyond the City, even. What about those weird upfluxers you told me about? The old man and his companions . . . curiosities from the wild. The upfluxers are Xeelee cultists, aren't they? Maybe they could tell us something; maybe they have preserved the knowledge we have foolishly destroyed.'

'Perhaps,' Muub said dutifully.

'Bring them to Parz, Muub.' Hork glanced down at his father. 'But first,' he said quietly, 'you must attend to your patients.'

'Yes. I . . . excuse me, sir.'

Gathering his strength, Muub Waved away from the grisly little tableau and returned to his work.

*

190

Dura glided to a halt against the soft resistance of the Magfield. She let her limbs rest, loose, against the field; they ached after so many days' Waving from the ruined ceiling-farm.

She stared around at the empty, yellow-gold sky. The Quantum Sea was a concave bruise far below her, and the new vortex lines arced around her, clean and undisturbed. It was as if the recent Glitch had never happened; the Star, having expelled its excess energy and angular momentum, had restored itself with astonishing speed.

It was a shame, Dura thought, that humans couldn't do the same.

She sniffed the Air, trying to judge the spacing of the vortex lines, the depth of redness of the distant South Pole. This must be about the right latitude; surely the sky had looked much like this at the site of the Human Beings' encampment. She dug her hand into the sack tied to the rope at her waist. The sack, massive and awkwardly full of bread when she had started this trek, was now depressingly easy to carry. She pulled out a small fistful of the sweet, belly-filling bread and began to chew. She could surely be no more than a centimetre or so from the Human Beings' site; she ought to be able to see them by now. Unless they'd moved on, of course – or, she thought, her heart heavy, unless they'd been destroyed by the Glitch. But even so she'd surely find their artifacts, scattered here – or their bodies. And . . .

'Dura! Dura!'

The voice came from somewhere above her, towards the Crust-forest. Dura flipped back in the Air and peered upwards. It was difficult to pick out movement against the misty, complex texture of the forest, but – there! A man, young, slim, naked, Waving alone – no, she saw, something was accompanying him: a slim, small form which buzzed around his legs as he Waved down towards her. She squinted. An Air-piglet? No, she quickly realized; it was a child, a human infant.

She surged through the Air, up towards the forest; she was still aware of the fatigue in her legs, but that felt distant, unimportant now.

The two adults came to a halt in the Air, perhaps a

mansheight apart; the infant, no more than a few months old, clung to the man's legs while the adults studied each other with an odd wariness. The man – no more than a boy himself, really – smiled cautiously. There seemed to be no fat in his face at all, and there were streaks of premature yellow in his hair; when he smiled his eyecups seemed huge, his teeth prominent. Under the superficial changes, wrought by hunger and fatigue, this face was as familiar as her own body, a face she had known for half her life. After the thousands of strangers to whom she'd been exposed in Parz, and later at the ceiling-farm, Dura found herself staring at this face as if rediscovering her own identity. It felt as if she'd never been away from the Human Beings, and she wanted to drink in this familiarity.

'Dura? We never thought we'd see you again.'

It was Mur, husband of Dia. And this must be Jai, the boy whom Dura had helped deliver, just after the Glitch which killed her father.

She moved towards Mur and folded him in her arms. The bones in Mur's back were sharp under her fingers, and his skin was filthy, slick with fragments of Crust-tree leaves. The baby at his leg mewled, and she reached down an absent hand to stroke his head.

'We thought you must be dead. Lost. It's been so long.'

'No.' Dura forced herself to smile. 'I'll tell you all about it. Farr and Adda are both well, though far from here.' She studied Mur more carefully now, trying to sort out the flood of her initial impressions. The signs of hunger, of poor living, were obvious. She ran her hand over the little boy's scalp. Through the sparsely haired flesh she could feel the bones of the skull, the plates not yet locked together. The child was pawing at her bag now, his tiny fingers poking at the lumps of food contained there. Mur made to pull the infant away, but Dura pulled out a handful of bread, crumbled it, and presented it to the child. Jai grasped the bread fragments with both hands and shoved them into his mouth; his jaw scraped across his open hands, raking in bread, his eyes unseeing as he fed.

'What's that?'

'Bread. Food . . . I'll explain it all. Mur, what's happening here?'

'We are – fewer.' His gaze shifted from her face, and he glanced down at his feeding son, as if in search of distraction. 'The last Glitch . . .'

'The others?'

The child had finished the bread already. He reached up his hands wordlessly to Dura, imploring more; she could see the fragment he'd devoured as a distinct bulge, high in his empty stomach.

Mur pulled the child away from Dura, soothing him. 'Come on,' he said. 'I'll take you to them.'

The Human Beings had established a crude camp in the fringes of the Crust-forest itself. The Air here was thin, unsatisfying in Dura's lungs, and the Quantum Sea curved away from her, far below. Ropes had been slung between branches of the trees, and garments, half-finished tools and scraps of food were suspended from the ropes. Dura touched one of the bits of food gingerly. It was Air-pig flesh, so old it was tough and leathery between her fingertips. The tree-branches for some distance around had been stripped of leaves and bark, revealing how the people had been feeding.

There were only twenty Human Beings left – fifteen adults and five children.

They crowded around Dura, reaching to touch and embrace her, some of them weeping. The familiar faces surrounded her, peering through masks of hunger and dirt. Her heart went out to these people – *her* people – and yet she felt detached from them, distant; she let them touch her, and she embraced in return, but a part of her wanted to recoil from their childlike, helpless pressing. She felt stiff, civilized. The very nakedness of these *upfluxers* was startling. She felt massive, sleek and bulky, too, compared to their starved scrawniness.

Her experiences, her exposure to Parz City, had changed her, she realized; perhaps she would never again be content to settle into the small, hard, limited life of a Human Being.

She gave Mur her bag of bread and told him to distribute it as he saw fit. As he moved among the Human Beings she saw how sharp eyes followed each move; the aura of hunger which hovered over the people, focussing on the bag of bread, was like a living thing.

She found Philas, the widow of Esk. Dura and Philas moved away from the heart of the crude encampment, out of earshot of the rest of the Human Beings. Oddly, Philas seemed more beautiful now; it was as if privation was allowing the bony symmetry, the underlying dignity of her features, to emerge. Dura could see no bitterness, no trace of the rivalry which had once silently divided them.

'You've suffered greatly.'

Philas shrugged. 'We couldn't rebuild the Net, after you left. We survived; we hunted again in the forest and trapped some pigs. But then the second Glitch came.'

The survivors had abandoned the open Air in favour of the fringe of the forest. It wasn't particularly logical, but Dura thought she understood; the need for some form of solid base, to have a feeling of protective walls around them, would dominate logic. She thought of the folk of Parz in their compressed wooden boxes, their thin walls affording illusory protection from the wilds of the Mantle not half a centimetre from where they lay. Perhaps people all shared the same basic instincts, no matter what their origins – and perhaps those instincts had travelled with humanity from whatever distant Star had birthed the Ur-humans.

It was impossible to find Air-pigs now, no matter how widely the Human Beings hunted. The latest Glitch, savage as it was, had scattered the herds of Pigs as well as devastating the works of humanity. The people were trying to survive on leaves, and were even experimenting with meals of spin-spider flesh.

Of course, it was impossible to subsist on leaves. Without decent food, the Human Beings would surely die. (*And so will I, now that my bread is gone,* she thought with a surprising stab of selfishness.)

Dura turned in on herself, trying to understand her own motives for returning to her people. After Rauc's death, and after she'd helped to cope with the worst of the destruction at Qos Frenk's farm, she learned that most of the coolies were to be released from their indentures. Qos, roots of yellow showing in his pink hair, his small hands wringing each other, had explained that he intended to save what he could of this year's harvest, and then start the slow, painful work of rebuilding

194

his holding. It would take many years before the farm was functioning again, and in the meantime it would not generate any income for Frenk; so he couldn't employ them any longer.

The coolies had seemed to understand. Frenk provided rides back to Parz City for those who wanted it; the rest, dully, had dispersed to seek work in the neighbouring ceiling-farms.

Dura slowly realized that she had lost the indenture which should have paid for Adda's Hospital treatment. Overwhelmed and shocked, she resolved to return to her people, the Human Beings. Later, perhaps, when things had settled down, she would return to Parz and address the problems of Farr, of Adda's debts.

Now, studying Philas's dull, silent face, she wondered what she'd been expecting to find, here among the Human Beings. Perhaps a hidden, childlike part of her had hoped to find everything restored to what it had been when she'd been a small girl . . . when Logue was strong, protecting her, and the world was – by comparison – a stable and safe place.

Of course, that was an illusion. There was nowhere for her to hide, no one who could look after her.

She raised her hands to her face. In fact, she thought with a stab of shameful selfishness, by returning here she'd only placed herself in danger of starvation, *and* had taken on responsibility for the Human Beings once more.

If only I'd gone straight back to Parz. I could have found Farr, and found a way to live. Perhaps I could have forgotten that the Human Beings ever lived . . .

She straightened up. Philas was waiting for her, her face grave and beautiful. 'Philas, we can't stay here,' Dura said. 'We can't live like this. It's not viable.'

Philas nodded gravely. 'But we have no choice.'

Dura sighed. 'We do. I've told you about Parz City . . . Philas, we must go there. It's an immense distance, and I don't know how we'll manage the journey. But there is food there. It's our only hope.'

'What will we do, in Parz City? How will we get food?'

Dura felt like laughing. *We'll beg*, she thought. *We'll be hungry freaks; if we're lucky they will feed us rather than Wheel-Break us. And . . .*

'Dura!'

Mur came crashing through the forest towards them; his eyes were wide with shock.

Dura felt her hands slip to the knife tucked into the rope at her waist. 'What is it? What's wrong?'

'There's something outside the trees ... A box of wood. Drawn by Air-pigs! Just as you've described it, Philas ...'

Dura turned, peering out through the thin foliage. There, easily visible beyond the stripped twigs of the forest fringe, was an Air-car, huge and sleek. It was calling, in a thin, amplified voice.

'... Dura ... upfluxer Dura ... If you can hear me, show yourself. Dura ...'

'Tell me about the Xeelee,' said Hork V.

The Palace anteroom was a hollow sphere about five mansheights across, anchored loosely in the Garden. Fine ropes had been threaded across the interior, and light, comfortable net cocoons were suspended here and there. Smaller nets contained drinks and sweetmeats.

Adda, Muub and Hork occupied three of the cocoons. The three of them faced each other close to the centre of the room. Adda felt as if he were trapped in the web of a Crust-spider.

Adda found Hork's demanding tone, his stare over that bush of ludicrous face-hair, quite offensive. This was the new Chair of the Parz Committee. So what? Such titles didn't mean a damn thing to Adda, and the day they did would be a sorry one, he reckoned.

Let them wait. Adda allowed his gaze to slide around the opulence of this chamber.

The painted walls were the ultimate folly, of course. They were designed to give an illusion of the open Air. He studied the drawn-in vortex lines, the purple paint that represented the Quantum Sea. How absurd, thought Adda, for these City people to close themselves away from the world in their boxes of wood and Corestuff, and then go to so much trouble to reproduce what could be found outside.

The centrepiece of the anteroom was a tame vortex ring. And, Adda conceded, it was impressive. It was contained in nested globes of clearwood which revolved continually about three independent axes, maintaining the spin of the Air trapped within. Every child knew that if an unstable vortex line threw off a ring, the torus of vorticity would rapidly lose its energy and decay away; but this trapped ring was fed with energy by the artful spinning of the globes, and so remained stable.

Of course, it wasn't as impressive as the million-mansheight-long vortex lines which spanned the Mantle and arced over the Garden, and which were available for viewing without charge or effort . . .

'I'm glad you're finding the room so interesting.' Hork's tone contained patience, but with an undercurrent of threat.

'I wasn't aware you were in a hurry. After all, you've lasted ten generations without talking to the Human Beings; what's the rush now?'

'No games,' Hork growled. 'Come on, upfluxer. You know why I've asked you here. I need your help.'

Muub interposed smoothly, 'You must make allowances for this old rascal, sir. He rejoices in being difficult . . . a privilege of age, perhaps.'

Adda turned to glare at Muub, but the doctor would not meet his eye.

'I ask you again,' Hork said quietly. 'Tell me of the Xeelee.'

'Not until you tell me that my friends will be returned from their exile.'

'From their *indentures*,' Muub said impatiently. 'Damn it, Adda, I've already assured you that they've been sent for.'

Adda watched Hork, his mouth set firm.

Hork nodded, the motion an impatient spasm which caused ripples to flow over the front of his chest. 'Their debts are dissolved. Now give me my answer.'

'I'll tell you all you need to know in five words.'

Hork tilted his head back, his nostrils glowing.

Adda said slowly, 'You – can – not – fight – Xeelee.'

Hork growled.

'That's your intention, isn't it?' Adda asked evenly. 'You want to find a way to beat off Xeelee as if they were rampaging Air-boars; you want to find a way to stop them smashing up your beautiful Palace . . .'

'They are killing the people I am responsible for.'

Adda leaned forward in his sling. 'City man, they don't

even know we're here. Nothing you could do would even raise you to their attention.'

Muub was shaking his head. 'How can you respect such – such primal monsters? Explain that, Adda.'

'The Xeelee have their own goals,' said Adda. 'Goals which we do not share, and cannot even comprehend . . .'

The Xeelee – moving behind mists of legend – were immense. They were to the Ur-humans as Ur-humans were to Human Beings, perhaps. They were like gods – and yet lower than gods.

Perhaps gods could have been tolerated, by the Ur-human soul. Not the Xeelee. The Xeelee had been *rivals*.

Hork twisted in his sling, angry and impatient. 'So the Ur-humans, unable to endure the aloof grandeur of these Xeelee, challenged them . . .'

'Yes. There were great wars.'

Billions had died. The destruction of the Xeelee had become a racial goal for the Ur-humans.

'. . . But not for everyone,' Adda said. 'As the venom of the assaults grew, so did Ur-human understanding of the Xeelee's great Projects. For instance the Ring was discovered . . .'

'The Ring?' Hork growled.

'Bolder's Ring,' Adda said. 'A huge construct which one day will form a gateway between universes . . .'

'What is this old fool babbling about, Physician? What are these universes of which he speaks? Are they in other parts of the Star?'

Muub spread his long, fine hands and smiled. 'I'm as mystified as you are, sir. Perhaps the universes reside in other Stars. If such exist.'

Adda grunted. 'If I knew all the answers I'd have spent my life doing a lot more than carve spears and hunt pigs,' he said sourly. 'Look, Hork, I will tell you what I know; I'm telling you what my father told me. But if you ask stupid questions you are only going to get stupid answers.'

'Get on with it,' Muub murmured.

'Even if they could have been successful,' Adda said, 'wise Ur-men came to see that to destroy the Xeelee might be as unwise as for a child to destroy its father. The Xeelee are working on our behalf, waging immense, invisible battles in order to save us from unknown danger. We cannot understand their ways; we are as dust in the Air to them. But they are our best hope.'

Hork glared at him, raking his fat fingers through his beard. 'What evidence is there for any of this? It's all legend and hearsay...'

'That's true,' Muub said, 'but we couldn't expect any more from such a source, sir...'

Hork shoved himself out of his sling, his bulk quivering in the Air like a sac of liquid. 'You're too damn patient, Physician. Legend and hearsay. The ramblings of a senile old fool.' He Waved to the captive vortex ring and slammed his fist into the elegant spheres encasing it. The outermost sphere splintered in a star around his fist, and the vortex ring broke up into a chain of smaller rings which rapidly diminished in size, swooping around each other. 'Am I supposed to gamble the future of the City, of my people, on such gibberish? And what about us, upfluxer? Forget these mythical men on other worlds. Why are the Xeelee interested in us?... and what am I to do about it?'

Past Hork's wide, angry face, Adda watched the captive vortex ring struggling to reform.

15

Bzya invited Farr to visit him at his home, deep in the Downside belly of the City.

The Harbour workers were expected to sleep inside the Harbour itself, in the huge, stinking dormitories. The authorities preferred to have their staff where they could call them out quickly in the event of some disaster – and where they had an outside chance of keeping them fit for work. To get access to the rest of the City, outside the Harbour walls, Bzya and Farr needed to arrange not only coincident off-shifts but also coincident out-passes, and they had to wait some weeks before Hosch – grudgingly and reluctantly – allowed the arrangement.

The Harbour, a huge spherical construction embedded in the base of the City, was enclosed by its own Skin and had its own skeleton of Corestuff, strengthened to withstand the forces exerted by the Bell winches. The Harbour was well designed for its function, Farr had come to realize, but the interior was damned claustrophobic, even by Parz standards. So he felt a mild relief as he emerged from the Harbour's huge, daunting gates and entered the maze of Parz streets once more.

The streets – narrow, branching, indecipherably complex – twisted away in all directions. Farr looked around, feeling lost already; he knew he'd have little hope of finding his way through this three-dimensional maze.

Bzya rubbed his hands, grinned, and Waved off down one of the streets. He moved rapidly despite his huge, scarred bulk. Farr studied the street. It looked the same to him as a dozen others. Why that one? How had Bzya recognized it? And . . .

And Bzya was almost out of sight already, round the street's first bend.

Farr kicked away from the outer Harbour wall and plunged after Bzya.

The area around the Harbour was one of the shabbiest in the City. The streets were cramped, old and twisting. The noise of the dynamo sheds, which were just above this area, was a constant, dull throb. The dwelling-places were dark mouths, most of them with doors or pieces of wall missing; as he hurried after Bzya, Farr was aware of curious, hungry eyecups peering out at him. Here and there people Waved unevenly past – men and women, some of them Harbour workers, and many of them in the strange state called 'drunkenness'. Nobody spoke, to him or anybody else. Farr shivered, feeling clumsy and conspicuous; this was like being lost in a Crust-forest.

After a short time's brisk Waving, Bzya began to slow. They must be nearly at his home. Farr looked around curiously. They were still in the deepest Downside, almost on top of the Harbour, and the buildings here had the shrunken meanness of the areas closest to the Harbour itself. But in this area there was a difference, Farr saw slowly. The walls and doors were patched, but mostly intact. And there were no 'drunks'. It was astonishing to him how in such a short distance the character of Parz could change so completely.

Bzya grinned and pushed open a doorway – a doorway among thousands in these twisting corridors. Once again Farr wondered how Bzya knew how to find his way around with such unerring accuracy.

He climbed after Bzya through the doorway. The interior of the home was a single room – a rough sphere, dimly illuminated by wood-lamps fixed seemingly at random to the walls. He felt his cup-retinae stretch, adjusting to the low level of light.

A globe-bowl of tiny leaves was thrust into his chest.

He stumbled back in the Air. There was a wide, grinning face apparently suspended over the bowl – startlingly like Bzya's, but half-bald, nose flattened and misshapen, the nostrils dulled. 'You're the upfluxer. Bzya's told me about you. Have a petal.'

Bzya pushed past Farr and into the little home. 'Let the poor lad in first, woman,' he grumbled good-naturedly.

201

'All right, all right.'

The woman withdrew, clutching her petal-globe and still grinning. Bzya wrapped a huge hand around Farr's forearm and dragged him into the room, away from the door, then closed the door behind them.

The three of them hovered in a rough circle. The woman dropped the petal-globe in the Air and thrust out a hand. 'I'm Jool. Bzya's my husband. You are welcome here.'

Farr took her hand. It was almost the size of Bzya's, and as strong. 'Bzya told me about you, too.'

Bzya kissed Jool. Then, sighing and stretching, he drifted away to the dim rear of the little home, leaving Farr with his wife.

Jool's body was square, a compact – if misshapen – mass of muscles. She wore what looked like the all-purpose coverall of the Harbour, much patched. One side of her body was quite damaged – her hair was missing down one side of her scalp in wide swathes, and her arm on that side was twisted, atrophied. Her leg was missing, below the knee.

He was staring at the stump of the leg, the tied-off trouser leg below the knee. Suddenly unbearably self-conscious, he lifted his eyes to Jool's face.

She clapped him on the shoulder. 'Not much point looking for that leg; you'll never find it.' She smiled kindly. 'Here. Have a petal. I meant it.'

He dug his hand into the globe, pulled out a fistful of the little leaves, and jammed them into his mouth. They were insubstantial, like all leaf-matter, and strongly flavoured – so strong that his head seemed to fill up with their sweet aroma. He coughed, spluttering leaf fragments all over his hostess.

Jool tilted back her head and laughed. 'Your upfluxer friend hasn't got very sophisticated tastes, Bzya.'

Bzya had gone to work in one corner of the cramped little room, beneath two crumpled sleeping-cocoons; his arms were immersed in a large globe-barrel full of fragments – chips of some substance – which crunched and ground against each other as he closed his fists around pieces of cloth. 'Neither have we, Jool, so stop teasing the boy.'

Farr picked up a petal. 'Is it a leaf?'

'Yes.' Jool popped one in her mouth and chewed noisily. 'Yes, and no. It's from a flower . . . a small, ornamental plant. They've been bred, here in Parz. You don't get them in the wild, do you?'

'They grow in the Palace, don't they? In their Garden. Is that where you work?' He studied her. From the way Cris had described the Committee Palace to him, Jool seemed a little rough to be acceptable there.

'No, not the Palace. There are other parts of the Skin, a little further Downside, where flowers, and bonsai trees, are cultivated. But not really for show, like in the Garden.'

'Why, then?'

She crunched on another leaf. 'For food. And not for humans. For pigs. I wait on Air-pigs, young Farr.' Her eyes were bright and amused.

Farr was puzzled. 'But these leaves – petals – can't be very nutritious.'

'They don't make the pigs as strong as they could be, no,' she said. 'But they have other advantages.'

'Oh, stop teasing the lad,' Bzya called again. 'You know, she used to work in the Harbour.'

'We met there. I was his supervisor, before that cretin Hosch was promoted. At the expense of this huge dolt Bzya, I'm afraid. Farr, do you want some beercake?'

'No. Yes. I mean, no thank you. I don't think I'd better.'

'Oh, try a little.' Jool turned to a cupboard set in the wall and opened its door. The door was ill-fitting, but the food store within was well stocked and clean. 'I'll bet you've never tried it. Well, see what it's like. What the hell. We won't let you get drunk, don't worry.' She withdrew a slab of thick, sticky-looking cake wrapped in thin cloth; she broke off a handful and passed it to Farr.

Bzya called, 'Cake is fine as long as you chew it slowly, and know when to stop.'

Farr bit into the cake cautiously. After the pungency of the petals it tasted sour, thick, almost indigestible. He chewed it carefully – the taste didn't improve – and swallowed.

Nothing happened.

Jool hung in the Air before him, huge arms folded. 'Just wait,' she said.

'Funny thing,' Bzya called, still working at his globe of crunching chips. 'Beercake is an invention of the deep Downside. I guess we evolved it to stave off boredom, lack of variety, lack of stimulation. The poor man's flower garden, eh, Jool?'

'But now it's a delicacy,' Jool said. 'They take it in the Palace, from globes of clearwood. Can you believe it?'

Warmth exploded in the pit of Farr's stomach. It spread out like an opening hand, suffusing his torso and racing along his limbs like currents induced by some new Magfield; his fingers and toes tingled, and he felt his pores ache deliciously as they opened.

'Wow,' he said.

'Well put.' Jool reached out and took the beercake from his numb fingers. 'I think that's enough for now.' She wrapped the cake in a fragment of cloth and stowed it away in its cupboard.

Farr, still tingling, drifted across the room to join Bzya. The big Fisherman's arms were still buried in the barrel of chips, and his broad hands were working at a garment – an outsize tunic – inside the chips, rubbing surfaces together and scraping the cloth through the chips. Bzya hauled the tunic out of the globe and added it to a rough sphere of clothes, wadded together, which orbited close to his wide back. Bzya grinned at Farr, rubbed his hands, and plunged a pair of trousers into the chips. 'Jool has been looking forward to meeting you.'

'What happened to her?'

Bzya shrugged, his arms extended before him. 'A Bell accident, deep in the underMantle. It was so fast, she can't even reconstruct it. Anyway, she left half herself down there. After that, of course, she was unemployable. So the Harbour said.' He smiled with unreasonable tolerance, Farr thought. 'But she still had her indenture to fulfil. So she came out of the Harbour with one leg, a dodgy husband, and a debt.'

'But she works now.'

'Yes.'

He fell into silence, and Farr watched him work the clothes curiously.

Bzya became aware of his stare. 'What's the matter? . . . Oh. You don't know what I'm doing, do you?'

Farr hesitated. 'To be honest, Bzya, I get tired of asking what's going on all the time.'

'Well, I can sympathize with that.' Bzya carried on rubbing the grit through his clothes, impassive.

After a few heartbeats of silence Farr gave in. 'Oh, all right. What are you doing, Bzya?'

'Washing,' Bzya said. 'Keeping my clothes clean. I don't suppose you do much of that, in the upflux . . .'

Farr was irritated. 'We keep ourselves clean, even in the upflux. We're not animals, you know. We have scrapers . . .'

Bzya patted the side of his barrel of chips. 'This is a better idea. You work your clothes through this mass of chips – bone fragments, bits of wood, and so on. You work the stuff with your hands, you see – like this – get it into the cloth . . . The chips are crushed, smaller and smaller, and work into the cloth, pushing out the dirt. Much less crude than a scraper.' He hauled a shirt out of the barrel and showed it to Farr. 'It's time-consuming, though. And a bit boring.' He eyed Farr speculatively. 'Look, Farr, while you're in the City you ought to sample the richness of its life to the full. Why don't you have a go?'

He moved eagerly away from the barrel, rubbing a layer of bone-dust from his arms.

Farr, well aware he was being teased again, took another shirt – this one stiff with grime – and shoved it into the barrel. As he'd seen Bzya do, he kneaded the cloth between his fingers. The chips crackled against each other and squirmed around his fingers like live things. When he drew the shirt out again the dust coated his hands, so that his fingers felt strange against each other, as if gloved. But the shirt hardly seemed any cleaner.

'It does need practice,' Bzya said drily.

Farr plunged the garment back into the barrel and pressed harder.

Jool had been fixing food; now she slapped Bzya on the shoulder. 'Every time someone comes to see us he gets them washing his smalls,' she said.

Bzya tilted back his battered face and bellowed laughter.

Jool led Farr to the centre of the little room. A five-spoked Wheel of wood hovered here, with covered bowls jammed into the crevices between its spokes. Hanging in the Air the three of them gathered close around the Wheel-table, enclosing it in a rough sphere of faces and limbs, the light of the wood-lamps playing on their skin. Now Jool lifted the covers from the bowls and let them drift off into the Air. 'Belly of Air-piglet, spiced with petals. Almost as good as Bzya can make it. Eggs of Crust-ray . . . ever tried this, Farr? Stuffed leaves. More beercake . . .'

Farr, with Bzya prompting, dug his hands into the bowls and crammed the spicy, flavoursome food into his mouth. As they ate, the conversation dried up, with both Bzya and Jool too intent on feeding. He couldn't help comparing the little home with the Mixxaxes', in the upper Midside. There was only one room, in contrast to the Mixxaxes' five. A waste chute – scrupulously clean – pierced another wall of the room they ate in. And Jool and Bzya were far less tidy than the Mixxaxes. The clump of cleaned clothes had been simply abandoned by Bzya, and now it drifted in the Air, sleeves slowly uncoiling like limp spin-spider legs. But the place was clean. And he spotted a bundle of scrolls, loosely tied together and jammed into one corner. The Wheel symbol was everywhere – carved into the walls, the shape of the table from which they ate, sculpted into the back of the door. There was a much greater feeling of age, of poor construction and shabbiness, than in the Midside . . . But there was more *character* here, he decided slowly.

He looked at the wide, battered, intelligent faces of Bzya and Jool as they worked at their food. The light of the lamps seemed to diffuse around them, so that their faces were evenly illuminated (the apparently random placing of the lamps was actually anything but, he realized). There was a quiet, unpretentious intelligence here, he thought.

He briefly imagined living with these people. What if he'd grown up *here*, deep inside Parz, in this strange, old, cramped part of the City?

It wouldn't have been so bad, he decided. His mood swung into a feeling of pigletish devotion to these two decent people.

Surreptitiously he shook his head, wondering if the beercake was affecting his judgement.

He became aware of Jool and Bzya watching his face curiously.

He blurted, 'Do you have children?'

Jool smiled over a fistful of food. 'Yes. One, a girl. Shar. We don't see much of her. She works out of the City.'

'Don't you miss her?'

'Of course,' Bzya said simply. 'Which is why I haven't mentioned her before, Farr. What can't be helped shouldn't be brooded on.'

'Why not bring her back?'

'It would be up to her,' Bzya said gently. 'I doubt if she'd want to come. But she's too far away. She's a ceiling-farm coolie. Like your sister, from what you say.'

Farr felt vaguely excited. 'I wonder if they'll meet.'

Jool laughed. 'The hinterland may seem a small place to an upfluxer, Farr, but it contains hundreds of ceiling-farms. Shar's serving out her indenture. It's hard for her to get home until that's through. Then, maybe, she'll get a more senior job on the farm. She's working for a decent owner. Equitable.'

'I don't understand.'

Jool frowned. 'What? How we can live apart, like this?' She shrugged. 'I'd rather have her away from us and safe, than here but in the Harbour. It's just the way things are for us . . .'

'Farr has family,' Bzya said.

Jool nodded. 'A sister. The coolie. Yes? And there's another with you from the upflux, an old man . . .'

'Adda.'

'And you're separated from them both. Just like us, with Shar.'

Farr nodded. 'But Dura's being brought back from her ceiling-farm. Deni Maxx has gone to get her.'

'Who?'

'A doctor. From the Hospital of the Common Good . . . And Adda has been taken to see the Chair of the City. It's all to do with sorting out the Glitches . . .'

'Hm,' Bzya said. 'Perhaps. Farr, I don't believe everything I hear from the Upside, and I'd suggest you grow a little scepticism too. Still, I hope you see your sister soon.'

Jool was working towards the bottom of the bowl of piglet meat. 'So what do you make of our part of the City?'

Farr finished his mouthful. 'It's different. It's . . .' He hesitated.

'Dark, dirty, threatening. Right?'

Farr shook his head. 'I was going to say cramped. Even more cramped than everywhere else.'

'Well, this is the heart of the City,' Jool said. 'I'm not sentimental about it, but that's the truth . . . It's the oldest part of Parz. The first to be built, around the head of the Harbour, when the Spine was first driven into the underMantle.'

Farr imagined those ancient days, the bravery of the men and women determined to extract the Corestuff they needed to build their City, and then constructing that immense structure with their bare hands and tools little more advanced, he guessed, than the average Human Being's today.

Jool smiled. 'I know what you're thinking, boy from the upflux. Why would anyone build a little box like this around themselves? Why shut out the Air?'

'Because,' Bzya said, 'they were trying to rebuild what they thought they'd lost, when the Colonists withdrew into the Core.' He looked thoughtful. 'So Parz is a representation in wood and Corestuff of an ancient dream . . .'

'You're both very intelligent,' Farr found himself saying.

Husband and wife together tilted back their heads and opened their throats with laughter. The pair of them made a ludicrous, outsized, merry sight in the room's cramped Air.

Jool wiped her eyecups. 'You say what you think, don't you?'

Bzya patted her arm. 'We aren't fair to laugh, Jool. After all, we know plenty of people – even in the lower Midside, let alone the Upside – who think Downsiders are all subhuman.'

'And,' Farr said, 'with Human Beings – upfluxers – worse than that.'

'But it's rubbish,' Bzya said fervently. He grabbed a ray egg from the bowl and waggled it before Farr's face. 'Humans are more or less equal, as far as I can see, no matter where they come from. And I'll go further.' He bit into the soft egg and spoke around his chewing. 'I believe humans throughout this Star are intelligent – I mean, more so than the stock on other human worlds; perhaps more intelligent even than the average Ur-human.'

Jool shook her head. 'Listen to him, the ruler of a hundred Stars.'

'But there's logic to what I say. Think about it,' Bzya went on. 'We're descended from a selected stock – of engineers, placed in the Star to modify it; to build a civilization in the Mantle. The Ur-humans wouldn't include fools in that stock, any more than they would have made us too weak, or too ill-adapted.'

'The analogous anatomists have worked out much of what we know about the Ur-humans' project from our ill-adaptation,' Jool said, her wide face lively and interested. 'From our inappropriate form, based on the Ur-human prototype. And . . .'

Their conversation, illuminating and informed, washed around Farr; he listened, mellow and relaxed, chewing surreptitiously on a little more beercake.

Jool turned to Farr. 'Of course, we weren't so clever as to avoid setting up a rigid, stratified society to control each other with.'

'Here in Parz, anyway,' Farr said.

'Here in Parz,' she conceded. 'You Human Beings are evidently much too smart to put up with it all.'

'We were,' Farr said mildly. 'That's why we left.'

'And now you've come back,' Bzya said. 'To the lowest strata, at the bottom of the City . . . Upside, Downside, bottom, top; all those up-and-down concepts are relics of Ur-human thinking – did you know that? . . . here in the Downside we're regarded as less intelligent, less aware, than the rest. In the past people here have reacted to that.' His large, battered, thoughtful face looked sad. 'Badly. If you treat people as less than human, often they behave like it. A couple of generations ago this part of the Downside was a slum. A jungle.'

'Parts of it still are,' Jool said.

'But we've pulled ourselves out of it.' Bzya smiled. 'Self-help. Education. Oral histories, numeracy, literacy where we've the materials.' He bit into a slice of beercake. 'The Committee does damn all for this part of the City. The Harbour does less, even though most of us are Harbour employees. But we *can* help ourselves.'

Farr listened to all this with a certain wonder. These people were like exiles in their own City, he thought. Like Human Beings, lost in this forest of wood and Corestuff. He told them of lessons and learning among the Human Beings – histories of the tribe and of the greater mankind beyond the Star, told by elders to little huddles of children suspended between the vortex lines. Bzya and Jool listened thoughtfully.

When the food was finished, they rested for a while. Then Bzya and Jool moved a little closer to each other, apparently unconsciously. Their huge heads dipped, so that their brows were almost touching. They reached forward and placed wide, strong fingers on the rim of the Wheel. Quietly they began to speak – in unison, a slow, solemn litany of names, none of them familiar to Farr. He watched them in silence.

When they finished, after perhaps a hundred names, Bzya opened his eyecups wide and smiled at Farr. 'A little oral history in action, my friend.'

Jool's face had resumed the sly, playful expression of earlier. She reached across the Wheel-table and touched Farr's sleeve. 'Have you figured out what my job is yet?'

'Oh, stop teasing the boy,' Bzya said loudly. 'I'll tell you. She gathers petals from the Upside gardens, and delivers them to the pig-farms – the small in-City ones scattered around Parz, where the pigs for the Air-cars that run within the City are kept.'

'Think about it,' Jool said. 'The streets of the City are hot and cramped. Enclosed. All those Cars. All those pigs . . .'

'The petals are ground up and added to the pigs' feed,' Bzya said.

Farr frowned. 'Why?'

'To make them easier to live with.' Solemnly, Jool bent forward, tilted her stump of leg, grabbed her wide buttocks through her coverall and separated them, and farted explosively.

Bzya laughed.

Farr looked from one to the other, uncertainly.

Then the smell hit him. Her fart was petal-perfumed.

Bzya shook his head, sighing. 'Oh, don't pay her any attention; it will only encourage her. More beercake?'

16

The driver of the car from Parz City was Deni Maxx, the junior doctor who had treated Adda. Dura wanted to rush to her, to demand news of Farr and Adda.

The Human Beings – all twenty of them, including the five children – emerged from their shelter in the forest and trailed after Dura. Deni Maxx peered out of the open hatch at her, staring indifferently past her at the ring of skinny Human Beings. 'I'm glad I've found you.'

'I'm surprised you managed it. The upflux is a big place.'

Deni shrugged. She seemed irritated, impatient. 'It wasn't so hard. Toba Mixxax gave me precise directions from his ceiling-farm to the place he first found you. All I had to do was scout around until you responded to my call.'

Philas crowded close to Dura. The widow pressed her mouth close to Dura's ear; Dura was aware, uncomfortably, of the sweet, thin stink of leaves and bark on Philas's breath. 'Who is she? What does she want?'

Dura pulled her head away. She was aware of Deni's appraising gaze. She felt a swirl of contradictory emotions: irritation at Deni's high-handed manner, and yet a certain embarrassment at the awkward, childlike behaviour of the Human Beings. Had she been such a primitive on her first encounter with Toba Mixxax?

'Get in the car,' Deni said. 'We've a long journey back to Parz, and I was told to hurry . . .'

'Who by? Why am I being recalled? Is it something to do with my indenture? Surely you saw Qos Frenk's ceiling-farm – or what was left of it; it's no longer functioning. Qos released us, and . . .'

'It's nothing to do with your indenture. I'll explain on the way.' Deni drummed her fingers on the frame of the car's door.

Dura was aware of the staring eyes of the rest of the tribe, as they waited mutely for her to make a decision. She felt a brief, selfish stab of impatience with them; they were dependent, like children. *She wanted to go back to Parz.* She could surely – she told herself – find out more about the situation of Farr and Adda there than if she stayed with the Human Beings as just another simple refugee upfluxer. And, in the long run – she justified to herself – she could maybe do more to help all the Human Beings by returning than by staying here. Something important must be required of her, for the City to send someone like Deni Maxx to fetch her. Perhaps in some odd way she would have *influence* over events . . .

Philas tugged at her arm, like a child, demanding attention. Dura pulled her arm away angrily – and instantly regretted the impulse.

The truth was, she admitted to herself, she was relieved that she had an excuse, and the means, to get away from the suffocating company of the Human Beings. But she felt such *guilt* about it.

She came to a quick decision. 'I'll come with you,' she told Deni. 'But not alone.'

Deni frowned. 'What?'

'I'll take the children.' She widened her arms to indicate the five children – the youngest was Mur's infant, Jai, the oldest an adolescent girl.

Deni Maxx launched into a volley of complaints.

Dura turned her back and confronted the Human Beings. They pulled their children to themselves in baffled silence, their eyes huge and fixed on her. She ran a hand through her hair, exasperated. Slowly, patiently, she described what awaited the children at Parz City. Food. Shelter. Safety. Surely she could prevail on Toba Mixxax to find temporary homes for the children. They were all young enough to seem cute to the City folk, she calculated, surprising herself with her own cynicism. And in a few short years they'd be able to turn their upfluxer muscles to gainful employment.

She was consigning the children to lives in the Downside, she realized. But it was better than starving here, or sharing their parents' epic trek across the devastated hinterland of Parz. And eventually, she insisted to the bewildered parents, they would reach Parz themselves and be reunited with their offspring.

The adults were baffled and frightened, struggling to deal with concepts they could barely envisage. But they trusted her, Dura realized slowly, with a mixture of relief and shame – and so, one by one, the children were delivered to Dura.

Deni Maxx glared as the grimy bodies of the children were passed into her car, and Dura wondered if Deni was even now going to raise some cruel objection. But when the doctor watched Dura settle little Jai – frightened and crying for his mother – in the arms of the oldest girl at the back of the car, Deni's irritation visibly softened.

At last it was done. Dura gathered the bereft adults in a huddle and gave them strict instructions on how to get to the Pole. They listened to her solemnly. Then Dura embraced them all, and climbed into the car.

As Deni flicked the team of Air-pigs into motion, Dura stared back through the huge, expansive windows at the Human Beings. Shorn of their children, they looked lost, bewildered, futile. Dia and Mur clung to each other. *I've taken away their future*, Dura realized. *Their reason for living.*

Or, perhaps, I've preserved their future.

When the Human Beings were out of sight – and despite the continuing crying of the frightened, disoriented children – Dura settled into one of the car's expensive cocoons, relief and guilt once more competing for her soul.

Deni steered the car with unconscious skill along the renewed vortex lines. 'The City is taking in injured from the hinterland. It's not been easy, for any of us.' The doctor was scarcely recognizable from the cheerful, rather patronizing woman who had treated Adda, Dura thought; Maxx's eyecups were ringed by darkness and crusty sleep deposits; her face seemed to have sunk in on itself, becoming gaunt and severe, and she hunched over her reins with tense, knotted muscles.

Dura stared moodily out of the car's huge windows at the Crust as it passed over them. She remembered how she had marvelled at the orderliness of the great hinterland with its ceiling-farms and gardens, as she had viewed it that first time with Toba Mixxax. Now, by contrast, she was appalled at the destruction the Glitch had wrought. In great swathes the farms had been scoured from the Crust, leaving the bare root-ceiling exposed. Here and there coolies still toiled patiently at the shattered land, but the naked ceiling had none of the vigour of the natural forest; obscenely stripped of its rectangles of cultivation it looked like an open wound.

Deni tried to explain how the Crust had responded to the Glitch by *ringing* – vibrating in sectors, apparently all over the Star; the devastation had come in orderly waves, with a lethal and offensive neatness. Dura let the words wash over her, barely understanding.

'The destruction persists right around the hinterland,' Deni said. 'At least half the ceiling-farms have stopped functioning, and the rest can only work on a limited basis.' She glanced at Dura. 'Parz City doesn't have much stock of food, you know; she relies on the daily traffic from the ceiling-farms. And you know what they say . . .'

'What?'

'Any society is only a meal away from revolution. Hork has already instituted rationing. In the long term, I doubt it's going to be enough. Still, at the moment people seem to be accepting the troubles we're having: patiently waiting their turn for medical treatment behind ranks of coolies, following the orders of the Committee. Eventually, I guess, they will blame the Committee for their woes.'

Dura took a deep breath. 'Just as you're blaming me?'

Deni turned to her, her eyes wide. 'Why do you say that?'

'Your tone. Your manner with me, ever since you arrived to bring me back.'

Deni rubbed her nose, and when she looked at Dura again there was a faint smile on her lips. 'No. I don't blame you, my dear. But I do resent being a ferry driver. I have patients to treat . . . At a time like this I have better things to do than . . .'

'Then why did you come to get me?'

'Because Muub ordered me to.'

'Muub? Oh, the Administrator.'

'He felt I was the only person who would recognize you.' She sniffed. 'Old fool. There aren't that many upfluxers on Qos Frenk's ceiling-farm, after all.'

'I still don't understand why you're here.'

'Because that friend of yours insisted on it.' She frowned. 'Adda? Worst patient in the world. But what beautiful work we did with his pneumatic vessels.'

The Air seemed thick in Dura's mouth. 'Adda is alive? He's safe?'

'Oh, yes. He was with Muub when the Glitch hit. He's quite well . . . or at least, as well as before. You know, with injuries like that it's a miracle he's able to move about. And . . .'

Dura closed her eyes. She hadn't dared ask of her kinsmen earlier – as if phrasing the very question would tempt fate. 'And Farr?'

'Who? Oh, the boy. Your brother, isn't he? Yes, he's fine. He was in the Harbour . . .'

'You've seen him? You've *seen* that he's safe?'

'Yes.' Some compassion entered Deni's voice. 'Dura, don't worry about your people. Adda had Farr brought to the Palace . . .'

'The *Palace*?'

'Yes, it was a condition of him working with Hork, apparently.'

Dura laughed; it was as if a huge pressure had been lifted from her heart. But still, what was Adda doing handing out orders at the Palace? Why were they so important, all of a sudden? 'Things have changed since I've been gone.'

Deni nodded. 'Yes, but don't ask me about it . . . Muub will tell you, when we dock.' She growled. 'Another Physician taken away from healing people . . . I hope this project of Hork's, whatever it is, really is important enough to cost so many lives.'

They were approaching the South Pole now; the vortex lines, deceptively orderly, were beginning to converge. Dura studied the Crust. The elegant, pretty farms and gardens of the ceiling-scape here had largely been spared the Glitch's devastation, but there was something odd: the Crust had a fine texture, as if it were covered by fine, dark furs – furs which Waved in slow formation towards the Pole.

Dura pointed this out to Deni. 'What's that?'

Deni glanced up. 'Refugees, my dear. From all over the devastated hinterland. No longer able to work on their farms, they are converging on Parz City, hoping for salvation.'

Dura stared around the sky. *Refugees*. The Crust seemed black with humanity.

The children started to cry again. Dura turned to comfort them.

When Hork heard that the two upfluxers – the boy from the Harbour and the woman, Dura – had been located and were being returned to the Upside, he called Muub and the old fool Adda to another meeting in the Palace anteroom.

Adda settled into his cocoon of rope, his splinted legs dangling absurdly, and he swept his revolting one-eyed gaze around the anteroom as if he owned the place.

Hork suppressed his irritation. 'Your people are safe. They are inside the City. Now I would like to continue with our discussion.'

Adda stared, eyeing him up as if he were a coolie in the Market. At last the old man nodded. 'Very well. Let's proceed.'

Hork saw Muub sigh, evidently with relief.

'I return to my final question,' Hork said. 'I concede the existence of the Xeelee. But I am not concerned with myths. I don't want to hear about the awesome racial goals of the Xeelee . . . I want to know what they want with *us*.'

'I told you,' Adda said evenly. 'They don't want anything of us. I don't think they even know we're here. But they do want something of our world – our Star.'

'Apparently they wish to destroy it,' Muub said, running a hand over his bare scalp.

'Evidently,' Adda said. 'Hork, the wisdom of my people – handed down verbally since our expulsion from . . .'

'Yes, yes.'

'. . . has nothing to say about any purpose of the Star. But we do know that humans were brought here, to this Star. By the Ur-humans. And we were adapted to survive here.'

Muub was nodding at this. 'This isn't a surprise, sir. Analogous anatomy studies have come to similar conclusions.'

'I am struggling to contain my fascination,' Hork said acidly. Restless, frustrated, he pushed his way out of his sling and began to swim briskly around the room. He watched the turning of the small, powerful cooling-fan set in one corner of the painted sky; he studied the captive vortex ring in its nest of clearwood spheres. He resisted the temptation to smash the spheres again, despite his mounting frustration; the cost of repair had been ruinous – indefensible, actually, in such times as now. 'Go on with your account. If humans were brought here, made to fit the Mantle – then why isn't the evidence of this all around us? Where are the devices which made us? Where are these "different" Ur-humans?'

Adda shook his head. 'At one time there *was* plenty of evidence. Marvellous devices, left here by the Ur-men to help us survive, and to work here. Wormhole Interfaces. Weapons, huge structures which would dwarf your shabby City . . .'

'Where are they now?' Hork snapped. 'And don't tell me they were suppressed, deliberately destroyed by some vindictive Parz administration of the past.'

'No.' Adda smiled. 'Your forebears did not have to conceal physical evidence . . . merely the truth.'

'Get on with it.'

'The Colonists,' Adda said slowly.

'What?'

Once, humans had travelled throughout the Star. The Quantum Sea had been as clear as the Air to them, in their marvellous machines. They had been able to venture even into the outer layers of the Core with impunity. And there had been marvellous gateways, called wormhole Interfaces, which had allowed humans even to travel *outside the Star itself*.

The humans, following the commands of their departed creators, the Ur-humans, had set about rebuilding the Star. And the mysterious Colonists, sleeping in their quark soup at the Core, had become hostile to the growing power of humans.

The Colonists had emerged from the Core. Brief, shattering wars were fought.

Human machines were destroyed or dragged into the Quantum Sea. The human population was devastated, the survivors pitched into the open Air virtually without resource.

Within generations, the stories of man's origin on the Star, the tale of the Colonists, became a dim legend, another baroque detail in the rich word-painting of human history, of the invisible worlds beyond the Star.

Muub laughed out loud, his long, aristocratic face creased with mirth. 'I'm sorry, sir,' he said to Hork. 'But here we are compounding myth on myth. How long are we to continue with this charade? I have patients to attend.'

'Shut up, Muub. You'll stay here as long as I need you.'

Hork thought hard. He had damnably little resource to spare. He had to tend the wounded and destitute, and, in the longer term, rebuild on the hinterland, alleviate the hunger of the people.

And yet, and yet . . .

If – by a small diversion of effort – he could remove the fantastic Xeelee threat from the City – the whole world, in fact – then he could become the greatest hero of history.

There was pride, self-aggrandizement in such a vision, Hork knew. So what? If he could repel the Xeelee, mankind would rightfully acclaim him.

But how to go about it?

He certainly couldn't devote armies of scholars to piecing together the fragmentary legends of man's origin. And he didn't have the years to wait while some such discipline as Muub's 'analogous anatomy' cogitated over its subject matter. He had to prioritize, to go for the most direct benefit.

He looked at Adda sharply. 'You say these beings – the Colonists – took the Interfaces, and the other magical machines, back into the Quantum Sea with them. Beyond the reach of our Fishermen. So we've no reason to believe the devices were destroyed?'

Adda looked up; the leech nibbling at his eye, disturbed, slid across his cheek. 'Nor any evidence that they survived.'

Muub snorted. 'Now the old fool has the effrontery to talk of evidence!'

What if this legend of Colonists and ancient technologies held some grain of truth? Then perhaps, Hork speculated, some of these devices *could still exist*, deep in the Quantum Sea. An Interface would be worth having . . .

'Muub,' he asked thoughtfully. 'How could we penetrate the Quantum Sea?'

Muub looked at him, as if shocked by the suggestion. 'We

cannot, of course, sir. It is impossible.' His eyes narrowed. 'You are not thinking of chasing after these absurd legends, of wasting resources on a . . .'

'You will not lecture me, Physician,' Hork snapped. 'Think of it as a – a scientific experiment. If nothing else we would learn much about the Star, and about our own capabilities . . . and, perhaps, disprove once and for all these fanciful legends of Colonists and antique wonders.' *Or*, he allowed himself to imagine, *perhaps I will uncover a treasure lost to mankind for generations.*

'Sir, I must protest. People continue to die, all over the hinterland. Parz itself may be overwhelmed by the flood of refugees approaching. We must abandon these fantasies of the impossible, and return our attention to the immediate, the practical.'

Hork studied the Physician – Muub was stiff, trembling in his cocoon of rope. His irritation with Muub's stiff anger was eclipsed, suddenly, by respect for this decent man. It must have taken a lot of courage for the Physician to speak out like that. 'Muub – my dear Muub – as soon as I close this meeting I will be immersed in the immediate, the practical . . . in the pain of ten thousand human beings.' He smiled. 'I want you to take charge of this project. Reach the Quantum Sea.'

Muub ground out, 'The task – is – impossible.'

Hork nodded. 'Of course. Bring me options, within two days.'

He turned from them then, and, straightening his back, thrust through the Air to the door and his duties.

17

After she'd endured a brief, unsettled sleep in Deni's cramped quarters, a messenger from the Committee called for Dura. The messenger was a small, rather sad man in a scuffed tunic; his skin was thin and pale and his eyes were bruised-looking, discoloured deep inside the cups. Perhaps he had spent too much of his life doing close work inside the City, Dura thought, shut away from fresh Air.

She was led away from the Hospital and through the streets. They passed through the Market, and Waved Upside along Pall Mall. The great avenue seemed quieter than she remembered. The lines of Air-cars moved much more easily than before, with clear Air between the sparsely spaced cars, and many of the shops were closed up, their wood-lamps dimmed. She began to understand how the disaster in the hinterland had impacted the economy of the City.

Even so, the noise was a constant, growling racket and the few fans and illumination vents seemed hardly sufficient. Soon Dura found herself fighting off claustrophobia. And yet, only days before, she had been feeling restless in the limited company of the upfluxers. Her experiences really had left her a misfit, she thought gloomily.

They took a turn off the Mall close to its Upside terminus and emerged, surprisingly, into clear Air-light. They had entered a huge open chamber, a cube a hundred mansheights on a side. Its edges were constructed of fine beams, leaving the faces open to the clear sky – this place must be clinging to the side of the City like some immense wooden leech – but, oddly, the Air was no fresher here than in the bowels of the City, and there was no discernible breeze. Looking more closely, she realized that the apparently open faces of this cube were coated with huge panels of clearwood; she was inside a transparent wooden box big enough to hold – she estimated quickly – a thousand people.

It was impressive, but utterly bizarre; Dura felt bemused – as so often before – by the strangeness of the City.

The messenger touched her elbow. 'Here we are. This is the Stadium. Of course it's empty today; when it's in use it's crammed with people . . . Up there you can see the Committee Box.' He pointed to a thin balcony suspended over the Stadium itself; his voice was thin, ingratiating. 'People come here to watch the Games – our sporting events. Do you have Games in the upflux?'

'Why have I been brought here?'

The little man shied away, his bruised-looking eyecups closing.

'Dura . . .'

Farr?

She whirled in the Air. Her brother was only a mansheight from her; he was calm and apparently well, and dressed in a loose tunic. There were people with him – Adda and three City men.

She saw all this in the heartbeat it took to cross the space between them and take her brother in her arms. He hugged her back – but not as an uninhibited child, she slowly realized; he put his arms around her and patted her spine, comforting her.

She let him go and held him at arm's length. His face was square and serious. He seemed to have grown older, and there was more of their father about him.

'I'm well, Dura.'

'Yes. So am I. I thought you might have been injured in the Glitch.'

'I wasn't in the Bells when the Glitch came. It was my off-shift, and I was in the Harbour . . .'

'That doesn't matter,' she said bitterly. 'You're too young to have been sent down in those things.'

'It's just the way things are,' he said gently. 'Boys younger than me have served in the Bells. Dura, none of it is your fault . . . even if I'd been hurt it wouldn't have been your fault.'

He *was* comforting her. He really was growing up.

'Anyway, I haven't been back to the Harbour for a while,' Farr went on. He smiled. 'Not since Adda had Hork send for me. I've been staying with Toba.'

'How are the family?'

'Well. Cris has been teaching me to Surf.' Farr held his arms out in the Air, as if balancing on an invisible board. 'You'll have to try it . . .'

'Dura. You've made it; I'm glad.' Adda came paddling through the Air towards them. Dura glanced quickly over the old man; his shoulders, chest and lower legs were still bound up with grubby bandages, but he was moving freely enough. He was towing an object which looked like the skin of an Air-pig; sewn up and inflated, it bobbled behind his clumsy progress like a toy.

She found a clear place on his face – away from the eye-leech – and kissed him. 'I'd hug you if I wasn't scared of breaking you.'

He snorted. 'So you got through the Glitch.'

Briefly she told her story; Farr's eyes grew round when she described the Xeelee ship. She told them how the Human Beings had fared in the Glitch – of their twenty dead. As she recited the familiar, lost names, she was reminded of the simple, moving name-litany ceremonial of the lumberjacks.

She told Adda and Farr of the five upfluxer children lodging, for today, with Deni Maxx. Farr and Adda smiled, and promised to visit the kids.

'Now tell me what we're doing here. And why you're towing a dead pig about the place.'

Adda grimaced, making the leech slither across his crumpling cheek. 'You'll find out . . . damn foolishness, all of it.' He glanced around to the rest of the party; Dura recognized Muub, the Hospital Physician, with two other men. 'Come on,' Adda said. 'We'd better get on with it.'

With Dura and Farr helping Adda, the three Human Beings made their way to Muub and his companions.

The six of them hovered together close to the centre of the huge emptiness of the Stadium; Dura felt cold and isolated despite the clamminess of the Pole. Ropes and guide rails were slung across the huge volume all around them, silent evidence of the crowds this place was designed to accommodate.

The Physician, Muub, was dressed in a severe, dark robe. As before, Dura found it impossible not to stare at the grand dome of his bald head. He greeted them with a smile which seemed professional enough but a little strained. 'Thank you for your time.'

Adda grinned. 'Oh, we had a choice?'

Muub's smile thinned. Briskly he introduced his two companions: a Harbour supervisor called Hosch, cadaverously thin, who seemed to know Farr, judging from the sour glances he cast at the boy; and a tall, wispy tree-stem of a man called Seciv Trop whom Muub described as an expert on the Magfield. Like Muub's, Trop's fine old head was shaven, in the style of the academics of the University.

Muub rapidly sketched in the background to Hork's directive. 'Frankly, I'm not certain about the value of this programme; I may as well tell you that from the start. But I do sympathize with Hork's thinking.' He looked about him, his expression hard. 'I only need to be here, in the fragility of this Stadium, to recognize that we have to find some way to protect ourselves from the random danger of Glitches.'

Dura frowned. 'But why are we here? We Human Beings, I mean. You need experts. What can we possibly add?'

'Two things. One is that you *are* experts – or the nearest we have – on the Xeelee. So Hork believes, at any rate. And second, there's no one else.' He raised his arms as if to embrace the City. 'Dura, Parz may seem a large and rich place to you, but the economy has taken a severe battering from the Glitches. All our resources are devoted to coping with the consequences, to rebuilding the hinterland . . . all but us, and we are all Hork felt able to spare.' He smiled at them. 'Six of us, including a boy. And our mission is to save the world. Perhaps we will succeed; and what plaudits we will earn if we do.'

He fell silent. The six of them hovered in a rough ring, studying each other warily – all but the Magfield expert Seciv Trop, who stared into the distance with his finely chiselled eyecups.

'Well,' Muub said briskly. 'Hork asked me to come up with

223

options to achieve the impossible – to penetrate the underMantle, more deeply than any human since prehistory. And I, in turn, asked Hosch and Adda to bring us suggestions to work with. The Bells from the Harbour descend to a depth of about a metre. Our first estimates indicate that we must penetrate at least ten times as deeply – to a depth of ten metres below Parz, deep into the underMantle. Seciv, you're here to comment, if you will, and to add anything you can.'

Trop nodded briskly. 'I'll do my feeble best,' he said in a thin, mannered voice. Seciv Trop was clearly the oldest of the group. His almost-bare scalp was populated by fine clumps of yellow-gold hair, left carelessly unshaven. And his suit – loosely fitting and equipped with immense pockets – was more battered and patched than Dura had come to expect of the grander City folk.

This old fellow was rather endearing, Dura decided. Farr asked, 'Why are we here? In this Stadium?'

'Because of your friend.' Muub eyed the pigskin doubtfully. 'Adda tells me he would prefer to demonstrate his idea rather than describe it. I thought I'd better obtain as much space as possible.'

The Harbour supervisor, Hosch, twisted his face into a sneer. 'Then maybe we'd better let the old fool get on with it before his damn pig corpse starts stinking out the building.'

Adda grinned and hauled on the short rope which attached the inflated pigskin to his belt. He held the grisly artifact before him, obviously relishing the squeamish reaction of the City men. The skin *was* revolting, Dura conceded; its orifices had been crudely sewn over and Air pumped in to inflate its boxy bulk, causing its six fins to become erect. Its sketchy, inhuman face seemed to be staring at her. And, she realized, it actually did stink a little.

Hosch sneered. 'Is this some kind of joke? The old fool thinks we could all don pigskins and swim to the bloody Core.'

Adda waved the inflated skin in the supervisor's face. 'Wrong, City man. You people travel around in chariots hauled by pigs. At first I wondered if humans could travel in one of those all the way to the Core . . . but of course the pigs could never survive the journey into the underMantle. So we

224

build a pig . . . an artificial pig, of wood and Corestuff. Strong enough to withstand the pressures of the underMantle.'

Seciv nodded. 'How is this device to be propelled?'

Adda jabbed a finger at the pig's jet orifice. 'With jetfarts, of course. Like the real thing.' He flicked the inflated fins. 'And these will keep it stable.' Now he pressed the skin between his arm and his bandaged ribs; Air squirted out of the jet orifice and the pig-corpse wobbled through the air in a ghastly, comic parody of life.

Hosch laughed out loud. 'And where do the farts come from, upfluxer? You?'

Seciv frowned, his crumpled hair waving. 'You could mimic the internal operation of the pig's anatomy. The car could carry tanks of Air, heated by a stock of wood in a nuclear-burning boiler and expelled through a valve orifice.' With a delicate finger he reached out and poked at one flabby fin, tentatively. 'You could even make an attempt at steering, by mounting these fins on gimbals worked from inside the craft. And the fart nozzles could be made directional, with a little ingenuity.' The old man nodded approvingly to Adda. 'A practical suggestion in many respects.'

Adda – despite himself, Dura realized – swelled at the praise; Hosch looked disgruntled.

Farr said seriously, 'But how could it survive the underMantle? Adda, I learned in the Bells that it's not pressure alone that would destroy such a craft, by crushing it . . .' He snapped his fist closed suddenly, making Dura flinch; she wondered where he'd learned such crude dramatic tricks. Farr went on, 'Nuclear matter – ordinary matter – would dissolve.'

Hosch said rapidly, 'Well, of course it would. Anyone with a fingernail of experience knows that. Our Bells are protected from the pressure by magnetic fields sent down from the turbines in the City.'

Seciv Trop shook his head. 'That's a misapprehension, Supervisor. To be precise, the Bells are fed by *electrical currents* which are generated in the Harbour . . . but the protective magnetic shell is generated at the Bell itself, by superconducting hoops which girdle the Bell.'

Hosch looked the old man up and down. 'You're a

Fisherman, I suppose. We must have been on different shifts . . .'

Muub touched Hosch's shoulder. 'Seciv designed the current generation of Bells – the Bells you ride every day. Hosch, your life depends upon his expertise; it suits you ill to mock him.'

Hosch subsided. 'Well, what of it? The boy's point stands.'

Seciv seemed impervious to offence. 'One would simply need to gird this artificial pig around with superconducting hoops, and carry equipment to generate the magnetic field from within.' He frowned. 'Of course, the bulk of the craft would be increased.'

Dura asked, 'Wouldn't it get hot inside the wooden pig, with nuclear burning going on all the time?'

Seciv nodded. 'Yes, that would be a difficulty . . . though not in itself insurmountable. A more serious problem would be the supply of propellant Air. Compression ratios in even our best-made tanks are not very high. Sufficient for a jaunt to the ceiling-farms in an Air-car, but hardly enough for an expedition of this magnitude.' He eyed Adda sadly. 'Again, perhaps this could be overcome. But there are two far more devastating flaws. First, a lack of stability. There is more to an Air-pig than an anus and a few fins, after all. The pig has six eyes to guide it . . .'

'Well,' Adda said defensively, 'you could have six windows of clearglass. Or more.'

'Perhaps. But the windows would each be manned by a pilot – yes? – who would then have to relay instructions to a crew – five or six men who would haul laboriously at the directing fins, hoping to adjust the motion. Adda, your wooden pig would flounder in the Air, I fear.'

Dura said, 'But you don't have to use fins. The thing doesn't have to be exactly like a pig, after all. Maybe we could use jetfarts, coming from the sides of the pig.'

'Yes.' Muub looked thoughtful. 'That could be far more precise.'

Seciv smiled indulgently. 'Still, I would expect instability. Besides, I fear my second objection is fatal.'

Adda glared at him, his eye-leech slithering across his cheek.

226

'Your mode of propulsion could not work within the underMantle, let alone the Quantum Sea. In high-pressure conditions Air could not be expelled; it would be forced back into the body of the pig.'

Hosch scratched his head. 'I hate to be constructive about this stupid idea,' he said, 'but couldn't you throw a magnetic field away from the pig's hull? Then the farts would be expelled into Air at normal pressure.'

Seciv looked at him and ran bony fingers through his scraps of hair, evidently searching for a simple explanation. 'But the expelled Air would still be inside the magnetic field, which in turn would be attached to the ship through the field lines. The Air would push at the magnetic shell, which would drag back the ship. It is a matter of action and reaction, you see . . .'

Muub waved him to silence. 'I think we can take your word for it, Seciv.' He smiled at Adda. 'Sir, the consensus seems to be that we can't proceed with your suggestion; but it was ingenious, and perhaps – do you agree, Seciv? – some aspects of it may survive in a final design. Also, it sounds to me as if we could use this idea to make Air-cars of a different design from those we have at present – Air-cars which wouldn't need pigs to draw them. None of the problems we've talked about would arise if the craft operated in the free Air, after all.'

Adda, clutching his retrieved pig with his one free arm, looked inordinately pleased with himself. Dura nudged him and said quietly, 'You're enjoying this. You're forgetting you're a miserable old bugger. You'll confuse them.'

Adda glared at her. 'Well? Who's next? This Fisherman's been so clever about my suggestions; now let's hear what he has to say.'

'Indeed. Hosch?'

The Harbour supervisor spread his empty hands, speaking only to Muub. 'My idea is straightforward and I don't need to send pigskins flying around to describe it. I say we stick to what we know. I say we extend the Spine . . . but build it as long as we need it to be, down into the underMantle.'

Seciv Trop rubbed his chin. 'Well, that has the merit of familiarity, as you say. The wooden Spine would need protecting against dissolution in the underMantle, but we could use superconducting coils to achieve that, as we do now . . . But what an awesome undertaking it would be. I doubt if such a Spine could sustain its structural integrity on the lengthscale required. And it might affect the stability of the City itself. Could the anchor-bands sustain our position, here at the Pole, with such a counterweight?'

Muub was shaking his head. 'Hosch, we can't conceivably spare the resources for this. You must know the timber convoys from the Crust have dried up since the Glitch, so we're not getting the wood. And we haven't the manpower to spare, in any case . . .'

'Besides,' Dura said, 'what if a Glitch hit? The Spine would be so fragile it would be destroyed in moments.'

Hosch folded his arms and crossed his legs, turning his wiry body into a ball of finality. 'Then it's impossible. We may as well stop wasting our time and tell Hork so.'

Muub turned to him. 'Frankly, Hosch, I won't be sorry if that is our conclusion. I'd rather not waste any more time and effort on this fool's errand than I have to.'

'Oh, no.' Seciv Trop's creased face showed irritation. 'We haven't reached such a conclusion at all. We've merely eliminated possibilities. And we do, perhaps, have some of the elements of a workable solution.'

Muub looked sour, and he pulled at a thread in his robe. 'Go on.'

'First, we know that this hypothetical device – this new, free-floating Bell – will need a protective magnetic field, to keep it from dissolution, and some means of propulsion. It will have to be self-sustaining; our traditional methods cannot be extended to such depths, so we've ruled out supply from the City. So the device would have to carry a simple turbine to generate a protective field.'

'How would it move?' Dura asked. 'I thought you said that jetfarts couldn't work.'

'And so they couldn't,' said Seciv. 'But there are other means of propulsion . . .'

'Waving,' said Farr, his round face animated. 'What about that? Maybe we could make a Bell that could swim freely, a Bell that could Wave.'

228

'Exactly.' Seciv nodded, looking pleased. 'We could haul ourselves along the Magfield, exactly as we do when we Wave in the Air. Well done, young man.'

Muub pulled at his lower lip. 'But maybe the Magfield doesn't penetrate the underMantle.'

'We believe it does,' Seciv said. 'The underMantle and the Sea are permeated by charged particles – protons, electrons and hyperons – which sustain the Magfield.'

Hosch sneered. 'What would we do, attach a pair of false legs to the back?'

Farr – whose imagination seemed to have been caught – said excitedly, 'No, you'd Wave using coils of superconductor. Like the anchor-bands. You could move them from inside the Bell, and . . .'

'Good thinking once more,' Seciv said smoothly. 'But you could go a little further. It wouldn't be necessary to move the coils themselves, physically; it is the movement of the current within them that could generate forward motion.'

Muub was nodding slowly. 'I see. So you'd make the current flow back and forth.'

'Have it alternate. Exactly. Then the coils could be fixed rigidly to the hull. And, of course, this design would have a certain economy: the craft's propulsion system would be one and the same as the magnetic shielding system.' He frowned. 'But we would still face the problem of the excessive heat in the interior of the craft generated by a nuclear-burning turbine in an enclosed space . . .'

Hosch looked reluctant to speak, as if, Dura thought, he genuinely hated to contribute anything positive. 'But you wouldn't need to use nuclear burning,' he said at last. 'Anything to power the turbine would be sufficient . . . maybe even human muscles.'

'No, I fear our muscles would be too feeble for such a task. But we *could* use the power of animals – a team of pigs, harnessed to some form of turbine – yes, indeed!' He laughed and clapped Adda on the back, sending the old man spinning slowly like a bandaged fan. 'So it seems after all that we will be riding pigs to the Core!'

Adda steadied himself, grinning widely.

Muub looked around the group. 'I don't believe it.' He

sounded disappointed. 'I think we've come up with something we could build . . . something that might actually work.'

Seciv pulled at his chin; Dura had never seen hands so bony and delicate. 'We should build a prototype – there may still be unforeseen problems with the design. And, of course, once the descent begins the craft will encounter conditions we can only guess at.'

'And then,' Dura said, her spine prickling and cold, 'there are the Colonists. In fact, the mission will be a failure if it doesn't encounter the Colonists. What then?'

'What indeed?' Seciv echoed gravely.

Muub ran a hand over his bald head. 'Damn you. Damn all of you. You've succeeded too well; I can't justify reporting to Hork that this idea of his is impossible.' He eyed the Harbour supervisor. 'Hosch, I want you to take charge of the design and construction of a prototype.'

Hosch glared back resentfully, his thin face livid.

Muub said icily, 'Call on these upfluxers, and you can have some of Seciv's time. As for labour, use some of your workers from the Harbour. But keep it simple and cheap, will you? There's no need to waste more of our energy on this than we have to.' He turned in the Air, dismissing them. 'Call me when the prototype's ready.'

The Human Beings, arms loosely linked, followed Muub and the others slowly out of the Stadium.

'So,' Adda said. 'A chance to confront gods from the past.'

'Not gods,' Dura said firmly. 'Even the Xeelee aren't gods . . . But these Colonists could be monsters, if they exist. Remember the Core Wars.'

Adda sniffed. 'This damn fool expedition will never get that far anyway. This Waving Bell will be crushed.'

'Perhaps. But you needn't be so stuffy, Adda. I know you enjoyed playing with ideas, back there. You have to admire the imagination, the spirit of these City folk.'

'Well, what now?' Adda asked. 'Do you want to find your friend Ito?'

'Later . . . I have something to do first. I need to find some-one – the daughter of a friend, from my ceiling-farm. A friend called Rauc.'

Adda thought about that. 'Does the girl know what's become of her mother?'

'No,' Dura said quietly. 'I'm going to have to tell her.'

Adda nodded, his crumpled face expressionless, seeming to understand.

And one day, Dura thought, *I will have to go to the upflux forests, and tell Brow . . .*

She glanced at Farr. The boy's eyes were fixed on an indefinite distance, and his face was blank. She felt as if she could read his mind. *Humans were going to build a ship to find the Colonists.* It was indeed an idea full of wonder . . . deep inside herself, too, she found, there was a small spark of awe.

And Farr was young enough to relish a ride.

But Adda was right. It was an utterly deadly prospect. And surely, she thought, as Hork's 'experts' on the Xeelee, at least one of the three Human Beings would be assigned to the voyage, if it were ever made . . .

She held Farr's arm tight and pulled herself closer to him, determined that Farr should never make the journey he was dreaming of.

18

Wakefulness intruded slowly on Mur.

Slowly, in shreds and shards, he became aware of the rustle of the Crust-trees, the tired stink of his own body, the endless yellow glow of the Air pushing into his closed eyecups. He'd used a few loops of frayed rope to bind himself loosely to a branch of an outlying tree, and now he could feel the undeniable reality of the ropes as they dug into the thin flesh of his chest and thighs.

Then the pain started.

His stomach, empty for so long, seemed to be slowly imploding, filling the centre of his body with a dull, dragging ache. His joints protested when he began to stir – stiff joints were a wholly unexpected side-effect of hunger, reducing his movements on bad days to those of an old man – and there was a sharp sheet of pain stretched round the inside of his skull, as if his brain were pulling away from the bone.

He jammed his eyes closed and wrapped his arms around himself, feeling his own bony elbows digging into his ribs. How strange it was that he had never slept more deeply in his life than in these impossibly difficult times. While waking life had become steadily more unbearable, sleep was ever more comfortable, seductive, a different realm in which his physical pain and mental distress dissolved.

If only I could stay there, he thought. *How easy it would be never to wake up again . . .*

But already the pain had dug too far into his awareness for that option to be available today.

With a sigh he opened his eyes and probed at the cups with one finger, working at rims sharp with crusty sleep deposits. Then he clambered slowly out of his loose sling of ropes. The rest of the Human Beings – the other fourteen – were scattered across the lower rim of the forest, bound by similar loops of rope. Dangling there half-asleep they looked like the pupae of insects, deformed spin-spiders perhaps.

Mur dropped out of the forest, avoiding the eyes of those others who were awake.

He stretched, his muscles still aching from yesterday's Waving. He pulled a handful of leaf-matter from the tree, and then flexed his legs and Waved stiffly down into the Mantle. Perhaps twenty mansheights below the fringe of the forest ceiling he lifted his tunic and raised his legs to his chest. His hips and knees protested, but he grabbed his lower legs and pulled his thighs close to his stomach. At first his bowels failed to respond to this prompting – like the rest of his system his digestive and elimination processes seemed to be failing, slowly – but he persisted, keeping his arms wrapped around his legs.

At last his lower bowel convulsed, and – with a stab of pain which lanced through the core of his body – a hard packet of waste was expelled into the Air. He glanced down. The waste, floating down into the Mantle, was compact, too dark.

He cleaned himself with his handful of leaves.

Dia, his wife, came drifting down from the impromptu camp in the forest. As she descended, he saw how she was blinking away the remnants of sleep and compressing her eyecups against the brightness of the Air; but she was already – just moments after waking – squinting along the vortex lines into the South, towards the distant Pole, trying to assess how far they had come, how much further was left of this huge odyssey.

When she reached Mur she looked into his face, kissed him on the lips, and wrapped her arms around his chest. He folded his arms around her and rubbed her back. Through her shabby poncho he could feel the bones of her spine. They had nothing to say to each other, so they clung to each other, hanging in the silent Air, with the Quantum Sea spread below them.

Since Dura and the City woman had left in their Air-car – taking away the children, including their own Jai – the fifteen abandoned Human Beings had trekked across the Mantle towards the Pole. The slow pulsations of the vortex lines marked out the endless days of the journey. With no stores of food, the Human Beings were forced to follow the fringe of the Crust-forest; the leaves of the trees were scarcely nutritious, but they did serve to fool the body into forgetting its hunger for a while. Every few days their food ran out and they were forced to interrupt the march. There was some game to be had but the forest was unfamiliar, and the animals, still scared and scattered after the most recent Glitch, were wary and difficult to trap.

Without their own herd, the Human Beings were slowly starving to death. And on this hopeless trek, with its endless days of slow, painful Waving, the Human Beings were probably burning off their energy faster than they could replace it. Mur couldn't forget the richness of the 'bread' Dura had brought to them, when she had come Waving out of the sky so unexpectedly with her startling stories of Cities in the Air.

Their progress round the Mantle's curve was imperceptible, a crushingly discouraging crawl. Every time he woke to another changeless Mantlescape Mur felt discouraged. And, even when the Pole was neared, the Human Beings would still have to cross the hinterland, the cultivated belt around the Pole. How would the inhabitants of those regions – themselves suffering after the Glitches – welcome this band of starving refugees as they came drifting beneath their ceiling-farms?

The logical thing for the Human Beings to do would be to give up this trek. Their best chance of survival would be to stay here, or even retreat a little further into the upflux, and try to establish a new home on the edge of the Crust-forest. Stop wasting their energies on this trek. They could build a new Net, establish a new herd of Air-pigs. They could even, he'd thought dizzily as he Waved across the silent Air, experiment with maintaining flocks of rays. The flesh of the ray was tough and not as palatable as Air-pig, but it softened when broiled using nuclear-burning heat; and the eggs were fine to eat and easy to store.

. . . But, of course, that wasn't possible; for their children had been taken from them, by well-meaning Dura, and transported to the South Pole. When he stared into the dull crimson glow of the Pole, in the far downflux, Mur felt as if a chain as long as a vortex line connected him directly to his child, a chain which dragged inexorably at his heart. Dura's action had surely been in the best interests of the children. But it left Mur knowing that his only chance of meeting his son again was to stay alive and to complete this trek, all the way to the City at the Pole.

He squeezed Dia once, and then they broke and prepared to return to the Crust-forest, to face the others and begin the day's work.

'Dia! Mur!' The voice, drifting down from the Crust-forest, radiated excitement.

Dia and Mur slowed their ascent, confused, and looked up. Philas was dropping towards them, her skinny legs pumping at the Air. When she reached the couple, she grabbed at their arms to stop herself.

Dia held Philas's shoulders. 'What is it? What's wrong?'

Philas, panting, the bones of her face prominent under her tied-back hair, shook her head. 'Nothing's wrong. But . . . look. Look down there.' She pointed, down past their feet into the Mantle.

The three of them separated and tipped forward in the Air. Mur peered down, trying to follow the direction of Philas's gesture. He saw the orderly array of vortex lines, the dull purple bruise of the Quantum Sea beyond the crystalline Air. There seemed nothing unusual, except . . .

There. A small, dark knot in the Air, a hint of motion.

He turned to Dia. 'Your eyes are sharper than mine. What is it?'

'People,' she said, squinting down. 'A group of them. Twenty or thirty, maybe. It looks like an encampment. But there's something at the centre . . .'

'What?'

Philas thrust her face forward at Dia. 'Do *you* see it?'

'I think so,' Dia said slowly. Her eyes narrowed. 'But it might not mean anything. Philas . . .'

Mur was baffled. 'What is it? What do you see?'

Uncertainty and fear creased Dia's small, pretty face. 'It's a tetrahedron,' she said.

The fifteen Human Beings gathered on the lower edge of the forest and debated what to do. Dia, fearful, uncertain, thought they shouldn't waste time on this chance encounter; she wanted simply to continue with the slog to the Pole. Mur sympathized. The Human Beings were already divided, listless, growing steadily more apathetic. It was becoming ever harder to maintain the momentum of this trek across the Mantle; and once that momentum was gone, it might be impossible to regain.

They would be stranded, wherever they stopped. And that, of course, would be unbearable for those with children at the Pole.

Philas and others argued strongly for doing something. 'Think about it,' she said vehemently, her thin arms raised over her head as she spoke, her fingers spread wide. 'What if that really is a wormhole Interface, left over from the past? What if it's still working?'

'That's impossible,' Dia said. 'The Interfaces were taken down into the Core, by the Colonists after the Core Wars.'

'The Mantle is a big place,' someone said. 'Maybe some of the Interfaces were left functioning. Maybe . . .'

'Yes,' Philas said eagerly, 'just think of that. We know that in the days before the Wars Human Beings could cross the Mantle in huge bounds, using the wormholes. If that is a working Interface down there we might complete this impossible journey in a heartbeat!'

Mur looked around at faces rendered sharp by hunger and exhaustion. Philas was weaving a dream of abandoning this ghastly journey, to reach their goal in moments with the aid of magical ancient technology. It was seductive, compelling, all but irresistible.

Despite his loyalty to Dia, he felt himself falling under the spell of that dream.

'There are already people there,' he said slowly. 'Around the Interface. If it is an Interface. Who's to say how they will react to us? Will they simply let us walk up and wander through?'

'Maybe they're Colonists,' Philas said.

'Anyway,' said someone, 'we won't know unless we go to find out . . .'

There was a murmur of agreement. Dia dropped her head.

Philas and Mur were named as scouts, to go ahead to the

artifact and investigate, leaving the rest of the Human Beings in the forest until their return.

Mur tried to comfort Dia. 'It won't take us long. And perhaps...'

'Perhaps what?' She stared at him bitterly. 'Perhaps there are wizards there who can restore little Jai to us. Is that what you expect?'

'Dia...'

She seemed to slump, as if the Air was collapsing out of her. 'We're going to spend the rest of our lives here. Right here. Dying off one by one. Aren't we, Mur?'

Philas and Mur dived away from the forest and into the Mantle. The tetrahedral artifact might be as much as a half-day away, so they each carried a bag containing a little of the tribe's precious, and dwindling, supply of pig-meat.

At first Mur looked back frequently into the Crust-forest. Dia's face, turned down like a small, round leaf, followed them as they descended, her expression soon too distant to read. Then she ducked back into the forest. For a while Mur was able to follow the movements of the other Human Beings as they worked through the forest, using the time to hunt and to repair damaged tools, ropes and clothes. But at last the site of the Human Beings' temporary camp was lost in the swirling, complex tapestry of trunks and branches that made up the Crust-forest.

Mur spent some time staring up at the forest, carefully committing the pattern of trunks to memory so they could find the Human Beings again.

Philas descended towards the artifact without speaking. Her thin face was intent on the goal, empty of expression; Mur hadn't seen her so focussed since the death of Esk. She dug into her pouch and, with efficient regularity, bit into a piece of meat.

Mur, alone with his thoughts, fell through the vortex lines. The artifact, and the little colony around it, grew in his vision tantalizingly slowly. But it wasn't long before he could see without ambiguity that the artifact was indeed a tetrahedron, around ten mansheights to a side.

The story of the Colonists, and their Core Wars, was part of

237

the lore of the Human Beings. When the Ur-humans first reached the Star, having travelled from their own unimaginable worlds, the Star was empty of human life. The Colonists had been the first generation to be established within the Star, by the Ur-humans. It had been their task to spawn the first of the Star's true inhabitants: all of them, the mortal, frail ancestors of the Human Beings, the people of Parz and the hinterland, all the inhabitants of the Mantle.

Compared to Human Beings the Colonists had been like gods. They had more in common with the Ur-humans, perhaps, Mur speculated. With Ur-human technology they had pierced the Mantle with wormhole links and established huge Cities which had sailed through the Mantle in vast, orderly arrays. The first generations of Human Beings had worked with their progenitors, travelling the wormhole links and building a Mantle-wide society.

Then the Core Wars had come.

As they neared the artifact, and the irregular little settlement around it, excitement gathered in Mur. Fatigue and hunger worked on him as he Waved, and he became aware that his thinking was becoming looser, more fragmented. His head seemed filled with visions, with new hopes; and the aches of his tired, protesting body seemed to fade. Could these really be Colonists, this artifact a fragment from the magical past?

He wanted to believe. He was tired – so tired – of pain, of death, of scraping his marginal existence from the unforgiving Air. To discover a Colonist artifact would be like returning to the arms of long-dead parents.

Glancing across at Philas, he recognized the same hunger to believe – to find a home – in her expression, the set of her body as she Waved.

With perhaps five hundred mansheights separating them from the artifact, two people broke from the grouping around the tetrahedron. The two came Waving cautiously up to meet Philas and Mur.

Mur slowed, and moved closer to Philas.

The pair from the tetrahedron halted a dozen mansheights below the Human Beings. They were a man and a woman, and they carried spears of wood. The woman came up a little further, and pointed her spear at Mur's belly. 'What do you want?'

Mur inspected the woman. She must have been aged around forty. The spear was well crafted, but it was just a spear – nothing more sophisticated than a sharpened stick of wood, nothing the Human Beings couldn't have manufactured for themselves. The woman wore a crude, pocketed poncho of what looked like pig-leather, and a wide-brimmed hat. Folds of cloth were tied up around the rim of the hat. The woman was well muscled but scrawny; her face was wide and flat, disfigured by a scowl. 'Well?' she demanded. 'Deaf, are you?'

Mur sighed, disappointment gathering in him. He turned to Philas. 'Obviously, these aren't Colonists.'

'Who are they, then?'

'How should I know?' he snapped back, irritated.

He moved forward a little, with arms spread wide, hands empty. 'My name is Mur. This is Philas. We're – refugees.' He decided not to mention the rest of the Human Beings. 'We lost all we possessed in the Glitch. We're trying to get to Parz City. Do you know it?'

The woman's eyes narrowed; she didn't reply. She raised the spear uncertainly and poked it towards Mur's stomach again, substituting aggressiveness for an answer.

'We're wasting our time,' Mur whispered to Philas. But Philas had broken away from him and was Waving down with irregular, trembling strokes of her thin legs towards the strangers.

'You have an Interface,' she said.

The man, similarly grimy and scowling, a little younger than the woman, joined his companion. He too was wearing a battered, wide-brimmed hat. They stared at the Human Beings as suspiciously, thought Mur, as a pair of tethered Airpigs.

'Please,' Philas said. 'We've come a long way. We're trying to reach the Pole. Can we . . .' She stumbled over her words, as if she'd become suddenly aware of how foolish they sounded. 'Will your Interface help us?' She looked from one to the other. 'Do you understand what I'm asking?'

The man opened a mouth devoid of teeth and laughed, but

239

the woman laid a restraining hand on his arm. Her voice remained stern, but it softened a little. 'Yes, I understand. And you're right; it is an Interface – from the olden days, from before the Core Wars. But you can't use it.'

Philas was trembling. 'We'll pay,' she said wildly. 'You must . . .'

Mur grabbed her shoulders and tried to still her shivering with his own inertia. 'Stop it, Philas. Don't you understand? Even if we could pay, *the Interface doesn't work any more.* These people are as helpless as we are.'

Philas stared into his face resentfully, then turned away; her body was wracked by shuddering.

The man and woman watched them curiously.

Mur turned to them wearily. 'Why don't you put away your weapons? You can see we're no threat to you.'

They lowered their spears carefully, but kept them aimed roughly in the direction of the Human Beings. The man said, 'You really are refugees from further upflux?'

'Yes. And we really are trying to reach a place called Parz City, which we've never seen. But it's at the Pole.'

'Which Pole?' the woman asked. 'The South Pole?'

The man cackled. 'If you're starting from here it hardly matters, does it?'

'Oh, shut up, Borz,' the woman said.

Mur put his arm around Philas. 'Will you let us see your Interface?'

To his shame, he read amused pity in the woman's expression. 'If you want,' she said. 'But stay close to the two of us. Do you understand? We see enough thieves and beggars . . .'

'We're no beggars,' Philas said with a spark of spirit. She drew away from Mur and pulled her shoulders straight. 'Come, then.'

Borz and the woman turned away from them and separated by a couple of mansheights. Hand in hand, Mur and Philas Waved cautiously forward.

Soon they were approaching the artifact, shepherded by spears and scowls.

Mur squeezed Philas's hand. 'You should have said we weren't thieves,' he whispered. 'I was thinking of trying a little begging.'

She managed a small laugh. 'It wouldn't have worked. These people have no more than we have . . . or had, before we lost our home.' She pointed at Borz, to their left. 'Look at the hat he's wearing.'

The hat's brim was piled with pleats of fine material, knotted into place by ties fixed through holes in the leather of the hat. Mur imagined undoing those ties; perhaps a kind of net would drop down, around the head.

'It's odd, but what about it?'

'Remember Dura's tales of her time on the ceiling-farm. The Air-tanks they made her wear, working high up, close to the Crust. The masks . . .'

'Oh. Right.' Mur nodded. 'Those hats must have come from coolies' Air-tanks.'

'So my guess is these people used to be coolies. Maybe they ran away.'

'But they ought to know about Parz.'

Philas laughed without humour. She seemed in control of herself again, but her mood was black. 'So they are concealing things from us. Well, we lied to them. That's what the world is like, it seems.'

Mur stared at Borz's hat. Apart from Deni Maxx's Air-car it was the first artifact even remotely related to the City he'd ever seen. And recognizing it now from Dura's description somehow lent veracity to Dura's bizarre tale. He felt oddly reassured by the confirmation of this small detail, as if somewhere inwardly he'd imagined Dura might be lying, or mad.

The people turned to stare, suspicious and hostile, as the Human Beings were brought into the encampment by Borz and his companion. There seemed to be around forty humans in the little colony, perhaps fifteen of them children and infants. The adults were fixing clothes, mending nets, sharpening knives, lounging in the Air and talking. Children wriggled around them like tiny rays, their bare skins crackling with electron gas. None of it would have looked out of place in any of the Human Beings' encampments, Mur thought.

The tetrahedral artifact loomed beyond the small-scale human activities. It was a skeletal framework, incongruous, sharp, dark.

Borz and the woman hung back as Mur and Philas hesitantly approached the tetrahedron's forbidding geometries. Mur peered up at the framework. The edges were poles a little thicker than his wrist, each about ten mansheights long. They were precisely machined of some dull, dark substance. The four triangular faces defined by the edges enclosed nothing but ordinary Air – in fact, the people here had slung sections of net to enclose a small herd of squabbling, starved-looking Air-pigs at the framework's geometric centre. Elsewhere on the framework rough bags had been fixed by bits of rope; irregular bulges told Mur that the bags probably contained food, clothes and tools.

Mur moved forward, reached out a tentative hand and laid his palm against one edge. The material was smooth, hard and cold to the touch. Maybe this was the Corestuff of which Dura had spoken, extracted from the forbidding depths of the underMantle by City folk (and now, unimaginably, by the boy Farr whom Mur had grown up with).

Philas asked, 'Can we go inside?'

The woman laughed. 'Of course you can. Your friend was right . . . nothing works, any more.'

The man grunted to Mur. 'We'd hardly keep our pigs in there if they were going to be whisked off to the North Pole at any moment.'

'I imagine not.'

Philas passed cautiously through one face of the tetrahedron. Mur saw her shiver as she crossed the invisible plane marked by the edges. She hovered close to the pigs and turned in the Air, peering into the corners of the tetrahedron.

The man – Borz – grunted. 'Oh, what the hell.' He dug into one of the bags dangling on the tetrahedral frame and extracted a handful of food. 'Here.'

Mur grabbed the food. It was stale, slightly stinking Air-pig flesh. Mur allowed himself one deep bite before stuffing the rest into his belt. 'Thank you,' he said around the mouthful of food. 'I can see you've little to spare.'

The woman drifted closer to him. 'Once,' she said slowly, 'this frame sparkled blue-white. As if it was made of vortex lines. Can you imagine it? And it really was a wormhole Interface; you could pass through it and cross the Mantle in a heartbeat.' For a moment she sounded sad – nostalgic for days she'd never seen – but now her dismissive expression returned. 'So they say, anyway. But then the Core Wars came...'

After raising several generations of Human Beings, the Colonists had suddenly withdrawn. According to the Human Beings' fragmented oral histories the Colonists had retreated into the Core, taking most of the marvellous Ur-human technology with them, and destroying anything they were forced to leave behind.

The Human Beings had been left stranded in the Air, helpless, with no tools save their bare hands.

Perhaps the Colonists had expected the Human Beings to die off, Mur wondered. But they hadn't. Indeed, if Dura's tales of Parz and its hinterland were accurate, they had begun to construct a new society of their own, using nothing but their own ingenuity and the resources of the Star. A civilization which – if not yet Mantle-wide – was at least on a scale to bear comparison with the great days of the ancients.

'The wormholes collapsed,' the woman said. 'Most of the Interfaces were taken away into the Core. But some of them were left behind, like this one. But its vortex-light died. Now it just drifts around in the Magfield...'

'I wonder what happened to the people inside the wormholes,' Mur said. 'When the holes collapsed.'

Philas came drifting out of the tetrahedron. 'Come on, Mur,' she said tiredly.

Mur thanked Borz for the scrap of food, and nodded to the woman – whose name, he realized, he'd never learned.

The pair barely reacted, and their scowls seemed to be returning. Their spears had never left their hands, Mur noticed.

They Waved out of the little encampment. A child jeered at them, until silenced by a parent; Mur and Philas didn't look back.

They began to Wave upwards, side by side.

Mur gazed up at the Crust-forest. 'That seems a hell of a long way back,' he said. 'To have come all this way, for a handful of meat...'

'Yes,' Philas said savagely, 'but we might have found riches. Riches beyond imagining. We had to come.'

'I wonder why they stay here, close to the Interface. Do you think it protects them, when Glitches come?'

'I doubt it,' Philas said. 'After all, the thing floats freely, they said. It's just a relic, a ruin from the past.'

'Then why do they stay?'

'For the same reason Dura's City folk built their City at the Pole.' Philas waved her hands at the empty Mantlescape, the arching vortex lines. 'Because it's a fixed point, in all this emptiness. Something to cling to, to call home.' She wiped her eyes with the back of her hand; already she seemed short of breath. 'Better than drifting, like we do. Better than that.'

Mur lifted his face to the Crust-forest and Waved hard, ignoring the gathering ache in his hips, knees and ankles.

19

Dura made sure it was she, not Farr, whom Hork chose to go on the journey into the underMantle.

At first Adda tried to explain Dura's reasoning to Farr, to provide a bridge between them; but he could see that Farr was devastated. The boy mooched around the Upside apartment Hork had loaned the Human Beings like a trapped Air-pig. Adda wistfully watched him prowl, recalling Logue as a young man. The underMantle journey had many potent elements for Farr – the chance to protect his sibling by taking her place, the intrinsic excitement of the jaunt itself. Farr was still such a melange of boy and man.

But – if one of the three Human Beings must go on this absurd trip – then Dura was the best choice. Farr didn't have the maturity, or Adda himself the strength, to cope with the challenges the journey would provide . . .

Adda cursed himself silently. Even in the privacy of his own mind he was starting to use the diluted language of the City folk, to be influenced by their grey thinking. Into the Core with that.

The truth was that whoever went down inside this ramshackle craft into the underMantle would almost certainly die there. Dura's qualification was only that she, of the three of them, had the skills and strength marginally to reduce that level of certainty.

So, knowing Dura's decision was right, Adda gave up trying to convince Farr. Instead he tried to support the decision in Farr's mind in subtle ways – by taking the decision as a given, not even trying to justify it. He concentrated on trying to distract Farr from his anxious, angry concern for his sister, which wound up tighter as the day of the Mantle-craft's launch neared. To this end Adda was pleased with the friendships Farr had made in his brief time in the City – with Cris, and the Fisherman Bzya – and tried to encourage them.

When Cris offered to take Farr Surfing again Farr at first refused, unwilling to break out of his absorption with Dura; but Adda pressed him to accept the invitation. In the end it was a little party of four – Cris, Farr, Adda and Bzya – who set off, two days before Dura's launch, through the corridors for the open Air.

Adda had taken a liking to the huge, battered Fisherman, and sensed that Bzya had given Farr a great deal of support – more than Farr realized, probably – during Farr's brief time in the Harbour. Now Farr was free of his indenture, thanks to the whim of Hork V, and – here was the boy showing his immaturity again, Adda reflected – now he seemed to sympathize little with Bzya, who was stuck with the situation Farr had escaped – the huge, stinking halls of the Harbour machines, and the depths of the underMantle. Instead, Farr complained at how little he saw of Bzya.

Adda had no qualms in accepting Bzya's help as they made their way through the busy corridors; the presence of Bzya's huge arm guiding him was somehow less patronizing, less insulting, than any other City man's.

As they travelled out from the core of the City the street-corridors became barer, free of doors and buildings, and the Air more dusty. At last they reached the Skin. It was dark, deserted here, almost disquietingly so, and the City hull stretched above and below them. Adda surveyed the workmanship critically: curving sheets of crudely cut wooden planks, hammered onto a thick framework. It was like being in the interior of a huge mask. From without, the City was imposing, even to a worldly-wise upfluxer like himself; but seen from within, its primitive design and construction were easy to discern. These City folk really weren't so advanced, despite their facility with Corestuff; the Ur-humans would surely have laughed at this wooden box.

They Waved slowly along the Skin, not speaking, until Cris brought them to a small doorway, set into the Skin and locked by a wheel. With Bzya's help Cris turned the stiff wheel – it creaked as it rotated, releasing small puffs of dust – and shoved the door open.

Adda hauled himself through the doorframe and into the open Air. He Waved a few mansheights away from the City and hovered in the Air, breathing in the fresh stuff with a surge of relief. The party had emerged about halfway up the rectangular bulk of the City – in the *Midside*, Adda reminded himself – and the skin of Parz, like the face of a giant, cut off half the sky behind him. The imposing curve of a Longitude anchor-band swept over the rough surface a few dozen mansheights off; electron gas fizzed around the band's Corestuff flanks, a visible reminder of the awesome currents flowing through its superconductor structure.

Adda's lungs seemed to expand. The vortex lines crossed the shining sky all around him, plunging into the crimson-purple pool that was the Pole beneath the City. The Air here was thick and clammy – they were right over the Pole, after all – but inside the City he always had the feeling he was breathing in someone else's farts.

The two boys tumbled away into the Air, hauling the Surf-board; Adda was pleased to see Farr's natural, youthful vigour coming to the surface as he Waved energetically through the Air, responding to the refreshing openness. Bzya joined Adda; the two older men hung in the Magfield like leaves.

'That door was a little stiff,' Adda said drily.

Bzya nodded. 'Not many City folk use the pedestrian exits.'

Pedestrian. Another antique, meaningless word.

'Most of 'em never leave the City walls at all. And those that do – because they have to, like your ceiling-farmer friend – take their cars.'

'Is that a good thing, do you think?'

Bzya shrugged. He was wearing a scuffed, ill-fitting cover-all, and under its coarse fabric his shoulder muscles bunched like independent animals. 'Neither one nor the other. It's just the way things are. And always have been.'

'Not always,' Adda murmured. He gazed around the sky with his good eye and sniffed, trying to assess the spin weather. 'And maybe not forever. The City isn't immune to the changes wrought by these unnatural Glitches. Even your great leader Hork admits that.'

Bzya nodded at the boys. 'It's good to see Farr looking a bit happier.'

'Yes.' Adda smiled. 'The body has its wisdom. When you're doing barrel-rolls in the Air, it's hard to remember your problems.'

Bzya patted his ample gut. 'I wish I could remember doing barrel-rolls even. Still, I know what you mean.' Now Cris had set up his board. Farr rested it against the soft, even resistance of the Magfield and Cris set his feet on it, flexing his legs experimentally. Adda saw the boy's muscles bunch as he pressed against the Magfield; his arms were outstretched and his fingers seemed to tickle at the Air, as if assessing the strength and direction of the Magfield. Farr pushed him off, recoiling through a mansheight or so, and Cris rocked the board steadily. He slid through the Air with impressive speed and grace; boy and board looked like a single entity, inseparable.

Cris performed slow, elegant turns in the Air; then – with a thrust at the board and a swivel of his feet almost too fast for Adda's rheumy eye to follow – he swept up and over, looping the loop in a single, tight motion. The boy flew across the blind face of Parz City, electron gas sparkling blue about his gleaming board.

He came to rest close to Bzya and Adda, and stepped away from his board gracefully. Farr Waved over to join them. Still a little dazzled by Cris's prowess, Adda saw the contrast with Farr: the Human Being had innate, Pole-enhanced strength, but beside Cris's athletic grace he looked clumsy, massive and uncoordinated.

But then, Farr hadn't had the luxury of a lifetime playing games in the Air.

'You ride that thing well.'

'Thanks.' Cris dipped his head with its oddly dyed hair; he seemed acceptably unself-conscious about his skill. 'And you're in the Games, I hear,' Bzya said.

Adda frowned. 'What Games?'

'They come once a year,' Farr said eagerly. 'Cris has told me about them. Sports in the Air – Surfing, the Luge, aerobats, Wave-boxing. Half the people in the City go out to the Stadium to watch.'

'Sounds fun.'

Bzya poked Adda in the ribs with a sharp thumb. 'It is fun, you old fogey. You should go along if you're still here.'

'It's more than fun.' Cris's tone was deeper than normal, earnest; Adda studied him curiously. Cris was a good boy, he had decided – shallow, but a decent friend to Farr. But now he sounded different: he was intense, his eyecups deep and dark.

Bzya said to Adda, 'The Games can make a big difference, for a talented young man like Cris. A moment of fame – money – invitations to the Palace...'

'This is the third year I've had an application in for the Surfing,' Cris said. 'I've been in the top five in my age group all that time. But this is the first time they've let me in.' He looked sour. 'Even so, I'm unseeded. I've got a lousy draw, and...'

Adda was aware of Farr hovering awkwardly close to them, his callused hands heavy at his sides. The contrast with Cris was painful. 'Well,' he said, trying not to sound hostile to the City boy's prattle, 'you should get your practice done, then.'

The boys peeled away once more. Cris mounted his board and was soon sweeping through the Air again, an insect sizzling with electron gas before the face of Parz; Farr Waved in his wake, calling out excitedly.

'Don't be hard on the boy,' Bzya murmured. 'He's a City lad. You can't expect him to have much sense of perspective.'

'The Games mean nothing to me.'

Bzya swivelled his scarred face to Adda. 'But they mean everything to Cris. To him, it's a chance – maybe his only chance – of breaking out of the life that's been set out for him. You'd have to have a heart of Corestuff, man, not to sympathize with the boy for trying to change his lot.'

'And what then, Fisherman? After his few moments of glory – after the grand folk have finished using him as their latest toy. What will become of him then?'

'If he's smart enough, and good enough, it won't end. He can parlay his gifts into a niche in the Upside, before he gets too old to shine on the Surfboard. And even if not – hell, it's a holiday for him, upfluxer. A holiday from the drudgery that will make up most of his life.'

There was a shout from above them. Cris had ridden his board high up the City's face, and was now sweeping through the sparkling Air close to the Longitude band. Electron gas swirled around his board and body, crackling and sparking blue. Other young people – evidently friends of Cris – had joined them, appearing from cracks in the Skin as if from nowhere – or so it seemed to Adda – and they raced around the Longitude band like young rays.

'They shouldn't do that,' Bzya murmured. 'Against the law, strictly speaking. If Cris goes too close to the Longitude the flux gradients could tear him apart.'

'Then why's he doing it?'

'To learn to master the flux,' the Fisherman said. 'To learn how to conquer the fiercer gradients he'll find when he's in the Games, and he Surfs across the face of the Pole.'

Adda sniffed. 'So now I know how you choose your rulers – on whether they can balance on a bit of wood. No wonder this City's such a damn mess.'

Bzya's laughter echoed from the blank, crudely finished wall of the City. 'You don't like us much, do you, Adda?'

'Not much.' He looked at Bzya, hesitating. 'And I don't understand how you've kept your sense of humour, my friend.'

'By accepting life as it is. I can question, but I can't change. Anyway, Parz isn't some kind of huge prison, as you seem to imagine. It's home for a lot of people – it's like a machine, designed to improve the lives of young people like Cris.'

'Then the machine's not bloody working.'

Bzya said calmly, 'Would you exchange Farr's life and experiences, to date, for Cris's?'

'But Cris's thinking is so narrow. The Games, his parents . . . as if this City was all the world, safe and eternal. Instead of . . .' He searched for the words. 'Instead of a box, lashed up from old lumber, floating around in immensity . . .'

Bzya touched his shoulder. 'But that's why you and I are here, old man. To keep the world away from boys like Farr and Cris – to give them a place that seems as stable and eternal as your parents did when you were a child – until they are old enough to cope with the truth.' He turned his scarred face to the North, staring into the diverging vortex lines with a trace of anxiety. 'I wonder how much longer we're going to be able to achieve that.'

Again and again, Cris Mixxax looped around the huge Corestuff band.

It was the day of the launch. The down-gaping mouth of the Harbour, here in the deepest Downside of the City, framed clear, yellow Air. A few people Waved beneath the entrance and peered up into the dark. Engineers talked desultorily as they waited for Hork to arrive, and to begin the launch proper. There was a smell of old, splintering wood.

Dura clung to a rail close to the lip of the access port, keeping to herself. She had already said her goodbyes. Toba had cooked them a fine meal in his little Midside home, but it had been a difficult occasion; Dura had had to work hard to break through Farr's resentful reserve. She'd asked Adda, quietly, to keep Farr away from the launch site today. She'd have enough to think about without the emotional freight of another round of farewells.

Even, she thought, wrapping her arms around her torso, if they turned out to be final farewells.

She looked down at the craft, studying lines which had become familiar to her in weeks of designing, building and testing. Hork V had decided to call his extraordinary craft the 'Flying Pig'. It was a clumsy, ugly name, Dura thought; but it caught the essence, maybe, of a clumsy, ugly vessel. The ship as finally constructed – after two failed prototypes – was a squat cylinder two mansheights across and perhaps three tall. The hull, of polished wood, was punctured by large, staring windows of clearwood. There were also clearwood panels set into the upper and lower cross-sections of the cylinder. The whole craft was bound about by five hoops of sturdy Corematter. The Air-pigs whose farts would power the vessel could be seen through the windows, lumps of straining, harnessed energy. The ship was suspended by thick cables from huge, splintered pulleys which – on normal days – bore Bells down towards the Quantum Sea.

This, then, was the craft which would carry two people into the lethal depths of the underMantle. In the dingy, dense Air of the City's Harbour the thing looked sturdy enough, Dura supposed, but she doubted she'd feel so secure once they were underway.

251

There was a disturbance above her, a sound of hatches banging. Hork V, Chair of Parz City, resplendent in a glittering coverall, descended from the gloom above. He seemed to glow; his bearded face was split by a huge smile. Dura saw that Physician Muub and the engineer Seciv Trop followed him. 'Good day, good day,' Hork called to Dura, and he clapped her meatily on the shoulder-blade. 'Ready for the off?'

Dura, her head full of her regrets and fears, turned away without speaking.

Seciv Trop wafted down, coming to rest close to her. He touched her arm, gently; the many pockets of his coverall were crammed, as usual, with unidentifiable – and probably irrelevant – items. 'Travel safely,' he said.

She turned, at first irritated; but there was genuine sympathy in his finely drawn face. 'Thanks,' she said slowly.

He nodded. 'I understand how you're feeling. Does that surprise you? – crusty old Seciv, good for nothing without his styli and tables. But I'm human, just the same. You're afraid of the journey ahead . . .'

'Terrified would be a better word.'

He grimaced. 'Then at least you're sane. You're already missing your family and friends. And you probably don't expect to make it back, ever.'

She felt a small surge of gratitude to Seciv; this was the first time anyone had actually voiced her most obvious fear. 'No, frankly.'

'But you're going anyway.' He smiled. 'You put the safety of the world ahead of your own.'

'No,' she snapped. 'I put my brother's safety ahead of my own.'

'That's more than sufficient.'

As she had suspected, the City men had insisted on one of the Human Beings taking this trip. Adda was ruled out because of age and injury. Farr's omission – which came to his frustration – hadn't been a foregone conclusion; his youth, in the eyes of those making the decisions, had barely out-weighed his experience as a novice Fisherman. Dura had been forced to argue hard.

The second crewman had been a surprise: it was to be Hork, Chair of Parz, himself. Now Hork was moving around the bay, glad-handing the engineers. Dura watched his progress sourly. He must be subject to the same fears as herself, and – in recent months anyway – to enormous personal pressure – and yet he looked relaxed, at ease, utterly in command; he had a natural authority which made her feel small, weak.

'He wears his fear well,' she said sourly.

Seciv pulled at the corner of his mouth. 'Perhaps. Or perhaps his fear of not taking the voyage, of remaining here, is the greater. He is gambling a great deal on this voyage, you know.'

This stunt . . . Yes, Dura did know; she'd become immersed enough in the politics of Parz to be able – with the help of Ito and Toba – to understand something of Hork's situation. However unreasonable it might be, the citizens of Parz expected Hork to resolve their troubles – to lift food rationing, to restore the lumber convoys and get the place working again. To open the *shops*, damn it. That he'd manifestly failed to do so (but how could he have succeeded?) had put his position in doubt; there were factions in his Court and on the larger Committee who were gunning for him, with varying degrees of openness.

This ludicrous jaunt into the underMantle was Hork's last gamble. All or nothing. If it succeeded then he, Hork, would return as the saviour of the City and all the peoples of the Mantle. But if it failed – well, Dura thought uneasily, perhaps it would be better for Hork to die in a glorious instant, in the deep underMantle, than at the hands of an assassin here in the bright corridors of Parz.

The crew members had to climb into the ship through a hinged hatch set in the upper end of the cylinder. Hosch, the former Harbour supervisor, had been checking the craft's simple systems; now Dura watched his thin, hunched shoulders emerge from the craft through the crew hatch. As Muub had expected, Hosch had turned out to be a good manager of the construction project, despite his sour personality; he'd been able effectively to draw out the mercurial expertise of the likes of Seciv Trop and to marry it to the practical skills of his Harbour engineers.

Hosch glanced up, saw that both Dura and Hork were ready. 'It's time,' he said.

Dura felt something within her recede. As if in a dream she watched her own hands and legs working as she clambered down towards the ship.

She climbed stiffly through the hatch and into the interior, squeezing past the row of bound, straining Air-pigs and the sleek turbine beside them. She experienced a mixture of gratified relief at being underway, and a tang of sheer, awful terror.

With bellowed goodbyes to the engineers, to Muub, Seciv and the rest, Hork shook Hosch's thin hand and clambered into the cabin, squeezing his sparkling bulk through the hatch. He seemed careless of the pollution of his gleaming suit by the dirt of the pigs. He dragged the hatch closed after him and dogged its wooden latches tight.

For a moment Hork and Dura hovered close to the hatch, alone in there for the first time. Their eyes met. *Now*, Dura thought, *now the two of them were bound to each other, for good or ill*. She could see a slow, appraising awareness of that in Hork's expression. But there was little fear there; she read humour, enthusiasm.

By the blood of the Xeelee, she thought. *He's actually enjoying this.*

Without speaking they descended into the craft.

The pigs were strapped in place close to the top of the cylinder. Dura climbed into her loose harness close to the pigs. The walls of the cabin were fat with Air-tanks, food stores, equipment lockers and a primitive latrine. Cooling fans hummed and wood-lamps, their green glow dim, studded the walls.

Towards the base of the ship Hork took his place at the craft's simple control panel, a board placed before one of the broader windows and equipped with three levers and a series of switches. He rolled his sleeves back from his arms with every evidence of relish.

There was a pounding on the hull.

Hork thumped back enthusiastically, grinning through his beard. 'So,' he said breathlessly, 'so it begins!'

The craft jolted into motion. Dura heard a muffled cheer from the engineers in the Harbour, the creaking of the pulleys as they began to pay out cable.

After a few seconds the craft emerged from the Harbour.

The golden brilliance of Polar Air-light swept the interior of the ship, filling Dura with a nostalgic, claustrophobic ache. The silhouetted forms of Waving people – some of them children – accompanied the craft as it began its descent from the City.

Hork was laughing. Dura looked down at him, disbelieving.

'Oh, come on,' Hork said briskly. 'We're off! Isn't this a magnificent adventure? And what a relief it is to be *doing* something, to be going somewhere. Eh, Dura?'

Dura sniffed, letting her face settle into sourness. 'Well, Hork, here I am going to hell in the belly of a wooden pig. It's a bit hard to find much to smile about. With respect. And we do have work to do.'

Hork's expression was hard, and she felt briefly uneasy – she'd been around him long enough now to witness several of his towering rages. But he merely laughed aloud once more. His noisy, exuberant presence was overwhelming in the cramped cabin; Dura felt herself shrink from it, as if escaping into herself. Hork said, 'Quite right, captain! And isn't it time you started working the pigs?'

He was right; Dura swivelled in her sling to begin the work. The craft wouldn't be cut loose of the Harbour cable for some time, but they needed to be sure the internal turbine and the magnetic fields were fully functioning. The animals' harness, slung across the width of the cabin, kept the pigs' rears aimed squarely at the wide blades of a turbine. A trough carved from unfinished wood had been fixed a micron or so before the pigs' sketchy, six-eyed faces, and now Dura took a sack of leaves from a locker and filled the trough with luscious vegetable material, crushing the stuff as she worked. Soon the delicious tang of the leaves filled the cabin. Dura was aware of Hork bending over his console, evidently shutting out the scents; as for herself – well, she could all but taste the protons dripping out onto her tongue.

The pigs could barely stand it. Their hexagonal arrays of eyecups bulged and their mouths gaped wide. With grunts of protest they hurled themselves against the unyielding harness towards the leaves, their jetfarts exploding in the cramped atmosphere of the cabin.

Under the steady pressure of the jetfart stream, the broad blades of the turbine began to turn. Soon the sweet, musky smell of pig-fart permeated the Air of the cabin, reminding Dura, if she closed her eyes, of the scents of her childhood, of the Net with its enclosed herd. She scattered a few fragments of food into the grasp of the pigs' gaping maws. Just enough to keep them fed, but little enough to keep them interested in more.

The anatomy of a healthy Air-pig was efficient enough to enable it to generate farts for many days on very little food. Pigs could travel metres allowing as much of their bulky substance to dissolve into fart energy as was required; these five, though terrified and frustrated by the conditions into which they had been penned, should have little problem powering the turbine for as long as the humans needed. And there was a back-up system – a stove powered by nuclear-burning wood – if they were desperate enough to need to risk its heat in the confines of the cabin.

Hork, grunting to himself, experimentally threw switches. The ship shuddered in response, and Hork peered out of the window, gauging the effect of the currents generated in the superconducting hoops.

Farr's face suddenly appeared outside the ship, at the window opposite Dura. His expression was solemn, empty. He was Waving hard, she realized; they must be descending rapidly already, and soon he and the other Wavers would not be able to keep up.

Farr must have given Adda the slip. And so, after all, here was a last goodbye. She forced herself to smile at Farr and raised her hand.

There was a thud from the hull of the 'Flying Pig'; the little craft shuddered in the Air before settling again.

Dura frowned. 'What was that?'

Hork looked up, his wide face bland. 'The Harbour cable cutting loose. Right on schedule.' He glanced out of the window at the dark shadows of the superconducting hoops. 'We're falling under our own power now; the currents in the hoops are Waving us deeper into the Star. And the hoops are the only way we're going to get back home . . . We're alone,' he said. 'But we're on our way.'

20

Three metres deep.

It was a depth Dura couldn't comprehend. Humans were
confined within the Mantle to a shell of superfluid Air only a
few metres thick. Her first journey with Toba to the Pole from
the upflux – so far that she had felt she was travelling around
the curvature of the Star itself – had only been about thirty
metres.

Now she was drilling whole metres into the unforgiving
bulk of the Star itself. She imagined the Star crushing their
tiny wooden boat and spitting them out, like a tiny infesta-
tion. And it was small comfort to remember that their journey
would be broken before reaching such a depth only if they
achieved their goal . . . if the unimaginable really did, after all,
emerge from the Core to greet them.

By the end of the second day they were already well below
the nebulous boundary of the habitable layer of Air. The
yellow brightness of the Air outside the windows had faded –
to amber, then a deeper orange, and finally to a blood-purple
colour reminiscent of the Quantum Sea. Dura pressed her face
against cold clearwood, hoping to see something – anything:
exotic animals, unknown, inhuman people, some kind of
structure inside the Star. But there was only the muddy
purple of the thickening Air, and her own distorted, indistinct
reflection in the wood-lamps' green light. She was trapped
in here – with her fears, and with Hork. She had expected to
feel small, vulnerable inside this tiny wooden box as it
burrowed its way into the immense guts of the Star; but the
thick darkness beyond the window made her claustrophobic,
trapped. She retreated into herself. She tended the fretting
pigs, slept as much as she could, and kept her eyes averted
from Hork's.

His determined efforts to talk to her, on the third day, were an intrusion.

'You're pensive.' His tone was offensively bright. 'I hope this adventure isn't causing you any – ah – philosophic difficulties.'

He'd left his console and had drifted up the cabin, close to her station near the pigs' harness. She stared at the broad, fat-laden face, the mound of beard around his mouth. When she'd first been introduced to Hork she'd been fascinated and disconcerted – as Hork intended, no doubt – by that beard, by this man with hair *on his face*. But now, as she looked closer, she could see the way the roots of the beard's hair-tubes were arranged in a neat hexagonal pattern over Hork's chin . . . The beard had been transplanted, either from Hork's own scalp or from one of his more unfortunate subjects.

So the beard wasn't impressive, she decided. Just decadent. And besides, it was yellowing more quickly than the hair on his head; another few years and Hork would look truly absurd.

How huge, how intrusive, how *irritating* he was. The tension between them seemed to crackle like electron gas.

'Philosophic difficulties? I'm not superstitious.'

'I didn't suggest you were.'

'We aren't religious about the Xeelee. I don't fear that we're going to bring down the wrath of the Xeelee, if that's what you mean. But Human beings – alone – would never have attempted this journey into the Star.'

'Because the Xeelee will look after you, like mama in the sky.'

Dura sighed. 'Not at all. In fact, quite the opposite . . . We have to accept the actions of the Xeelee without question – for we believe that their goals will prove in the long term to be of benefit to us all, to humans as a race. Even if it means the destruction of the Star – even if it means our own destruction.'

Hork shook his head. 'You upfluxers are full of laughs, aren't you? Well, it's a chilly faith. And damn cold comfort.'

'You don't understand,' Dura said. 'It's not meant to be comforting. Back up there . . .' – she jerked her thumb upward, to the world of light and humans – '*there* is my comfort. My family and people.'

Hork studied her. His face, under its layers of fat, was

broad and coarsely worked, but – she admitted grudgingly – not without perception and sensitivity. 'You fear death, Dura, despite your knowledge.'

Dura laughed and closed her eyes. 'I told you; knowledge is not necessarily a comfort. I've no reason not to fear death . . . and, yes, I fear it now.'

Hork breathed deeply. 'Then have faith in me. We'll survive. I feel it. I know it . . .'

His face was close to hers, so close she could smell sweet bread on his breath. His expression was clear, set. Determination seemed to shine from him; just for a moment Dura felt tempted to let herself wallow in that determination, to relax in his massive strength as if he were her father reborn.

But she resisted. She said harshly, 'So you've no fear of death? Will your power in Parz help you overcome the final disaster?'

'Of course it won't,' he said. 'And I'm not without fear. That surprises you, doesn't it? I'm not a fool without the imagination to be afraid, upfluxer; nor am I so arrogant as to suppose myself beyond the reach of death. I know that in the end I am as weak as the next man in the face of the great forces of the Star – let alone the unknowns beyond it. But, just at this moment, I'm . . .' He waved a hand in the Air. 'I'm *exhilarated*. I'm doing something more than waiting for the next Glitch to hit Parz, or coping with the devastation of the last one. I'm trying to *change the world*, to challenge the way things are.' His eyecups were dark wells. 'And I couldn't bear to allow anyone else to go into the dark at the heart of the Star, and not be there.' He looked at her. 'Can you understand that?'

'Some say you're running away from the real problems. That genuine courage would lie in staying behind and wrestling with the disaster, not flying off on a spectacular, wasteful jaunt.'

He nodded, his smile grim. 'I know. Muub's among them. Oh, don't worry; I won't do anything about it. It's a point of view. Even one I share, in my darkest moments.' He grinned. 'But I like to think my father would have been proud of me, if he could have seen me now. He always thought I was so – *practical*. So unimaginative. And yet . . .'

There was a thud from the hull of the 'Flying Pig'; the little craft shuddered in the Air. The pigs squealed, thrashing in their stall, and with a single, involuntary movement Dura and Hork grabbed at each other.

The craft settled. Hork's expansive belly, liquid beneath its covering of glittering material, was heavy against Dura's stomach and breasts.

'What was that?'

The small, regular arrays of hair at the fringe of his beard wafted as he breathed. 'Corestuff bergs,' he said, his voice tight. 'That's all. Corestuff bergs. If either of us was a Fisherman we'd not have been startled – that's why they come down here in the first place: to fish for the Corestuff bergs. The 'Pig' is designed to cope with little impacts like that; there's nothing to fear.' His arms were still around her – and her arms were in turn wrapped around his torso, her hands clutching at the layers of material over his back – and now he reached up to stroke her hair. She wanted, suddenly, to bury herself in this bulky strength, to hide deep inside the warm darkness of the eyecups which were huge before her.

She scrabbled at his clothing, found a line of buttons down the seam at his side; and she felt his thick, clumsy fingers travelling over her own coverall.

A last shred of rationality made her assess his expression, his open mouth and flaring, shining nostrils, and she saw that his need was as great as hers.

His clothing came apart, and she peeled a layer of thick, expensive material away from his belly and chest. She ran her left hand down the curve of his stomach and found his cache; with a deft, tender motion she pulled out the small penis, wrapped it in her fingers and squeezed it gently. It swelled rapidly, pushing at her palm like a small animal. He'd opened her coverall now, and she shrugged out of it, kicking her legs impatiently out of the clinging material and letting the garment drift away into the Air. She felt Hork's hand slide, dry and hot, up her thigh and between her legs; she opened her thighs softly and he ran his fingers over her cleft, as clumsily and eagerly as an adolescent. There was a coolness inside her, and she knew that she was ready, that membranes inside her were already sighing lubricating Air into her. Now she took Hork's penis – it was pulsing, rhythmically – and pushed it deep inside her; it entered her easily. He sighed, and buried his face in her shoulder; she turned her head, resting her cheek on his hair. His penis was like a warm, beating heart inside her. His legs, still clothed, were warm and rough against hers as she began to scissor her thighs, back and forth, letting the pattern of her movements stimulate the muscle walls inside her.

At last she felt herself clench at him, hard; she shuddered, and she heard him gasp, his bulk heavy against hers as they drifted in the Air. Her muscles pulsed around him, and for a few seconds she felt flutters, beats, as the rhythms of their bodies strove to merge. But soon they coalesced, and she felt a surge of triumph as the walls of her vagina throbbed in unison with Hork.

He came quickly, and she only heartbeats later. They cried out and shuddered against each other; she felt the muscles of his back move under her fingers.

Hork slumped against her. She held him against her body, curling her fingers in his hair, unwilling to release his warmth and mass. She felt his penis still inside her, small and hot. The moment of closeness stretched on, and she thought of how strange this liaison would have seemed to her – deep in the lethal depths of the Star with the ruler of an astonishing City – if she could have imagined it, in the days before she left the upflux. For some reason she thought of Deni Maxx, the brisk doctor from Muub's Hospital. *But your coupling would have seemed much stranger to a watching Ur-human,* Dura imagined her saying. *We believe their sexual mechanism was based – not on compression, like ours – but on frictional forces. That's obviously impossible for us, embedded in superfluid as we are, so when they designed us . . .*

Slowly the closeness faded. The sounds of the craft – the snuffling of the feeding Air-pigs, the soft whirr of the turbine axle, the slow hissing of the wood-lamps – seeped back into her awareness. Hork's bulk seemed separate from her once more, and she became aware of folds of cloth trapped uncomfortably between their bodies, of a stiffness in her back as her body leaned forward over his belly.

Gently she pushed him away. His penis fell out of her with a soft, warm sound.

He looked into her eyes, smiled – he looked as if he had been *crying*, she thought briefly, startled – and tucked his penis back into its cache. He hauled his coverall around the circumference of his stomach, and she reached for her discarded clothes.

'Well,' she said at last. 'Where did that come from?'

He drifted away from her and settled back into the small seat close to the control console; she saw how his sparkling coverall was noticeably less elegant now, crumpled and sitting askew on his shoulders. 'Fear,' he said simply. His composure was restored, she saw, but he wasn't bothering to restore his usual abrasive front. The atmosphere between them had changed; the tension which had pervaded the ship in the days since its launch had dissipated. 'Fear. Obviously. I needed – comfort. I needed to lose myself. I don't know if that's enough of a reason; I'm sorry.'

'Don't be.' Absently she reached up and fed more leaf fragments into the pigs' hopper. 'I wanted it too.'

He ran his hands over the simple instruments before him. 'I meant what I said, you know. For myself, I'd rather be here, running this ship, than anywhere in the Star. In Parz, the problems I have to deal with, day to day . . .' For a brief, empathetic moment she could imagine how it must be to be in a position like Hork's – with the welfare of not just himself, not just his family, but of *thousands* resting on his shoulders. She watched the set of his face and recalled the hint of weeping she thought she'd detected; briefly she felt she understood him. He said, 'Nothing ever gets solved, you see. That's the trouble. Or if it does, the next day it is worse. At least here . . .' He grasped the simple controls. 'At least here, I am doing something. Going somewhere!'

'Yes, but doing what? Going where?'

He looked up at her. 'You know there's no reply to that. We're seeking help, from whatever came out of the Core once before to destroy us.'

'And how are we supposed to find it?'

'You sound like the Finance sub-Committee,' he said sourly. 'All we can do is put ourselves into a position where *they* can find *us* . . . whoever *they* are.'

She felt her mood swinging away from him now; she felt

hot and vaguely soiled, and once more the tight curves of the walls seemed to close in around her. She recalled, now, that they hadn't kissed once. She didn't even *like* this man. 'So you're happy to be going somewhere. Anywhere. Is that what this is really all about? – providing you with recreation from your awful burdens? And if it is, did you really have to drag me down into the depths with you?'

For a moment there was an element of hurt in his face, and his lips parted as if he were about to protest; but then he smiled, and she saw his defensive front enclose him once more. 'Now, now. Let's not bicker. We don't want to be found at odds when our host from the Core comes to meet us, do we?'

'I don't think I can restrain myself for such a long wait,' she said with contempt, and she turned back to her pigs, stroking and soothing them.

There was another thud at the hull, a scrape along the length of the ship. This one was softer than before, but still Dura found herself shuddering. She calmed the nervous pigs with quiet words, and wondered if she had been right – if it really would be such a long wait, after all.

Electron gas crackling from its superconducting hoops, the tiny wooden ship laboured centimetre after centimetre into the thickening depths of the neutron star.

Bzya was to be put on double shifts, inside the Bells. He didn't know when he would next have enough free time to get away from the Harbour between dives. So he invited Adda and Farr to come see him off, in a place he called a 'bar'.

Adda found the place with some difficulty. The bar was a small, cramped chamber tucked deep inside the Downside. The only light came from guttering wood-lamps on the walls; in the green, poky gloom Adda was strongly aware of how deep inside the carcass of the City he was buried.

In one corner of the bar was a counter where a couple of people were apparently serving something, some kind of food. Rails criss-crossed the chamber with no apparent pattern; men and women clustered together in small groups on the rails, slowly eating their way through bowls of what looked like bread, and talking desultorily. Adda saw heavy workers' tunics, scarred flesh, thick, twisted limbs. One or two appraising stares were directed at the upfluxer.

Bzya was alone at a length of rail, close to the far wall. He saw Adda and raised an arm, beckoning him over; three small bowls were fixed to the rail beside him.

Adda pushed forward, feeling self-conscious in his bandages, and clambered stiffly through the crowded place, aware of the babble of conversation all around him.

'Adda.' Bzya smiled through his distorted face, and waved Adda to a clear space of rail. Adda hooked one arm over the rail, hooking himself comfortably into place. 'Thanks for coming down.' Bzya glanced, once, past Adda towards the door, then turned back to his bowls.

Adda caught the look. 'No Farr,' he said heavily. 'I'm sorry, Bzya. I couldn't find him.'

Bzya nodded. 'I expect he's Surfing again.'

'I know you did a lot for him, when he was working in the Harbour; he should have . . .'

Bzya held up his thick palm. 'Forget it. Look, if I was his age I'd rather be losing myself in the sky with the Surfers than sitting in a poky place like this with two battered old fogeys. And with the Games coming up in a couple of days, they'll only have one thing on their minds. Or maybe two,' he said slyly. He nodded at the three bowls on the rail. 'Anyway, it just means there's more of this stuff for us.'

Adda looked down at the row of bowls. They were crudely carved of wood and were little larger than his cupped palm, and they were fixed to the rail by stubs of wood. The bowls contained small slices of what might have been bread. Adda, cautiously, pulled out a small, round slice; it was dense, warm and moist to the touch. He turned it over doubtfully. 'What the hell's this?'

Bzya laughed, looking pleased with himself. 'I didn't think you'd have heard of it yet. No bars in the upflux, eh, my friend?'

Adda glared. 'I'm supposed to eat this stuff?'

Bzya extended his fingers, inviting Adda to do so.

Adda sniffed at the plastic stuff, squeezed it, and finally took a small nibble. It was as hot, dense and soggy as it looked – unpleasant inside the mouth – and the taste was sour, unidentifiable. Adda swallowed the fragment. 'Disgusting.'

'But you've got to treat it right.' Bzya dipped into the bowl, drew out a thick handful of the stuff, and crammed it into his mouth. His big jaws worked as he chewed the stuff twice, then swallowed it down in one go. He closed his eyes as the hot food passed down his throat; and after a few seconds he shuddered briefly, suppressing a sigh. Then he belched. '*That's* how you take beercake.'

'Beercake?'

'Try it again.'

Adda reached into the second bowl and lifted a healthy handful of cake to his mouth. It sat in his mouth, hot, dense and eminently indigestible; but, with determination, he bit into it a couple of times and then swallowed, forcing his throat to accept the incompressible stuff. The cake passed down his throat, a hard, painful lump. 'Fabulous,' he said when it was gone. 'I'm so glad I came.'

Bzya grinned and held up his palm.

. . . And a heat seemed to surge smoothly out from Adda's stomach, flooding his body and head; his palms and feet tingled, as if being worked by invisible fingers, and his skull seemed to swell in size, filling up with a roomy, comfortable warmth. He looked down at his body, astonished, half-expecting to see electron gas sparking around his fingertips, to hear his skin sighing with the new warmth. But there was no outward change.

After a few seconds the heat-surge wore away, but when it had receded it left Adda feeling subtly altered. The bar seemed cosier – friendlier – than even a moment before, and the smell of the remaining beercake was pleasing, harmonious, enticing.

'Welcome to beercake, my friend, and a new lifelong relationship.'

The pleasing warmth induced by the cake still permeated Adda. He poked at the cake with a new wonder. 'Well, I've not eaten anything with such an impact before, up- or downflux.'

'I didn't think so.' Bzya picked up a piece of cake and compressed it between his fingers. 'Farr is developing a taste too, I ought to say. It's a mash, mostly of Crust-tree leaf. But it's fermented – in huge Corestuff vessels, for days . . .'

'Fermented?'

'Spin-spider web is put into the vats with the mash. There's something in the webbing, maybe in the glistening stuff that makes it sticky, which reacts with the mash and changes it to beercake. Magic.'

'Sure.' Adda took another mouthful of the beercake now; it was as revolting as before, but the anticipation of its after-effects made the taste much easier to bear. He swallowed it down and allowed the warmth to filter through his being.

'What does the stuff cost?'

'Nothing.' Bzya shrugged. 'The Harbour authorities provide it for us. As much as we want, as long as we're able to do our jobs.'

'What do you mean? Is it bad for you?'

'If you overdo it, yes.' Bzya rubbed his face. 'It works on the capillaries in your flesh – dilates them – and some of the major pneumatic vessels in the brain. The flow of Air is subtly altered, you see, and . . .'

'And you feel wonderful.'

'Yeah. But if you use it too often, you can't recover. The capillaries stay dilated . . .'

Adda gazed around the bar, at this safe, marvellous place. 'That seems all right to me.'

'Sure. Your head would be a wonderful place to live in. But you couldn't function, Adda; you couldn't do a job. And if it gets bad enough you couldn't even feed yourself, without prompting. But, yes, you'd feel wonderful about it.'

'And I don't suppose this City is so forgiving of people who can't hold down jobs.'

'Not much.'

'Don't the Harbour managers worry they're going to lose too many of their Fishermen, to this cake stuff? Why dole it out free?'

Bzya shrugged. 'They lose a few. But they don't care. Adda, we're expendable. It doesn't take long to train up a new Fisherman, and there're always plenty of recruits, in the Downside. And they know the cake keeps us here in the bars,

266

happy, quiet, and available. They gain more than they lose.'
He chomped another mouthful. 'And so do I.'

Adda worked his way slowly through the bowl, cautiously observing the cake's increasing effects on him. Every so often he moved his fingers and feet, testing his coordination. If he got to the point where he even thought he might be losing control, he promised himself, he'd stop.

The Fisherman had fallen silent; his huge fingers toyed with the cake.

'I hear you're on double shifts. Whatever that means.'

Bzya smiled, indulgent. 'It means I'm assigned to the Bells twice as frequently as usual. It's because they're running twice as many dives as usual.'

'Why?'

'The upflux Glitch. No wood coming into the City. Not enough, anyway. People bitch about food rationing, but the wood shortage is just as important in the longer term. And let's hope the day never comes when they have to ration beer-cake . . . Anyway, they want more Corestuff metal, to use as building material.'

'Building? Are they extending the City?'

'Rebuilding. It goes on all the time, Adda, mostly deep in the guts of the place. Small repairs, maintenance. Although,' he said, leaning forward conspiratorially, 'there are rumours that it isn't just the need to keep up routine repairs that's prompted this increased demand.'

'What, then?'

'They're trying to strengthen the City's structure. Rebuild the skeleton with more Corestuff. They're not shouting about it for fear of causing panic; but they're endeavouring to make it more robust in the face of future problems. Like a closer Glitch.'

Adda frowned. 'Can they do that? Will it work?'

'I'm not an engineer. I don't know.' Bzya chewed on the cake, absently. 'But I doubt it,' he said without emotion. 'The City's so huge; you'd have to rip most of its guts out to strengthen it significantly. And it's a ramshackle structure. I mean, it *grew*; it was never planned. It was built for space, not strength.'

Parz had been one of the first permanent settlements

founded after humanity was scattered through the Mantle following the Core Wars. At first Parz was a random construct of ropes and wood, no more significant than a dozen others, drifting freely above the Pole. But at the Pole the bodies of men and women were significantly stronger, and so Parz grew rapidly; and its position at the only geographically unique point in the southern hemisphere of the Mantle gave it strategic and psychological significance. Soon it had become a trading centre, and had wealth enough to afford a ruling class – the first in the Mantle since the Wars. The Committee had been founded, and the growth and unification of Parz had proceeded apace.

Parz's wealth exploded when the Harbour was established – Parz was the first and only community in the Mantle able to extract and exploit the valuable Corestuff. Soon the scattered community of the cap of Mantle around Parz, the region eventually to be called the hinterland, fell under Parz's economic influence. Eventually the hinterland and City worked as a single economic unit, with the raw materials and taxes of the hinterland flowing into Parz, with Corestuff and – more importantly – the stability and regulation provided by Parz's law washing back in return. Eventually only the far upflux, bleak and inhospitable, remained disunited from Parz, home to a few tribes of hunters, and bands of Parz exiles like the Human Beings themselves.

Adda bit into more cake. 'I'm surprised people accepted being taken over like that. Didn't anybody fight?'

Bzya shook his head. 'It wasn't seen as a conquest. Parz is not an empire, although it might seem that way to you. Adda, people remembered the time before the Wars, when humans lived in safety and security throughout the Mantle. We couldn't return to those times; we'd lost too much. But Parz was better than nothing: it offered stability, regulation, a framework to live in. People gripe about their tithes – and nobody's going to pretend that the Committee get it right all the time – but most of us would prefer taxes to living wild. With all respect to you, my friend.' He bit into his cake. 'And that's still true today; as true as it ever was.'

Two of the bowls were already empty. Adda felt the seduction of this place, that he could have sat here in this companionable glow with Bzya for a long time. 'Do you really believe that? Look at your own position, Fisherman; look at the dangers you face daily. Is this really the best of all possible lives for you?'

Bzya grinned. 'Well, I'd exchange places with Hork any day, if I thought I could do his job. Of course I would. And there are plenty of people closer to me, in the Harbour, who I'd happily throttle, if I thought it would make the world a better place. If I didn't think they'd just bring in somebody worse. I accept I'm at the bottom of the heap, here, Adda. Or close to it. But I believe it's the way of things. I will fight injustice and inequity – but I accept the need for the existence of the heap itself.' He looked carefully at Adda. 'Does that make sense?'

Adda thought it over. 'No,' he said at last. 'But it doesn't seem to matter much.'

Bzya laughed. 'Now you see why they give us this stuff for free. Here.' He held out the third bowl. 'Your good health, my friend.'

Adda reached for the cake.

A couple of days later Bzya's shifts should have allowed him another break. Adda searched for Farr, but couldn't find him, so he went down to the bar alone. He entered, awkward and self-conscious in his dressings, peering into the gloomier corners.

He couldn't find Bzya, and he didn't stay.

21

In the interior of the Star there were no sharp boundaries, merely gradual changes in the dominant form of matter as pressures and densities increased. So there was no dramatic plunge, no great impacts as the 'Flying Pig' hauled itself deeper: just a slow, depressing diminution of the last vestiges of Air-light. And the glow cast by the wood-lamps fixed to the walls was no substitute; with its smoky greenness and long, flickering shadows, the gloom in the cabin was quite sinister.

To Dura, hunched over herself in her corner of the ship, this long, slow descent into darkness was like a lingering death.

Soon, though, the ride became much less even. The ship swayed alarmingly and at one point was nearly upended. The labouring pigs, their shadows huge on the ship's roof, bleated pathetically; Hork laughed, his eyecups pools of green darkness.

Dura's fingers scrabbled over the smooth wooden walls in search of purchase. 'What's happening? Why are we being pummelled like this?'

'Every Bell hits underMantle currents. The only difference is, we've no Spine to steady us.' Hork spoke to her slowly, as if she were stupid. Since their single physical encounter, his aloof hostility had been marked. 'The substance of the Mantle at these depths is different from our Air . . . or so my tutors used to tell me. It's still a superfluid of neutrons, apparently, but of a different mode from the Air: it's *anisotropic* – it has different properties in different directions.'

Dura frowned. 'So in some directions it's like the Air, and it doesn't impede our progress. But in others . . .'

'. . . it feels thick and viscous, and it batters against our magnetic shield. Yes.'

'But how can you tell which directions it's Air-like?'

'You can't.' Hork grinned. 'That's the fun of it.'

'But that's dangerous,' she said, uneasily aware of how childlike she sounded.

'Of course it is. That's why the Harbour suffers so many losses.'

. . . *And this is where I sent my brother*, she thought with a shiver. She felt strangely, retrospectively fearful. Here, drifting through this anisotropic nightmare, it was as if she were fearing for her brother for the first time.

Still, after a while Dura found she could ignore – almost – the constant, uneven buffeting. Immersed in the hot, fetid atmosphere of the ship, with the warm stink of the pig-farts and the patient, silent work of Hork at his control box, she was even able to doze.

Something slammed into the side of the ship.

Dura screamed and jolted fully awake. She felt herself quiver from the blow, as if someone had punched her own skull; she looked around, wild-eyed, for the source of the disaster. The pigs were squealing furiously. Hork, still at his controls, was laughing at her.

'Damn you. What was that?'

He spread his hands. 'Just a little welcoming card from the Quantum Sea.' He pointed. 'Look out of the window.'

She turned to stare through the clearwood. The Mantle here was utterly dark, but the lamps of the ship cast a green glow for a few microns through the murky, turbulent stuff. And there were forms drifting through that dim ocean – blocky, irregular shapes, many of them islands large enough to swallow up this tiny craft. The blocks slid silently upwards past the ship and towards the distant Mantle – or rather, Dura realized, the 'Pig' herself was hurtling down past them on her way towards the Core.

'Corestuff bergs . . . Islands of hyperonic matter,' Hork said. 'No Fisherman would tackle bergs of such a size . . . but then, no Fisherman has ever been so deep.'

Dura stared gloomily out at the vast, slow-moving bulks of hyperonic matter. If they were unlucky enough, she realized – if they were caught by a combination of a large enough mass and an adverse current – their little ship would be crushed like a child's skull, magnetic protection or no. 'How deep are we?'

Hork peered at the crude meters on his control panel; his beard scratched softly at the meters' clearwood covers. 'Hard to say,' he said dismissively. 'Our tame experts were very clever at finding ways for us to travel so far, but not so clever at letting us know where we are. But I'd guess . . .' He scowled. 'Perhaps five metres below the City.'

Dura gasped. *Five metres* . . . Five hundred thousand mansheights. Why, surely even an Ur-human would be awed by such a journey.

'Of course, we've no real control over our position. All we've the capability to do is to descend and, if we live through that, to come up again. But we could emerge anywhere; we've no idea where these currents are taking us.'

'We've discussed this problem. Wherever we emerge we need only follow the Magfield to the South Pole.'

Hork smiled at her. 'But that could be tens of metres from the City . . . It could take months to return. And then we will rely on your upfluxer survival skills to enable us to endure, in the remote wilds of the Star. I will place myself in your hands, and I anticipate that the journey home will be . . . interesting.'

The impacts from the hyperonic bergs were coming thick and fast now. Hork pulled at the wooden levers on his control panel and slowed their progress down to a crawl; Dura watched through the windows as the thickening masses of Corestuff clustered around the 'Pig', held back from crushing her only by the invisible walls of the magnetic shield.

At last Hork flicked over his controls and pushed himself away from the panel. 'You may as well let the animals rest,' he said to Dura. 'That's as far as we're going.'

Dura frowned and peered out of the windows. 'We can't penetrate any deeper?'

Hork shrugged, and yawned elaborately. 'Not unless a channel through the bergs opens up. The bergs are like a solid mass from here on in – you can see for yourself. No, this is the end of the journey.' He drifted up through the cabin, took some fragments of untouched leaf matter from the pigs' trough and chewed it without enthusiasm. He handed more handfuls of food to Dura. 'Here,' he said.

Dura took the food and bit into it thoughtfully. The whine of the turbine was stilled now, and she was suspended in a silence broken only by the hoarse wheezing of the pigs and by the soft thumping of hyperonic fragments against the magnetic shield. The pigs, still bound into their harnesses, were trembling with the panic of their blocked flight; their sixfold eyes rolled. As she ate, Dura ran her hands over the dilated pores of their flanks; the simple action of soothing the frightened animals – of tending creatures even more scared than herself – seemed to calm her.

Hork folded his arms, his massive shoulder muscles bunching under his glittering costume. 'Well, this is the strangest picnic I've ever had.'

'What do we do now?'

'Who knows?' He grinned at her, a fragment of his professional charm showing. 'Maybe that's all we've come so far to find.' He pointed out of the window. 'Corestuff. Hard, dangerous, and dead. Anyway, it's not over yet. We've only just arrived, after all. We can stay here for days, if we have to.'

Dura laughed. 'Maybe you should go out and make a speech. Wake the Colonists out of their thousand-year slumber.'

Hork studied her impassively, his heavy jaw working; then he turned away from her, rebuffing her completely.

She felt alone and a little foolish. In the renewed silence of the cabin, her fear crowded in once more. She stroked the quivering pigs and sucked on leaf-matter.

She wondered how long they would have to wait here, before Hork would give up – or, terrifyingly, before *something happened*.

In the end, they didn't have to wait very long at all.

Hork screamed, his voice thin and high with terror.

Somehow Dura had fallen asleep again. She jolted awake, the muggy Air thick in her lungs and eyes. She looked around quickly.

The green glow of the lamps filled the cabin with eerie, sharp shadows. The pigs were squealing, terrified, arching in their restraints. Hork, all his arrogance and cockiness gone, had backed against a wall, his coverall rumpled and stained, his hands fruitlessly seeking a weapon. It was as if the inhabitants of the 'Flying Pig', human and animal alike, had radiated away from the heart of the cylindrical craft, like fragments of a slow explosion. Dura blinked, trying to clear her vision. No, not an explosion, she saw; hovering at the geometric centre of the cylinder – the focus of all this terror – was *another person*. A third human, here where it was impossible for any human to be . . .

Or rather, she realized as she stared more closely, it was – something – with the form of a human. She saw a bulky woman, evidently older than herself, dressed in what might have been a Fisherman's tunic. But the material glowed, softly crimson, and it looked seamless. Hair, deep black, was tied tightly around her scalp. A purple glow shone out of eyecups, nostrils and mouth.

. . . But there was something in those eyecups, she saw. There was *flesh* in there, spheres which moved independently of the face, like animals trapped inside the skull.

She felt the leaves rise in her throat; she wanted to scream, scrabble at the walls of the craft to escape this. She held herself as still as she could, forcing herself to study the vision.

'It's like a woman,' she whispered to Hork. 'A human. But that's impossible. How could a human survive down here? There's no Air to breathe, or . . .'

Hork sounded impatient, though his breath still rattled with fear. 'This isn't a human, obviously. It's . . . something else, using the form of a human. A human-shaped sac of fire.'

'*What* else? What is it?'

'How am I supposed to know?'

'Do you think it's Xeelee?'

'No human has ever seen a Xeelee. Anyway, the Xeelee are just legend.'

Astonishingly, she found anger building inside her. At a time like this, she felt *patronized*. She glared at him and hissed, 'Legends are why you brought me here, remember?'

The Chair of Parz City shot an exasperated glance at her; then he turned to face the woman-thing, and when he spoke Dura found herself admiring the steadiness of his tone. 'You,' he challenged. 'Intruder. What do you want with us?'

The silence, broken by the wheezing of the pigs, seemed to

stretch; Dura, staring at the ugly flaps of flesh which covered the woman-thing's ear-cavities, wondered if it could hear Hork, still less answer him.

Then the woman-thing opened its mouth. Light poured out of its straining lips, and a sound emerged – deeper than any voice originating in a human chest – and, at first, formless.

But, Dura realized, wondering, words were beginning to emerge.

I . . . We've been expecting you. You took your own sweet time. And we had a devil of a job to find you. It looked around at the 'Pig', its neck swivelling like a ball joint, unnaturally. *Is this the best you could do? We need you to come a lot deeper than this; transmission conditions are awful . . .*

Hork exchanged an astounded glance with Dura.

'Can you understand me?' he asked the thing. 'Are you a Colonist?'

'Of course it can understand you, Hork,' Dura hissed, exasperated in her turn. She felt fascinated beyond her horror of this bag of skin. 'How is it you can speak our language?'

The thing's mouth worked, obscenely reminiscent of an Airpig's, and the flesh-balls in the eyecups rolled; as she watched, it seemed to Dura that the woman-thing appeared less and less human. It was merely a puppet of some unfathomable hyperonic creature beyond the hull, she realized; she found herself glancing through the window, wondering what immense, dark eyecups might be fixed on her even now.

The woman-thing *smiled*. It was a ghastly parody.

Of course I can understand you. I'm a Colonist, as you call us . . . but I'm also your grandmother. Once or twice removed, anyway . . .

A week before Games Day, Muub, the Physician, sent Adda an invitation to join him to view the Games from the Committee Box, high over the Stadium. Adda felt patronized: he had no doubt that in Muub's eyes he remained an unreconstructed savage from the upflux, and to Muub, Adda's reactions to the City's great events would be amusements – entertainments in themselves.

But he didn't refuse immediately. Perhaps Farr would enjoy seeing the Games from such a privileged vantage point. Farr's mood remained complex, difficult for Adda to break into. In fact he saw little of Farr these days; the boy seemed determined to spend as much time as possible with the rebellious, remote community of Surfers who lived half their lives clinging to the City's Skin.

In the end, Farr wouldn't come to the Games.

The City wasn't what it was. Even in Adda's short time of acquaintance with it, Parz, battered by the consequences of the Glitches, had lost some of its heart. In the great avenues half the shops and cafés were closed up now, and the ostentatiously rich with their trains of perfumed Air-piglets were conspicuous by their absence. There was a sense – not exactly of crisis – but of austerity. Times were difficult; there was much to be done and endured before things improved and the City could enjoy itself again.

But the Games were going to be different, it seemed. As the Day approached he sensed a quickening of the City's pulse. There seemed to be more people on the streets, arguing and gambling over the outcome of the various strangely named events. The Luge. The Slalom. The Pole-Divers . . . The Games would be like a holiday for the City, a relief from drudgery.

Adda was *curious*.

So, in the end, he decided to accept Muub's invitation.

The Stadium was a huge, clearwood-walled box fixed to one of the City's upper edges. The Committee Box was a balcony which hung over the Stadium itself from the City's upper surface, and to reach it Adda had to travel to the uppermost Upside, to the Garden surrounding the Palace itself. Feeling more out of place than ever in the opulent surroundings, he Waved past the miniature, sculpted Crust-trees, brandishing his begrimed bandaging like a weapon. He was subjected to scrutiny by three layers of contemptuous Guards before he reached the Box itself; he enjoyed insulting them as they searched his person.

At last he was ushered into the Box, a square platform twenty mansheights on a side domed over by clearwood. Neat rows of cocoons filled the platform, bound loosely to the structure by soft threads. About half the cocoons were already full, Adda saw; courtiers and other grandees nestled in the soft leather of the cocoons like huge, glittering insect larvae.

Their talk was bright and loud, their laughter braying; there was a heavy, cloying scent of perfume.

Adda was escorted to the front row of the Box by a small, humble-looking woman in a drab tunic. Muub was already there. He rested in his cocoon with his long, thin arms folded calmly against his chest, and his bare scalp shone softly as he surveyed the Stadium below. He turned to greet Adda with a nod. With ill grace Adda let the woman servant help him into a spare cocoon; his legs remained stiff and his right shoulder barely mobile, so that, embarrassingly, he had to be levered into the cocoon as if he were a statue of wood. Another woman, smiling, approached him with a box of sweetmeats; Adda chased her away with a snarl.

Muub smiled at him indulgently. 'I'm glad you decided to come, Adda. I believe you will find the Day interesting.'

Adda nodded, trying to be gracious. After all, he had accepted Muub's invitation. But what was it about this man's manner that irritated him so? He nodded over his shoulder at the sparkling ranks of courtiers. 'That lot seem to agree with you.'

Muub regarded the courtiers with aloof disdain. 'Games Day is a spectacle which does not fail to excite the unsophisticated,' he said softly. 'No matter how many times it is viewed. And besides, Hork is absent. As you know very well. And there is something of a vacuum of authority, among my more shallow colleagues, until the Chair's return.' He listened to the jabber of the courtiers for a moment, his large, fragile head cocked to one side. 'You can hear it in their tone. They are like children in the absence of a parent.' He sighed.

Adda grinned. 'Well,' he said, 'it's nice to know that your superciliousness isn't restricted to upfluxers.' He deliberately ignored Muub's reaction; he leaned forward in his cocoon and stared through the clearwood wall below him.

He was perched at the upper rim of the City. Its wooden Skin swept away below him, huge, uneven, battered; the great Corestuff anchor-bands were arcs of silver-grey cutting across the sky. Far below the City the Pole was a mass of bruised purple. Vortex lines shimmered across the sky around the City, on their way to their own rotation pole around the curve of the Star . . .

Adda stared at the vortex lines for a moment. Were they more tightly packed than usual? He tried to detect a drift through the Air, a presage of another Glitch. But he wasn't in the open Air – he wasn't able to smell the changes in the photons, to taste the Air's disturbance – and he couldn't be sure there was any change.

The Stadium was thronged with people who swarmed through the Air, hauling themselves over each other and along the ropes and rails strung across the great volume. Even through layers of clearwood, Adda could hear the excited buzz of the crowd; the sound seemed to come in waves of intensity, sparkling with fragments of individual voices – the cry of a baby, the hawking yells of vendors working the crowd. Sewage outlets sprayed streams of clear waste from the shell of the Stadium into the patient Air.

Away from the bulk of the City, aerobats Waved silkily through the Air in a prelude to the Games proper. They were young, lithe, nude, their skins dyed with strong primary colours; with ripples of their legs and arms they spiralled around the vortex lines and dived at each other, grabbing each others' hands and whirling away on new paths. There must have been a hundred of them, Adda estimated; their dance, chaotic yet obviously carefully choreographed, was like an explosion of young flesh in the Air.

He became aware that Muub was watching him; there was curiosity in the Physician's shallow eyecups. Adda let his jaw hang open, playing the goggling tourist. 'My word,' he said. 'What a lot of people.'

Muub threw his head back and laughed. 'All right, Adda. Perhaps I deserved that. But you can scarcely blame me for my fascination at your reaction to all this. Such scenes can scarcely have been imaginable to you, in your former life in the upflux.'

Adda gazed around, trying to take in the whole scene as a gestalt – the immense, human construct of the City itself, a thousand people gathered below for a single purpose, the scarcely believable opulence of the courtiers in the Box with their fine clothes and sweetmeats and servants, the aerobats flourishing their limbs through the Air in their huge dance. 'Yes, it's impressive,' he said. He tried to find ways of expressing what he was feeling. 'More than impressive. Uplifting, in a way. When humans work together, we can challenge the Star itself. I suppose it's good to know that not everyone has to scratch a living out of the Air, barely subsisting as the Human Beings do. And yet . . .'

And yet, why should there be *wealth* and *poverty*? The City was a marvellous construct, but it was dwarfed on the scale of the Star – and it was no bigger than an Ur-human's thumb, probably. But even within its tiny walls there were endless, rigid layers: the courtiers in their Box, walled off from the masses below; the Upside and Downside; and the invisible – yet very real – barriers between the two. Why should it be so? It was as if humans built such places as this with the sole purpose of finding ways to dominate each other.

Muub listened to Adda's clumsy expression of this. 'But it's inevitable,' he said, his face neutral. 'You have to have organization – hierarchy – if you are to run the complex, interlinking systems which sustain a society like the City with its hinterland. And only within such a society can man afford art, science, wisdom – even leisure of the most brutish sort, like these Games. And with hierarchies comes power.' He smiled at Adda, condescending once more. 'People aren't very noble, upfluxer. Look around you. Their darker side will find expression in any situation where they can best each other.'

Adda remembered times in the upflux, when he was young, and the world was less treacherous than it had become of late. He recalled hunting-parties of five or six men and women, utterly immersed in the silence of the Air, their senses open, thrilling to the environment around them. Completely aware and alive, as they worked together.

Muub was an observer, he realized. Believing he was above the rest of mankind, but in fact merely detached. Cold. The only way to live was to be yourself, in the world and in the company of others. The City was like a huge machine designed to stop its citizens doing just that – to alienate. No wonder the young people clambered out of the cargo ports and lived on the Skin, riding on the Air by wit and skill. Seeking *life*.

The light had changed. The rich yellow of the Air over the Pole seemed brighter. Puzzled, he turned his head towards the upflux.

There was a buzz of anticipation from the Box, answered by a buzz from the Stadium. Muub touched Adda's arm and pointed upwards. 'Look. The Surfers. Do you see them?'

The Surfers were a hexagonal array, shining motes scattered across the Air. Even Muub, despite his detachment, seemed thrilled as he stared up, evidently wondering how it would be to ride the flux so high, so far from the City.

But Adda was still troubled by the light change. He scoured the horizon, cursing the distortion of the clearwood wall before him.

Then he saw it.

Far upflux, far to the north, the vortex lines had disappeared.

Its – *her* – name was Karen Macrae. She had been born in a place called Mars, a thousand years ago.

That's Earth-standard years, she said. *Which are about half of Mars' years, of course. But they're the same as your years . . . We designed your body-clocks to match the standard human metabolic rate, you see, and we got you to count the rhythms of the neutron star so that we have a common language of days, weeks, years . . . We wanted you to live at the same rate as us, to be able to communicate with us.* Karen Macrae hesitated. *With them, I mean. With standard humans.*

Dura and Hork looked at each other. He hissed, 'How much of this do you understand?'

Dura stared at Karen Macrae. The floating image had drifted away from the centre of the cabin, now, and seemed to be growing coarser; it was not a single image, in fact, but a kind of mosaic formed by small, jostling cubes of coloured light. Dura asked, 'Are you an Ur-human?'

Karen Macrae fizzed. *A what? Oh, you mean a standard human. No, I'm not. I was, though . . .*

Karen Macrae and five hundred others had come to the Star from – somewhere else. Mars, perhaps, Dura thought. They had established a camp outside the Star. When they'd arrived the Star had been empty of people; there were only the native lifeforms – the pigs, the rays, the spin-spiders and their webs, the Crust-trees.

Karen Macrae had come to populate the Star with people.

The structure of a neutron star is astonishingly rich, whispered Karen Macrae. *Do you realize that? I mean, the Core is like a huge, single nucleus – a hypernucleus, laced with twenty-four per cent hyperonic matter. And it's fractal. Do you know what that means? It has structure on all scales, right down to the . . .*

'Please.' Hork held up his hands. 'This is a storm of words, conveying – nothing.'

The blocks of Karen's face jostled like small insects. *I am a first-generation Colonist,* she said. *We established a Virtual environment in the hypernucleus – in the Core. I was downloaded via a tap out of my corpus callosum – downloaded into the environment here, in the Core.* Karen Macrae brought veils of skin down over the pulpy, obscene things nestling in her eyecups. *Do you understand me?*

Hork said slowly, 'You are – a copy. Of an Ur-human. Living in the Core.'

Dura said, 'Where is the Ur-human Karen Macrae? Is she dead?'

She's gone. The ship left, once we were established here. I don't know where she is now . . . Dura tried to detect emotion in the woman-thing's voice – was she resentful of the original who had made her, who had thrust her into the Core of the Star? Was she envious? – but the quality of the voice was coarse, too harsh to tell; Dura was reminded of the Speaker system on Toba Mixxax's Air-car.

The colony of human copies, downloaded into the Core, had devices which interfaced with the physical environment of the Star, the woman-thing told them. They had a system to produce something called exotic matter; they laced the Mantle with wormholes, linking Pole to Pole, and they built a string of beautiful cities.

When they'd finished, the Mantle was like a garden. Clean, empty. Waiting.

Dura sighed. 'Then you built us.'

'Yes,' Hork said. 'Just as our fractured history tells us. We are made things. Like toys.' He sounded angry, demeaned.

The world had been at peace. There had been no need to struggle to live. There were no Glitches (few, anyway). The downloaded Colonists, still residing in the Core, had been there for the Human Beings like immortal, omniscient parents.

One could Wave from upflux to Pole, through the worm-hole transit ways, in a heartbeat.

Hork pushed forward, confronting the woman-thing. 'You expected us to come here, to seek you.'

We hoped you would come. We could not come to you.

'Why?' He seemed to be snarling now, Dura thought, unreasonably angry at this ancient, fascinating woman-shell. 'Why do you need us now?'

Karen Macrae turned her head. The light-boxes drifted, colliding noiselessly – no, Dura saw, they drifted through each other, as smoothly as if they were made of coloured Air.

The Glitches, she said slowly. *They are damaging the Core . . . they are damaging us.*

Dura frowned. 'Why don't you stop them?'

We haven't a physical interface any more. We withdrew it. Karen's voice was growing more indistinct, her component blocks larger; the form of a human was gradually being submerged in loss of detail.

Hork pushed himself forward from the cabin wall, his heavy hands outspread against the wood. 'Why? Why did you withdraw? You built us, and took away our tools, and abandoned us. You waged war against us; you took our trea-sures, our heritage. Why? *Why?*'

Karen turned to him, her mouth open, purple boxes stream-ing from her coarsely defined lips. She expanded and blurred, the boxes comprising her image swelling.

Hork threw himself at the image. He entered it as if it were no more than Air. He batted at the drifting, crumbling light-boxes with his open palms. *'Why did you make us? What purpose did we serve for you here? Why did you abandon us?'*

The boxes exploded; Dura quailed from a monstrous, bal-looning image of Karen Macrae's face, of the pale forms infest-ing her eyecups. There was a soundless concussion, a flood of purple light which filled the cabin before fleeing through the walls of the ship and into the ocean beyond. The human-thing, the simulacrum of Karen Macrae, was gone. Hork twisted in the Air, punching at emptiness in his frustration.

But there were new shadows in the cabin now, blue-green shadows cast by something behind Dura. Something outside the ship. She turned.

The object was a tetrahedron, she recognized immediately; a four-faced framework of glowing blue lines, like fragments of vortex lines. Sheets of gold, rippling, glistened over the faces. The construct was perhaps ten mansheights to a side, and its faces were easily wide enough to permit a ship the size of the 'Pig' to pass.

It was a gate. A four-sided gate . . .

Dura felt like a child again; she found a smile, slow and heavy with wonder, spreading across her face. This was a wormhole Interface, the most precious of all the treasures lost in the Core.

It could be a gateway out of the Star.

She grabbed at Hork's tunic, wonder flooding out her fear. 'Don't you understand what it means? We'll be able to travel, to cross the Star in a moment, as we could before the Wars . . .'

He pushed her away roughly. 'Sure. I understand what this means. Karen Macrae can't stop the Glitches. And so – for the first time since dumping us in the Mantle all those years ago, since leaving us to our fate – she and her Core-infesting friends need us. We – you and I – are going to have to travel through that thing, to wherever it takes us, and *stop the Glitches ourselves*.'

22

Cris Mixxax climbed onto his board. The wood under his bare feet was polished, warm, familiar; his soles gripped the ridged surface, and the ribs of Corestuff embedded in the wood felt like cold, hard bones. He flexed his knees experimentally. Electron gas hissed around his ankles and toes as the board cut through the flux lines. The Magfield felt springy, solid.

Cris grinned savagely. It felt *good*. It all felt good. At last this day had come, and it was going to be his.

The sky was a huge diorama, all around him. The South Pole, with its brooding purple heart sunk deep in the Quantum Sea, was almost directly below him; he could feel the massive Polar distortion of the Magfield permeating his body. Above him the Crust seemed close enough to touch, the dangling Crust-trees like shining hairs, immensely detailed; patterns of cultivation showed in rectangular patches of colour and texture – sharp, straight-line edges imposed by humans on the vibrant nature of the Star.

The City hovered in the Air over the Pole. Parz was so far below him he could cover it with the palm of his hand, and imagine he was alone in the sky – alone, save for his fellow racers. Parz looked like some elaborate wooden toy, surrounded by its cage of shining anchor-bands and pierced by a hundred orifices from which the green light of wood-lamps seeped, sickly. Sewage cascaded steadily from its underside, around the Spine of the Harbour. He could see the shining bulge that was the Stadium; it clung to the City's upper lip like a fragile growth, with the Committee Box a colourful balcony over it. Somewhere in there his parents would be watching, he knew – praying for his success, he'd like to think. But perhaps they were wishing he might fail –

give up this dream, this distraction of Surfing, and join them in their quiet, constrained lives once more.

He shook his head, staring down on the City as if he were some god, suspended over it. Out here the inwardness, the frustration of his life in and around the City, seemed remote, reduced to the trivial; he felt exalted, able to view it all with compassion, balance. His parents loved him, and they wanted what was best for him – as they saw it. The cries of the race marshals, tiny in the huge, glowing sky, floated to him. *Almost time.* He glanced around. There were a hundred Surfers, drawn into a rough line across the sky; now they were drawing precisely level, into line with the squads of marshals in their distinctive red uniforms. Cris flicked at his own board, once, twice; he felt it kick at the Magfield and bring him exactly into his place in the line. He stared ahead. He was facing along the direction of the vortex lines, towards the rotation pole; the closest line was a few mansheights from him, and the lines swept around him like the walls of some intangible corridor, beckoning him to infinity.

The challenge of the race was to Surf along the vortex lines, far across the roof of the world – across the Pole – to a finishing cross-section; there another group of marshals marked out an area of the sky, like human spin-spiders. The race was won – not just by the fastest, the first to complete the course – but by whoever applied the most technical skill, the most style in following the course.

He looked along the line. Ray, he knew, was three places down from him – the only other of his friends to have qualified for the Games this year. There she was, her lithe, bare body coiled over her board, her hair swept back and her teeth shining in a broad, hungry grin. He caught her eye, and she raised a fist, her smile broadening.

The Surfers were all in place now; he saw how they settled over their boards, concentrating, spreading their feet and lifting their arms. The marshals continued to scurry around the line like worried little animals, checking positions, adjusting boards with small pushes and shoves. Silence spread along the line; the marshals were withdrawing. Cris felt his senses open up. The board under his feet, the fizz of the Magfield, the freshness of the Air so far from the womb of the City as it sighed through his mouth and capillaries – these were vital and real things, penetrating his head; he had never felt so *alive*.

And perhaps, a distant, unwelcome part of him said, he never would again.

Well, if that was to be so – if his life was to be a long-drawn-out anticlimax after this superb moment – then let it be; and let this be his finest time.

The marshals glanced along their line at each other. In unison they raised their right arms – and brought them down with a chop, a cry of 'Begin!'

Cris thrust savagely at his board. He felt the Magfield surge through the board and his limbs, dragging at the currents of charged particles there. He lunged forward with a roar, lancing through the Air. The tunnel of vortex lines seemed to explode outwards around him; blue-white electron gas sparkled over his body. He was half-aware of similar yells around him, from the rest of the line, but he shut out the other Surfers; he focussed on his board, the Magfield, his balance and position in the Air.

The line of marshals, ragged and breaking up, hurtled beneath him.

He opened his mouth and yelled again, incoherent. In his peripheral vision he saw that only Ray, and one or two others, had matched his start. He was in the lead, already ahead of the other Surfers! And he knew his style was good, his balance right; the Magfield surged through his body like a wave of heat. He raised a hand before his face and watched electron gas shower from his fingertips; shrouded in blue light he must look like a figure from a dream racing across the sky . . .

His board slammed upwards, into his feet.

He gasped, almost thrown off the board with the shock. It had been like hitting something solid in the Magfield. He let his knees bend, trying to absorb the upward surge; but still he was hurled up into the Air, balanced perilously on his board. The vortex lines slid down the sky around him, and the Magfield flux lines tore at his stomach and chest as he was dragged brutally across them.

He heard screams from the Surfers around him.

The surge passed. Shaken, his knees and ankles aching, he straightened up. He risked glances to left and right. The line of Surfers was ragged, scattered, broken up. Whatever had caused that surge had hit the others as hard as it had him.

. . . Ray had gone. He saw a glinting sparkle which might have been her board, turning end over end through the Air; but of the girl herself there was no sign.

He felt a stab of concern – an awful, unfamiliar sense of *waste* – but the feeling was drowned by a flood of triumph. By luck or skill, or both, he had survived. He was still on his board, still in the race, and still determined to win.

But there was still something wrong. He was drifting downwards through the hexagonal array of lines. He corrected his line of flight, pushed himself hard along the Magfield – but again there came that damnable drift downwards. He felt confused, disoriented, as if his instincts were betraying him.

. . . No, he realized slowly; his instincts, his skill, were fine. He was holding his line. *The vortex lines themselves were drifting upwards, towards the Crust.*

He was a City boy, but he knew what that meant.

The Mantle was expelling its rotational momentum. *Glitch.*

Suddenly, for the first time, he felt lost, vulnerable, alone in the sky. He couldn't help but cry out, longing to be back in the remote wooden womb of Parz.

He forced himself to concentrate. He wasn't in any direct danger yet. With luck, and skill, he could still get through this.

Still he pushed across the sky, keeping in line with the drifting vortex lines. But now he slowed a little, glancing around. He was virtually alone now; of the hundred starters in the race, perhaps thirty were still on their boards, paralleling his path through the Air. Of the rest – of the marshals – there was no sign. The City still hung in the Air like a dusty lantern, solid and unperturbed.

The vortex lines were drifting faster. They looked tangled, untidy. Looking more closely he saw instabilities searing along the lines from both upflux and downflux; the huge, complex waveforms passed through each other, seeming to drag and reinforce each other.

He looked over his shoulder at the far upflux. There the Air glowed yellow, empty. *No vortex lines at all.*

Now purple light flooded up through the Air, sudden, shocking, so that his board cast a shadow over his legs and arms. He leaned over his board, glanced down.

The Quantum Sea had exploded, right under the City; a neutrino fount rose steadily towards Parz, like an immense fist.

Resentment flooded Cris. *No*, he thought. *Not today. Not on my day . . .*

The Magfield surged again, ramming upwards into his board with force and immediacy.

I was winning! Oh, I was winning!

Like a fragment of food swimming towards its own consumption, the crude wooden cylinder with its precious cargo of people and animals laboured towards the unblemished mouth of the Ur-human artifact.

Dura worked with the Air-pigs, feeding and patiently soothing as their farts drove the turbine. To bring the 'Pig' to the wormhole mouth Hork had taken the ship through a long, flat sweep to a position above one facet of the Interface. Through the wide windows she watched the wormhole gate sink briefly into the turgid glimmering of the underMantle, to reemerge as if surfacing as they approached it once more.

Now the Interface rose towards them, like an outstretched hand framed in the clearwood panel set into the base of the ship; within it light flashed, impossibly distant and vortex-line blue.

Hork worked his controls with savagery. For all his outer flippancy in the earlier stages of the voyage, he seemed to have become enraged since the encounter with Karen Macrae. Or perhaps that anger had been there in him all along, Dura thought; perhaps he had always resented the position of humans, left stranded and helpless in this Star. But now, for the first time, he had a focus for that rage: Karen Macrae, and her intangible Colonist companions in the Core of the Star.

Dura wondered at her own composure. She was fearful, yes; and an inner fluidity threatened to overwhelm her as she stared into the approaching maw of the wormhole. But at the same time, she realized, *she was not confronting the unknown*, as was Hork. The lore of the Human Beings was calm, detailed and analytical. The universe beyond the Star, the universe of the past beyond the here-and-now: those realms were abstract, remote, but they were as real to Dura as the world of Air, pigs, trees. Although she had never seen them she had grown up with the Xeelee and their works, with the artifacts of the Ur-humans, and to her they were no more exotic than the wild Air-boars of the Crust.

Perhaps, in the end, the lore of the Human Beings – their careful, almost obsessive, preservation of apparently useless knowledge from the past – was actually a survival mechanism.

The Interface was very close now, Dura saw; the fine, perfect vertices of the upper face spread away from the curving window of the ship, and the rest of the frame was foreshortened by perspective.

Then the clean lines of the artifact began to slide *across* the windows of the ship, as slow as knife-blades drawn across skin. The ship's downward trajectory had been carrying it steadily towards the centre of the face; but now they were clearly drifting, sliding towards one knife-sharp edge.

Something was wrong.

Hork hauled at his levers and slammed his hand into the fragile console. 'Damn it. She won't respond. The Magfield here is disrupted – maybe by the presence of the Interface – and . . .'

'Look!' Dura pointed downwards.

Hork stared at the edge, its fizzing blue light painting deep, shifting shadows on his face as it approached. He swore. 'It's going to hit us.'

'We might be safe. Maybe the Ur-humans designed this wormhole to be as safe as possible; maybe the ship will just rebound, and . . .'

'Or maybe not. Maybe the Ur-humans didn't expect anyone to be stupid enough to go careering through their doorway in a wooden ship. I think that damn thing is going to cut us in two.'

The Interface edge, wheeling past the windows, had widened from the abstraction of a line into a glowing rod as broad as a human arm.

Dura wrapped her arms around herself. Behind her the pigs

were a comforting, warm mass, an oasis of familiarity. 'At least try, damn you. Maybe you can get a purchase on the Interface's magnetic field.'

Now, beyond the walls of the ship, there was a spectacular flash, a sudden storm of blue-white light which flooded the cabin and made her cry out. The pigs squealed, terrified again. The ship lurched. Hork rolled in his seat and Dura grabbed at the pigs' restraining harness.

'We've hit!' she cried.

Hork dragged at his levers. 'No. It's the ship's own field; it must be brushing against the edge . . . The ship's responding. Dura, I think you're right; I think we're starting to work against the artifact's field. Keep feeding those animals, damn you!'

The flashing persisted and the shuddering of the ship assumed a steady, violent rhythm. Dura clung to the pigs' harness, striving to feed the pigs with an unwavering rhythm of her own.

Slowly, painfully slowly, the wheeling of the edge lessened, and the blue glare which had filled the cabin began to diminish. Dura glanced through the windows; the edge was receding and the magnetic flashes lessened, growing fitful and irregular, before dying completely.

The three edges of the face were all around the ship now, a fence of pale light slowly ascending past her. At last the ship was passing through the face, Dura realized; they were actually entering the Interface.

'Yes,' she murmured. 'But we're hardly safe.'

Hork raised his hands over the control panel. Then he pushed all three of his levers forward, deliberately; the ship surged forward into the Interface. She heard the hum of current in the Corestuff bands around the hull. 'We go on,' Hork said.

Dura had expected to make out the blue lines of the Interface, this box of light, from the inside. But there was no sign of the other faces, the rest of the wormhole; instead, beyond the walls of the ship, there was only a darkness even deeper than the twilit glow of the underMantle. It was as if they were entering – not a box of light – but the mouth of a corridor, like one of Parz's dingy alleys. In fact, it seemed that she *could* make out the lines of a corridor, stretching through the wormhole and on into infinity; black on black, it was like staring into a throat. Deep in the corridor there were flashes – sharp, silent and distant, light which splashed briefly over the dim walls. Slowly a picture assembled in her mind, each flash providing another fragment; the corridor was a smooth-walled cylinder perhaps five mansheights across and . . .

And how deep?

The walls were all around them now; the ebony throat enclosed the fragile craft as if it had been swallowed. She felt a rush of Air through the capillaries of her head; illuminated in stabs, fragments of the walls raced upwards past the ship like pieces of a dream. The walls seemed to converge at a great distance, closing around a point at infinity. But that was impossible – wasn't it? – because the Interface itself, the four-faced frame of light, was only ten or a dozen mansheights across.

But of course the corridor was immensely long – impossibly long – for the very purpose of a wormhole was to connect far-distant places. And now she was entering such a worm-hole; soon the ship would be passing through the device to emerge . . .

Somewhere else.

For a moment, fear, primitive, irrational and stark, surfaced in her mind; it was as if the mystery of it all was ramming itself into her eyes, ears and mind. She closed her eyes and wrapped her fingers in the soft leather of the pig harness. Was she, now, going to crumble into superstitious panic?

The wormhole was an artifact, she told herself. And an arti-fact built by humans – by Ur-humans, perhaps, but by humans nonetheless. She should not cringe before a mere device.

She forced her eyes open.

The ship shuddered.

Dura cried, 'Too fast! You're going too fast, damn it; we'll turn over if you don't slow down . . . Are you crazy?'

The control levers were still buried inside Hork's fleshy hands, but when he turned to her his wide face was empty, wondering. 'It's not me,' he said slowly. 'I mean, it's not the ship . . . we're no longer propelling ourselves. Dura, we're being drawn into the wormhole.' He stared at the little control console, as if seeking an answer there. 'And there's nothing I can do about it.'

Cris rode the turbulent Magfield almost automatically. He stared at the neutrino fount, fascinated, almost forgetting his own peril. The fount was a tower, dark, unimaginably massive, thrusting out of the turbulent mass of the Quantum Sea. As it rose into Mantle Air, the viscous purple Sea-stuff crusted over, shattering, the fragments spiralling upwards around the dense-packed flux lines of the Magfield.

Here was stuff from deep in the heart of the Star – deeper than any Bell had gone, deeper perhaps even than Hork's wooden ship would reach. Here was an expulsion of material from the immense, single nucleus that was the soul of the Star, from within the nebulous boundary between Sea and Core. The fount's material was hyperonic; each hyperon was a huge cluster of quarks far more massive than any ordinary nucleon, and the hyperons were bound together by quark exchanges into complex, fractal masses. But as the material spewed up through the throat of the Pole its structure was collapsing, unable to sustain itself in the lower-density regime of the Mantle. The quark bags were breaking apart, releasing a flood of energy, and reforming as showers of nucleons; and the free nucleons – protons and neutrons – were congealing rapidly into chunks of cooling nuclear matter.

That deadly hail was now lancing through the Mantle, and would soon come streaming upwards around the City. And he felt the energy released by that huge wave of hyperonic decay as it surged upwards, the neutrinos sleeting through his body, hot and needle-sharp, on their way to the emptiness above the Crust.

Now, even as he watched, the spiralling paths of the charged chunks of freezing Core-matter seemed to be distorting – flattening – as if the Magfield itself were changing, in response to the disaster.

Suddenly Cris understood.

The Magfield *was* changing. The irruption of this immense freight of charged material from the Core had disrupted the field; the Sea-fount was like an electrical current, unimaginably strong, passing through the heart of the Star's Magfield Pole, temporarily competing with the great magnetic engines at the Core of the Star itself. What he'd felt – the unexpected surges in the field – had been no more than distant echoes of that huge disturbance.

. . . But now another of those magnetic echoes hurtled up around him. This time his feet slipped from the board and he fell forward, crying out; the board slammed against his chest and thrust him upwards towards the Crust. He clung to the board helplessly, his legs scrabbling across its smooth surface, as he rose faster than he could ever have Surfed. If he lost the board he was finished, he knew. His mind raced. Perhaps he would be thrown beyond the Crust, board and all! What then? Would his body collapse into cooling fragments in the emptiness beyond, just as the Core material froze in the Mantle?

As it happened, would he be *aware*?

But the upward surge subsided, as suddenly as it had come.

The board stabilized in the Air. Gasping, Cris dragged himself forward across the board; his chest ached from the pressure of the board in its flight. There was the City, far below him, but still close enough for him to make out detail – the Spine, the gaping cargo ports, the encrustation of Garden on its upper surface. He felt a surge of relief, and even a little shame; he couldn't have been thrown so impossibly high after all.

Carefully, cautiously, he tucked his knees under him, rested his feet against the board, and stood up. The Magfield was quivering like a live thing under him, and he rocked the board against it, tilting his aching ankles; but, for the moment, the field was fairly stable. Predictable. He could Surf on it . . . and he was going to have to, if he was to make it through this.

He glanced around the sky. He was alone now; there was no sign of any of the other hundred Surfers. Again he felt a burst of triumph, accompanied by shame. Had he survived because he was the best? Or the luckiest, perhaps?

And, he reminded himself, he might join the rest in the anonymity of death yet, before this day was through.

The vortex lines around him writhed, tortured by instabilities, by impossible, ungainly forms which warped as they propagated, gathering energy. The *end* of the vortex lines – the boundary of the volume of Air in which there were no vortex lines – was rushing towards him, a wall of emptiness. In that region, he knew, the turbulence of the Air, lashed by the neutrino storm from the Core, was such that its superfluid properties had broken down. He wouldn't be able to Surf; the friction would be impossible. Damn it, he wouldn't be able to *breathe*. His capillaries would clog, his heart strain at the thickening Air . . .

He shook his head, tried to focus. He looked down. He had to get back to the City before the turbulence reached him. (That remote part of him prodded his mind over this. Why should he be any safer in the City than outside?) Again he shook his head, growling at himself. The City was the only place to go, safe or not. Therefore he would go there. But already the chunks of frozen Sea-stuff were hurtling up around the City. A graze from one of those . . .

Thinking about it was pointless. He spread his feet against the board, bent his legs, and thrust.

He Surfed as he'd never Surfed before – perhaps as nobody had Surfed before. He thrust at the board again and again, ramming its Corestuff web across the shaking Magfield. He soared between rippling vortex lines, ducking and swooping. Soon he was moving so quickly that the residual normal-fluid component of the Air whipped at his hair, his face. But still he accelerated, slamming his feet against the board until his soles ached.

There was something in the distance, a new factor in the chaos the sky had become. He risked a brief glance. He saw lines crossing the sky, lancing down through the Crust across the vortex lines, and penetrating the Core – blue-white beams which stirred the Core like spoons.

Now he was entering the inverted rain from the exploded Sea. The frozen Sea-fragments were irregular, solid chunks, two or three mansheights across. They tumbled upwards through the Air around him, sharp edges sparkling, Sea-purple laced through their interior. The fragments had their own, whirling magnetic fields; ghostly flux-fingers plucked at Cris as they passed him. He followed a curving path, dipping down over the Pole towards the City; flexing his legs, his hips, his neck, he slalomed through the crumbling vortex lines, the Sea-fragments.

What sport! It was wonderful! He roared aloud, yelling out his exhilaration.

The City was ahead of him now. It seemed to balloon out of the Air, its Skin swelling before him, uneven, ugly, as if being inflated from within.

He was almost home.

By the blood of the Ur-humans, he thought. *I might actually live through this.* And if he did, what a tale he would have to tell. What a hero he would become . . .

But now the Magfield surged again, betraying him.

This time he fell back; his spine was slammed against his board. The breath was knocked out of him, and he tumbled off the board, vainly clutching for its rim.

The board fell away from him, tumbling across the face of the City.

Falling naked through the Air, he watched the board recede. He tried to Wave, to rock his legs through the Air, but his strength was gone; he could get no purchase on the Magfield.

He was moving too fast, in any case.

Oddly he felt no fear, only a kind of regret. To have come so close and not to have made it . . .

The Skin of Parz was huge before him, a wall across the sky.

23

All around the City, cooling fragments of the Quantum Sea, huge and threatening, streamed upwards from the Pole.

In the Stadium, there was panic.

Adda leaned forward in his cocoon and peered down. The bulk of the Stadium was a turbulent mass of human torsos and struggling limbs; even as he watched, the network of delicate guide ropes which had criss-crossed the Stadium collapsed, engendering still more chaos as a thousand people struggled to escape. The crowd, screaming, sounded like trapped animals. Lost in the melee, Adda saw the purple uniforms of stewards and food vendors scrambling along with the rest.

They all wanted to get out, obviously. But get out to what? Where was safety to be found – inside the cosy Skin of the City? But that Skin was just a shell of wood and Corestuff ribs; it would burst like scraped leather if . . .

He was kicked in the back, hard. He gasped as the Air was forced out of his lungs, and he fell forward; then the rope fixing his cocoon on one side parted, and he was spun around.

He struggled out of his cocoon, ignoring the protests of stiff joints, and prepared to take on whoever had struck him. But it was impossible to tell. The Committee Box was full of panicking courtiers, their made-up faces twisted with fear, fighting free of cocoons and restrictive robes. Adda opened his mouth and laughed at them. So all their finery, and fine titles, offered no protection from mortal terror. Where was their power now?

Muub was struggling out of his own cocoon with every expression of urgency.

Adda said, 'Where will you go?'

'The Hospital, of course.' Muub gathered his robes tight around his legs and glanced around the Box, looking for the

fastest way out. 'It's going to be a long day's work...'
Apparently on impulse, he grabbed Adda's arm. 'Upfluxer.
Come with me. Help me.'

Adda felt like laughing again, but he recognized earnestness in Muub's eyes. 'Why me?'

Muub gestured to the scrambling courtiers. 'Look at these people,' he said wearily. 'Not many cope well in a crisis, Adda.' He glanced at the upfluxer appraisingly. 'You think I'm a little inhuman – a cold man, remote from people. Perhaps I am. But I've worked long enough as a Physician to gain a functional understanding of who can be relied on. And you're one of them, Adda. Please.'

Adda was surprisingly moved by this, but he pulled his arm free of Muub's grasp. 'I'll come if I can. I promise. But first I have to find Farr – my kinsman.'

Muub nodded briskly. Without another word he began to work his way through the crowd of courtiers still blocking the Box's exit, using his elbows and knees quite efficiently.

Adda glanced down at the crowded Stadium once more. The crush there was becoming deadly now; he saw imploded chests, limp limbs, Air-starved faces like white flowers in the mass of bodies.

He turned away and launched himself towards the exit.

Farr could be in any of a number of places – with the Skinriders outside the City itself, or up somewhere near the Surfer race, or down in the Harbour with his old work-friends – but he would surely make for the Mixxaxes' to find Adda. The Mixxaxes' part of the mid-Upside was on the opposite side of Parz, and Adda began the long journey across a City in turmoil.

It was as if some malevolent giant, laughing like a spinstorm, had taken the City and shaken it. People, young and old, the well-dressed rich and drab manual workers alike, fled through the corridor-streets; screams echoed along the avenues and Air-shafts. Perhaps each of these scurrying folk had some dim purpose of their own in the face of the Glitch – just as Adda did. But collectively, they swarmed.

To Adda it was like a journey through hell. Never before had he felt so confined, so enclosed in this box built by lunatics to contain lunatics; he longed to be in the open Air where he could *see* what the Star was doing. He reached Pall Mall. The great vertical avenue was full of noise and light; people and cars swarmed over each other, Speakers blaring. Shop-fronts had been smashed open, and men and women were hastening through the crowds with arms full of goods – clothes, jewellery. Above his head, at the top of the Mall – the uppermost Upside – the golden light of the Palace Garden filtered down through the miniature bushes and ponds, as peaceful and opulent as ever. But now lines of guards fenced off the grounds of the Palace from any citizen who thought that might be a good direction to flee.

Adda, close to the centre of the Mall now, felt an absurd impulse to laugh. *Guards. Looters . . .* What did these people hope to achieve? What did they think was happening to the world around them? It would be a triumph if their precious City survived this disaster intact enough for the looters to find an opportunity to flaunt their ill-gotten wealth.

As if in response to his thought, the City *lurched*.

The Mall – the huge vertical shaft of light and people around him – *leaned* to the right. He flailed at the Air, scrabbling for balance. The street had shifted with shocking suddenness. There was an immense groan; he heard wood splintering, clearwood cracking, a high-pitched scream which must be the sound of a Corestuff rib failing.

People rained through the Air.

Helpless, they didn't even look human – they were like inanimate things, carvings of wood, perhaps. Their bodies hailed against shop-fronts and structural pillars; the Mall echoed with screams, with small, sickening crunches.

A woman slammed against Adda's rib-cage, knocking away his breath once more. She clung to him with desperate strength, as if she thought he might somehow save her from all this. She must have been as old as Adda himself. She wore a rich, heavy robe which was now torn open, revealing a nude torso swathed in fat, her loose dugs dangling; her hair was a tangled mess of blue-dyed strands with yellow roots. 'What's happening? Oh, what's happening?'

He pulled the woman away from his body, disengaging her as kindly as he could. 'It's a Glitch. Do you understand? The

Magfield must be shifting – distorted by the charged material erupting from the Quantum Sea. The City is trying to find a new, stable . . .'

He stopped. Her eyes were fixed on his face, but she wasn't listening to a word.

He pulled her robe closed and tied it shut. Then he half-dragged her across the Mall and left her clinging to a pillar before a shop-front. Perhaps she'd recover her wits, find her way to her home. If not, there was little Adda could do for her.

He found an exit to a side-street. He Waved his way down it with brisk thrusts of his legs, trying to ignore the devastation around him.

The journey through the wormhole lasted only heartbeats, but it seemed an eternity to Dura. She clung to her place, feeling as helpless and as terrified as the squealing pigs.

Out of control, despite all Hork's vain heavings at the console, the 'Flying Pig' rattled against the near-invisible walls of the corridor. Spectacular flashes burst all around the clumsy vessel.

The end came suddenly.

Light – electric blue – blossomed from the infinity point, beneath the plummeting craft at the terminus of the corridor. The light hurtled up the corridor like a fist, unavoidable. Dura stared into it, feeling its intensity sting her eyes.

The light exploded around them, flooding the ship and turning the cabin's lanterns into green wraiths. The pigs screamed.

Then the light died away – no, she realized; the light had *congealed* into a framework around them, another tetrahedral Interface. The finely drawn cage of light turned around them with stately grace; evidently the 'Pig', spewed out of the wormhole, had been brought almost to rest, and was now tumbling slowly.

Beyond the cage of light there was only darkness.

Dura glanced around the ship. There wasn't any obvious sign of damage to the hull, and the turbine was still firmly fixed in place. The squeals of the pigs, the stink of their futile escape-farts, slowly subsided.

Hork remained in the pilot's seat. He stared out of the

windows, his large mouth gaping like a third eyecup in the middle of his beard.

Dura drifted down towards him. 'Are you all right?'

At first her question seemed not to register; then, slowly, his head swivelled towards her. 'I'm not injured.' His face twisted into a smile. 'After that little trip, I'm not sure how healthy I am, but I'm not injured. You? The pigs?'

'I'm not damaged. Nor are the animals.'

'And the turbine?'

She admired his brisk dismissal of the wonders of the journey, his focus on the practical. She shrugged.

He nodded. 'Good. Then we have the means to move.'

'. . . Yes,' she said slowly. 'I suppose so. But only if the Magfield extends this far.'

He studied her face, then peered out of the craft uncertainly. 'You think it mightn't? That we've moved beyond the Magfield?'

'We've come a long way, Hork.'

She turned away, dropping her eyes to her hands. The shadows cast on her skin were soft, silvery; the diffuse glow seemed to smooth over the age-blemishes of her flesh, the wrinkles and the minute scars.

. . . Silvery?

Outside the ship, the light had changed.

She moved away from Hork and peered out of the ship. The vortex-blue tetrahedron had disappeared. There was a *room* around the ship now, a tetrahedral box constructed of some sheer grey material. It was as if this skin-smooth substance had plated over the framework, turning the Interface from an open cage into a four-sided box which encased the 'Pig'.

The walls weren't featureless, though. There was some form of decoration – circular, multicoloured patches – on one wall, and, cut in another, a round-edged rectangle which could only be a door.

. . . A door to what?

Hork scratched his scalp. 'Well. What now? Did you see where these walls came from?'

Dura pressed her face to a clearwood window. 'Hork, I don't think we're in the underMantle any more.'

'You're guessing.' His face was creased with frustration.

She pointed to the room beyond the window. 'I think that's Air out there. I think we could live out there.'

'How can you know that?'

'Of course I can't *know*.' Dura felt a calm certainty fill her. She was starting to feel safe, she realized, to trust the powers into whose hands she'd delivered herself. 'But why would we be brought to a place which is lethal for us? What would be the point?'

He frowned. 'You think this is all – designed? That our journey was *meant* to be this way, to bring us here?'

'Yes. Since we entered the wormhole we've been in the hands of the ancient machines of the Ur-humans. Surely they built their machines to protect us. I think we have to trust them.'

Hork took a deep breath, the fine fabric of his costume scratching over his chest. 'You're saying we should go out there. Shut down the turbine and our magnetic shell – leave the "Pig" and go outside.'

'Why else did we come here?' She smiled. 'Anyway, I want to see what those markings on the wall are.'

'All right. If we're not crushed in the first instant we'll know you're right.' The decision made, his manner was brisk and pragmatic. 'And I guess the pigs need a rest anyway.'

'Yes,' Dura said. 'I believe they do.'

Hork turned to his control console and threw switches. Dura tended to the pigs, providing them with healthy handfuls of leaves. As they fed, their flight-farts died to a trickle and the turbine slowed with a weary whirr.

The cabin fell silent, for the first time since the departure from Parz.

Hork whispered, 'It's gone. Our magnetic field. It's shut down.'

For a moment Hork and Dura stared at each other. Dura's heart pounded and she found it impossible to take a breath.

Nothing had changed; the ship still tumbled slowly within the cool grey walls of the wormhole chamber.

Hork grinned. 'Well, we're still alive. You were right, it seems. And now . . .' He pointed to the hatch in the upper end of the craft. 'You first,' he said.

*

The hatch opened with a soft pop.

Dura winced as gas – *Air?* – puffed into the ship past her face. She found herself holding her breath. With an effort of will she exhaled, emptying her lungs, and opened her mouth to breathe deeply.

'Are you all right?'

She sighed. 'Yes. Yes, I'm fine. It's Air all right, Hork . . . We were expected, it seems.' She sniffed. 'The Air's cool – cooler than the ship. And it's – I don't know how to describe it – it's fresh. Clean.' Clean, in comparison to the murky Air of the City to which she'd grown accustomed. When she closed her eyes and drew in the strange Air it was almost like being back with the Human Beings in the upflux.

. . . Almost. Yet the Air here had a flat, lifeless, artificial quality to it. It was scrubbed clean of scents, she realized slowly.

Hork pushed past her and out into the room beyond. He looked around with fists clenched, aggressively inquisitive, his robe garish against the soft grey light of the walls. Dura, suppressing pangs of fear, followed him away from the wooden ship's illusory protection.

They hung in the Air of the wormhole chamber. The 'Flying Pig' tumbled slowly beside them, a scarred wooden cylinder crude and incongruous within the walls of this finely constructed room.

'If the Ur-human builders could see us now, I wonder what they would say?'

Hork grunted. 'Probably, "Where have you been all this time?"' He Waved experimentally and moved forward a mansheight or so. 'Hey. There's a magnetic field here.'

'Is it the Magfield?'

'I don't know. I can't tell. If it is, it's weaker than I've ever felt it before.'

'Maybe it's artificial . . . put here to help us move around.'

Hork grinned, his confidence growing visibly. 'I think you're right, Dura. These people really were expecting us, weren't they?' He looked over his shoulder at the 'Pig', inspecting the ship briskly. He pointed, his embroidered sleeve flapping. 'Look at that. We've brought a passenger.'

Dura turned. There was something clinging to the side of

the craft; it was like a huge, metallic leech, spoiling the clean cylindrical lines of the ship. 'It's Corestuff,' she said. 'We've brought a Corestuff berg with us, all the way through the wormhole. It must have stuck to our field-bands . . .'

'Yes,' Hork said. 'But by no accident.' He made a mock salute to the lump of Corestuff. 'Karen Macrae. So glad you could accompany us!'

'You think she's in there? In that berg?'

'Why not?' He grinned at her, his eyecups dark with excitement. 'It's possible. Anything's possible.'

'But why?'

'Because this trip is as important to Karen Macrae as it is to us, my dear.'

Dura flexed her legs; the Waving carried her easily through the Air. She moved away from the hulk of the 'Pig' and towards the walls of the chamber. Tentatively she reached out a hand, placed it cautiously on the grey wall material. Beneath her fingers and palm its smooth perfection was unbroken. It was cool to the touch – not uncomfortably so, but a little cooler than her body.

'Dura.' Hork sounded excited; he was inspecting the wall display Dura had seen from within the 'Pig'. 'Come and look at this.'

Dura Waved briskly to Hork; side by side they stared at the display.

Two circles, differing in size, had been painted on the wall. The larger was coloured yellow and was perhaps a micron wide. The colour was deepest at the heart of the circle and lightened, becoming almost washed out, as the eye followed the colour out to the edge of the circle. The disc was marred by a series of blue threads which swept through its interior – a little like vortex lines, Dura thought, except that these lines did not all run in parallel, and in places even crossed each other.

Each blue line was terminated by a pair of tiny pink tetrahedra, one at each end. Most of the tetrahedra had been gathered into the centre of the disc, so that the lines looped around the heavy amber heart of the disc. But five or six of the lines broke free of the knot at the centre. One of them terminated at a pole of the disc, just inside its surface. The rest of the lines led, in wavering spirals, out of the disc itself, and crossed the empty space of the intervening wall to the second, smaller circle; a half-dozen tetrahedra jostled within the small circle like insects.

Dura frowned, baffled. 'I don't understand. Perhaps these little tetrahedra have something to do with the wormholes . . .'

'Of course they do!' Hork's voice was brisk and confident. 'Can't you see it? It's a map – a map of the entire Star.' He traced features of the diagram with his fingertip. 'Here's the Crust; and within it – this outermost, lighter band – is the Mantle, which contains the Air we breathe. All the world we know.' His fingertip gouged a path into the heart of the Star image. 'These darker sections are the underMantle and the Quantum Sea – and here's the Core.'

'And the tetrahedra, the threads connecting them . . .'

'. . . are maps of the wormholes!' His eyecups were wide and filled with the grey light of the chamber. 'Isn't it obvious, Dura? Look.' He jabbed at the 'Core'. 'And here are the wormhole Interfaces, brought into the Core by the Colonists after the Core Wars. Most of the Interfaces, anyway. And so the wormhole corridors – marked by these threads – lead nowhere but back to the Core.'

The implications of his words slowly sank into her. 'So there are many wormholes – dozens, hundreds – not just the one we travelled in?'

'Yes. Just think of it, Dura; once the wormholes must have riddled the Star.' He shook his head. 'Well, the Colonists put a stop to that. Now we're reduced to crawling around the Star in wooden boxes drawn by Air-pigs.' Again anger, resentment welled in his voice.

'Do you think we're still here?' She pointed to the Core of the Star map, at the knot of wormholes which looped around it.

'No,' he said briskly. 'Why would we be given an Interface which took us into the Core? Remember, the Colonists have a goal too – they also have to find a way to stop the Glitches. They surely can't use the wormholes themselves – after all, we know the wormholes were built for humans. Real humans, I mean. Us. So they have to rely on us.'

She found herself shivering. 'Then if we're not in the Core, we must be *here*.' She drew her finger along the threads of wormhole paths which left the main circle and crossed the grey spaces to the second, smaller disc. '. . . *Outside the Star.*' She looked at him. 'Hork – what are we going to find when we open the door to this chamber?'

He stared into her eyes, his brashness gone, utterly unable to answer.

Farr was waiting for Adda at Toba Mixxax's home. Ito Mixxax was there, but not Toba or Cris. The City-tilt had made a mess of the Mixxaxes' domesticity: crockery and other material had been smashed against the walls, and fragments drifted in the Air.

Ito had her arm around Farr, trying to comfort or reassure him; when Adda opened the door to the home, Farr greeted his arrival with relief, a smile, while Ito looked merely disappointed that it wasn't her husband or son. They were both uninjured, though Farr looked shocked. Adda came to them both and placed a hand on their shoulders. The three of them drifted there, at the centre of the Mixxaxes' cosy room, their human warmth sufficient for a brief moment.

Then they pulled apart. Ito Mixxax looked drawn, but composed. 'What are you going to do? Do you want to stay here?'

He looked at Farr. The boy must be worried sick about his sister. But it would do no good to stay here and let him brood. Besides, despite its lingering domesticity, what sanctuary was this place, any more than the rest of Parz? 'We're going to the Hospital,' he said firmly. 'Or at least, we'll try to get there. We'll find work to do there. What about you?'

'Toba was with me at the Games. In the Stadium.' She sighed, looking more weary than afraid. 'We got separated. I'll have to wait for him here. Then we'll start searching for Cris, I suppose. We ought to be able to get the car out of the City.' She looked at Adda, appraising him, evidently trying to concentrate on his needs. 'Do you want to rest here? Are you hungry?'

'No.' He reached for Farr; the boy took his hand, meekly, like a child. 'Come on, Farr. It's not food they'll be short of in that damn Hospital, but strength, and courage, and ingenuity. And . . .'

There was an explosion from the heart of the City – no, not an explosion, Adda thought, but an immense tearing sound, a huge exhalation.

There was a moment of stillness. Then a shock passed through the City.

The very fabric of the structure seemed to flex. The little room rattled around them, and the fragments of crockery, already smashed, rattled in a thin hail against the walls.

When the tremor had passed, Farr asked, 'What was that? Another settling in the Magfield?'

'I don't think so. That was sharper – more abrupt . . . Come, lad. Let's move.'

Ito kissed them both quickly on the cheek. 'Be safe,' she said.

The Hospital of the Common Good was in the upper Downside, and Adda decided that the quickest way to get there – the most likely to be clear – would be through Pall Mall. So he and Farr Waved along one of the main artery streets towards the broad axis of the City. It was a little easier to move now, Adda found; most people must have reached whatever destination they had been looking for – or, he reflected sadly, be lying hurt in some corner of the City. But the Air-cars were an increased menace. The cars soared along the emptying streets behind teams of terrified Air-pigs; several times the Human Beings had to lurch aside to stop themselves being run down. Once they came across a car which had embedded itself nose-first into a shop-front. There was no sign of the driver, but the Air-pig team was still attached to its harness. The pigs strained against their restraints, their circular mouths wide as they screamed.

Farr loosened the harness. Released, the pigs fled away into the shadows of the corridors, caroming from the walls like toys.

They reached the junction of the artery-street and the Mall. Adda rested at the street's rectangular lip for a moment, then prepared to launch himself out into the main shaft. But Farr grabbed his arm and held him back. The boy pointed downwards. Adda stared into his face, then squinted down, blinking to clear his good eyecup.

The lower end of the Mall – the huge spherical Market

– was filled with light. Too much light, which glinted from the guide rails, stall sites, the huge execution Wheel . . . Yellow Air-light, which flooded into the heart of the City from a new, ragged shaft that cut right through the Mall itself, just above the Market.

So here was the cause of the shock they had experienced with Ito.

The edges of the shaft were neat – so neat that Adda might almost have thought it was man-made, another avenue. But the cross-section of this shaft was irregular – formless, nothing like the precise rectangles and circles which defined Parz – and it was off-centre, askew, too wide.

Adda drifted out into the Mall a little way and stared down at the gash.

The inner skin of the Mall had been sloughed away, shops and homes scoured off as cleanly as if by a blade. And within the gash itself he could see the cross-sections of cut-open homes, shops. There were splashes of broken flesh. He heard human voices, but no screams: there were groans, and low, continuous weeping.

Farr joined him in the Air. 'What is it? What's happened?'

'A Sea-fragment,' Adda said grimly. 'The City has been hit. Looks as if the berg passed straight through . . . We're lucky the City wasn't smashed wide open . . . Come on, Farr. Let's see if that damn Hospital is still working.'

They dropped down the wide, almost empty shaft of the Mall, searching for a way to get to the Hospital.

24

Hork ran his thick fingers round the seam of the door. Then, impatient, Waving to give himself leverage, he laid his hands flat against the door and shoved.

The door swung back on invisible hinges, heavy and silent; Air hissed.

Through the doorway Dura caught glimpses of another, larger chamber, walled by more of the featureless grey material.

For a moment Hork and Dura hesitated before the doorway.

'Let's get on with it,' Hork growled. He grasped the edges of the doorframe. With a single fluid movement he hauled his bulk through; his small feet, Waving gently, disappeared into the frame.

With a sigh, Dura took hold of the frame. Like the rest of the wall material the frame edges were cool to the touch, but the walls seemed knife-thin and the edges dug into her palms. She laid her hands carefully on the outer surface of the wall, beyond the frame, and pushed herself through.

The outer chamber was another tetrahedron – and constructed of the ubiquitous grey-bland material – but perhaps ten times as large, a hundred mansheights across or more. This room would be as large as any enclosed space in Parz City. The chamber from which she had emerged floated at the heart of this new room, its vertices and edges aligned with the chamber within which it was embedded. Dura wondered vaguely what was holding the smaller chamber in place; there were no signs of struts, supports or ropes.

Perhaps they were in a nest of these tetrahedral chambers, one contained in the other, she speculated; perhaps if they went beyond these walls they would swim into a third chamber, ten times larger again, and then onwards . . .

But there was no door in this outer chamber. The walls were featureless: unbroken even by the map device which had adorned the inner cell. There must be no way out; maybe this was the end of their journey.

Hork came Waving towards her. 'Dura. I've found something.' Taking her by the hand he half-dragged her around the inner cell. He Waved to a stop, causing Dura to bump against him, and pointed to his find. 'There. What do you think of that?'

It was a box, irregularly shaped, about half a mansheight across. Dura circled the thing warily a few microns from where it hovered in the Air. Sculpted of the familiar grey wall material, it consisted of a massive block from which a thinner rectangular plate protruded; smaller cylinders stretched forward from the sides of the rectangle . . .

Its function was unmistakable.

'It's a *seat*,' she said.

Hork snorted impatiently. 'Obviously it's a damn seat.' He prowled around the object, poking boldly at its surfaces. Levers – thick stumps apparently designed for human fists – protruded from the end of each of the chair's arms. A swivelling pointer was inset into the left arm.

Dura asked, 'Do you think it's meant for us . . . I mean, for humans?'

Hork groaned. 'Of *course* it is.'

Dura was offended. 'There's nothing obvious about this situation, Hork. If that map was right, we've travelled across space – away from the Star itself. Why should we expect anything but utter strangeness? It's a miracle we've found Air to breathe, let alone . . . *furniture*.'

He shrugged; the fat-covered muscles flowed under his coverall. 'But this is obviously meant for humans. See how the back, the seat have been moulded?' And, before Dura could protest, Hork swivelled his bulk through the Air and settled into the chair. At first he wriggled, evidently uncomfortable – he even looked alarmed – but soon he relaxed and assumed a broad smile. He rested his hands on the arms of the chair; it seemed to match the shape of his massive body. 'Perfect,' he said. 'You know, Dura, this chair must be three hundred generations old. And yet it looks as good as new, and it fits my bulk as well as if it had been designed by the best Parz craftsmen.'

Dura frowned. 'You didn't seem so happy when you got into the seat.'

He hesitated. 'It felt odd. The surfaces seemed to flow around me.' He grinned, his confidence recovering. 'It was adjusting to me, I suppose. It was disconcerting, but it didn't last long . . . What do you think these levers are for?' His massive fists hovered over the rods protruding from the seat-arms.

'No!' She laid her hands over his.

After a moment he relaxed and lifted his hands away from the levers, leaving them untouched. 'Interesting,' he said mildly. 'These look just like the control levers in the "Flying Pig". Maybe there are some basic commonalities of human design, a certain way things just have to be . . .'

'But,' she said firmly, 'unlike with the "Pig" we don't have the faintest idea what these controls are for.'

Hork looked like a reprimanded child. 'Well, as you told me earlier, we're not going to make any progress unless we take a few chances.' He glanced down at the arrow device inset in the left arm of the seat. 'What about this, for instance?'

Dura Waved closer. The arrow was a finger-thick cylinder hinged at its centre; it lay at the heart of a small crater gouged out of the chair. The crater's rim was marked by a band divided into four quarters: white, light grey, dark grey, black. The arrow was pointing at the black quadrant. It seemed obvious that the arrow was designed to be twisted by the occupant of the chair.

Hork looked up at her. 'Well? This seems harmless enough.'

Dura suppressed a manic giggle. 'You haven't the faintest idea what it *is* . . .'

'Damn you, upfluxer, we didn't come all this way to cower.' And with a convulsive movement he grabbed the arrow and twisted it.

The device clicked through a quarter of a turn.

Dura flinched, wrapping her arms around her body. Even Hork could not help but wince as the arrow came to rest, pointing to the dark grey quadrant of the scale band. Then he exhaled heavily. 'See? No harm done . . . In fact, nothing seems to have happened at all. And . . .'

'No.' She shook her head. 'You're wrong.' She pointed. 'Look . . .'

Hork twisted in the seat.

The walls of the chamber had turned transparent.

Bzya was dozing, hands loosely wrapped around the Bell's axial support pole, when the blue flashes started.

He snapped awake.

This had been a long, fruitless dive, and he had been looking forward to home, to breaking some beercake with Jool. But now something was wrong.

He scanned quickly around the cabin. Hosch, his only companion on this trip, was awake and alert; they shared a brief, interrogative glance. Bzya placed his hands gently on the polished, worn wood of the support pole. No unusual vibration. He listened to the steady hum of the great Corestuff hoops which bound about the hull of the Bell; the sound was an even thrumming, telling him that the current from the City still flowed down the cables as steadily as ever, throwing a magnetic cloak around their frail ship. He looked through the nearest of the Bell's three small windows. The Air outside – if it could be graced with the name, this far down – was a murky yellow, but bright enough to tell him that they were somewhere near the top of the underMantle. He could even see the shadow of the Spine; they were still close to its lower tip, not much more than a metre below the City . . .

There. Another of the blinding blue flashes, just beyond the window. It was electron-gas blue and it seemed to surround the ship; shafts of blue light shone briefly through the small round windows into the cabin.

The Bell lurched.

Hosch wrapped his thin hands around the support pole. 'Why aren't we dead?'

It was a good question. Clouds of electron gas around a Bell usually meant current surges in the Corestuff hoops. Maybe the cable from the Harbour was fraying, or a hoop failing. But if that was so the Bell's field would fail almost immediately. The Bell should have imploded by now.

'The current supply is still steady,' Bzya said. 'Listen.'

They both held their breath, and looked into the Air; Hosch

adopted the empty-eyed expression of a man trying to concentrate on hearing.

Another flash. This time the Bell actually rocked in the soupy underMantle, and Bzya, clinging tightly to the pole, was swung around like a sack. He pulled himself closer to the pole and wrapped his legs around it.

The supervisor's breath stank of meat and old beercake. 'Okay,' he said. 'We know the Harbour supply is steady. What's causing the flashes?'

'There have to be current surges in the Corestuff hoops.'

'If the City supply is steady that's impossible.'

Bzya shook his head, thinking hard. 'No, not impossible; the surges are just caused by something else.'

Hosch's mouth pursed. '*Oh*. Changes in the Magfield. Right.'

The Bell wasn't malfunctioning; *the Magfield itself was betraying them*. The Magfield had become unstable, and it was inducing washes of charge flow in their protective hoops and dragging them away from their upward path to home.

'What's causing the Magfield to vary?' Bzya asked. 'Another Glitch?'

Hosch shrugged. 'Hardly matters, does it? We're not going to live to find out.'

There was an upward jolt, this time without the accompanying blue flash.

Bzya grasped the pole. 'Feel that? That was the Harbour. They're pulling us up. We're not dead yet. They're trying to . . .'

And then the blue light came again, and this time stayed bright. Bzya felt the writhing Magfield haul at his stomach and the fibres of his body, even as it tore at the Bell itself.

Electron gas sparked from his own fingertips in streamers. It was really quite beautiful, he thought absently.

The Bell was hurled sideways, away from the Spine. Bzya's hands were torn from the support pole. The Bell's curving wall came up, like a huge cupped palm, to meet him. His face rammed into a window, hard. His body bent backwards as it crammed itself into the tight inner curve of the wall. The structure of the Bell shuddered and groaned, and there was a distant, singing sound above him. That was the cables breaking, he thought through his pain. He felt oddly pleased at his own cleverness at such a deduction.

The walls wrenched, settled; the Bell rolled.

He fell into darkness.

Beyond the transparent walls, huge, ghostly buildings hovered over the humans.

The third chamber was immense, sufficient to enclose a million Parz Cities. The walls – made of the usual grey material, it seemed – were so far away as to be distant, geometric abstractions. Maybe this strange place was a series of nested tetrahedra, going on to infinity . . .

She Waved to Hork and reached out for him, blindly; still in the chair, he took her hands, and although his grip was strong she could feel the slick of fear on his palms. For a heartbeat she felt an echo of the passion they'd briefly found, in flight from terror during the journey.

The transparent structures hovered around them like congealed Air. They were translucent boxes hundreds of thousands of mansheights tall. And within some of the buildings more devices could be seen, embedded; the inner structures were ghosts within ghosts, grey on grey.

The tetrahedral box containing the 'Pig', the solid little chair, Hork and Dura themselves, were like specks of wood adrift in some mottled fluid. In fact, she realized, the whole of the tetrahedron they occupied was embedded *inside* one of the huge buildings; its grey lines sectioned off the space around them, and she looked out through its spectral flesh.

'Why do you suppose we can't see these things clearly? And I wonder what their purpose is. Do you think . . .'

Hork was peering up at the 'building' they were embedded in. He stared into its corners and at its misty protuberances, and then glanced down quickly at the chair he sat in.

'What's wrong?'

'The ghost-building we're inside. Look at it . . . It has the same shape as this chair.' The grey light of the translucent forms pooled in his eyecups. 'It's a hundred thousand times the size, and it's made of something as transparent as clearwood and thinner than Air . . . but nevertheless, it's an immense – spectral – *chair*.'

She lifted her head. Slowly she realized that Hork was right. This immense 'building' – at least a metre tall – had a seat, a back; and there, so far above her it was difficult to see, were two arms, each with its control lever.

Hork grinned, his face animated. 'And I think I know what it's all for. Watch this!'

He twisted his body. His chair swivelled in the Air.

She gasped, Waving away in alarm; but the chair came to rest, and no damage seemed to have been done. 'What are you doing?'

'Don't you understand yet? Look up!'

She tilted her head back.

The other 'chair' – the ghostly analogue – *had turned too*, swivelling to match Hork's lurch.

'See?' he crowed. 'The chair is keyed to mine, somehow; whatever I make mine do, the big one must follow.' Hork swung this way and that, laughing like a child with a toy. Dura watched the giant analogue dance clumsily, aping Hork's movements like some huge pet. Presumably, she thought, when the device swivelled, its substance must be moving around her – *through* her, in fact, like an unreasonable breeze. But she felt nothing – at least, no more than an inner chill which could as easily be caused by her awe and fear.

At last Hork tired of his games. 'I can make it do whatever I want.' He looked a little more thoughtful. 'And so if I pull these levers . . .'

'No. We need to work this out, Hork.' She looked up. 'This – ghost, this City-sized artifact – is a seat big enough for a giant . . .'

'That's obvious. But . . .'

'But,' she interrupted, 'a giant of a certain form . . . a human-shaped giant, metres tall.' She studied his face, waiting for him to reach the same conclusions.

'*Metres* . . . The Ur-humans.'

She nodded. 'Hork, I think the ghost-seat is an Ur-human device. I think we're in a little bubble of Air, floating inside an Ur-human room.'

She tilted her head back on her neck, feeling the flesh at the top of her spine bunch under her skull, and looked up into a ghost-room which abruptly made sense.

They were *inside* a huge Ur-human chair. But there were other chairs – four of them, she counted, receding into mistiness, like a row of cities. The chairs were placed before a long, flat surface, and she caught hints of a complex structure beneath and behind that surface. Perhaps that was some form of control panel. Looking further out, the tetrahedral structure surrounding all of this was a sketch drawn against fog.

Hork touched her arm. 'Look over there.' He pointed. On the side of the Ur-human room opposite the row of seats there was a bank of billowing gas – but that must be wrong, of course; she tried to forget her smallness, to see this through Ur-human eyes. It was a structure made up of something soft, pliable, piled up on a lower flat surface. It looked like a cocoon, laid flat.

Did the Ur-humans *sleep*?

Again Hork was pointing. 'On top of that surface before the chairs. See? Instruments, built for giant hands.'

Dura saw a cylinder longer than a Crust-tree trunk. Its end was sharp, protruding over the lip of the surface. Perhaps it was a stylus, as she'd seen Deni Maxx use in the Hospital. She tried to imagine the hand that could grasp a tree trunk and use it to write notes . . . Beside the 'stylus' there was another cylinder, but this was set upright. It seemed to be hollow – the cylinder was transparent to Dura's eyes, and she could make out a structure of thick walls surrounding an empty space – and there was no upper surface.

She frowned and pointed out the second cylinder to Hork. 'What do you think that is? It looks like a fortress. Perhaps the Ur-humans needed to shelter – perhaps they came under attack . . .'

He was laughing at her, not unkindly. 'No, Dura. You've lost the scale. Look at it again. It's maybe – what? – ten thousand mansheights tall?'

'Ten times as big as your glorious Parz City.'

'Maybe, but that's still only ten centimetres or so. Dura, the Ur-humans were *metres* tall. The *hand* of an Ur-human could have engulfed that cylinder.' He was watching her slyly. 'Do you see it yet? Dura, that's a food vessel. A cup.'

She stared. A cup, large enough to hold a dozen Parz Cities?

She tried to keep thinking. 'Well,' she said, 'then it's a damn odd cup. All the food would float out of the top. Wouldn't it?'

Hork nodded grudgingly. 'You'd think so.' He sighed. 'But then, there are many things about the Ur-humans we can't understand.'

She imagined this little box of Mantle-stuff from the outside. 'It's as if they created this inner chamber, around the wormhole Interface, as an ornament. A little section of the Star, so they could study Human Beings. We would look like toys to them,' she murmured. 'Less than toys; little animals, perhaps below the level of visibility.' She looked at her hand. 'They were a hundred thousand times taller than us; even the "Pig" would have been no more than a mote in the palm of an Ur-human child . . .' She shivered. 'Do you think any of them are still here?' She imagined a giant Ur-form floating in through some half-seen door, a face wider than a day's journey billowing down towards her . . .

'No,' Hork said briskly. 'No, I don't. They've gone.'

She frowned. 'How do you know?'

He grinned. 'For one thing, that's what your precious legends tell us. But the clincher is this seat.' He patted its arms. 'The Ur-humans set up this place so that *we* could work their machines. If I move the chair I can mimic anything an Ur-human could have done . . . Dura, they have made me as powerful as any of them. Do you see?' He probed at the unyielding surface of the chair. 'If we had the wit we could operate other devices.' He looked around the ghostly chamber greedily. 'There must be wonders here. Weapons we've never dreamed of.'

The Ur-humans had meant Star people to come here, to work the devices they left behind, maybe when the Glitches got too bad. Perhaps there was something they were meant to do now . . . But what?

'Your arrow device doesn't have an analogue, in the Ur-human chair,' she said slowly, pointing up. 'See? So the arrow-thing must be something meant for us alone. Maybe to help us see what's going on.' She frowned. 'It only turned one quarter. What if you turned it again?'

'Only one way to find out.'

He reached for the arrow.

At first he turned it back towards the darkest sector of the scale. Reassuringly the walls of smooth grey material congealed around them, shutting out the chamber of the Ur-humans. And when Hork twisted the arrow the other way the walls vanished, to reveal the vast devices.

'All right,' he said. 'Going from the black to the dark grey allows us to see a little more. A little further. And what if I turn it another quarter, to the light grey?'

Dura shrank back despite herself. 'Just turn it,' she said hoarsely.

Confidently he twisted the arrow to the third of the four quarters.

Light seemed to bleed out of the Air.

The devices of the Ur-humans, the walls of their ghostly chamber, became still more translucent. And there was darkness beyond those distant walls, darkness which settled on the two humans, huddled as they were within layers of immensity.

Points of light hung in that darkness.

Dura twisted in the Air, staring around. 'I don't understand. I can't see the walls of the next chamber. And what are those lights?'

'There are no more walls,' Hork said gently. 'Don't you see? No more chambers. *We're looking out into space*, Dura, at volumes even the Ur-humans couldn't enclose.'

She found her hand creeping into his. 'And those lights . . .'

'You know what they are, Dura. They're *stars*. Stars and planets.'

'Wake up, Bzya, you useless asshole.'

Hosch was slapping him. Bzya shook his head, blinking to clear his eye. He was surprised to be alive; the Bell should have imploded.

His bad eyecup blazed with pain. He raised a tentative fingertip to it to find the cup filled with sticky matter. His back ached, right at the base, where it had been bent backwards against the curve of the Bell.

'So we're not dead,' he said.

Hosch grinned, his thin face drawn tight with fear. 'We aren't that deep in the underMantle. We can't be, or the Bell

317

would have collapsed already.' He was kicking at the rim of the hatch frame, trying to splinter it with his heel.

Bzya flexed his hands and toes. He felt a vague disappointment. Fishing wasn't the safest of occupations; he'd always known it would finish him one day. But not today – not so close to home, and after such a futile, wasted dive. 'You'll make the hatch collapse in if you keep that up.'

'That's . . .' Kick. '. . . the idea.' Kick. Kick.

'And what then? Wave for it?'

'You've got it.' Kick, kick. 'We've lost the cable. We haven't any better options.' The frame was already starting to splinter. The hatch was a disc of wood, held in place by external pressure against the flanged frame. Once Hosch damaged enough of the flange, the hatch would fall in easily.

Bzya glanced out of the window. 'We're not deep enough to crush the Bell, but we're surely too deep for *us*. No one's ever come so deep unaided. We must still be ninety centimetres.'

'Then we'll become damn legends. Unless you've a better idea, you useless jetfart. Help me . . .'

But Bzya didn't need to.

With a thousand tiny explosions all around the frame the flange splintered. Bits of wood rattled across the cabin; they flew into Bzya's face and he batted at them dimly. Then the hatch fell forward, yielding in a moment. Bzya had an instant's impression of a mass of fluid – dense, amber and incompressible – crowding into the breached cabin.

The wood-lamps died, overwhelmed.

Then it was on him.

It washed over his limbs, forced its way into his mouth and throat and eyecups; it was a hard physical invasion, like fists pushing into him. He could not see, hear or taste anything. He panicked, and twisted his head back and forth, trying to spew the vile stuff out of his lungs. But he could not expel it, of course; he was embedded in this dense, unlivable material – in a layer of it ninety centimetres deep.

His lungs expanded, tearing at the material.

. . . And they found *Air*. Fragments, splinters of Air which stung as they forced their way out of his lungs and into his capillaries. His chest heaved, dragging at the fluid around him. There *was* Air here, but with just a trace of its normal fractional density.

Damn it, maybe I can make it out of this . . .

Then the burning started.

It was all over his body, like a thousand needles. And inside him too – *by the Wheel!* – scorching into his lungs and stomach; it flooded the capillaries that coursed through his body, turning the network of fine tubes that permeated him into a mass of pain, every threadlike capillary electric-alive with it.

Too dense. Too dense . . .

In these extremes of density and pressure the tin nuclei at the surfaces of his body were seeking a new stable configuration. The nuclei were breaking apart from each other and crumbling into their component nucleons, which were then swarming into the fire-Air in search of the single, huge nucleus which filled the heart of the Star . . . Bzya was dissolving.

He kicked at the fluid, driving his legs through it. He felt a dull impact as his head struck something. It must be the wall of the Bell. He felt vaguely surprised to find that there was anything left of the familiar, external universe, beyond this pain-realm of dissolution. But he'd managed to move himself. He'd *Waved*.

He dragged his hand through the fluid, made a sign of the Wheel against his chest. He couldn't see, but he could breathe, and he could Wave. He was going to get out of here.

He'd bumped his upper face. He must be facing the rear wall of the cabin, then; he must have been spun around by the incoming underMantle fluid. He turned round, spread his hands behind him across the wall. The pain eclipsed his touch, but he could feel the curve of the wall, the round profile of a window. He pictured the cabin, as it had been in that last instant before the hatch came in. Hosch had been somewhere to his right.

He pushed away from the wall and Waved that way, groping ahead of him.

His hands found something. Hosch, it had to be. He ran his hands over Hosch's chest and head; Hosch didn't respond. Hosch's skin crumbled under Bzya's touch – or maybe it was the flesh of Bzya's own fingers and palms.

He found Hosch's hand, wrapped it in his own.

Two strong kicks and he'd found the open hatchway. He was still blind, and his sense of touch was fading – perhaps, he thought with horror, it would never return; even if he survived perhaps he would have to live in this shell of pain, without light or sound . . . But he could feel the rim of the hatchway, the splinters left by Hosch's brave kicking.

He tried to fall forward, out of the Bell, but something was holding him back. Something hard, unyielding, which pressed into his chest and legs – the Corestuff hoops, wrapped around the Bell. He lifted his feet against the lower hoop, grabbed the upper with a numbing hand, and tried to straighten his body. His lower back, already injured, blazed with pain. He felt an abrupt shift as the hoops slid apart. He lifted his feet and let his body slide forward through the gap; he held his hands over his head and felt the limp form of Hosch rattle against the hoops, following him.

He tumbled out of the Bell, dragging the supervisor after him.

He had to find the Spine. He turned to his left and kicked out. He held Hosch's hand tight – at least he thought he did; only pain reached him now from his hands, feet and face. He felt a whispering drag pull at his own body . . . No, he thought, it was more than that; there were a thousand discrete tugs at his flesh, like hooks dragging into the skin. His flesh was *ablating*, he realized slowly, crumbling off him as he Waved.

He reached ahead with his free hand. His sight was gone, both eyecups useless now. This was the way back to the Spine, as best he remembered it from the moment the Bell had been torn away by the Magfield surges. Of course, since then he'd been unconscious. The Bell could even have turned upside down . . .

But he didn't have any better guesses. He thrashed at the scouring liquid, trying not to estimate how far he'd Waved from the Bell, how much further before he was *sure* he'd missed the Spine.

Mercifully the pain seemed to be lessening. The burning, the decomposition of his flesh, must be damaging the nerve endings themselves. Soon he genuinely would be isolated inside his body.

Well, I'll never Surf again. Or sculpt. Or, and now his inner smile faded, *or feel a woman's skin.*

There was a new stab of pain from his outstretched arm, his useless stub of hand. The arm buckled, forced back by something solid.

His body collided with a hard surface. He tried to feel with his chest, thighs and face.

The Spine. The blessed Spine.

He dragged his free arm across the surface until it snagged on something. There, he had it – a Bell cable. He made his hand into a hook and wrapped it around the cable. With Hosch still towed limply behind him, he flattened himself against the wooden surface of the Spine, and began to Wave once more, along the length of the Spine, using the Cable as a guide.

How ironic, he thought, if he were Waving the wrong way, down towards the Core.

By the time he was lifted out of the fluid, he was almost isolated from the world, inside a deadened body. He felt as aware, as alert as ever, but he could feel little. Even the pain had gone now. But he could feel his chest expand, dragging in the thinning, clearing Air, and he could feel the Magfield pull at his stomach, the centre of him.

He was still here, he thought. Just a little battered around the edges.

He thought he'd kept Waving until the end, and he thought he'd kept hold of Hosch. But it was hard to be sure.

And now he was being moved again, more delicately. He tried to smile. The Fishermen must have come down for him and Hosch, in a second Bell.

He was glad he couldn't see the looks on their faces, as they nursed him.

25

With a final heave from the team of volunteers, the patient
was loaded through the kicked-out Hospital wall and into the
car waiting in the Air beyond. Adda watched the car recede
cautiously from the Hospital, and then turn to join the streams
of refugees fleeing to the upflux.

Once the evacuation of the City had begun, this ward of the
Hospital of the Common Good, directly behind the Skin of
Parz, had rapidly been adapted to serve as a loading bay.
Now it was a three-dimensional swarm of Hospital staff,
volunteers, patients and those close to them. Patients
screamed or moaned, and staff called desperately to each
other for splints, bandages, drugs. And as fast as the patients
were shipped off in the cars outside, more – ever more – were
crowding in from the rest of the broken City. Adda felt overwhelmed, daunted, dismayed, exhausted. *Perhaps I've finally
seen too many changes. Too many disasters; too many shattered
bodies . . .*

He leaned out into the Air beyond the Skin. He opened his
mouth, trying to expel from his lungs the Hospital stink of
stale capillary-Air. But even outside the Skin the Air was
sour; he could smell nuclear-burning wood, Air-pig jetfarts,
the smell of human fear. It was as if the City, in its death
throes, was wrapped in an invisible cloud of sour-smelling
photons, like an immense dying creature leaking its last
capillary-Air.

The City, suffering hugely with groans of wood and the
shearing scream of failing Corestuff metal, shuddered around
him. The Hospital was lodged in the Downside belly of the
City, so that Adda was peering out of the Skin like an insect
gazing out of a wall. The anchor-bands were still functioning;
electron gas shone around them in response to the huge

currents surging through their superconducting interiors as the City fought to maintain its position.

The Skin was a blur of motion. All over the City the fragile hull had been kicked away. People clambered out of the City and into waiting cars; most of them dragged possessions after them through the ragged holes they'd made. Cars and free-Waving people diffused away from the City in a widening, blurring cloud. The Air was filled with the yells of people, the braying commands of Speakers.

Beyond the pathetic human river the Glitch-wracked vortex lines were mere sketches, scribbles of instability. The Magfield shuddered perceptibly as the massive upwellings from the Quantum Sea continued.

And in the far distance, the blue-violet fire of Xeelee ships raked through the Mantle. It was a sight he never thought he'd live to see.

'Adda!'

Reluctantly, he turned away from the open Air and concentrated on the ward once more.

The next patient to be evacuated, a woman, was screaming in pain. She was so swaddled in stained bandages that all that could be seen of her was a gaping mouth. Deni Maxx trailed after this grotesque package, stroking the woman's hair and murmuring futile words of comfort. Deni looked to Adda with a mute appeal. He tried to mask his reluctance to touch the injured woman. He moved closer to the woman and stared into her face, muttering gruff, calming words. It was like soothing a wounded Air-pig. But the woman's eyecups were black with bruising, and he doubted that she'd heard him.

They moved quickly to load the woman into a waiting Air-car. At last the car pulled away from the building, and the screams of the woman dwindled slowly.

Deni lingered by the improvised doorway and gulped in breaths of dank Polar Air. She looked into the mists of distance, at the violet limbs of the Xeelee starbreaker beams walking easily through the Star.

'Let's hope those damn things keep away from the City,' Adda said.

She brushed back a handful of filthy hair. 'And from your

323

people, wherever they are . . . Anyway, if the beams do hit us directly, it will be mischance. The purpose of the Xeelee is obviously to disrupt the Core; they wouldn't waste effort on a tiny, helpless construct like a City.'

'Yes. So much for Hork's expedition into the underMantle.'

'Perhaps. But, Adda, that brave and foolish expedition was the only hope any of us had. I have clung to it far beyond any rational point.' She smiled thinly. 'In fact I still cling to it. Why not? As long as it keeps me functioning.'

He surveyed the thin trails of Air-cars and people dispersing into the roiling Air. In the distance the larger cars showed up as silhouettes, fleeing insects against searing Xeelee light.

Deni rubbed her chin. 'You may not understand this, Adda, but most of the City's people have never strayed outside Parz before. To them, the City has always been the safest place in the world. Now that it's falling apart around them, they feel – betrayed. Like a child abandoned by its parents.' She hesitated. 'We're talking of hope. But in a way, for many the worst has already come to pass.'

'Do you think we're doing any good here?'

She looked strained. 'Well, we're shoving the patients out of this improvised port as fast as they are coming in – crushed in the Stadium, or burned and sliced open by that Corestuff berg incursion through the Midside . . . But whether they are any safer out there than in what's left of the City, I don't care to judge.' She smiled without humour. 'But at least it makes us feel better to help them. Don't you agree?'

Another patient was shouldered past them and out into a waiting car. Farr was in this latest work party, and as soon as the patient – an unconscious child – was delivered, Farr turned to make his way back into the chaos of the ward. Adda laid a hand on his shoulder, restraining him. There were deep bruises around the boy's eyes; his shoulders were hunched and his mouth was working as if he was mumbling to himself.

Adda shook him gently. 'Farr? Are you all right, lad?'

Farr focussed on the old man. 'I'm fine,' he said, his voice high and thin. 'I'm just a little tired, and . . .'

'Listen, you don't have to carry on with this.'

Farr looked offended. 'Adda, I'm not a kid.'

'I'm not suggesting you are, you damn . . .'

Deni moved smoothly between them, something of her old sheen of competence returning to her. 'Farr, you're doing a marvellous job . . . and I need you to keep on doing it. So I agree with Adda; I think you should take a short break – find something to eat, a place to rest.'

Farr looked ready to protest further, but Deni pushed him gently in the chest. 'Go on. That's an order.'

With a thin smile the boy complied.

Deni turned a quizzical face to Adda. 'I can tell you were never a parent.'

Adda growled wordlessly.

A new Air-car approached the rough lip of the opened-up wall; five nervous pigs jostled together, bumping against the Skin like inflated toys. The car's door opened and the driver leaned across. 'Adda,' Toba Mixxax said, his broad, weary face splitting into a grin. 'I'm glad to find you. Ito said you were trying to get here, with Farr.'

'Well, he's here. He's fine. He's working hard.' Adda had always found Toba's round, flat face rather bland and unexpressive; but now Adda could see real pain in the set of Toba's eyecups, the small lines at the corners of his mouth. 'Cris isn't here. I'm sorry.'

Toba's expression barely changed, but Adda could see a small light go out of him. 'No. I, ah – I didn't expect he would be.'

'No.'

The two men let their gazes slide away from each other, briefly embarrassed.

'How's Ito? Where is she?'

'At the ceiling-farm. What's left of it. She's found plenty to do. She's a craftswoman, Adda, and she's launched herself into repair work, with the coolies who've stayed.' He shook his head. 'Everything's smashed, though. You wouldn't believe it.' There was bitterness in Toba's voice. 'This latest Glitch has done for us, Adda.'

Toba's words made him think of what Deni had said – that the Xeelee were here to disrupt the Core, to devastate *the Star itself*. Adda wasn't very imaginative; he focussed on the here-and-now, on what was achievable. But, he suddenly wondered, what if Deni Maxx was right – that the Xeelee truly had come, this time, to finish the Star – to do for them all?

He glanced around the lurid sky. Inside himself, he'd been expecting this Glitch to come to an end, eventually – just like all the other Glitches in his long life, no matter how severe. But what if that wasn't true, this time? After all, the Xeelee were *manufacturing* this Glitch; his previous experience wasn't a reliable guide. What if the Xeelee kept on, persisted until the Core itself welled out from rents in the Quantum Sea . . .

Up to now Adda had been anticipating only his own death, and the death of many others – even of those close to him. But perhaps this new catastrophe was destined to go much further – to encompass the destruction of the race itself. He was overwhelmed suddenly by a vision of the Star scoured clean of Human Beings, of all future generations – everything Adda had worked for – snuffed out, rendered meaningless.

Toba was still talking. Adda hadn't heard a word he'd said for a long time.

Adda pulled himself away and took a deep breath. If the world was to finish today – well, there was little Adda could do about it. In the meantime he had work to do.

Deni Maxx joined Adda in the improvised doorway. 'Thanks for coming to help us, citizen.'

Toba shrugged. 'I needed something to keep me busy.' Another patient was being brought through the ward now; Toba Mixxax stared past Adda at the broken body, and his round face set into a mask of grimness.

'Well, you found it,' Adda said darkly.

Deni Maxx touched his arm. 'Come on, upfluxer. Let's get back to work.'

In the distance the starbreakers, like immense daggers, continued to pierce the Mantle. Adda stared out for one moment longer; then, with a final nod to Toba, he turned away.

Once the Star had seemed huge to her. Now here she was stranded in the immensity of this Ur-sky, of stars and planets, and she thought back almost nostalgically to the cosy world of the Mantle – with the smooth purple floor of the Quantum Sea below her, the Crust a blanket above her, the Mantle itself like an immense womb succouring her. All of that had been stripped away by this astonishing journey, and by the seeing-gadgets of the Ur-humans.

She tilted back her head and opened her eyes as wide as she could, trying to take it all in, to bury her awe and build a model of this new universe in her head.

The sky around them – the space between the stars – wasn't utterly black. She made out hints of structure: clouds, whorls, shadings of grey. There must be some kind of air out there, beyond the transparent walls – air but not Air: thin, translucent, patchy, but sufficient to give the sky an elusive shape. It was a little like the fugitive ghost-patterns she could see in the darkness of her own eyecups if she jammed her eyes tight shut.

And beyond the thin shroud of gas lay the stars, suspended all around the sky. They were lanterns, clear and without flicker; they were of all colours and all levels of brightness, from the faintest spark to intense, noble flames. And perhaps, she thought with an almost religious awe, those lights in the sky were worlds in themselves. Maybe there were other forms of humans on those distant lights, placed there by the Ur-humans for their own inscrutable purposes. Would it ever be possible to know? – to speak to those humans, to travel there across such immensities?

She tried to make out patterns in the distribution of the stars. Perhaps there was a hint of a ring structure over there – and a dozen stars trailed in a line across that corner of the sky . . .

But as fast as she found such bits of orderliness in the unmanageable sky, she lost them again. Slowly she came to accept the truth – that *there was no order*, that the stars were scattered over the sky at random.

For the first time since leaving the 'Flying Pig', panic spurted in her. Her breath scraped through her throat and she felt her capillaries expand throughout her flesh, admitting more strength-bearing Air.

Why should randomness upset her so? Because, she realized slowly, there were no vortex lines here, no neat Crust ceiling or Sea floor. All her life had been spent in a ruled-off sky – a sky where any hint of irregularity was so unusual as to be a sign of deadly danger.

But there were no lines here, no reassuring anchor-points for her mind.

'Are you all right?' Hork sounded calmer than she was, but his eyecups were wide and his nostrils flared, glowing like nuclear-burning wood above his bush of beard.

'No. Not really. I'm not sure I can accept all this.'

'I know. I know.' Hork lifted up his face. In the starlight the intrinsic coarseness of his features seemed to melt away, leaving a calm, almost elegiac expression. He waved a hand across the sky. 'Look at the stars. Look how their brightness varies . . . But what if that variation is an illusion? Have you thought about that? What if all the stars are about as bright as each other?'

Her mind – as usual – plodded slowly behind his flight of logic. If the stars were all the same intrinsic brightness, then some of them would have to be further away. Much further away.

She sighed. No, damn it. She *hadn't* thought of that.

Somehow she'd been picturing the starry Ur-universe as a shell around her – like the Crust, though much further away. But it wasn't like that; she was surrounded by an unbounded sky throughout which the stars – themselves worlds – were scattered like spin-spider eggs.

The universe ballooned around her, reducing her to a meaningless mote, a spark of awareness. It was oppressive, beyond her imagination; she cried out, covering her face in her hands.

Hork sounded uncomfortable. 'Take it easy.'

Irritation burrowed through her awe. 'Oh, sure. And you're quite calm, I suppose. Sorry to embarrass you . . .'

'Give me a break.'

She turned away from him, striving for calm. 'I wish I knew what *is* an appropriate response to all this – to be here in this ancient place, to be seeing through the eyes of the Ur-humans . . .'

'Well, not quite,' Hork said gently. 'Remember there are still walls around us, which must somehow be helping us to see. The Ur-humans didn't see things the same way we do. Ask Mur o about it when we get back . . . We "see" by sound waves which are transmitted through the Air.' He waved a hand. 'But beyond this little bubble, there isn't any Air. The

Ur-humans didn't live in Air, in fact. And they "saw" by focussing beams of photons, which . . .'

She wrinkled her nose. 'They could *smell* the stars?'

'Of course not,' he snapped. 'In Air, photons can travel only slowly, diffusing. So we use them to smell. And we "hear" temperature fluctuations.

'In empty space, it's different. Phonons can't travel at all – so we would be blind. But photons travel immensely fast. So the Ur-humans could have "seen" photons . . . Anyway, that's Muub's theory.'

'Then how did they hear? Or smell, or taste?'

He growled impatiently. 'How the hell should I know? Anyway, I think this third chamber is designed to let us see the universe the way the Ur-humans did.' He rubbed his chin thoughtfully. 'And there's still a setting left on the arrow-console, the fourth one . . . we haven't finished with our ways of seeing yet.'

She'd forgotten about that last setting. Some core of her, buried deep inside, quailed a little further.

Turning in the Air she looked around, still searching for patterns. The sky wasn't uniformly dark, she realized; the elusive gas faded up from grey to a deep, crimson glow on the far side of the room. 'Come on. I think there's something beyond the wormhole chamber . . .'

Still holding hands, they Waved past the control chair and around the darkened tetrahedron which contained the wormhole portal and the 'Pig'. Through the open door, Dura glimpsed their craft; its roughly hewn wooden walls, its bands of Corestuff, the slowly leaking stink of Air-pig farts, all seemed unbearably primitive in this chamber of Ur-human miracles.

The sky-glow intensified as they neared its source. At last the glow drowned out the stars. Dura felt herself pull back, shying away from new revelations. But Hork enclosed her fingers in a tight, smothering grip and coaxed her forward. 'Come on,' he said grimly. 'Don't fold on me now.' At the centre of the glowing sky was a single star: tiny, fierce and yellow-red, brighter than any other in the sky. But this star wasn't isolated in space. A ring of some glowing gas circled the star, and – still more astonishing – an immense globe of light hung close to the fierce little star. The globe was like a star itself, but attenuated, bloated, its outer layers so diffuse as almost to merge with the all-pervading gas cloud. Tendrils of grey light snaked from the globe-star and reached far into the ring of gas.

It was like a huge sculpture of gas and light, Dura thought. She was stunned by the spectacle, and yet charmed by its proportion, scale, depths of shading and colour.

She was seeing the gas ring around the star from edge-on . . . in fact, she realized slowly, the Ur-human construct around her was actually *inside* the body of the ring. And she could see beyond the central star to the far side of the gas ring; distance reduced the ring's far limb to a line of light on which the little star was threaded, like a pendant.

She could see turbulence in the ring, huge cells big enough to swallow a thousand of the Ur-human colonies. The cells erupted and merged, changing as she watched despite their unthinkable scale. And there seemed to be movement around the star, a handful of sparks dipping into its carcass . . .

'Then it's true,' Hork breathed.

'What?'

'That we're not in the Star any more. That we've been transported, through the wormhole, to a planet outside it.' Ring-light bathed his face, casting complex highlights from his beard. 'Don't you see? That's our star – *the Star* – and, just like the map said, we're on a planet circling the Star. But the map didn't show the ring.' He turned to her, excitement in his eyes. It was the excitement of understanding, she realized, of piecing together a puzzle. 'So now we know how our Star's system is put together.' He mimed with his hands. 'Here's the Star, at the centre of it all. The gas ring encircles it, like this. The planet must drift within the ring. And hanging above it all we have the globe-thing, glowing dully and leaking gas.'

Dura stared at their Star. It was small and mean, she thought, disappointing compared to the glorious lanterns which glittered in other parts of the sky. And yet it was *home*; she felt a strange dislocation, a pang of sadness, of loss. 'Our world is so limited,' she said slowly. 'How could we ever have known that beyond the Crust was so much wonder, immensity, beauty . . .'

'You know, I think that big sphere of gas has a glow of its own. It isn't just reflecting the Starlight, I mean.'

The globe was like an immense pendant on the ring, utterly dwarfing the Star itself. Hork seemed to be right; the intensity of its grey-yellow glow increased towards its rough centre. And it wasn't actually a sphere, she realized slowly; perhaps it had once been, but now it was drawn out into a teardrop shape, with a thin tip attached to the ring by an umbilical of glowing gas. The outer layers of the globe were misty, turbulent; Dura could see through them to the darkness of space.

'It's like a star itself. But . . .'

'But it doesn't look right.' Dura searched for the right word. 'It seems – *unhealthy*.'

'Yes.' He pointed. 'It looks as if stuff is being drawn out of the big star and put into the ring.' He glanced speculatively at Dura. 'Perhaps, somehow, the Star is drawing flesh from the big star to create the ring. Perhaps the planet we're on is constructed of ring-stuff.'

She shuddered. 'You make the Star sound like a living thing. Like an eye-leech.'

'A star-leech. Well, perhaps that's as good an explanation as we'll ever get . . .' He grinned at her, his face spectral in the ring's glow. 'Come on. I want to try the arrow's last setting.'

'Oh, Hork . . . Do you have *any* capacity for awe?'

'No.' His grin broadened through his beard. 'I think it's a survival characteristic. Mental toughness, I call it.' He led her back around the inner portal-chamber and eyed her roguishly. 'So we've seen the stars. Big deal. What's left?'

'Twist the arrow and find out.'

He did so.

The universe – of stars and starlight – imploded.

Dura screamed.

26

The stars – all except *the* Star – had disappeared, dragging all the light from the sky. The Star, with its ring and its huge, bleeding companion, hung in an emptied sky . . .

No, she realized, that wasn't quite true. There was a bow around the sky – a multicoloured ribbon, thin and perfect, which hooped around the Ur-humans' habitat – and, she saw, passed *behind the Star itself.*

It was a ribbon which encircled the universe, and it contained all the starlight.

Hork loomed before her, the starbow adding highlights to the grey illumination of his face. 'Well?' he demanded irritably. 'What now?'

She rubbed her forehead. 'Each setting of that device has shown us more of our surroundings – more of the universe. It's as if successive layers, veils, have been removed from our eyes.'

'Right.' He lifted his eyes to the starbow. 'So this must be the truth? The last setting, which strips away all the veils?' He shook his head. 'But what does it mean?'

'The sky we saw before – of stars, scattered around the sky – was strange to us . . . even awesome. But it looked *natural*. The stars were just like our Star, only much further away.'

'Yes. Whereas this seems distorted. And how come we can still see our Star? Why isn't its light smeared out into this absurd hoop, too?'

Smeared starlight . . . Yes. I like that. Good; that's very perceptive . . .

Dura whirled in the Air, trying to suppress a scream. The voice, dry and soft, emanating from the emptiness of the huge room behind her had been utterly terrifying.

'Karen Macrae,' Hork said, his voice thick with hostility.

A sketch of shoulders and head wrought in pale, coloured cubes of light hung in the Air a mansheight from them. The definition was poorer than within the underMantle – the colours washed out, the jostling light-cubes bigger. Karen Macrae opened her eyes, and again Dura was repulsed by the fleshy balls nestling within the cups.

Hork had been right; somehow Karen Macrae had ridden with them in the lump of Corestuff attached to the side of the 'Pig', all the way from the depths of the Star to this remote, austere place.

The starlight is smeared; yes. And it's crucial that you understand why it's smeared, what's happening to you. The walls of this place aren't windows; they have processing capacity – they're virtually semi-sentient, actually – capable of deconvolving the Doppler distortions of . . .

Hork growled and Waved forward. 'Talk straight, damn you.'

The blurred head rotated slowly. *Doppler distortion. Blue shift. You – we – are travelling enormously quickly through space. Almost as fast as light itself. Do you see? And so . . .*

'And so we outrun starlight,' Hork said. '. . . I think I understand. But why is it we still see the Star itself, and its system of ring and giant companion?'

The Colonist seemed to be retreating into her own half-formed head; the fleshy things in her eyecups slid around like independent animals.

Dura struggled to answer Hork. 'Because the Star is travelling with us. And that's why we can still see its light.' She looked at him doubtfully. 'Does that make sense?'

Hork growled. 'This Colonist and her riddle-talk . . . All right. Let's assume you're right. After all, we haven't any better explanation. Let's assume we, and the Star, are travelling through space as fast as light. *Why?* Where are we coming from? And where are we going?'

There was no answer from Karen Macrae. Light-cubes crawled over her face like leeches.

Hork and Dura stared at each other, as if seeking the answers in each other's exasperated faces.

They looked around once more, trying to make sense of the distorted sky. Dura felt small, fragile, helpless in this ensemble of hurtling worlds. There was a symmetry to the smeared light around them, and after some argument they decided that their departure point and destination must lie at the poles of an imaginary globe around them, the globe whose equator was marked by the starbow.

Hork reached for the arrow device. 'All right. Then let's see if we can see what lies there . . .' He set the pointer at its penultimate setting.

The stars fled from the crumbling starbow and back to their scattered homes around the sky.

Hork Waved towards one of the imagined poles, peering through the blocky Ur-human cloud devices and into space. To Dura, who remained close to Karen Macrae, he looked like a toy, a speck swimming against the Ur-humans' vague immensities.

'Nothing here,' he called at last, sounding disappointed. 'Just an anonymous patch of stars.'

'Then it must be at the other end of the chamber. The other pole. Come on.'

She waited for him to return. Then, hand in hand, they Waved in the Star's direction of flight.

. . . And there *was* something at the pole of the sky: something set against the backdrop of stars, something huge – if diminished by distance – and precisely defined.

Karen Macrae was saying something. The rustling words sighed across the huge silences of the chamber.

Dura and Hork hurried back and pressed their faces close to the Colonist's cloudy lips. 'What is it?' Dura demanded, almost despairing. 'Won't you try again? What are you saying to us?'

. . . *The Ring. Can you see it? I've so little processing power here . . . hard to . . . the Ring . . .*

Dura turned away and looked at the artifact; and a fear borne of childhood tales, of old, distorted legends, welled up in her.

The car sailed away.

Adda hung on to the ward's improvised doorframe and sucked Air into his lungs. He glanced around the sky. The panorama, now sombre and deep yellow, grew less and less like the secure, orderly Mantlescape he'd grown old with: the vortex lines were discontinuous shreds of spin loops struggling to reform, and the starbreaker beams continued to cut down through the Air and into the Core, unnaturally vertical.

Tired as he was, something probed at the edge of his awareness. It seemed *darker* than before. Why should that be? He pushed himself out of the ward and Waved a few weary mansheights into the sky. Behind him, the Skin was a limitless wooden wall which cut away half of the sky. It was bounded about by the huge anchor-bands and punctuated by a hundred crude gashes; a slowing trickle of cars and people still dribbled from the opened-up walls and diffused into the wastes of the Air. The Skin was dark, intimidating . . .

Too dark. That was it.

Adda Waved a little further and twisted his head around, surveying the Corestuff anchor-bands. The huge hoops were like a grey cage over the City's wooden face – but they were dull, lifeless, where a little earlier they had crackled with blue electron gas.

The glow of the gas had gone.

So the dynamos, the huge, wood-burning lungs of the City, had failed at last. Perhaps they had been abandoned by their attendants; or maybe some essential part of the City's infrastructure had failed under the strain of holding the City against the fluctuating Magfield.

It scarcely mattered.

There was a sharp explosion. A hail of splinters fanned out from the base of the City, at the junction of the Spine and the main inhabited section. The splinters sailed away through the showers of sewage material still falling from the base of Parz.

There might be no more than heartbeats left.

Adda Waved strongly back to the improvised Hospital port and dived into the melee of swaddled patients, harassed staff and volunteers. He found Farr helping Deni Maxx to fix a patient's bandages. He grabbed Farr's and Deni's arms roughly; he hauled them away from the unconscious patient and towards the exit.

'We've got to get out of here.'

Deni stared at him, the deep yellow Air-light scouring shadow-lines in her face. 'What is it? I don't understand.'

'The anchor-bands have lost power,' Adda hissed. 'They can't sustain the City, here above the Pole. The City's going to drift – come under intense stress . . . We have to get away from here. The City will never withstand it . . .'

Farr glanced back to the patients and helpers. 'But we're not finished.'

'Farr,' Adda said with all the persuasiveness he could muster, '*it's over*. You've done a marvellous job, but there's nothing more you can do. Once the effects of the band failure hit we won't be able to complete the evacuation anyway.'

Deni Maxx stared into his face, her mouth tight. 'I'm not leaving.'

Adda felt his scarred old heart break once more.

'But you'll die,' he said, hearing a plea in his voice. 'These wretched people can never survive anyway. There's no point . . .'

She pulled her arm from his grasp. She looked back into the ward, as if all this had been a mere distraction from her work.

When he placed his hand on the crude doorframe he felt a deep, shuddering vibration, coming from the very bones of the City, and shivers of turbulence crept across the bare skin of his arms and neck.

Maybe it was already too late. He pulled himself through the improvised doorway and into the open Air.

He looked back into the ward. Deni Maxx was making her way back into the chaos of patients and helpers, her face set. Already she'd dismissed his warning. Forgotten it, probably. But Farr still lingered close to the doorway; he looked back into the ward, apparently torn.

Well, Deni was lost; but not Farr. Not yet.

Adda grabbed Farr by the hair and, with all his remaining strength, hauled the boy backwards out of the Hospital and hurled him into the Air. Farr came to rest in the empty Air, struggling; he looked like some stranded insect, dwarfed by the immense, wounded face of the City. He glared at Adda. 'You had no right to do that.'

'I know. I *know*. You'll just have to hate me, Farr. Now Wave, damn you; Wave as hard as you've ever Waved in your life!'

There was a glow from the North, a deep, ominous red glow from all around the sky. It was a light Adda had never seen before. It soaked the Mantle in a darkness in which the starbreakers of the Xeelee glowed like opened-up logs.

Another shout of tearing wood and failing Corestuff was wrenched from the guts of the City. The Skin *rippled;* waves perhaps a micron high spread over its surface, and the wood broke open in tiny explosions.

Adda dropped his head and kicked at the seething Air, Waving away from Parz as hard as he could.

The Ring was reduced by distance to a sparkling jewel, lovely and fragile.

'I believed most of it,' Dura said slowly, 'most of the stories my father told me . . . But I don't think I ever quite believed in the Ring itself.'

Bolder's Ring, the greatest engineering construct in the universe. So massive – rotating so rapidly – that it had ripped a hole in space itself.

'The Ring is a doorway in the universe, a way for the Xeelee to escape their unknown foe,' she told Hork.

His fists clenched; dwarfed by the huge sky around him, his belligerence looked absurd. 'I know your legends. But what foe?' He crowded close to Karen Macrae and drove his fist into the cloud of jostling cubes which comprised her face. His hand passed through, apparently unaffected. 'What foe, damn you?'

Slowly Karen Macrae began to talk, the globes in her eyecups glinting. She spoke hesitantly, in fragments.

The Star was spawned in a *galaxy,* a disc of a hundred billion stars. It was actually ancient, the cooling remnant of an immense explosion which had driven away much of a massive star's bulk and devastated the grey companion which still accompanied it. As time wore on the Star had drawn material from the companion, knitted gas into planets.

Then the Ur-humans came.

They downloaded the Colonists – images of themselves – into the Core; and the Colonists built the first Star-humans.

For five centuries the Colonists and the Star-humans

worked together. Huge engines – *discontinuity drives*, Karen called them – were built at the North Pole of the Star. Teams of Star-humans wielded mighty devices under the instruction of the Colonists.

Hork's eyes narrowed. 'Ah,' he breathed. 'So they *do* need us, these Colonists. We are the hands, the strong arms which built the world . . .'

The discontinuity drive engines hurled the Star from its birthplace. It soared out of its galaxy and sailed free across space.

The Ring was close to the Star's native galaxy – so close that light would take no more than ten thousand years to cross the void to the Ring, Karen Macrae said; so close that the immense mass of the Ring was already distorting the galaxy's structure, pulling it apart. The Star – with its companion, its planets and gas ring, and its precious freight of life – fell across space towards the Ring, glowing in the darkness like a wood-burning torch.

A century passed inside the Star. Thousands of years fluttered by in the universe outside the Crust. (Dura could make nothing of this.)

The Ring neared.

The Colonists grew afraid. The Star-humans grew afraid.

'Why?' Dura demanded. 'Why should they fear the Ring? What will happen when we reach it?'

The Colonists retreated into the Core. They had constructed a wonderful virtual world for themselves in there – unreal Earths . . . And they believed they would be safe there, that they could ride out any disaster which might befall the Star.

The Star-humans were left bereft in the Mantle like abandoned children. They had their wormholes and other gadgets, but without the guidance of the parent-Colonists the devices were like so many gaudy toys.

Resentment grew, displacing fear. The Star-humans determined that they would follow the Colonists into their Core haven if they could – or if not, they would make the complacent Colonists as fearful as themselves.

Wormhole Interfaces were ripped from their anchor-sites in the Mantle and hurled downwards into the Core. Armies, grim-faced, lanced through the wormholes in improvised ships. The technologies which had once built the discontinuity drives were pirated to craft immense weapons.

'The Core Wars,' Hork said slowly. 'Then they really happened.'

Hork's anger was intense; it was as if, Dura thought, the huge injustice of abandonment had occurred only yesterday, not generations before.

The Colonists, insubstantial Core-ghosts as they were, had nevertheless retained immense material power. The War was brief.

Power failed; weapons exploded, or dissolved, killing their operators. The Interfaces were dragged into the Core, or fell into uselessness, their linking wormhole tunnels collapsed. Once the Mantle had sustained a single community of Star-humans, united by the wormhole network. In a few heartbeats that Star-wide culture collapsed.

Humans, naked, defenceless, fell into the Air.

A huge silence fell over the Star.

With the War ended, the Colonists retreated into the Core and prepared for eternal life.

Hork pounded his fist into his palm. 'The bastards. The cowardly bastards. They abandoned us, to generations of suffering. Illness, disease, Glitches. But we showed them. We built Parz City, didn't we? We survived. And now, five centuries after dumping us, they need us again . . .'

Dura couldn't drag her eyes away from the Ring. Lights flickered over the huge construct, dancing silently. 'What's happening to the Ring? I don't understand.'

Hork snorted. 'Isn't it obvious? The Ring is under attack. It's a war, Dura; someone is attacking the Xeelee.'

He pointed at the incongruously delicate patterns of light. 'And it would be too much of a coincidence for us to arrive here, aboard this Star, just as the first battle is being waged. Dura, this war – the assaults on the Ring – must have been enduring for a long time.' He rubbed his chin. 'Generations, perhaps; centuries of war . . .'

She felt a pulse pound in her throat. 'Humans? Are they Ur-human ships?' She stared at the tableau, willing herself to see more clearly, seeking the huge ships of those spectral giants.

The battle unfolded, slowly, even as she watched. Some of the sparkling ships disappeared, evidently destroyed by Xeelee defenders. Others plummeted through the Ring, she saw; and if the old stories were correct those ships were now lost in different universes. She wondered if the crews of those ships would survive . . . and if they did, what strange tales they would have to tell.

'Oh, yes,' Hork said grimly. 'Yes, the assailants are humans. Ur-humans, anyway.'

'How can you be so sure?'

'Because the Star is *heading straight for the Ring*. Don't you see it yet, Dura? The Star has been aimed at the Ring. We're going to collide with it . . .'

Dura stared at the remote, twinkling battlefire. Was Hork right? 'I don't know how big the Ring is. Perhaps it's bigger than the Star; perhaps it will survive. But surely the Star is going to be devastated.'

Hork raised his fists to his chest. 'No wonder the Xeelee have been attacking the Star; they're trying to destroy it before it gets to the Ring. Dura, the Star has been launched on this trajectory, straight at the Xeelee artifact, as a *missile*.' His tone had become hushed, almost reverent. Dura looked at him curiously; his eyes were locked on the images of distant battle, evidently fascinated.

She wondered if he were still quite sane. The thought disturbed her.

So that is why we are here, she thought. *That's the purpose of the whole project. The Colonists, the manufacture of Star-humans . . . That is the meaning, the purpose of my race. My life.*

We are expendable weapons' manufacturers, serving a huge war beyond our comprehension.

And when the Star destroyed itself against the Ring – or was destroyed first, by the Xeelee starbreakers – then they would all die with it, their purpose fulfilled.

No.

The word was like a shout in the turmoil of her mind. She had to *do* something.

Without allowing herself to think about the consequences, she Waved briskly across the chamber towards the floating control seat.

'What are you doing? Dura, there's nothing we can do here. We're in the grip of immense forces; forces we barely understand. And . . .'

She took her place in the seat. Around her the ghostly Ur-human seat swivelled, trembling in response to her touch. She grasped the twin handles fixed to the seat's arms.

A globe swelled into existence in the Air, fat and sullen red; a neat grid covered its surface, laid out like the anchor-bands around Parz City.

Dura, startled by this sudden apparition, lost her nerve; she screamed.

Hork laughed at her. His voice, thin and shrill, betrayed his own tension. 'Damn it, Dura, you've just witnessed a battle, immense beyond our capacity to comprehend. You've learned that our world is doomed. And yet you're scared by a simple conjuring trick like this!'

'But what is it?'

The globe was about a mansheight across; it hovered just in front of the seat. 'Isn't it obvious?' Hork snapped. 'Take your hands off the levers.' She did so; the globe persisted for a few seconds, then deflated gracelessly, finally disappearing. 'It's an aid,' Hork said briskly. 'Like . . .' He gestured vaguely. 'Like a window in an Air-car. An aid to a pilot.'

She tried to focus on this new puzzle. She glanced across the chamber and out at the Star, that scowling yellow-red speck at the centre of its immense setting of gas and light. 'But that globe looked like the Star itself.'

Hork laughed, the shrill edge still present in his voice; his eyecups were wide with excitement. 'Of course it did! Don't you see? Dura, one is meant to *pilot the Star* with these wonderful levers . . .'

'But that's absurd,' she protested. 'How can a Star – a whole world – be driven, directed like one of your Air-cars?'

'But, my dear, someone has *already done so*. The Star has been launched at the Ring, with deliberate intent. That we have found a device to do this is hardly a surprise. And this is a map-Star, to help you pilot a world . . .'

She grasped the handles again and the globe sprang into existence, wide, delicate and ominous. She gathered her scattered courage. 'Hork, we can't let our world be destroyed.'

He moved closer to her. His eyecups were wide and empty, his breathing shallow. He seemed huge. His hands were held away from his body. She closed her fingers tighter around the chair handles, watching, half-expecting him to lunge at her.

'Dura, get out of the chair. For a thousand years our Star has crossed space. We have a duty to fulfil, a destiny.'

She shook her head. 'You've lost yourself in this, Hork. In the glamour of it all . . . It's not our battle.'

He frowned at her, his bearded face a ferocious mask. 'If it wasn't for the battle we wouldn't even exist. Generations of humans have lived, died and suffered for this moment. This is the purpose of our race, its apotheosis! I see this now . . . How can a person like you take the fate of a world in your hands?'

'But I can't – *accept* – this. I've got to try something. We must try to save ourselves.'

Doubt – a kind of longing – spread across Hork's broad face. 'Then consider this. Suppose we're right. Suppose our world really is a missile aimed at the Xeelee. Then – if it really is possible to aim the Star with this device – *why is the device here?*'

She was frightened of him – not just physically, but of this new, unexpected side of his character, this self-immolating fanaticism.

'Think,' he demanded. 'If you were the designer, the Ur-human who planned this fantastic mission, what would you intend the occupant of that seat to do, now, at the climax of the project?'

She hesitated, thinking. 'It's meant to be used to refine the trajectory. To direct the Star even more precisely at its goal.'

He threw his arms wide. 'Exactly. Perhaps there are devices lying dormant here, messages instructing us – or whoever was planned to be here – how to do just that. And *what if we don't, Dura?* What if we don't complete our mission? Perhaps the Ur-humans themselves will intervene, to punish our arrogance.'

Her palms were slick with sweat; his words were like the

articulation of the conflict inside her. Who was she to decide the fate of a world, of generations?

She thought back over her life, the extraordinary, unfolding sequence of events that had led her to this point. Once, not a very large fraction of her life ago, she had been adrift in the Mantle, at the mercy of the smallest stray Glitch along with the rest of the Human Beings. Stage by stage, as events had taken her so far from her home, her understanding of the Mantle, the Star, and the role of mankind had opened out, like the layers of perception opened up gradually by the seeing-walls of this Ur-human construct.

And now she was here, with more power over events than any human since the days of the Core Wars. She was dizzy, vertiginous, a feeling she remembered from her first trips to the fringes of the Crust-forest, as a little girl with her father.

Her awareness seemed to implode. She became aware of her body – of the wide, dilated pores over her skin, the tension in her muscles, the knife still tucked into the frayed rope tight around her waist. She looked into Hork's wide, staring eyes. She saw recklessness there, exhilaration, intoxication, the fringes of insanity. Hork, overwhelmed by the journey, the realm of Ur-humans, Colonists and stars, had forgotten who he was. She hadn't. *She knew who she was*: Dura, Human Being, daughter of Logue – no more, and no less. And she was no more, no less qualified to speak for the peoples of the Star, at this moment, than anyone else. And that was why it was she who would have to act, now.

Her uncertainty congealed into determination. 'Hork, I don't care about the goals of these damn monster-men from the past. All I care about are my people – Farr, my family, the rest of the Human Beings. I won't sacrifice them for some ancient conflict; not while I have some hope of changing things.'

The wide, distorted mouth of Karen Macrae was opening again; as she spoke, Dura saw, distracted by the detail, that Karen's lips were not quite synchronized with her rustling words.

Time is long, inside our virtual world. But still, it is coming to an end. The Glitches have damaged us. Some have already lost coherence.

343

Stop the flight. We discover we do not want to die.

Dura closed her eyes and shuddered. The Colonists could no longer act. And so they had brought Star-humans – they had brought *her* – to this place, to save their world.

When she looked at Hork he was grinning, throwing his head back like some animal. 'Very well, upfluxer. It seems I am outvoted, and not for the first time – although it doesn't usually stop me. We are humans too, whatever our origins, and we must act, rather than die meekly as pawns in somebody else's war!' He shouted, 'Do it!'

She cried out; she felt remote, numb. She hauled on the levers as hard as she could.

Crimson fire erupted from the base of the map-Star.

27

Blue Xeelee light illuminated the Air. Fragments of shattered vortex lines hailed around Adda. He Waved furiously, squirming in the Air to avoid the deadly sleet, disregarding the pain in his back and legs. But even Waving wasn't reliable; the strength and direction of the Magfield was changing almost whimsically, and he had to be constantly aware of its newest orientation, of which way his Waving would take him among the lethal vortex fragments.

He came to a clearer patch of Air. He twisted, his hips and lower back protesting, and Waved to a halt. He looked back towards the City, now about a thousand mansheights away. The great wooden carcass was tilting noticeably, leaning across a Magfield which no longer cradled it. Its Skin was still a hive of activity, of kicked-out panels and scrambled evacuations; Adda was reminded of corruption, of swarms of insects picking over a dying face.

There was no sign of Farr.

Adda looked back to the upper Downside, to the location of the Hospital. He could see motion inside that widened gash in the Skin, but he couldn't make out Farr himself. *Damn, damn* . . . He shouldn't have let go of the boy; he should have dragged him physically away from the City, from the damn Hospital, until either his strength ran out or the City fell apart anyway.

I'm an old man, damn it. He'd had enough; he'd seen enough. Now all he wanted was rest.

Well, it looked as if he still had work to do. Shaking his head, he dipped his body in the Air and Waved back towards the groaning City.

In the Hospital of the Common Good, patients continued to be brought to the exit. Another dull explosion sounded somewhere in the guts of the City, but – to Adda's disbelief – the labouring volunteers scarcely looked up. He wanted to scream at them, to slap faces, to force these brave, foolish people to accept the reality of what was happening around them.

There were no cars returning to the port now. But nevertheless a volunteer hauled a helpless bundle – age and sex unidentifiable – to the breached Skin. The volunteer climbed out after the patient, gripped the bandaging with both hands, and, Waving backwards, began to drag the patient away from the collapsing City. The volunteer was a young man, nude, his skin painted with elaborate, curling designs. This was evidently one of the aerobats who should have been taking part in the great Games spectacle today; instead here he was, his body-paint smeared and stained with pus, dragging a half-dead patient out from a dying City. Adda stared at the boy's face, trying to make out how the aerobat must feel at this implosion of his life, his hopes; but he read only fatigue, a dull incomprehension, determination.

'Adda!'

It was Farr's voice. Adda peered into the gloom of the ward, blinking to clear his one working eyecup.

'Adda – you must help me . . .'

There. Farr was close to the rear of the ward; he was hovering over another patient, a massive, still form wrapped in a cocoon. The boy seemed unharmed still, Adda saw with relief.

He pushed his way over the heads of the crowd.

The patient was lost in the cocoon with only a little flesh showing: a huge, crumpled fist, an area of shoulder or chest about the size of Adda's palm. The exposed flesh was surfaceless, chewed up.

Adda suppressed a shudder and looked at Farr. The boy's face was drawn, the fatigue showing in his eyecups, the dilated Air-pores like craters on his cheeks.

'I'm glad you returned.'

'You're a damn fool, boy. I want you to know that now, in case I don't get a chance to tell you later.'

'But I had to return. I heard Bzya's voice. I . . .'

Something moved deep inside the cocoon – a head turning, perhaps? – and a claw-like finger protruded from the lip of the material, to pull the neck of the cocoon tighter closed. The tiny motion was redolent of shame.

'This is *Bzya*?'

'They had to pull him up from the underMantle. He was nearly lost – Adda, he had to abandon his Bell. He dragged back Hosch, but he was dead.' The boy looked down at his friend, his hands twisting together. 'We've got to get him out of here – away from the City.'

'But...'

There was another dull impact, deep in the guts of the City. The very Air seemed to shake with it, and the ceiling of the ward settled, wood splintering with a series of snaps. Then a mansheight-square section of the ceiling imploded, raining sharp wood splinters. This time the workers and patients had to take notice; screams were added to the bedlam of orders and frantic activity, and patients threw bare or bandaged arms over their faces.

'All right,' Adda said. 'You take the head; I'll push at the feet. Move, damn you...'

They scrambled for the entrance to the ward, hauling the cocoon beneath the splintered ceiling. They had to work through the melee, pushing with their feet at slow-moving limbs and heads.

Deni was nowhere to be seen.

It seemed to take a lifetime to reach the open mouth of the ward. They bundled Bzya out into the Air, over the port's splintered lip; Bzya rolled in the Air, helpless in his cocoon. Adda and Farr scrambled after him. Farr made to grab the head end of Bzya's cocoon once more, but Adda stopped him. He hauled Bzya around lengthways, so that the Fisherman was almost lying across their laps. 'We'll take him like this,' Adda said. 'Get hold. We'll both Wave backwards...'

Farr nodded, understanding quickly. He took handfuls of the cocoon, and soon he and Adda were kicking backwards in parallel through the Air, hauling the massive cocoon after them.

The City, looming huge over them, settled once more, this time with screeches from deep within its fabric. Adda imagined the huge Corestuff girders, the bones of the great carcass, twisting, failing one by one. Explosions of shattering wood erupted all over the Skin. Huge, rectilinear creases emerged over the wooden face, as if the Skin were starting to fold over on itself.

Adda kicked desperately at the thick Air, ignoring the numb ache of his legs, the pain of fingers which were turning into claws as they dragged at cocoon material. Vortex fragments continued to hail through the Air, rings and other fantastic forms sleeting past them.

Suddenly Bzya's body twisted in the Air. The Fisherman's heavy legs thumped into Adda's chest, causing him to lose his grip. Adda heard the Fisherman groan from within his cocoon at this latest disruption.

Adda slithered to a halt and scrabbled at the slick, expensive material of the cocoon, trying to regain purchase.

Farr had stopped Waving. He'd simply come to a halt in the Air and had dropped the cocoon, and was staring back at the City.

'By the blood of the Xeelee, boy . . .'

'Look.' Farr pointed back at the Hospital entrance. 'I think it's Deni.'

Adda rubbed dirt from his good eye and stared at the figures in the port. They were dwarfed by the huge wooden panorama of Skin all around them. Yes, it was Deni Maxx; the little doctor, all energy and competence, was working in the entrance to bring out still another patient.

There was a new sound from within the bulk of the City – a yielding sigh which slid rapidly to a higher pitch, almost as if in relief. Skin crumbled away in huge rafts of wood, revealing the Corestuff girder framework beneath. It looked like bones emerging through corrupt flesh. And, even as Adda watched, the girders, dully shining, were creasing, folding over.

Adda grabbed at the cocoon and kicked at the Air. His hands slid over the material and the inert bulk of Bzya barely stirred in the Air; but Adda clung to the material and tried again. In a moment Farr joined him, and soon the two of them were lunging backwards away from the City, their Waving ragged, spurting.

The face of the City – huge rents gaping – collapsed under its mask of anchor-bands and folded forward over them. The Corestuff structure showed no more resistance than if it had been constructed of soft pig-leather. Splinters of wood rained forward, bursting from the crumpling Skin.

Farr screamed: 'Deni!'

Through the chaos of the crumpling face of the Hospital port, Adda could see the compact form of the doctor, still working. She looked up, briefly, at the collapsing Skin above her. Then she turned back to her patients.

The port of the Hospital ward closed like a mouth.

In the very last heartbeat Adda saw Deni raise her arm against the huge jaw of wood and Corestuff which closed over her, as if – at last – trying to save herself. Ragged edges of wood met like meshing teeth, bursting her body. A cloud of wood fragments and dust billowed from the crushed face of the City, obscuring the Hospital from Adda's view.

Farr was screaming incoherently, but he was still Waving, dragging at Bzya's cocoon.

'Scream!' Adda yelled over the crashing roar of the City. 'Scream and cry all you want, damn you! But *don't – stop – Waving!*'

Hork pressed his face close to the surreally silent display. 'It's a jetfart,' he said wonderingly. He laughed. 'I can scarcely believe it. A jetfart, from the North Pole of a Star!'

Dura gripped the control levers, forcing her hands to remain clenched. The levers were warm, comfortable; they seemed to fit well in her palms. She felt as if she were trapped inside her head, an impotent observer of her own actions. She tried to imagine what must be happening inside the Mantle, if that map-globe really did represent the Star itself.

Hork Waved to the transparent wall, and stared at the tiny image of the battle. Eventually he turned to Dura and shouted, 'I think that's enough . . . You can let go.'

Dura stared at her hands. Her fingers wouldn't open; she had to glare at her rebellious hands, consciously willing them to uncurl.

Released, the levers slid gently back to their rest positions.

The fount from the map-Star dwindled, thinning to a fine plume before dying completely; the map itself folded up and disappeared.

'Is it over? We're not aimed at the Ring any more?'

Hork Waved back across the huge chamber. He turned the chair's arrow device this way and that, alternately studying the starbow and the field of stars, trying to judge the changes Dura had made.

Dura settled back in the chair, watching starfields explode silently across the sky.

'We haven't turned the Star around, if that's what you mean,' Hork said. 'But we've turned it aside. I think so, anyway . . . The Ring has moved away from the centre of that wall.' He pointed. 'We're still heading for the battlefield but we've deflected the Star; we're going to miss the Ring.'

She frowned, her feeling of distance, of unimportance, lingering. 'Will that be enough, do you think?'

'To stop the Xeelee destroying us?' He shrugged. 'I don't know, Dura. But we've done all we can.'

Dura looked at Hork, seeing a match in his broad face for her own sense of bewilderment, of anticlimax.

Hork held out his hand. 'Come. We need to rest, I think, after such epic deeds. Let's return to our wooden ship. We'll eat, and try to relax.'

She allowed him to pull her out of the chair. Hand in hand, they Waved back to the inner tetrahedron.

As they entered it, Dura made her way towards the 'Pig's' open hatchway; but Hork held her arm. 'Dura. Wait; look at this.'

She turned. He was pointing to the map on the inner wall of the tetrahedron – the map-Star, the wormhole diagram they had studied earlier. One of the wormhole routes – a path which snaked from the Core of the Star to its Crust, at the North Pole – was flashing, slowly and deliberately.

Hork nodded slowly. 'I think I understand. This is how the Star-fount was made.' He traced the wormhole with a finger-tip. 'See? When you hauled on your levers, Dura, this wormhole must have opened up. It took matter from the heart of the Star and transported it to the Crust. The Core material must have exploded at once in the lower pressure, releasing immense energy.'

Dura felt odd; she seemed to see Hork as if at the far end of a long, dark corridor.

'At the North Pole there must be huge engines to exploit

this energy – the *discontinuity drive engines* Karen Macrae spoke of, which propel the Star itself.' His gaze was distant. 'Dura, some day we must reach those engines. And I wonder how the Colonists fared, when that wormhole belched . . .'

In Dura's eyes all the colour had leeched from Hork's face; even the lurid map on the tetrahedron wall had turned to shades of brown, and there was a strange, thin taste on her tongue.

She was exhausted, she realized. There would be time enough in the future for plans and dreams. For now, she longed for the comparative familiarity and security of the 'Pig', for food and sleep.

The rich, sweet stink of Air-pigs greeted her as she reached the ship's entrance.

He touched Farr's arm. 'Wait. We stop here. That's enough.'

Farr looked confused. He Waved through a couple more strokes, as if automatically; then, uncertainly, his legs came to rest. He released his grip on the cocoon material and looked down at his hands, which were bent into stiff claws.

Adda let himself drift away from the cocoon and hang in the Air, giving way to his fatigue for the first time since the start of the disaster. The Magfield supported him, but he could feel its continuing shudders. The aches in his legs, arms, back and hands had gone beyond mere fatigue, beyond exhaustion now, he realized, and had transmuted into real pain. He inflated his chest, hauling in dank Polar Air, and felt the thick stuff burn at his lungs and capillaries. He remembered the dire warnings of poor, lost Deni Maxx: that after his encounter with the Air-sow his body would never regain its pneumatic efficiency. Well, this day he'd tested that diagnosis to its limits.

The City was a battered wooden box almost small enough to be covered over by the palm of a hand, with the long, elegant Spine spearing down from its base to the under-Mantle. A cloud diffused around the upper City, a mist of rubble and dispersing refugees.

The Xeelee starbreakers continued to walk through the Mantle. Vortex strings hailed all around them, deadly and banal.

He felt his eyes close; weariness and pain lapped over his

351

mind, shutting out the world. This was the worst part of growing old: the slow, endless failure of his body that was slowly isolating him from the world, from other people, immersing him instead in a tiny, claustrophobic universe of his own weakness. Even now, even with the Mantle in its greatest crisis . . .

Well, a small, sour part of him thought, *at least I won't grow any older, to find out how much worse it gets.*

'. . . Adda.' There was more wonder than fear in Farr's voice. 'Look at the City.'

Adda looked at the boy, then turned his aching neck to the distant tableau of Parz.

The City had already drifted far from its usual site directly over the Magfield Pole, tilting and twisting slowly as it travelled. Now that drift was accelerating. Parz, with all its precious freight of life, swung through the Air like a huge spin-spider. It was oddly graceful, Adda thought, like a huge dance. Then there was a cracking noise, a sharp sound which travelled even to this distance, uneasily like breaking bone. Wood fragments burst around the junction of the City and its Spine – splinters which must be the size of Air-cars to be visible at this distance.

The Spine had snapped off.

The Spine remained suspended in the depths of the Polar Magfield, like an immense, battered tree trunk. The Spine must have been supplying much of the City's residual anchoring in the Magfield, for now the box-like upper section of Parz, with green wood-lamp light still gleaming from its ports, rolled forwards like an immense, grotesque parody of a lolling head.

The structure could not long stand such stress.

The Corestuff anchor-bands, dull and useless, folded, snapped and fell away in huge pieces. The clearwood bubble which enclosed the Stadium burst outwards, popping. The Palace buildings on the upper surface, like elaborately coloured toys with their miniature forests and displays, slid almost gracefully away into the Air, exposing the bare wooden surface beneath.

And now the City itself opened, coming apart like rotten wood.

The carcass split longitudinally, almost neatly, around the central structural flaw of Pall Mall. From the cracked-open streets and shops and homes, Air-cars and people spilled into the Air. The Market opened up like a spin-spider's egg, and the huge execution Wheel tumbled out into the Air.

The sounds of cracking wood, of twisting Corestuff, carried through the Air, mercifully drowning the cries of the humans.

Adda tried to imagine the terror of those stranded citizens; perhaps some of them had never ventured beyond the Skin before, and now here they were cast into the Air, helpless amid clouds of worthless possessions.

Now the residual structure of Parz imploded into fragments. All traces of the City's shape were lost. The cloud of rubble, of wood, Corestuff and struggling people, drifted through the Air away from the amputated Spine, slowly diffusing.

Adda closed his eyes. There had been a grandeur about that huge death. Almost a grace, a defiance of the Xeelee's actions which had been, in its way, magnificent.

'Adda.' Farr was pulling at his arm and pointing.

Adda followed the boy's finger. At first he could see nothing – only the lurid crimson glow around the Northern horizon, the yellow chaos of the Air . . .

Then he realized that the boy was pointing out an *absence*.

The starbreaker beams were gone.

Adda felt something lift from his heart. Perhaps some of them might yet live through this.

But then more vortex fragments came gusting towards them, precluding thought; gripping the boy's hand as hard as he could, Adda stared into the mouth of the storm and grabbed at Bzya's cocoon.

28

The Interface was glowing.

The shouting woke Borz from a deep, untroubled sleep. He stretched and scowled around, looking for the source of the trouble. He reached to his belt and pulled out his Air-hat, jammed it on his head. He didn't really need the hat, of course, but he thought it gave him a bit more authority with the scavenging, thieving upfluxers who came by all the time and . . .

The Interface was glowing. The edges around its four triangular faces were shining, vortex-line-blue, so bright he was forced to squint. And the faces themselves seemed to have been covered over by a skin of light, fine and golden, which returned reflections of the yellow Mantle-light, the vortex lines, his own bulky body.

A deep, superstitious awe stirred in Borz.

There was no sign of the pigs, which had been stored at the heart of the tetrahedron. And the various possessions – clothes, tools, weapons – which had been attached to the tetrahedron's struts by bits of rope and net now tumbled around in the Air. A length of rope drifted past him. He grabbed it and laid it in his huge palm; the rope looked scorched.

People, adults and children alike, were Waving away from the Interface, crying and wailing in their panic. Borz – and two or three of the other men and women – held their place.

The Interface hadn't worked for generations – not since the Core Wars; everyone knew that. But it was obviously working now. Why? And – Borz ran a tongue over his hot, Airless lips, and he felt the pores on his face dilate – and what might be coming through it?

The face-light died, slowly. The faces turned transparent once more. The glow of the tetrahedral frame faded to a drab blackness.

The Interface was dead again; once more it was just a framework in the Air. Borz felt an odd, unaccustomed stab of regret; he knew he'd never again see those colours, that light.

The pigs had gone from the heart of the framework. But they'd been replaced by something else – an artifact, a clumsy cylinder of wood three mansheights tall. There were clear panels set in the walls of the cylinder, and bands of some material, dully reflective, surrounded its broad carcass.

A hatch in the top of the cylinder was pushed open. A man – *just a man* – pushed his face out; the face was covered by an extravagant beard.

The man grinned at Borz. 'What a relief,' he said. 'We needed some fresh Air in here.' He looked down into the cylinder. 'You see, Dura, I knew Karen Macrae would get us home.'

'Hey.' Borz Waved with his thick legs until his face was on a level with the strange man's. 'Hey, you. Where are our pigs?'

'Pigs?' The man seemed puzzled, then he looked around at the dead Interface. 'Oh. I see. You kept your pigs inside this gateway, did you?'

'Where are they?'

The man looked amused, but sympathetic. 'A long way from here, I fear.' He sniffed the Air and stared around, his gaze frank, confident and inquisitive. 'Tell me, which way's South?'

29

Toba Mixxax, his round face pale in the heat, stuck his head out of his Air-car. 'Sounds like Mur and Lea are arguing again.'

Toba's car had approached unnoticed. Dura had been labouring to fix ropes to a section of collapsed Skin. She backed away from her work, her arms and hands aching. Even here, on the outer surface of the dispersing cloud of debris that marked the site of the ruined City, the heat and noise were all but unbearable, and the work was long, hard and dangerous. As she listened now, she could hear the raised voices of Lea and Mur. She felt a prickle of irritation – how long was she going to have to hand-hold these people, before they learned to work together like adults?

But as she studied Toba's familiar round face – with its uncertain expression, its pores dilated in the heat – the irritation vanished as soon as it had come. She straightened up and smiled. 'Nice to see you, farmer.'

Toba's answering smile was thin. 'You look tired, Dura. . . We're all exhausted, I suppose. Anyway,' with a touch of strain entering his voice, 'I'm not a farmer any more.'

'But you will be again,' Dura said, Waving towards him. 'I'm sorry, Toba.'

Stretching the stiffness out of her back, she looked around the sky. The vortex lines had reformed and now crossed the sky in their familiar hexagonal arrays, enclosing, orderly and reassuring; the Magfield, restored to stability, was a firm network of flux in the Air – a base for Waving, for building again.

She studied the lines, examining their spacing through her fingers. Their slow pulsing told her that it would soon be time for Hork's Wheel ceremony, at the heart of the ruined City.

'How's the farm?' she asked carefully. 'Is Ito . . .'

'We're putting it back together again,' Toba said. 'Slowly. Ito is . . . bearing up. She's very quiet.' For a moment his small, almost comical mouth worked as if he were struggling to express his feelings. 'You know Farr's there with her. And some of Cris's friends, the Surfers. Cris has gone. But I think Ito finds the young people around her a comfort.'

Dura touched his arm. 'It's alright. You don't have to say anything. Come on; maybe you can help me sort out Lea and Mur . . .'

Toba climbed out of his car.

Together, they made their way through the City site. Parz had become a cloud of floating fragments of Skin, twisted lengths of Corestuff girder, all suffused by the endless minutiae of the human world, spilled carelessly into the Air. She could see, at the cloud's rough centre, the execution Wheel, cast adrift from the old Market. Even from this vantage point – close to the cloud's outer edge – Dura could see clothes, toys, scrolls, cocoons, cooking implements: the contents of a thousand vanished homes. Those few sections of the City which had survived the final Glitch continued to collapse spasmodically – even now, weeks after the withdrawal of the Xeelee – and to the careless eye the swarms of humans crawling over the floating remains must look, she thought, like leeches, scavengers hastening the destruction of some immense, decomposing corpse, adrift in the turgid Air of the Pole. Many of the City's former inhabitants, recently refugees, had returned to Parz to seek belongings and to help with the reconstruction. There had been some looting, true – and too many people had come back here, intent on picking over the remains of a City which would not be restored to anything like its former completeness for many years.

But Hork's emergency edicts against a mass return to the City seemed to be holding. Enough of the City's former inhabitants had dispersed to the recovering ceiling-farms of the hinterland – and stayed there to work – to reduce fears of famine. And genuine reconstruction and recovery was progressing now. Already teams of workers had succeeded in locating the surviving dynamos. The great engines – which had once powered anchor-band currents – had been cleared of rubble and stumps of infrastructure. Now the dynamos floated in clear spaces, their lumpy Corestuff hides gleaming dully in the purple light of the Quantum Sea as if they were immense, protected animals.

It could still go wrong, Dura thought uneasily. The fragile society left adrift by the Xeelee Glitch could still fall apart – disintegrate into suicidal conflict over dwindling resources, over once-precious goods from the old Parz which had been reduced in value to trinkets by the disaster.

But not just yet. Now, people seemed – on the whole – to be prepared to work together, to rebuild. This was a time of hope, of regeneration.

Dura welcomed her own aching muscles and stiff back. It was evidence of the hard work that comprised her own small part of the Mantle-wide rebuilding effort. She felt a surge of optimism, of energy; she suspected that the days to come would comprise some of the happiest of her life.

In a clear space a few mansheights from the car, the Human Being Mur had been showing Lea – a pretty girl who had once been a Surfer – how to construct nets from the plaited bark of Crust trees. The two of them were surrounded by a cloud of half-coiled ropes and abandoned sections of net. Little Jai – reunited with his father – wriggled through the Air around them, nude and slick, grasping at bits of rope and gurgling with laughter. Lea was brandishing a length of rope in Mur's face. 'Yes, but I don't see why I have to do it over.'

Mur's voice was cracking with anger, making him sound very young. Compared to the City girl, Mur still looked painfully thin, Dura thought. 'Because it's wrong,' he said. 'You've done it wrong. Again! And I –'

'And I don't see why I should put up with that kind of talk from the likes of you, upfluxer.'

Toba placed his hands on the girl's shoulders. 'Lea, Lea. You shouldn't speak to our friends like that.'

'Friends?' The girl launched into an impressive round of cursing. Toba looked pale and pulled away from her, dismayed.

Dura took the rope which Lea was rejecting. 'Perhaps Mur

didn't explain,' she said smoothly. 'You have to double plait the rope to give it extra strength.' She hauled at sections of it, demonstrating its toughness.

'But the way he speaks to me –'

'This plaiting is finely done.' She looked at Lea. 'Did you do this?'

'Yes, but –'

Dura smiled. 'It takes most Human Beings years of practice to learn such a skill, and you've almost mastered it already.'

Lea, distracted by the praise, was visibly struggling to stay angry; she pushed elaborately dyed hair from her forehead.

Dura passed the rope to her. 'With a bit more help from Mur, I'll be coming to you for instruction. Come on, Toba, let's take a break; I'd like to see how Adda is getting on.'

As they moved away Dura was careful not to make a show of looking round, but she could see that Mur and Lea were moving back towards each other, warily, and picking up sections of rope once more.

She felt rather smug at her success at defusing the little situation. And she was secretly pleased at this evidence that the Human Beings were managing to adjust to the situation they'd found here at the Pole – better than some of Parz's former inhabitants, it seemed. Dura had expected the Human Beings to be shocked, disappointed to arrive at the Pole after their epic journey across the sky, only to find nothing more than a dispersing cloud of rubble. In fact they'd reacted with much more equanimity than she'd anticipated . . . especially once reunited with their children. The Human Beings simply hadn't known what to expect here. They couldn't have imagined Parz in all its glory – any more than she herself could have, before Toba brought her here for the first time. For the little band of Human Beings, the immense number of people, the huge, mysterious engines, the precious artifacts scattered almost carelessly through the Air, had been wonder enough.

One section of the rough, expanding City-cloud had been cordoned off, informally, to serve as a Hospital area. Dura and Toba pushed through the cloud of debris until they were moving through arrays of patients, drifting comfortably in the Air and loosely knotted together with lengths of rope. Dura cast a cursory, slightly embarrassed glance at the patients. Many people had been left so damaged by the Glitch that they would never function fully again; but the care they were receiving was clearly competent. The bandaging and splints seemed undamaged and clean. One of the blessings of the destruction of Parz was that its scale had been so immense many smaller, more robust items in the City – like medical equipment – had simply been spilled into the Air, undamaged.

As they neared the heart of the improvised Hospital, Muub, once Court Physician, emerged to meet them. Muub had abandoned his impractical finery, replacing it with what looked like a Fisherman's many-pocketed smock. His smile was broad and welcoming beneath his shining bare scalp, and the Physician looked as happy as Dura could remember seeing him – liberated, even.

Muub led them to Adda. The old upfluxer was standing a sullen guard over an outsized, sealed cocoon. Dura knew that the cocoon contained Bzya, the crippled Fisherman, who still could do little more than bellow half-coherent phrases from his ruin of a mouth. Bzya was evidently asleep. But Adda seemed content to spend much of his waking time with his friend, keeping watch over him and serving as a clumsy nurse when necessary, helping Jool and their daughter – Shar, who had returned from the ceiling-farms – to tend to him.

Adda embraced Dura, and asked after the rest of the Human Beings. Dura told him about Mur and Lea, and Muub added, 'There are points of friction. But your upfluxers are working well with the citizens of Parz. Don't you agree, Adda?'

The old man growled, his face as sour as ever. 'Maybe. Maybe not. Maybe we're "fitting in" too damn well.'

Dura smiled. 'You're too much of a cynic, dear Adda. Nobody forced the Human Beings to come here, to help the City folk dig their way out of the rubble.'

'Although we're delighted you're here,' Muub said expansively. 'Without your upflux-hardened muscles we wouldn't be making half the progress we've managed so far.'

'Sure. As long as we're not using our "upflux-hardened muscles" to build another nice, neat cage for ourselves.'

Dura said, 'Now, Adda –'

Toba Mixxax said nervously, 'But you were never in a cage. I don't understand.'

Muub held up his hands. 'Adda has a point. And while we're rebuilding our City, it's a time to think about rebuilding our hearts as well. The Human Beings were in a cage, Toba. As were we all: a cage of ignorance, prejudice and suppression.'

Dura looked at him carefully. 'You genuinely accept that?'

'Do we need a City at all?' Adda asked sourly. 'Maybe it's time for a fresh start without one.'

Dura shook her head. 'I don't think I agree with that. Not any more. The benefits of a City – stability, a repository of understanding, the access to medicine – all of these will help us all, everyone in the Mantle.' She fixed Muub with a sharp glance. 'Won't they?'

He nodded seriously. 'We could never advance from a base of subsistence farming. But the City must never again become a fortress-prison. That's why we're planning a whole series of satellite communities, with the City as the hub. We should not trap most of humanity in one place, so vulnerable to disasters from without – and from our own hearts.'

Adda snorted. 'You talk about human nature. What's to stop human nature from reasserting itself where prisons and fortresses are concerned?'

'Only the strong and continuing efforts of good men and women,' Muub said evenly. 'Hork shares these goals. He's talking about new kinds of power structures – representative councils which would give all of the Mantle's people a say in the way things are run.'

'Knowing Hork,' Dura admitted, 'I find that a little hard to swallow.'

'Then try harder,' Muub said sternly. 'Hork is no sentimental dreamer, Dura. He faces realities and acts on them. He knows that without the ancient wisdom of the Human Beings – without the clues you people brought about the Core Wars, the possibility of retrieving some of the ancient technology – the City would have been wiped out by the Xeelee attack, without even knowing why. Perhaps the race itself would have perished . . . We need each other. Hork accepts that, and is going to make sure we don't lose what we've gained. Surely his litany, today, is evidence of his goodwill. Perhaps we could construct a new, integrated philosophy, incorporating the best elements of all these strands – the Xeelee philosophy, the Wheel followers – and build a new faith to guide us...'

Dura laughed. 'Maybe. But we'll have to put the City back together first.'

Adda rubbed his nose. 'Perhaps. But I don't think we'll have Farr here to help us.'

'No,' Dura said. 'He's determined to return to the Quantum Sea, in a new, improved "Flying Pig". To find the Colonists again. But he's accepted he needs to put in some time rebuilding his own world first, before flying off to win new ones...'

'Not a poor ambition to have,' Muub said, smiling thinly. 'Quite a number of us are intrigued by what you learned of the Colonists... and the huge Ur-human engines at the North Pole. Of course, we don't know any way of travelling more than a few tens of metres from the South Pole, let alone of crossing the Equator... but we'll find a way.'

'Why should there be a way at all?' Adda asked cynically. 'This Star is a hostile environment, remember. The Glitches have forced that home into our heads, if nothing else. We've no guarantee we'll ever be able to achieve much more than we can do now. After all the Ur humans left us to die with the Star; they didn't believe in any future for us.'

'Perhaps.' Muub smiled. 'But perhaps not. Here's a speculation for you. What if the Ur-humans didn't intend us to be destroyed when the Star impacted the Ring? What if the Ur-humans left us some means of escaping from the Star?'

Dura said, 'Like the wormhole to the planet –'

'Or,' Muub said, 'even a ship – an Air-car that could travel outside the Star itself.' He looked up at the Crust, a look of vague dissatisfaction on his face. 'What lies beyond that constraining roof over our world? The glimpses you saw, Dura, of other stars – hundreds, millions of them – each one, perhaps, harbouring life – not human as we are, and yet human, descended from the Ur-stock... And then, behind it all, the Ur-humans themselves, still pursuing their own aloof goals. To see it all – what a prize that would be! Yes, Adda; many of us are very curious indeed about what might lie at the far Pole...

'Yet even that will tell us so little of the true history of our universe. What is the true purpose of Bolder's Ring? What are the Xeelee's intentions – who, where is the enemy they seem to fear so much?' He smiled, looking wistful. 'I will resent dying without the answers to such questions, as I surely will...'

In the distance, in the opened heart of the City hundreds of mansheights away, pipes began to bray: Hork calling his citizens to him. Muub bid a hasty farewell to his friends.

With Adda, Dura began to make her way towards the heart of the debris cloud. As they Waved, peacefully, she slipped her hand into his.

'We've come a long way, daughter of Logue,' Adda said.

Dura looked at him with a little suspicion, but there was no sign of irony in his expression; his good eye returned her gaze with a softness she hadn't often seen there before.

She nodded. 'We have...' And some of us a little further than others, she thought. 'How's Bzya?'

He sniffed. 'Surviving. Accepting what he has. Which is a lot, I suppose; he has Jool and Shar both with him now...'

'And you,' she said.

He didn't reply.

'Do you think you'll stay with them?'

He shrugged, with an echo of his old cantankerousness, but his expression remained soft.

She squeezed his hand. 'I'm glad you've found a home,' she said.

As they neared the Wheel at the heart of the debris cloud, they could hear once more the thin, clear voice of Physician Muub as he addressed the crowd gathering there.

'...The cult of the Xeelee, with its emphasis on higher goals than those of the here-and-now, was impossible for Parz's closed, controlled society to accommodate. It was only by the suppression of these elements – the expulsion of the Xeelee cultists, the Reformation's expunging of any genuine information about the past – that the authorities thought the City could survive.

'Well, they were wrong.

'Human nature will flourish, despite the strictest controls.

The upfluxers kept their ancient knowledge almost intact – across generations, and with little recourse to records or writing materials. New faiths – like the cult of the Wheel – bloomed in the desert left by the destruction of beliefs and knowledge.' Muub hesitated, and – unable to see him – Dura remembered how his cup-retinae characteristically lost some of their focused shape, briefly, as he turned to his inner visions. 'It's interesting that both among the exiled Human Beings – and among the almost equally disadvantaged Downsiders, here in Parz – a detailed wisdom from the past survived, by oral tradition alone. If we are all descended from Stellar engineers – from a highly intelligent stock – perhaps we should not be surprised at such evidence of mentation, crossing generations. Indeed, the systematic waste of such talent seems a crime. How much more might man have achieved in this Star by now, if not for petty prejudice and superstition . . .'

Adda snorted. 'Unctuous old fart.'

Dura laughed.

'And I wish I could see Hork's face, as he Waves around having to listen to that.'

'Maybe you misjudge him, Adda.'

'Maybe. But then,' he said slowly – carefully, she thought – 'I've never been as close to him as you have.'

Again she studied the old man sharply, wondering how much he knew – or what he could read, in her face. He was watching her, waiting for some reaction, his battered face empty of expression.

But what was her reaction? What did she want, now?

So much had happened since that first Glitch – the Glitch that had taken her father from her. Several times she had thought her life was finished – she'd never really believed she'd return to the Mantle, from the moment she boarded the 'Flying Pig' in Parz's Harbour. Now, she realised, she was simply grateful to be alive; and that simple fact would never leave her, would inform her enjoyment of the rest of her time.

And yet . . .

And yet her experiences had changed her. Having seen so much – to have travelled further, done so much more than any human since the days of the Colonists themselves – would make it impossible for her to settle back into the cramped lifestyle of a City dweller – and still less of a Human Being.

Absently she folded her arms across her stomach, remembering her single moment of passion with Hork – when she had allowed her intense need for privacy to be overcome, when she thought her life was almost lost, deep in the underMantle. She had found a brief spark of human warmth there; and Hork was surely wiser than she had first realised. But still, she had seen into Hork's soul in the Ur-human chamber, and she had recoiled from what she had found – the anger, the desperation, the need to find something worth dying for.

Hork could not be a companion for her.

'I've changed, Adda,' she said. 'I . . .'

'No.' He was shaking his head sadly, reading her face. 'Not really. You were alone before all this – before we came here – and you're still alone, now. Aren't you?'

She sighed. A little harshly, she said, 'If that's how I'm meant to be, then maybe I should accept it.' She turned; beyond Parz's cloud of rubble she could see the ceiling fields of the hinterland: bare, scrubbed clean of their cultivation – and yet, in a way, renewed. 'Maybe that's where I will go,' she said.

He turned to see. 'What, and become a farmer? Making pap-wheat for the masses? You?'

She grinned. 'No. No, making a place of my own . . . a little island of order, in all of this emptiness.'

Adda snorted with contempt, but the pressure of his fingers around hers increased, gently, warmly.

The pipers' calls were bright and harsh. From all around the cloud-City people were Waving into the Air, converging towards the Wheel at the heart of the cloud. Peering that way now, Dura could see the massive form of Hork – a colourful speck in his robes, his massive arms resting on the huge Wheel. She imagined she could already hear his voice as he recited the litany – the first legal Wheel-litany, a list of all those known to have died in the final Glitch, whether they were from Parz, the hinterland, the upflux, the Skin.

It was a litany intended to conciliate and heal.

The two Human Beings, Waving strongly, joined the shoal of people converging on the Wheel. Around them, the shimmering vortex lines marched steadily across the sky, renewed and strong.

Voyage

Stephen Baxter

A novel of the right stuff

Voyage takes place in a world that almost existed but never was. John F. Kennedy survived the assassination attempt in Dallas. From his wheelchair in 1969, the former president sets NASA a new, daunting challenge: '*...to continue the building of our great ships, and to fly them onward to Mars.*'

His voice carries beyond the clamour of military and industrial lobbies keen to develop the Space Shuttle. Instead, Apollo flights continue, boosted by Wernher von Braun's cherished nuclear rocket. Both are high-risk technologies . . .

When the first Ares mission lifts off for Mars in 1986, it is both a triumphant climax and the end of a long saga of technical and human over-ambition. Ares carries three dedicated people, one of them a woman, who have sacrificed everything to achieve the single goal of reaching another planet: their stories weave through a decade of political drama leading to the transfiguring experience of a year-long journey away from Earth.

'Arthur C. Clarke, Isaac Asimov, Robert Heinlein . . . now Stephen Baxter joins their exclusive ranks'   *New Scientist*

ISBN 0 00 648037 3

Arthur C. Clarke

The Songs of Distant Earth

The Voyagers Awoke in Paradise

When Earth's sun went nova, the *Magellan* barely escaped in time with its precious cargo of one million sleepers and gene banks of plants and animals.

Five hundred years into the voyage they stopped for repairs on the idyllic planet of Thalassa. But whilst the awakened Earth people envied them their stable, harmonious world, the hospitable Thalassans were drawn by the long quest of the interstellar voyagers. And when Lieutenant Commander Loren Lorenson met beautiful Thalassan Mirissa, their alien destinies became inextricably – and tragically – entwined.

The Songs of Distant Earth blends sound scientific speculation with a moving story of life and love on an alien and beautiful world.

ISBN 0 586 06623 3